ASHES OF THE EARTH

ACROSS TIME - BOOK 2

STEPHANIE E. DONOHUE

UCHEN
Furness
Dunbar
Ashborne
Thorne
Norhall
IDRIL
Detha
Lenwick
Onryx
Lundy
Solaris
AECKLAND
Exeter
DAIGH
Oakwell
Keld
Nascombe
NERDANEL
Kald
APRA
Salkire
Mortham
ECHA
SAKAR
Mulnigan Sea
VATRA
Muirin
Darfield
Kilerth
Ilragorn
Laewaes
Vaporia
Swindon
Harthwaite
VICTARION
Niall
Pantmawe
Hadleigh
NETHERIDGE
Glenarm
Bullmar
Marren
Sanadrin
Lamex
Ecrin
Dalry
Emall
Aramore
Cullfield
Jabbart
Sharpton
Sanlow
Haran
MARACH
Pella
Pirn
Alryne
Sanlow
BAFRUS
Mirfield
Landow
Berkton
Merton
Cynerik
Fallholt

CONTENT WARNING

This book contains violence, graphic descriptions of blood/gore, general language (lots of F-bombs), and occasionally crude jokes. Also includes scenes depicting the loss of family members/loved ones and scenes showcasing mental health issues, including (but not limited to) anxiety and depression.

CONTENTS

Life's Short.

Have More Sex.

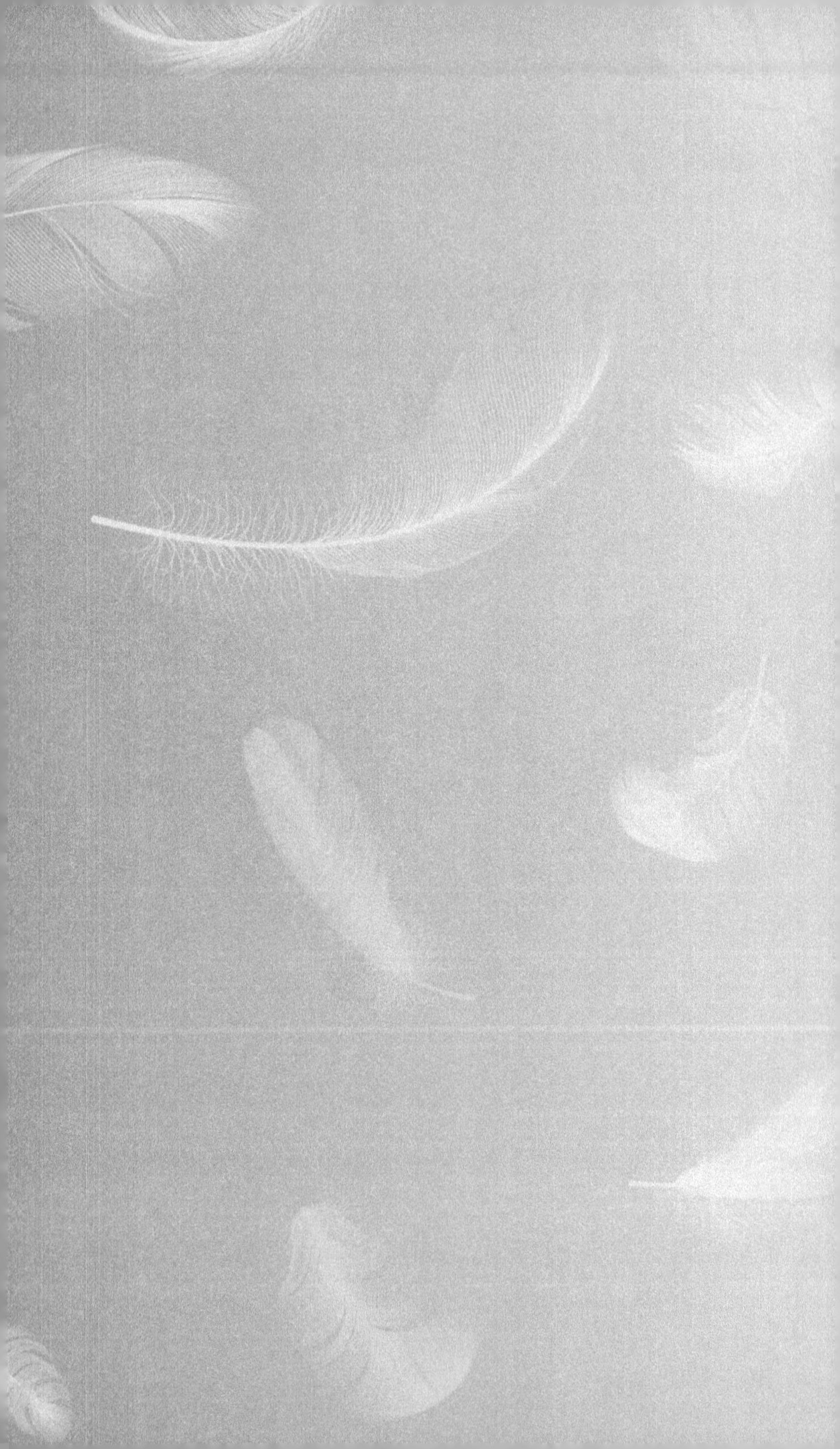

PREVIOUSLY ON..

FIRES OF THE FORSAKEN

Addie Collins—hairstylist extraordinaire, food junkie, and badass pop culture nerd—is rudely abducted in front of her pizza and blasted into an alternate world known as Sakar. A place not only grossly primitive (the Sakarians have never met the lovely lady named hygiene) but also teeming with monsters. In her first day, Addie is chased by a Wraith (disfigured humans who lost their souls), nearly bitten by a Púca (black-scaled, venomous horses), and upchucks all over Cheriour, the fierce-looking Viking who was kind enough to save her. Oh, and she also learns that she was sent to this world by a Celestial (cosmic beings who started an apocalypse-level war over a petty power grab) and only a Celestial can send her back. The problem? These Celestials placed the humans of Sakar right smack in the middle of their bullshit biblical war and then they abandoned them.

With no chance of catching a ride home, Addie reluctantly (*very* reluctantly) adapts to this world. She travels across the land on horseback, learns about the people and the abilities some of them possess (called "hybrids," these humans have a touch of Celestial power), sees the harsh reality these people are living in (not only are they regularly attacked, but an incurable disease is wiping out entire towns), and she learns how to fight...*somewhat.* All while trying (and failing) not to tip head over heels for the gruff and grumpy Cheriour, the commander of the human army. Except he's not gruff and grumpy at all. The more time she spends with him, glimpsing the soft, compassionate heart he keeps buried beneath his brutish Viking Viktor exterior, the more attached to him she becomes. And the more he falls for her, the more protective he gets. But his fighting prowess can't shield her from everything.

Addie has enemies waiting for her in Sakar. One of them is Quinn, the ruler of the human city of Niall, who does everything in his power to get rid of her, including dumping her into a full-fledged battle. She gets through the melee by the skin of her teeth...and with the help of a rogue Púca, who seems hellbent on being her bodyguard. But instead of a celebration, the aftermath of the battle turns into a clusterfuck. The group are attacked by diseased birds and chased into a deadly ambush. Cheriour almost dies. The rogue Púca saves the day and gets a new name: Abby Normal. And

Addie learns she is, in fact, a hybrid, one who is totally fireproof.

Which then leads to her discovering her *second* set of enemies: the deranged Firestarter Seruf and the lethally suave Ramiel. Both are Celestials. Both seem to know her from a past she can't remember. And both push her to the brink, unlocking a second hybrid power that is strong enough to poof Seruf out of existence but one that also poses a threat to Addie's soul.

Although destroying Seruf helps save the people of Niall, nothing Addie does can stop the city from falling. As the survivors move to Sanadrin, the last human-ruled country left in Sakar, Addie grapples with everything she's seen and done and wonders how the heck she's going to move forward...

AND NOW IT'S TIME FOR BOOK TWO!

CHAPTER 1
A TRASHCAN SOME HOBO SHAT IN

Today was a shit day.

To be fair, every day since I got drop-kicked into the hellhole known as Sakar two months ago had been a shit day. Just varying degrees of it. You had the pitiful shit days: the stubborn little turds that pinged into the bowl. Then you had normal shit days: the good ole steaming loaf. There were also no-shit days where nothing happened, but the eruption was inevitable. And then... *explosion days*. With the super-special *"OMG, I'm never eating spicy food again"* stomach pain. The stink. The *mess*.

It happened to everyone.

Today was an explosion day.

Not literally. But y'know what was worse than having stomach cramps and a stanky bathroom? Getting a chunk of someone's rotted flesh stuck to your hand. Especially when that someone was your friend.

"Was that a piece of me arm?" Belanna asked groggily when I tried (and failed) to suppress a gag.

"Nope," I trilled.

"Ye liar." Belanna made a soft whiff, as though fighting a laugh or a moan of pain. She didn't open her eyes.

Which meant she missed my epic dry-heave face.

OMG! *The smell*! The rotted flesh had a stench worse than any vat of diarrhea; more like curdled milk and rancid eggs left sitting in a sweaty gym bag.

Yum!

It got even *more* yummy when mixed with the noxious cloud of odors clinging to the raftered ceiling in Sanadrin's dining hall. I was surprised the radioactive smog hadn't snuffed out the candles on the black metal chandeliers. And these weren't *just* bodily odors—although there was plenty of that to go around, with the rows of infected people criss-crossing the craggy stone floor. But herbs also burned in the fireplace on the far wall: rosemary, thyme, and...well, I didn't know what else. I *barely* recognized the first two scents.

Maddox, the burly but soft-spoken leader of Sanadrin, claimed they were *cleansing*. I mean...*sure*. If you were looking for a stomach cleanse, this vile concoction of smells would work. Especially when combined with the *lovely* visuals.

My stomach burbled as I unstuck Belanna's hunk of flesh from my hand—*not* an easy task. That sucker was superglued on. It made a loud *pwwapttt* when I finally wres-tled it off and splattered globs of blood over my shirt. Which, thank *fuck* I'd rescued this shirt from the mud a few weeks ago. Because this sparkly Celestial-made material never stained. Ever. My pants had blobby blotches all over them, and crusties covered my boots. But the shirt? Still looked brand new and freshly pressed. Not a single blemish to be found.

And its chameleon color-changing ability was a fun bonus. In the dim candlelit hall, it had more of a violet/blue hue, but the second I stepped out into sunlight, it would pop into a rogue pink. Nighttime turned it into a dusky purple. And *all* of its technicolor shades would've clashed with the crimson droplets seeping from Belanna's skin flap—so thankfully, the ick squeegeed right off.

"Ye should keep that piece of me arm. Something to remember me by." Belanna's dried, bleeding lips curled into a smile.

I held the mottled flap between my forefinger and thumb. *Jiggle it! And wiggle it!* Zombie jello. *Bleh.* "No thanks. It's a very thoughtful gift. Really. But I'll pass."

There was an empty waste bucket next to Belanna's lump of bedding, although it wouldn't stay empty for long. A grim-faced trash crew circled the room every hour to dispose of the never-ending supply of vomit, diarrhea, blood, and the occasional juicy clods of flesh.

The skin flap *splatted* against the bottom of the bucket.

"How about a strand of me hair?" Belanna pressed.

I chuckled. "What hair?"

And, okay, it wasn't funny. But it was one of those "I'm either gonna laugh or cry" scenarios.

Belanna once had wild, carroty-orange hair.

It was all gone now.

It had started coming out in clumps three or four days ago (as did hunks of her scalp). Now she was almost totally bald, save for a few stubborn curlicues. And her oozing scalp had turned funky shades of purplish-black. Rot. Her flesh was *literally* rotting away. The decay and blood left swirly, multicolored bloodstains on her pillow.

"Ach, I've got some left for ya." Belanna patted one of the stubborn curls. "Ye can fashion yerself a bracelet. Or a ring. This way, ye'll be thinking of me whenever ye use that hand." The wheezing laugh rattled through her crusty lips.

"Umm...naw. I think I'm good," I said.

"'Twas only a suggestion..."

"Well, I've got a better one. How 'bout this..." I raised my hands, touching the tips of my fingers together to make a square. "I'll commission a painting of your face..."

"I'm not lookin' my finest, Addie..."

"Your pre-plague face. *Obviously*. And I'll hang it over my bed. So your gorgeous mug'll be the first and last thing I see every day."

Belanna gave a thin, wet guffaw. "I like the way ye think. But ye should—"

The man on Belanna's right side suddenly bolted from his blood-stained bedding with a pale, bug-eyed *"oh shit"* look on his face. He clamped a hand over his mouth.

"*Oooh*, hang on!" I scuttled over and shoved a waste bucket under his chin as a wave of bubbling, steaming vomit cascaded from his mouth.

Plague puke was basically tar: thick, dark gloop that smelled worse than a trashcan some hobo had shat into (don't ask me why or how I knew that smell). And it looked *excruciating*. The man's body went rigid as his muscles spasmed. Tears coursed down his face, mixing with the goop in the bucket. The poor bastard could barely breathe between the violent bouts of vomiting. But he kept gasping apologies. "I'm sorry"—*blurgh*—"I didn't"—*balcch*.

"It's alright, bud." I knelt beside his frumpy, stinky bedding and patted his shoulder. My knees popped as the bucket sat heavy in my lap. The stench and sound effects made my stomach go *swish-swatch*. I gulped the fizzing nausea down. "You're doing good," I said. The man's shoulder trembled beneath my hand. "Once you get it all up, you'll feel better." *Lies.* Elion's disease (a fucked-up plague handcrafted by a fucked-up Celestial) created an *endless* supply of upchuck.

But that was what Freda had always cooed to me when I'd been sick as a kid: *"You'll feel better once your tummy gets rid of the bad stuff."* It'd helped calm me down.

And the poor bastards stuck in the sickroom could definitely use some soothing lies. These people had spent the last few days suckling on water droplets and munching on air, and yet they spewed gallons and *gallons* of tar vomit. If you could sell this stuff as black-market gasoline, one person produced enough *per day* to fill a few trucks.

Okay, it wasn't *that* much. But ten minutes of straight vomiting nearly overflowed the bucket.

"We've all upended our guts before. This is no biggie," I kept babbling even as the man stilled and rested his sweaty cheek against the rim of the bucket. "Wanna know my best gross-out story?" I ran my hand down his shuddering back.

To be clear, I didn't know this man. His name was Harry...

Urm, no. Henry?

Something like that.

He and I only ever talked when he had his head in a bucket. So the petting was probably a little out of bounds, but I always found it comforting when someone stroked my back while I was sick. So I kept doing it. And kept talking.

"I had this job interview," I started. "I was eighteen and had snagged a fake ID—gotta be twenty-one to play in America, y'know? So I went to the bar the night before my interview, mainlined tequila shots, and stumbled home at three AM. And my roommate...well, Amy and I hadn't always gotten along great to begin with. So when I staggered through the door singing *Baby Got Back*... It's—never mind."

The man's eyes drooped. His breathing slowed.

I rambled on. "Long story short: Amy kicked me out. I spent the night sleeping in the alley behind our apartment. But I still got up at dawn, nursing the mother of all hangovers, and convinced Amy to unlock the door so I could shower. I didn't want to smell like Splinter the Sewer Rat, y'know? And I still got to my interview *on time*. I was pretty damn proud of myself. But then the manager walked in, and I caught a whiff of whatever God-awful drug store cologne he'd bathed in that morning, and I blew chunks all over him, the table, and the floor. The *whole room* had to be disinfected after I left. Needless to say, I blew that interview. Haha—get it? Like, *blew chunks*?"

The man snored into the bucket.

Belanna let out a strangled chuckle. "I knew ye couldn't hold yer liquor."

"Listen, I was eight—*shit!*" I scurried across the room when Belanna did an abrupt panic-lurch off her bedding, but she retched before I could get the bucket in place.

"*Ugggghhhh,*" I groaned when black vomit splattered over my lap and used my sleeve to swipe it off my pants. Then I joggled my arm to shake the excess goop off and *voila!* Goop Be Gone.

"Are you alright, Addie?" Maddox called from the other

side of the room as he flipped a seizing woman sideways on her bed, trying to stop her from swallowing her tongue. He didn't look at me, but he had his head cocked in my direction.

"I'm good." *Bull-friggin'-shit.* But maybe if I kept lying, some of it would become the truth.

I stroked Belanna's neck, soothing her as she heaved.

"Denis!" Somewhere nearby, a man screeched.

I jerked my head up, and my hand shot forward onto the nape of Belanna's neck, squelching my fingers into her corroded scalp...*ick*!

"Sorry!" I drew my hand back to her shoulders.

"Denis!" the man wailed again.

I craned my head, scanning the vast, dark-stoned hall, and rose onto my haunches, ready to make the dash once I figured out who was screaming.

Kaelan beat me to it. He scampered across the room, swiping an errant strand of gold hair out of his eyes, and stooped beside a writhing, hawk-nosed man.

"It's alright, Darren," Kaelan soothed. "Try to take a deep breath."

"Where is my son?" the man boomed.

A solemn expression distorted Kaelan's face, making him look decades older than the late-teens kid he was. "He died, Darren. Remember? A few years ago, now. You'll"—Kaelan squeezed the man's hand—"you'll be seeing him soon."

More heartbreaking cries and mournful words rippled around the room. Sometimes the sick called out to lost loved ones; sometimes they begged us to stop the pain. Us nurses (aka, those of us who were healthy, uninjured, and able to stomach being in the sickroom—because who needed trained clinicians, right?) did what we could to ease their distress. Some offered comfort. Like Kaelan, who spewed mollifying lies, telling Darren all the things he and his son would do together once Darren was better. Some were all business. Like Maddox, who spent much of the time silently cleaning up the muck and managing symptoms as best he could. Some told shitty jokes to raise people's spirits. Me. I was the only one who did that. And Quinn patrolled the room, trying to keep all the nurses on their feet. His job was to make sure we ate, drank, took breaks, and didn't end up putting ourselves in a sick bed. He was obnoxious about it, though. Every hour or so, he tried to boot me from the room, claiming I needed more time to recover, even though I wasn't injured. The petty bastard probably wanted me to GTFO so he didn't have to keep staring at my (stunningly attractive) face.

This had been our lives for the last few days...weeks... however the hell long it'd been since we'd arrived at Sanadrin. It was tough to tell time when the *entire goddamn building* was windowless.

"Windows are weak spots," Belanna slurred, then spat another mouthful of tar into the bucket.

"Huh?"

"Sanadrin doesn' have windows"—*blugh*—"because they're weak spots. Without them"—*bleeek*—"the fortress is secure. Or, as"—*bluuuugh*—"secure as it can be..."

I patted the top of her head. "How 'bout you wait 'til you're done puking before you talk?"

"I was"—*buuurgh*—"...only answering ye..." Her breath came out in ragged gasps.

Right. Because *of course* I'd been blabbing out loud. "Blabber" should've been my middle name.

"Maddox needs to fecking get this over with." Belanna dry-heaved one more time and lowered herself back onto the bed. "This is why Healers make shite leaders, Addie. Too fecking sentimental. Always thinkin' if they try somethin' different or…" Blood dribbled down her chin when she coughed. "Bloody useless. We all know how this will end."

Ooooh, yes. I knew.

There was no cure for Elion's disease. Only an escape (aka, death).

"Anyway." Belanna batted my hand away when I tried to wipe the blood off her chin. "What do ye have to drink?" She smacked her lips.

I strained to get a smile plastered on my face. "Well," I unhooked the two flasks from my belt, "you've got water—" I gave the one in my left hand a shake—"or wine." The right flask was almost empty and made a louder *sloosh*.

"Did ye need to ask?"

"Wine it is." I popped the cork and took a sip, relishing the rancid, vinegary burn.

"Ye plannin' to share?" Belanna huffed.

"Hold your horses, Calamity Jane. There's enough for both of us." I pressed the flask to Belanna's crusted lips, tipping a small mouthful onto her tongue.

She choked, spitting wine all down her front.

"Whoa there," I chuckled. "And you accuse *me* of not being able to hold my liquor…"

"Give me another sip," she said. "*Now!*"

"How 'bout you stop choking on the first one—"

"Addie!" Belanna's eyes were wide. Wild. "*Please.*" Her shaking hand stretched toward the flask.

"Er…okay. But drink it *slowly* this time. The wine's not gonna disappear on ya."

I drizzled a bit into her mouth. When the first drop hit her tongue, her jaw closed with a snap. Her throat bobbed, muscles tightening. The deer-in-headlights expression never left her face, even as her lips turned blue.

"Belanna. Hey. C'mon, now. It's cheapo wine. You don't need to savor the flavor notes." I tapped her shoulder. "*Swallow*. And take a breath."

Instead, she horked it all back up.

"Maybe you should stick with water." I dabbed at her chin. "This stuff is kinda strong. Might be too much for your stomach."

"I can't..." Belanna spat. "Fecking...*Feck!*" She clapped her mottled hands over her face.

"Chill out." A weird feeling slithered around my gut. Belanna had been in mostly good spirits throughout this nightmare. Not happy. *Hell* no. But calm. And still willing to crack jokes. This meltdown was coming out of left field. "Let your stomach settle a bit and...oh, *shoot*! Hang on..."

The woman on Belanna's left had expelled her guts all over herself, and on her bedding, and the floor...the *ick* was everywhere.

"Alrighty...it's Geraldine, right?" I crab-crawled to her side and snatched the bucket.

"Y-yes." She was about my age, give or take a few years.

"I got ya." I propped the bucket on top of her bedding and patted her back. "Try to sit up a bit. I don't want you choking."

She'd been curled in a fetal position. As she moved, I bundled blankets behind her back to support her upper body. But then the kid (an under-twenty-something who looked like a baby to my old eyes) on her left darted up with hearty *urk-urk-urk-urk* gags, and I had to go help him.

It was a domino effect: once one person upchucked, vomit *whoosed* around the whole room.

"It's Sean, right?" I rubbed the boy's thin, bony shoulders as he went heave-ho.

He didn't answer. Not surprising. This poor kid hadn't spoken since he'd arrived in the sickroom. Most of the time, he laid on his bedding and gave the ceiling a dead-eyed stare.

"Here." I held the water out to him once he finished vomiting. "You're alright, bud. I got you."

He took a slow, mechanical sip. Sputtered. And spat it all back up.

Normally, I'd've thought it was his outraged stomach saying *fuck no*. But Belanna had done the *exact* same thing. And with the way she'd reacted...

I peered over at her. She still had her hands clasped over her face, and her body pulsed with tremors.

A deep pain rocketed through my chest.

"Can you try again?" I coaxed the boy to take another sip.

This time, he didn't attempt to swallow. Just let the water trickle out of his mouth.

I shifted back to Geraldine.

She lay sideways with her brow pressed against the bucket rim. But she looked up when I tapped her hand.

"You think you can keep some water down?" I asked.

"Have you anything stronger?" she groaned.

"I do. But let's start with water. Gotta walk before you can run, right?" My heart thrummed in my chest. Okay, one weird occurrence was...well, *weird*. Two was a coincidence. But three...

I held my breath when Geraldine took a long gulp of water—

Only to ralph it into the bucket.

She stared at me, her lower jaw twisting, throat convulsing, exactly as Belanna had done. And then she wailed, a full-on animalistic scream.

Something was wrong. *Really* wrong.

"Umm," I started. What the hell was I supposed to do? "Where does it hurt?" I turned to Belanna, who still wouldn't look at me. Geraldine kept screaming. "Give me something to work with here. Is it your stomach? Is the pain more in the front or—"

"It's the fecking disease!" Belanna spat.

"Well, yeah. I get that. But why—"

"This is what happens at the end." Belanna whacked her bedding. "Every. Fecking. Time. *They shouldn't have let it get this fecking far!*" Her voice cracked on a sob, and her face was redder than a stoplight.

"Belanna...hey..." I moved toward her.

"DON'T!" she shrieked. "Unless yer coming to put a blade to me throat, ye don't need to be coming near me anymore, Addie. It's *over*. I can't—" Her breath hitched. "*I can't fecking swallow!*" She turned her red, teary eyes to me. "It always starts with the swallowin'. I've seen it before. Today, I can't drink. Tomorrow, I'll be choking on me own spit. Then me head turns to rot and me innards will leak through me arse. But I won't *die*—not until me lungs stop drawin' air. I could be trapped in this feckin' decaying body for *weeks*. This is the worst part of the disease, ye see." She covered her face with her hand. "Maddox...Quinn...the whole lot of those useless sods should've ended this *days* ago."

I had an awful sensation in my chest, as though I'd tried to shove a whole slice of pizza down my gullet. "Well"—I reached for the wine flask—"*fuck*."

I didn't care that Belanna's diseased lips had been the last thing to touch the mouthpiece; I tipped that sucker back and drained it in three big gulps.

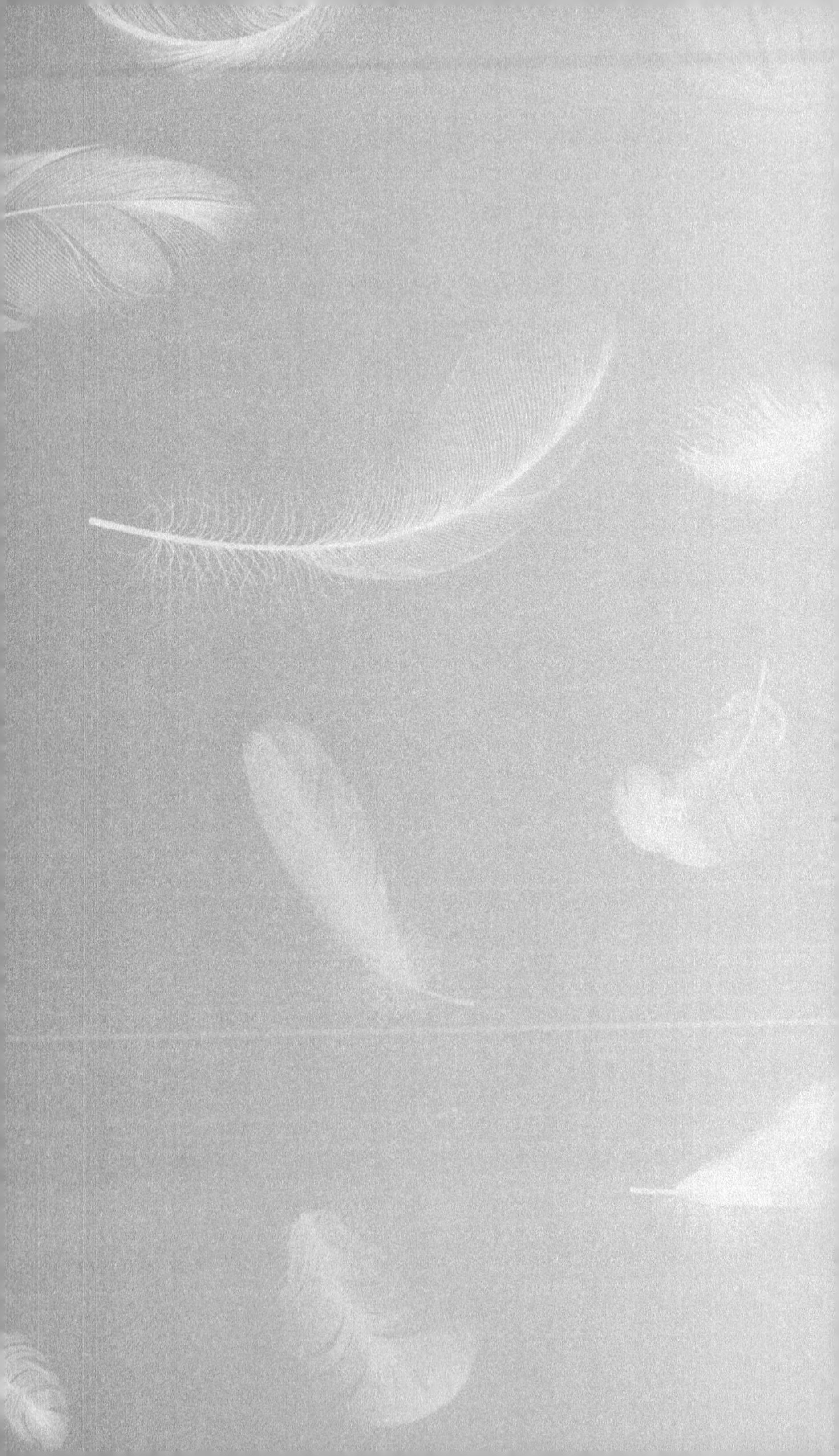

STUPID, STUBBORN VIKING

I couldn't breathe.

On my one side, Belanna screamed a colorful array of profanities, most of which I'd never heard before. Which was impressive considering I had a potty mouth and an eclectic collection of curses. But Belanna's vocabulary beat mine by a country mile.

On my other side, Geraldine cried, her sobs soft and hiccupping.

Or maybe that was me making those *hic-huck* noises.

My chest *hurt*. A raw, sharp, acidic kinda pain, as though a radioactive creature had shimmied down my throat and made my lungs its happy home. But it was too big, so it clawed at the confining walls (aka, my bones), trying to remodel, and getting pissy when the foundation wouldn't budge...

Thunk.

The wineskin slipped out of my hand and plopped against the toe of my left boot. I squinted at it, struggling to make out its shape through the white spots bursting in front of my eyes.

Oh, fuck. *I'm gonna faint.*

The white spots got bigger and bigger. The ground bucked and thrashed beneath my feet. I was going down. Right in the middle of the sickroom. With my luck, I'd land face-first in one of the puke buckets. And I couldn't stop it. Even as my brain went, *Get out of here! Go get fresh air!* the rest of my body was going, *Hmm, smell that lovely decay perfume? It's better than lavender. Why don't we lay down and take a nap?*

My knees buckled.

"Don't!"

The voice snapped in my ear a half second before a hand snatched my right bicep and wrenched me sideways.

"Move your feet!" the voice barked.

I blinked and shooed enough white spots away to catch a glimpse of Quinn's disheveled, sandy-colored hair as he walked in front of me, dragging me across the room.

"Dude…" The chortle that came out of my mouth sounded weird. Hollow. "Do any of you Sakarians know how to brush your fucking hair? And, y'know, you've got a lot of gray back here…"

Quinn's jaw clenched, and he gave my arm a firm tug as he whipped me out of the room and into the claustrophobic, mold-scented foyer that connected the kitchen to the dining hall.

This place resembled a dorm room from the deepest bowels of the underworld. It was as roomy as a janitor's closet and coated in about fifteen layers of mud and blood from the people traipsing through to get to the dining hall or the spindly staircase on the left side. Its only furnishings included a wad of puke-soaked blankets and a three-legged table.

And, to my googly eyes, that three-legged table seemed to be doing a funky jig.

Quinn had whipped me into the foyer too fast.

My already spinning head did a full loop-de-loop. I hissed. Blinked. And through the barrage of angrily buzzing white gnats hovering over my eyes, I saw...

Cheriour?

"*Ughmph!*" The incoherent sound guggled out of my mouth when Quinn stopped.

Because I *didn't* stop. The pesky floor kept moving, lurching me up, down, sideways, and then spinning me in circles.

Cheriour said something—to me or to Quinn, I couldn't tell. My ears were making a high-pitched *squeeeeeeee*, reveling in the wild dance the floor was doing beneath my feet.

"*Oooof...*" My ass whammed onto the ground. Hands had encircled my arms, guiding me down, but I wasn't exactly a lightweight, and gravity was a strong bitch.

"...between your knees..."

Snippets of Cheriour's droning voice slipped through the screaming in my ears. But it was Quinn's clammy palm that shoved my head down, forcing it between my thighs. Which helped. Kinda. It made the earth steadier, at least. But the ringing wouldn't stop, so the jabber of voices over my head became just that: incoherent jibber-jabber, distinguishable only by the tone: Cheriour's had the low, droning quality of a bumble bee, while Quinn's more resembled the roar of a rushing river.

They talked. And *talked*. Their meaningless blather

skated through my ears as I pressed my sweaty forehead to my thighs, praying my lungs would remember how to breathe again. Wishing someone would snuff out the teakettle that still *squeeeeeeeed* inside my head.

Because that *squeeing* sounded a lot like screaming. The kinda piping shrieks a human made while they were getting burned alive.

My parents had made similar noises on the night they died. So had the citizens of Niall. Actually, their cries had been *worse*. More of a siren-like wail...

I flung my head up, cracking the back of my skull on something solid but also...moveable? And something that made a barely audible grunt.

"Oh, freaking hell." I opened my eyes, wincing when a momentary wall of white exploded in front of my vision, and tilted my chin up.

Cheriour peered down at me.

My belly did a little *swoop-swoop* at the sight of those *gorgeous* green eyes of his. And that rugged, high-cheeked face, even if it was partially obscured beneath his wild beard and crazy, curling, chocolate-brown hair...

Hmmm.

Apparently, I had a taste for the dingy lumberjack type now.

Sakar had definitely given my brain a good rattling.

Cheriour blinked, and the left side of his mouth slanted into a faint smile.

Swoop-swoop went my stomach again.

But it soured a bit when I angled my head farther back (so I could properly eye-hump him) and I realized the thing I'd head-butted earlier had been his leg.

His *good* leg. If you could call it that. He'd broken bones in both, but the right was eighty percent healed. And my big-ass head had almost demolished it. Which kinda pissed me off because Cheriour should've been *in bed*, a safe distance from my bulbous noggin.

"Do you need me to spell out the definition of *'bed rest?'*" I grumbled. "Because I can tell ya...it does *not* include taking a joyride through the castle with your—your...Jesus, *that's* what you're using as a cane?" I eyed the spindly strip of wood he clutched in his left hand. "That's a jumbo *toothpick!*"

Cheriour said nothing. Just raised his head and turned his gaze toward Quinn, who paced in front of the sickroom doors, doing a weird snappy thing with his fingers, as though directing an invisible orchestra.

"It has to be done, Quinn," Cheriour said.

"I know!" Quinn gave his fingers a few hard, agitated snaps. "It's *past* time. But Maddox wanted...and I couldn't go against him...we'd never tried it before..."

"Fumigation has never worked. Against any disease." The bored tone of Cheriour's voice never gave anything away. He might as well have been telling Quinn about the weather. *"Oh, yes. Those are clouds in the sky, huh? Darn, I guess it's gonna rain."* But his leg twitched—a subtle sign of the agitation brewing inside him.

"*I know!*" Quinn snapped again. "But this isn't a *human* disease, so he hoped...*feck!* It doesn't matter." He ran a hand over his face.

Behind me, Cheriour shifted his weight, pressing his right calf more firmly into my back. His joints snapped, crackled, and popped more than a bowl of Rice Krispies. Har, har, har.

"You wanna join me on the floor?" I asked him. "Before you fall and break something else?"

He exhaled.

"And, let me guess..." I pinched the bridge of my nose when a final spattering of white spots peppered my vision. "You two wanna pull the plug—kill the sick," I amended when Quinn shot me a hard stare, "but Maddox doesn't wanna give you the go-ahead? He'd prefer to...what? Hotbox the room and hope the stench drives the disease away?"

"It's not your concern," Quinn said. "If you feel steady, you may go. You've been in the sickroom half the day. That's more than enough."

"I'm not leaving them."

A strange look passed over Quinn's face, as though a toxic glug of gas had rumbled through his gut. "You won't be much use to them if you're sick."

"Good thing I'm as healthy as a fucking horse," I said. "I just inhaled too much of Maddox's chemical cloud." *Lies.* The virulent air had made my head woozy, sure, but it wasn't why I'd nearly fainted. Or why, even now, my muscles jittered, my head throbbed, and my chest seemed to have shrunk several sizes, forcing my heart and lungs to war for space.

I'd been like this since I'd left Niall.

Or, to be more accurate, I'd been like this since I'd taken a jaunty stroll through Seruf's soul and then gone on an unwanted walk down my forgotten memory lane with Ramiel.

That whole night had been a friggin' nightmare, one I wanted *desperately* to forget. But the images had dug their claws into my brain and were refusing to let go.

I flinched when Cheriour's calf bumped my back. A

deliberate move this time, and not in a prodding *"get on your feet and GTFO"* kinda way. This was a comforting nudge. A reminder that he was there.

I angled my head back as he tilted his down. "Was I talking?" I muttered.

"No." Cheriour tapped his calf against my back again and looked up at Quinn. "We can do it tonight," he said, "while the rest of Sanadrin sleeps."

Quinn nodded. "Maddox will prefer that." He stopped pacing and pulled on his knuckles until they made a series of soft pops. "We'll take the bodies over the hill to burn. Away from the city—he's worried about inciting a panic. Rightfully so. Of course, we won't be able to conceal the smoke..." Quinn turned back to the sickroom, still muttering under his breath as he threw the door open and walked inside.

A shudder ripped along my spine as another monstrous memory shoved to the forefront of my brain: the day we'd arrived at the doomed Lamex, a town decimated by Elion's disease. We'd lit that whole town ablaze so there would be nothing but ashes for the Wraiths to find.

By tomorrow morning, ashes would be all that remained of Belanna. And Geraldine. And the dozens of others I'd spent the last few days tending and talking to, trying to keep their minds distracted from their deteriorating bodies.

Now I'd have to lie through my teeth and spew platitudes while we gave them the good ole Columbian bowtie...

"Addie," Cheriour murmured, "you need not kill anyone."

Apparently that time, I *had* burped my thoughts up.

"I'm not leaving them," I repeated.

"I know," Cheriour said. "But your hand won't be steady

enough to wield a knife. *Properly*," he added when I started to tell him I was a regular pro at dicing veggies. "You would make too many cuts trying to bleed the vein. And I'll not let them suffer more than they already have. So you'll help me."

"Help you," I scoffed when he took a step (two, three) away from me. "The only thing I should *help* you do is get back to bed."

His pain scale had to be pushing fifteen outta ten now. *Had to be.* The dude had a slow shuffle that even a crotchety ninety-year-old with a walker could've outpaced. And he didn't look so hot.

I mean, he was still *hot*. Definitely. But a sickly hot.

In the week or so since leaving Niall, he'd lost a noticeable amount of weight—enough to hollow his cheeks. Heavy, dark rings encircled his eyes. He *never* slept. Once he'd shaken the fever slumber, he'd been awake every single time I'd seen him, no matter if it was in the middle of the day or the middle of the night. Not that you could freaking tell the difference in this dark AF castle...

"You'll get used to the darkness," Cheriour grunted.

"No one gets used to 24/7 darkness," I said. "Unless they're a vampire. And—*God*." I winced when he took another stutter step. "At least let me push you around in a wheelchair. That walk looks *painful*."

Cheriour's puffy left leg was encased in a mis-matched boot twice the size of his right one. He'd made himself a brace: a thick hunk of leather belted his calf and ankle, supporting the barely healed bones. But he still wobbled—badly—whenever he put weight on that leg.

"*You should not be walking!*" I grimaced on his behalf as he limped over to the narrow, arched passageway leading to the kitchen area. "Am I gonna have to drag your ass back to bed and tie you down? I'm good at tying knots. *Really* good. I can—oh, okay, cool. That's nice. Just walk away. It's not like I'm talking to you or anything."

He went right through to the kitchen, completely ignoring me.

I dropped my head into my hands. "Stupid, stubborn Viking asshat..."

From the depths of the black passageway came his response—in his usual dry voice but with a touch of warmth, as though he'd folded the words around a smile. "I'm going to sit down."

CHAPTER 3

WHY IS THE RUM GONE?

These Sakarians were tough freaking cookies.

When a country leader announces, "Hey kids! I'm gonna be murdering your friends at midnight. But I need help. Who wants to volunteer?" (my paraphrased version of Maddox's speech), most people would've shouted "not it!" and run like a bat outta hell. But not the Sakarians.

(Serial killers wouldn't have run either, but they were a whole other breed of crazy).

A dozen people gathered in that dingy foyer outside the sickroom. Some I recognized: Kaelan slumped against the wall closest to the doors, staring at his feet; Maddox sat in the center of the floor, his face pale as he sorted clean cloths into a bucket; Quinn mixed cocktails on the three-legged table, using his left thigh to support the rickety structure; and Braxton, Belanna's identical twin brother, reclined against the wall next to Quinn, swaying and slurping from his flask. But the others were strangers. I'd seen them before and I'd heard their names floating around, but I didn't *know* them. Not like I'd gotten to know Belanna.

Or Garvin, who'd died during the attack on Niall.

Or Moira, who'd died on the battlefield at Sanadrin.

Christ. Almost everyone I'd gotten close to had kicked the bucket. Pretty soon, my face would be on the cover of *All My Friends Are Dead*.

"'Lo, Addie," Braxton said glumly when Cheriour and I joined the group. "Whiskey?" He held out his wineskin.

"Umm...*yes*." I grabbed it from him and took a *loooong* pull, enough to light my insides on fire and burn some of the feeling out of my heart. Then I passed it back to him.

He glugged several mouthfuls, drooling most of it along the side of his chin. "Awch, bugger me." He flicked the droplets off his carrot-colored beard...

Right onto Quinn's face.

I snorted. *Bullseye!*

"You don't have to be here, Braxton." Quinn scowled and used his sleeve to mop up the regurgitated whiskey.

"She's me sister. First out of the womb, ye ken? She never let me forget that." Braxton belched and took another slurp from his flask. "'S'no' fair she's also the first of us to die."

"Oh, Braxton..." I started.

He waved me off. "Anyway, if I don't see her, she'll haunt me for the rest of me days. She will. Always was a persistent bitch." He staggered, gave the wall a dirty *"hey asshole, why'd you push me?"* look and mumbled, "I need more whiskey."

He pinged off the wall, tripped over Quinn's table, and rammed into Cheriour. And since Braxton was about five sheets to the wind, and Cheriour wasn't exactly steady on his feet, I grabbed both their arms, making sure they stayed upright.

Braxton shrugged my hand away with an ultra-slurred, "Suuureee, Churoar."

"Braxton," Cheriour murmured, "Belanna *will* forgive you. If you choose not to stay."

Braxton rubbed his glassy and unfocused eyes. "I'll be sssssaying goodbuh to me sssester." And with that, he stumbled sideways, bounced off the wall again, and did a *stellar* Jack Sparrow swagger all the way to the kitchen.

On any other occasion, his less-than-graceful exit might've been comical.

But no one laughed. They all watched him with the same strained expression on their faces, probably all feeling the same achingly hollow sensation that filled my chest.

"Right, well...we should not waste any more time." Quinn drummed his fingers against the table. Not in a scattered, nervous kind of way (although he was all pasty and sweaty). The dude had rhythm. Enough to create a coherent, catchy tune.

One that sounded vaguely familiar.

Like a sea shanty, with that heavy, repetitive rhythm I could picture sun-roughened men hi-ho-ing to as they marched to work.

There once was a lass...

I blinked as the fragment of a lyric hummed through my brain. "Uh...*what?*"

Cheriour angled his head toward me. Quinn abruptly stopped drumming.

I wasn't sure if they were reacting to my startled "what?" or if I'd started singing (if it was the latter...R.I.P. their eardrums). And I didn't care. Because...because...

I *knew* that tune. The words had been *right there.* And, for some unfathomable reason, the song made me *sad.*

I was losing my dang mind. Seruf and Ramiel had fucked with something in my head. Knocked some screws loose. Or...

"Shit!" I jumped almost a foot into the air when Cheriour's jumbo toothpick scraped against the stone floor. The harsh sound was way, way, way too similar to a sword being drawn.

Cheriour touched my arm, as though apologizing for startling me, before he began speaking. "It will be easier to do this in two stages..." He turned to Maddox.

"Let them say their goodbyes. Be gentle but firm with the ones who are frightened." Maddox's normally deep voice came out in a thin, croaky rasp. Yelling gave the vocal cords a strenuous workout—and he'd done a good bit of shouting when Quinn gave him the ultimatum earlier. Cheriour and I had heard snatches of their verbal spar from the kitchen...a pretty damn impressive feat considering Quinn had (wisely) taken Maddox to the next floor up.

"You should bleed the vein with your first stroke. Do *not* make unnecessary cuts." Cheriour gave his directive in his usual bored drawl.

He was always so freaking calm, even while giving instructions on how to murder a room full of people. It should've made me squeamish.

But that stupid fragment of a song had hijacked my brain.

There once was a lass...there once was a lass...there once was a lass who laughed—

BANG!

Quinn had abruptly shoved away from the three-legged table. It seesawed, sending parts of his science experiment crashing to the floor. He cursed, righted the piece of furniture, and shoved the remaining bowls and cups away from the edges. And then he fixed me with an icy stare, as though it was *my* fault he'd brain farted and forgotten the table was broken.

Bastard...

"Does anyone have questions?" Maddox called.

"I have—*hic*—one." Braxton moseyed back to the group, clutching a wineskin that looked ready to burst at the seams. "Who drank all the whiskey?"

A few people gave him "*dude, c'mon, you're embarrassing yourself*" side-eyes. Kaelan snorted and clapped a hand over his mouth. Cheriour leaned more heavily on his toothpick.

And I couldn't help myself. "Why is the rum gone?"

"Eh?" Braxton blinked at me.

"It's...never mind." My bad jokes were a lot funnier when people actually understood the references. "But you realize you've got a full bottle of whiskey in your hand, right?"

"Yesh," he slurred. "But the cask is"—*hic*—"empty. Someone"—*huc*—"drank it."

"It was probably *you.*"

Braxton took another pull and shook his head.

"If no one has a *serious* question," Cheriour said, "we should begin."

"Agreed." Quinn divvied up his science experiment into six lopsided bowls and three warped buckets and began passing them around the group. "This is all we have," he added as he shoved a bucket into my chest. "Do *not* be wasteful."

"What—" I started.

But Quinn harrumphed and turned away.

Cheriour's hand brushed my back. A slight, soothing stroke.

I craned my head toward him. Just in time to catch the flash of pain in his normally toneless eyes.

He drew his gaze away from my face and started his usual restless roaming, hiding his discomfort.

"You okay?" I murmured.

He nodded.

I nudged my elbow lightly into his side before I stared at the bucket in my hands.

My *very shaky* hands. The gelatinous blob of...whatever Quinn had cooked up joggled. And wobbled. And it was *potent*. I stuck my head into the bucket to take a whiff and came away feeling woozy. It reminded me of walking into an old lady's house and getting assaulted by her mismatched bowls of potpourri.

"What is this?" I asked.

"Herbs. To help them sleep," Cheriour said. "They're aware of what we're doing, but some might still panic. I'd rather they go peacefully."

"Are they going to be able to drink this? Because from what I saw earlier—" I cut myself off as Maddox passed his clean linens down the line, and the burly woman in front of me (her name might've been Sara? Or Cara? Or something like that) turned and draped a long, dingy rag over the edge of my bucket. "Oh. *Oh*, I see," I muttered. "This is like chloroform, huh? They need to *inhale* it."

Cheriour nodded.

I twined the rag around my arm as Maddox paced in front of the group, instructing us on what to do with the bodies after we were done. Which was *not* something I wanted to focus on. So I fiddled with the rag, staring at its pockmarked red, brown, green, and yellow stains, wondering if it had been used to stem a gushing wound at one point. Or to mop up a pile of sick. Or to scrub the inside of a dirty toilet (aka, a stanky bucket). Sakarians didn't have stain remover or bleach to get fabrics looking brand new again. Once a stain settled into the cloth, it was there to stay, like a scar, and each one had a story. The people this rag had saved. The diseases it had seen. The lives it'd lost...

"Addie." Cheriour's voice was barely a whisper in my ear.

I blinked because—*oh, shoot*—everyone in front of me was gone. They'd all moved into the sickroom, and I'd been too zoned out to notice.

"Bleeding hell!" I scrambled, tripping over my own feet, and pitched myself clumsily through the door.

Cheriour said nothing. It wasn't his style to offer words of comfort, even though he knew my nerves were frayed. Nah. The most I'd ever gotten from him was a "breathe," usually said with about as much enthusiasm as Ben Stein talking about dry eyes. And tonight, with him walking in an unsteady cadence behind me, his own breathing now growing harsher...well, the dude was in too much pain (physically and probably mentally) to remind me to breathe.

So I reminded myself.

Breathe. Breathe. Breathe...shit. Too fast! My vision got fuzzy as I borderline hyperventilated.

Braxton gave me an odd look when I weebled by him. Probably because I made that *hic-hic-heave* sound. Or maybe his crumpled expression wasn't aimed at me at all. Because he tottered backward, sticking himself in the corner of the room and grasping onto the wall as though the floor would disappear from under his feet if he ventured away from the "safe zone."

The floor sure felt ready to collapse beneath me. I didn't kneel beside the first man I came across. I *fell*, smacking my knees against the ground. Sharp, white-hot needles punctured my kneecaps, dragging down into my shins. But then the man coughed, sending a plume of blackish-reddish phlegm into the air, and my pain vanished.

The man's eyes rolled from Cheriour to me, then back to Cheriour before he made a sound halfway between a cry and a grunt.

"It will be alright, Dominic," Cheriour said with that low, monotone voice.

Dominic blinked a few times, forcing back tears. Every time he tried to say something, his words got lost in violent, wet bouts of coughing.

I touched his shoulder as he arched his back, straining to breathe. Blood oozed from his nose, trickling down his cheeks to smear across his already stained pillow.

"We'll let him sleep first." With a long, pained huff, Cheriour lowered himself into a half-kneeling position beside me, his good knee braced on the ground, his other leg stretched out in front. A position that looked awkward and *excruciating*.

"Dude, you should *not*—"

"Hold the rag over his mouth." Cheriour inclined his head toward my bucket. "It will only take a moment with as weak as they are."

Dominic stilled. No more coughing. But his breath came out in short, wet, rattling pants.

I dipped the rag into the bucket, wincing when the slimy mush glopped over my hands.

Dominic watched me with wide, scared eyes as I laid the

sopping fabric over his mouth. His warm breaths puffed through the rag, unsteady at first, but then they slowed. His eyes closed, and his face slackened.

"That's all you need to do, Addie." Cheriour freed a knife from his belt.

My stomach gave a sticky spasm as I threw myself to my feet. "I'll, uh, okay. Yeah. I guess I'll keep walking down this row..." I gestured to the line of bedding. "And you can come up behind me, yeah?"

I didn't wait for him to respond before I snatched the rag and bucket and bolted for the next person.

But after I soothed a hysterical woman and sent her to herbal la-la-land, I had to look over my shoulder. *Had to.* Because I was a glutton for fucking punishment.

Cheriour gently pulled a blanket over Dominic's face. Blood saturated the sheets, drizzling from the long slash on Dominic's throat.

I spun back around, pressing my potpourri-scented fingers to my eyes as a heavy pulse thrummed behind my temple.

We were *helping* them. By letting them go rather than making them suffer through the disease.

But I wished it *felt* like we were helping.

Instead, guilt gnawed at my heart, and every instinct I had screamed "this is wrong!"

I didn't look at Cheriour, or anyone else, as I made my way down the row. I couldn't watch them kill people. *Wouldn't.* So I kept my head down, shuffling from person to person, soothing them when they whimpered or cried and holding their hands while the herbal chloroform whisked them off to dreamland.

I knelt by Geraldine's bed—my fifth...no, sixth patient?

Could I even call her a patient at this point? *Victim* seemed more fitting.

"Geraldine?" I touched the back of her hand.

Her watery gaze sluggishly moved over my face. "It's time?"

"Yeah. Sorry."

"Nothing you need to be apologizing for." She gave a barking laugh. "You've been the best part of this mess. I loved listening to your stories."

I smiled. "Really? I figured I gave you all headaches."

She huffed.

Belanna also scoured out a laugh. "Ach, we already had headaches. But ye never gave us a quiet moment to dwell on them. Speakin' of headaches...where's me brother?"

"On the other side of the room," I said. "He's trying to work up the courage to come over here."

Braxton was a *wreck*. He still stood in the corner, his red-rimmed eyes blearily watching the room as he drank his whiskey.

"Did he find out I emptied the whiskey cask?" Belanna chuckled.

"Oh, Belanna," Geraldine did a cough-laugh, "you're *incorrigible*."

I snorted. "You're so full of shit."

"Eh?"

"There is *no way* you emptied that cask."

"Aye." Belanna grinned.

"How? With the power of your mind?"

"No. I had Kaelan do it." Belanna's smile was lopsided and her teeth bloodstained, but her eyes were bright. "I couldn't go to me grave without playin' one last trick on me wee brother, could I?"

A laugh bubbled out of me. "Oh...my...God. That's *terrible*. A really badass prank, though—I thought he drank himself to the bottom of the cask and was too smashed to remember."

"Ha! I'm sure that's what everyone'll be thinkin'. This will drive him mad." She winked. "Ye should have yerself a drink of that whiskey, Addie. Or two. It's the only good alcohol ye'll find here..."

"That's debatable..."

"Just make sure ye give the rest to me brother when yer done." Her smile faded. "He'll be needin' it."

"I'll tell ya what." I flinched when the guilt took a big munch out of my heart. "I'll have a drink for you. A toast. 'To Belanna. She may have seemed like your typical back-stabbing, slut-faced ho-bag, but she was so much more than that.'"

"Hoes are not typically bagged," Geraldine said.

"I didn't understand half of what ye said, but I like it!" Belanna grinned. Then she started coughing and bringing up big clods of blood, and that prompted Geraldine to start puking, and...yeah. The good times were officially over.

It was so fucking unfair. Belanna had become a good friend. I'd barely gotten to know Geraldine, but I liked her. A lot. The three of us probably could've had a blast going out to bars, drinking too much, and doing a ton of stuff we'd regret in the morning. Poor Geraldine probably would've been stuck as the Voice of Reason (she seemed the type). But we would've had *fun*. We could've been friends.

And now I'd never see them again.

I didn't speak as I mopped the bile off Geraldine's chin. I couldn't.

"It's alright," Geraldine said. "You're doing us a favor."

I swirled the rag in the gloopy herbal chloroform and bit my lip until it bled, keeping all the things I *wanted* to say to myself. Geraldine and Belanna didn't need to leave this world riding a tide of angry tirades and curses. So I waited for the words to pass, and then I let Geraldine drift to sleep on a gentle current of quiet platitudes.

"Addie..." Belanna muttered as I got back to my feet and moved to her side.

"You should wait for your brother," I said. "He was pretty damn adamant about being here..."

"I know. And I'll start yellin' if he doesn't work up the courage soon. But I wanted to say...well..." She stretched a hand up, fingers shaking.

I reached down, clasping her knuckles.

"It was a pleasure knowin' ye, Addie. Truly."

"You too." I gave her fingers a squeeze. "You're totally not gonna get this reference, but... 'I think I'll miss you most of all.'"

Belanna's head lolled back. Blood glistened against her teeth and lips. "Ye finally said something I *do* understand." She flashed a wry smile. "'There's no place like home,' eh?"

A response that had me so fucking flabbergasted—she knew about the *Wizard of Oz*??—that I didn't even realize Braxton had approached until he sideswiped me. And even then, I said *nothing*.

Or at least I didn't *think* I said anything. But I was sure a string of barely coherent words ruptured from my mouth.

Belanna knew about the *Wizard of Oz*!

Holy *shit*!

Seriously...*Ho-ly SHIT!*

Wha-how-when-HOW??

Belanna laughed. A deep, gleeful bray that stayed in my head long after she was gone.

With her last words, she'd broken my brain.

I really would miss her most of all.

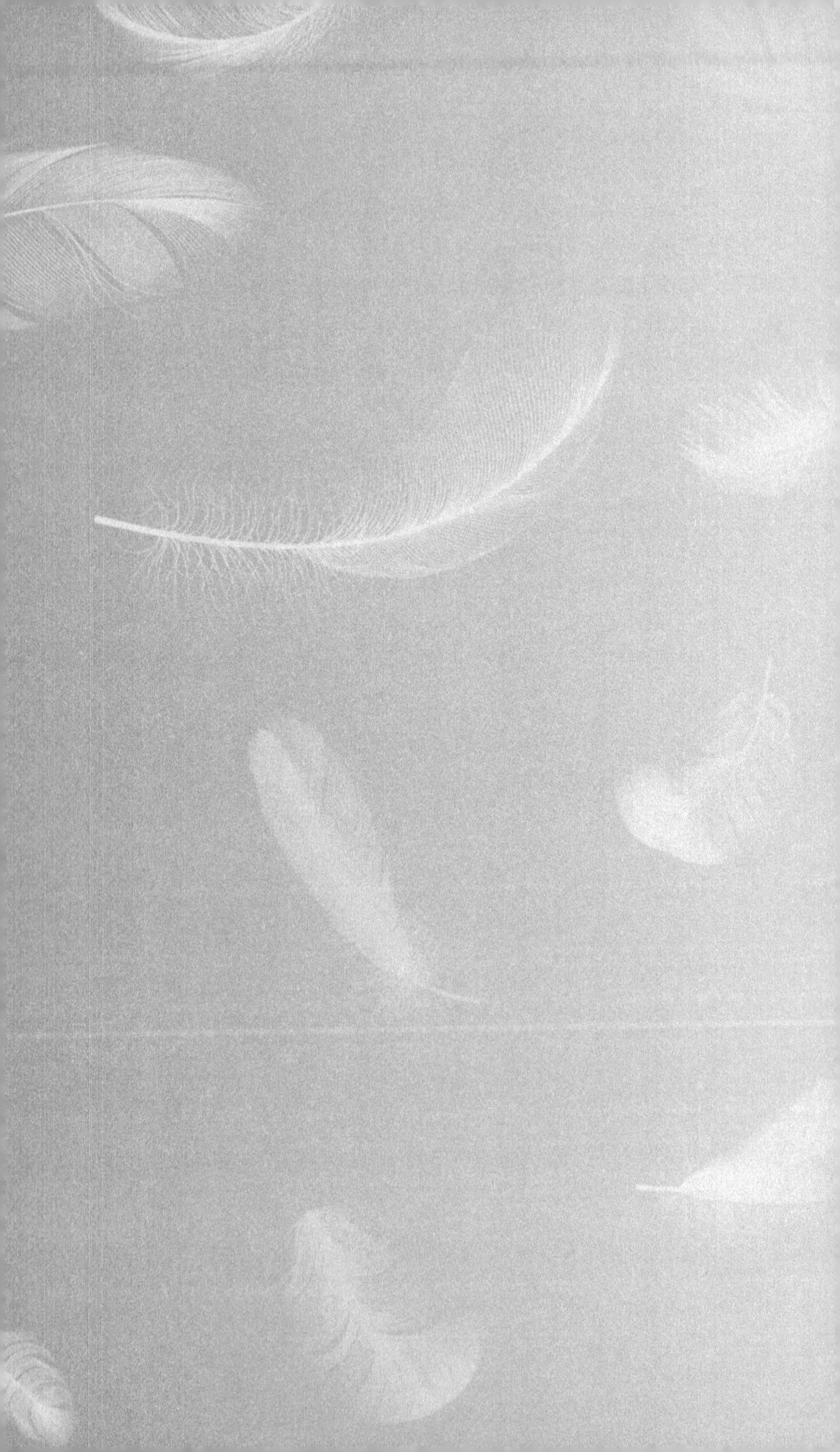

CHAPTER 4

A TOAST TO MOURN THE LIVING

There were no funerals. No memorials. Nothing.

I mean, that wasn't a shock. Funerals were for the living.

And there weren't many living left in Sakar.

But it seemed cold, carting the bodies across the rocky field—the same field we'd once battled on—and stacking them into neat rows and piles. As though they were planks of wood, crisscrossed and set for an epic bonfire, instead of a group of people who'd been breathing a few hours before. People with lives. Loved ones. Hopes. Dreams.

And we lit them all ablaze.

We couldn't stay there, either. Couldn't pour drinks and toast the glorious dead. Because the stench that rose from their bodies as they burned...

Well, burnt human flesh smelled like pork chops. But burnt disease-mangled flesh had a rancid ground-beef odor. Very ammonia-y and zesty as hell. My eyes immediately started watering. Which made the walk back to the castle, across the hilly and rugged terrain, treacherous.

"Cover your nose with this." Cheriour flopped a damp piece of cloth over my shoulder. A cloth he'd been using to mop the sweat off his forehead. Because, y'know, the dude *still had a broken leg.* But he'd *insisted* on limping to the crematory with us. Now he hobbled back to the castle beside me, pale, shaky, and sweating bullets. And his kankle looked ready to bust out of his boot and brace.

"Thank—*oooh, shit!*" I made a hasty grab for his arm when he hit a pothole and took half a second too long to catch himself. "Maybe we should throw your stubborn ass in one of the carts." I'd said the same thing on the way out.

And Cheriour gave me the same response both times. "Hmmm."

It was amazing how that sound could be both sexy and infuriating.

"*Hnnnn,*" I mimicked in a nasally voice that didn't even remotely resemble his. But then a breeze walloped the fetid odor across my face, and I clamped that wet rag over my nostrils, inhaling the oniony tang of Cheriour's sweat. It settled my stomach but did nothing to soothe the deep, yawning ache in my chest.

My God, I wanted a drink.

Not wanted, *needed.* I needed to take a shot of something strong enough to mush my brain.

"Where's Kaelan?" I asked.

Cheriour jutted his chin forward.

And there he was, walking a few feet in front of us, his golden head hanging in a glum bow: the Keymaster to one of the strongest drinks in all of Sakar.

"Hey! Kaelan!" I jogged to his side.

He jolted and snapped his head away from me, not-so-discretely blotting tears from his cheeks.

I slowed down a touch, staying a step behind him, waiting until he composed himself.

His smile, when he turned to face me, was more of a strained grimace. "Hi, Addie."

"Hey yourself, kid." I dropped my voice to a whisper. "Word on the street is you're the keeper of the whiskey."

At that, his smile loosened. His puffy, red-rimmed eyes scanned the field, making sure Braxton was out of earshot, before he nodded.

"Mind if I steal some?"

"You won't tell Braxton where it is, right? Belanna and I —" He gulped. "We made a wager. Although I suppose it doesn't matter now."

"I wouldn't *dream* of telling Braxton." I touched Kaelan's shoulder. "Scout's honor. I don't want Belanna haunting you from beyond the grave because you lost her bet—*kidding*," I added when an odd look crossed his face. "That was a bad—"

But he laughed—a soft, sad sound. "She told me she would hunt me down to collect her winnings. I wish she could." His lip quivered.

Kaelan was too fucking young for this kinda suffering. He and the other kids of Sakar had seen more trauma in their short years than most people back home would endure in an entire lifetime. Maybe *two* lifetimes.

And the adults of Sakar...*ooh, buddy*. A childhood bursting with trauma and loss led to a long adulthood teeming with war and heartbreak.

"I miss her," Kaelan murmured.

My heart was already breaking for the poor kid. That anguished whisper shattered it.

I rubbed his trembling arm. "Me too."

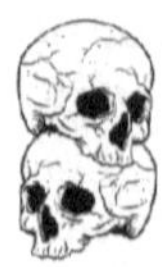

By the time we got back, the scraggy, black-stone castle was bathed in a silvery-gray light. It was almost dawn, although no one would get to see the sunrise today. Not with those big, fat, black smoke and ash clouds smearing the horizon.

I spent the day scouring the sickroom. Seriously, if someone had given me a toothbrush, I'd've used it to get right down to the cracks in the stone floor. Instead, I had to make do with rags. And elbow grease. Lots and lots of elbow grease. I was pretty sure I threw my back out with my overly animated scrubbing, but the throbbing between my shoulder blades dulled the ache in my chest, so...two negatives made a positive.

Or so I kept telling myself.

The castle was quiet. I worked with a big group, including Kaelan and Quinn, but no one spoke.

Well, *I* spoke. But everyone had learned to ignore my wild babbling.

Cheriour disappeared around mid-morning, hopefully to take himself to bed (I'd threatened to tie him up, *again*, and had gotten another aggravating "hmmmm"). Braxton drank himself under the table. *Literally.* He'd passed out under one of the kitchen benches.

And everyone else...well, it wasn't exactly a cheery day on the job. People went through their daily routines, but they resembled ghosts—pale and silent—as they roamed the halls.

The smoke still lingered in the sky at sunset.

And the rank scent of burning humans wound itself around the castle, seeping through the stone walls. It plastered itself in my nostrils as I returned to my room that night. But thankfully, I had a plump flask filled to the brim with whiskey to dull my senses.

Kaelan had barely moved the big whiskey cask, opting to swap it with the wine cask right beside it. "Belanna thinks —*thought* it would be too easy," he had told me. "I disagree. Braxton *despises* wine. He won't drink from this cask until he's desperate."

"Hidden in plain sight," I'd chuckled. "I like it."

Now I sat on the edge of my straw bed (aka, the bundle of cloth-wrapped straw perched atop a slat of wood masquerading as a bed) in my dark, cramped, and windowless room. And I suckled from the flask until my gut gave an unhappy gurgle. Then I stopped, breathing shallowly as the petrol booze (this stuff was the bottom shelf's anus) burned my esophagus.

We should've had a fucking funeral.

Viewing, luncheon, open bar...the whole nine. We could've done shots. A toast. To mourn the living.

Wait. That wasn't right, was it?

Mourn the dead?

Ah, fuck, I liked it better the other way. *Mourn the living.* Appropriate. The dead were...*wherever*. The spirit world. Heaven. Hell. Limbo. Didn't know. Didn't care. Whatever fate awaited them, it was sure as fuck better than being alive in Sakar.

"How much did you drink?"

I jerked my head up when Cheriour hobbled into the

room and—*whoa*, when the *fuck* did he get so tall? Even leaning on his jumbo toothpick, he looked ten feet high.

"Dude. You're like Clifford," I snorted. "Y'know, the Big Red Dog? Started out as this teeny-weeny puppy and then... *poof*. He's bigger than the house."

Cheriour sighed.

"How's the weather up there?" I yelled.

"You're sitting on the floor," he said.

"Am not." But I totally was. My bed towered over me too, a massive, insect-infested no-tell-motel.

"Fuck." I rubbed my eyes. "How'd I end up on the floor?"

Cheriour gestured to the bedsheets spilling off the mattress. "It seems you fell. How much did you drink?"

"Not enough, apparently." I took another swig.

How had I ever thought this whiskey was nasty? It was delicious. Went down smoother than a baby's bottom.

Er, no. That wasn't the saying. At all. Kinda creepy.

Smoother than...?

Butter? Was that the word I was looking for?

"Addie," Cheriour murmured. "It's late..."

"How can you fucking tell? It's always so goddamn dark in here...y'know vitamin D deficiency is a thing, right?"

"You should go to bed."

"*You* should go to bed," I grouched. "Your body's broken. Mine's—" *Hic!* "Oooh man, that burned. *Ouch*." The deep, wet hiccup stabbed my throat like a proverbial flaming sword. "Anyway...my body is A-okay. Okay? It's my *mind* that's messed up. Bed rest won't make that better."

"Addie." Cheriour stretched a hand toward me. "Why don't you give me that wineskin?"

I batted his arm away. "Get your own...*urrgghh*." I

flopped sideways. And, y'know, it was all the floor's fault. Damn thing bucked harder than a bronco.

But once I was down, my cheek resting against the coarse rock, I couldn't get back up. My whole body seemed... unmovable. As though I'd turned to stone.

Except stones felt no pain.

I still hurt. *Everywhere.*

"She knew about the *Wizard of Oz,*" I mumbled.

Cheriour said nothing except his usual "hmmm," but more softly this time. Questioningly.

"*The Wizard of Oz,*" I repeated. "A movie from back home. Er, it's a book too. But I only ever saw the movie. Always kinda hated it—Dorothy annoys the crap outta me. But it's got some good quotes. And Belanna *knew* about it! She..." My unshed tears stabbed white-hot pokers into my eyes. "She lived in my world once, didn't she? Sometime after 1939. Before the fuckhead Celestials brought her here. And-and *you*...you-you were one of those fuckhead Celestials once. Don't think I've forgotten about that." Although I *had* forgotten for a hot second. But now that fun fact was added to the dirty laundry running in a wobbly spin cycle around my brain. "Did you ever rip a kid away from their family?"

Cheriour was silent for a while, watching me. "No," he said. "I've done worse."

"Define *worse?*"

He shifted his toothpick and slowly, *slowly,* lowered his blank gaze toward me. The gaze that wasn't blank at all but was good at burying. Pain. Fear. Anger. Buried deeper and deeper and deeper—like the food I used to shove to the bottom of my freezer. Out of sight, out of mind. Left alone to rot. Only noticed when something exploded or leaked or started stinking.

"Never mind. I don't think I wanna know what *worse* is." I closed my eyes, slapping my hand over my face. This was too much. Not just what Cheriour had hinted at, or Belanna's death, *all* of it. Sometimes it seemed impossible that it'd been barely two months since I'd left home. Those weeks had seemed like a *decade*, one jam-packed with more drama than a soap opera scriptwriter could ever dream of...

"Gah!" I squealed when hands slipped beneath my shoulders and ass, hefting me off the ground. Cheriour's harsh breaths filled my ears.

"Yo! The doctor hasn't cleared you to lift—*oh no*." My vision spun as Cheriour moved toward my bed. The walls ran around my head screeching *he-he-he-he* like a damn cartoon villain. And my stomach didn't appreciate that. Nope.

The mattress sank when Cheriour deposited me onto it. And sank. *And sank.*

Was this a drop ride? Where was the bottom?

"I'm gonna..." Whiskey flooded my mouth. *Regurgitated* whiskey. OMG it burned.

I heaved forward to spit it out and whacked my chin on something hard. A bucket.

Cheriour held a bucket beneath my mouth. And thank *Christ*. Because once I spat out that first mouthful, more came up. And more. *And more.*

I'd morphed into a petrol-breathing dragon (I sure sounded like one) as I spewed enough whiskey to fill three-quarters of the bucket.

I expected to feel better afterward as I rested my sweaty

chin on the edge of the pail. Puke and rally, right? I'd made room for more alcohol!

Instead, I felt worse. A chill gripped my body. "Ooh man, I think Belanna told me to drink her whiskey because she'd poisoned it," I ground out as my teeth chattered. This wasn't the kinda cold bundling into blankets would fix. It was a chilled fever quake...one that came from somewhere deep inside.

"Addie..." Cheriour rubbed the back of my neck as he lowered the bucket to the floor and sat beside me.

And his touch, the rough scuff of his calloused fingers, the tender way he grazed my skin...

I hiccupped. Gave a treacly burp that tasted *foul* but was, thankfully, a false alarm. No more puke. My stomach was empty.

But my heart and my mind were overstuffed, and there wasn't an *easy* way to empty those out. I didn't know what the right outlet would be (yelling, throwing a tantrum, grabbing the hot Viking next to me and yanking his clothes off, or doing a sloppy combo) when I couldn't understand what I was feeling.

I didn't even notice when I'd finally started crying. Not until Cheriour's fingers grazed my cheeks, drying them.

Then the tears turned ugly—deep sobs that left my throat raw and my face snotty. I dropped my head into my hands, digging my nails into my scalp, trying to snuff out the thoughts that tumbled around and around and around inside my brain.

It was always the traumatic crap that started the spiraling.

My parents' piercing shrieks as the fire (one I kinda-sorta started?) gobbled them alive.

The oh-so-alluring aroma of piss-cheap beer and filet fish on Freddie Hawkins' (foster mom number three's closeted pedo boyfriend) breath as he slopped his mouth over my cheek.

Freda (foster mom number one; #1...aka, the *best* mom ever) staring blankly at the ceiling, her corpse already growing cold even as I crouched on the floor, chaffing her arms to warm her and *begging* her to look at me.

The sick woman I'd seen in Lamex, dazedly stumbling through her laundry and vomiting that black tar into her clothes basket.

Belanna, still cracking a mischievous smile even as the disease masticated her flesh.

The fire gallivanting through Niall's streets, devouring everything in its path. Except me. And the Celestial Seruf.

Seruf snapping that little boy's neck.

Cheriour's legs cracking when Seruf kicked them out from under him.

"He was a Celestial. Once."

The Fallen Celestial Gabriel careening through the smoke, hiding his freshly shorn hand behind his back.

"He suffers, dies, and rises. Again, and again, and again. That is the true curse of the Fallen."

The way Seruf had cackled this at me—*delighting* in the pain and confusion Gabriel had endured and eagerly anticipating the torment awaiting Cheriour.

Cheriour's hand slid from my neck.

"W-wait!" I snapped my head back only to lower it again, *gingerly*, when the world gave another violent buck. "Don't—" I sponged the sleeve of my shirt against my snotty nose. "Please? I—was I talking? I'm sorry...I...don't go. Please."

"Be still, Addie." Cheriour's fingers skated over my side before he bent and slowly, painfully, wriggled his puffy kankle from his boot and brace.

Once his other foot was freed as well, he scooted backward, drawing me against him, and reclined us both on my thin feather pillow.

I shuddered and pressed my face to his chest, inhaling his Au Naturel B.O. musk. "I-I don't actually care that you were a Celestial. But...I..." Questions swirled around my brain. Questions that seemed too big, too exhausting, to vocalize. So I didn't. "I still like you. 'Kay? Even when you're a stubborn ass."

Cheriour's body twitched on a soft chuckle. "I like you as well." He traced soft, languid circles around my ribcage.

His arms were heavy around me, and stiflingly hot. But beneath their warm weight, my body went soupy and relaxed. The world was still moving, but it'd become less of a breakneck amusement ride and more of a rowboat, gently rocking me to a faraway place where there were doctors and medicine and funerals.

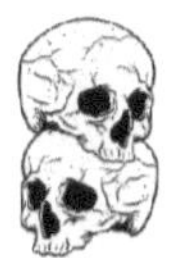

Scrape, scrape, scrape.

"This is fucking disgusting." I dragged the cock-eyed wooden rake across the prickly dead grass in Abby Normal's paddock. It made an awful *chirr* as it chaffed the ground. And the whiskey from last night had split my skull in half, so this noise was driving needles of pain right into that jagged crack.

Hangovers were no fun.

Hangovers from shit alcohol were always twice as painful.

Scrape, scrape, scrape.

If ya did it in a rhythm, it made a nifty tune.

"Shake, shake, shake…" I belted, even though it made my head thrum. "Shake ya booty!"

Beside me, Abby Normal grunted and laid her ears flat against her head.

"Look, if I'm stuck cleaning up your shit, you're stuck listening to my singing," I said. And, *literally*, I was cleaning up her poop. Her runny, mucusy, bloody poop.

Yes, her poo came out in blood globs.

Which I assumed (*hoped*) was normal for a Púca. She'd been pooping this way for…well, the entire time I'd known her. But since she wasn't a horse (she was a red-eyed, poisonous viper in a horse-shaped body), no one seemed to know whether her bowel movements were normal or not. And I'd asked *dozens* of people, including Cheriour. They'd all more or less given me the same answer: "I dunno."

"I think we need to have a talk about your diet, Abs. This "all liquid, no carb" B.S. isn't working for you." I swiped the gelatinous mess onto a shovel and waggled the rake in front of her face.

In response, Abby Normal turned to bite an itch on her shoulder. Her fangs made a long *scrrriippt* as she ran them across her black-scaled skin. And then she sneezed, sending snot projectiles across the paddock.

"Ew." I wiped one of the droplets off my arm. "Abs, you're kinda nasty…" I bit back a gag as a glutinous bit of blood poo plopped off my shovel right onto the toe of my freaking boot. And the sight of the crimson jello jiggling in the early morning sunlight combined with the scent (think a chemical plant operating inside a sewer)...

Welp, I *thought* I'd purged all the whiskey. I'd been wrong.

"Ugh...Belanna..." I leaned my hands against my knees, spitting the last bit of puke out of my mouth. "I definitely think you poisoned that—Abs! Hey!"

Abby Normal had emitted her god-awful *mowow* and lunged for the fence, teeth bared.

A boy was walking to the stables, carrying a heavy bucket on each arm. Although he was several feet from the paddock, he still let out a *"gugggh"* when he saw Abby Normal and jumped about a foot into the air, sloshing a steaming mix of bran mash down his side.

"Sorry!" I called to him as I rushed to shove Abby Normal back.

The kid gave me a bug-eyed stare and then hauled ass to the stables, spilling bran mash all along the loose stone path.

Abby Normal watched him like a hawk, ears still flattened.

"Congratulations," I told her dryly. "You made the thirteen-year-old shit his pants. And it's not even eight AM! What *hardened criminals* are you gonna bust next, oh mighty guard horse?" I slumped against the fence, pressing the heel of my palms to my palpitating head.

Abby Normal shuffled over, making a wet *sluup-sluup* as she licked her lips.

"Y'know, you're stuck living with these people," I told her.

She blew out a warm puff of air. It tickled as it brushed my hair.

"You ain't making any friends by bulldozing the fence every time someone gets too close."

It didn't help that Abby Normal's paddock was located in Grand Central Station (aka, along the castle's main walkway). Hordes of people and animals strolled back and forth all day long. Sometimes to get to one of the long, blackstone barns that wrapped in a giant horseshoe shape around the castle's perimeter, sometimes to get to the city a jaunty half-mile stroll down the walkway. And there were other fields too: A herd of cattle lounged in the rocky terrain behind the castle, shadowed by the building's barbarous eaves. Mares and foals were kept in a paddock on the other side of the walkway, as far away from Abby Normal's hungry eyes as they could get. There was a training field behind the right side of the barn, and a potato field somewhere to the left, beyond the city entrance.

Sanadrin was *massive*. And always bustling with activity. So this was *not* an ideal spot for a brambly, bloodthirsty horse. But the location was by design. Abby Normal was out in the open, where everyone could keep a careful watch on her. Because people distrusted her nearly as much as she despised them.

Abby Normal's muzzle touched the top of my head a half second before she blew me a kiss (aka, sneezed in my face).

"Abs"—I wiped the snot off my cheek—"*gross.*"

She bobbed her head.

"Yes, I'm glad you agree with me. It's disgusting. Like your radioactive poop—Hey! Abs! *Again?*"

The change happened so damn fast. There she was, being all affectionate and sweet, and then she abruptly spun, *mowowing* as she blitzed for the fence on the other side of the paddock.

Heading right for Quinn.

"Hey!" I called. "Quinn! *Back off the fence*! Abs, don't!" I got to my feet, my head *whomping* because I'd moved too fast, and sprinted across the grass. "Abs!"

Quinn paled and took a step back, putting several feet between himself and the paddock. In response, Abby Normal raised her head, readying to *jump* the damn fence.

Fuckfuckfuckfuck.

"Abs! *Stop!*" My feet skidded in a puddle of blood poo.

At the last second, Abby Normal hit the brakes. Clumps of dirt sprayed out from beneath her hooves. Her bulky body smashed into the fence, making the boards rattle almost right out of their fasteners.

Quinn's cheeks puffed as he blew out a breath.

I staggered into Abby Normal's side as she raked her teeth against the top slat.

"Bad...*bad!*" I gave her shoulder a hard shove. "Jesus, Abs. Didn't we *just* talk about making friends?"

Tension still rippled across Abby Normal's back, but she moved away from the fence. She never took her eyes off Quinn, though. Never unpinned her ears or relaxed her furled lips.

"You'll need to break her of this habit," Quinn said. "*Before* she hurts someone."

Abby Normal and I had almost the same reaction to the sound of his voice: she clicked her fangs, I ground my teeth.

"It's a work in progress. But if you *know* she's grouchy..." I whirled to face him. "*Why* did you get so close to the fence?"

Quinn sighed, shifted, and gave me this contorted, constipated look, as though he found me as unpleasant as a feculent turd that had festered in his bowels for a week. But then he pinched his bottom lip between his forefinger and thumb and smoothed his face into something more resembling a concerned pucker. "I need your help."

"*Hoo-hoo-hoo!*" I crowed. "How'd those words taste coming out of your mouth?"

"Cheriour," Quinn spoke over me, "is not yet fit to be training."

"Ummm, no shit. He's still got broken bones—"

"And he won't accept more healing. Not while Maddox and I are…" Quinn pressed his thumb into his lip. "Cheriour's been leading a training session all morning."

I gaped at him. "He—what?"

"He doesn't look well, but he's insisting he's fit to continue. And I—" Quinn pinched his lower lip again. "He listens to you. Sometimes."

"Oh, he's gonna listen to me, alright." I saw red as I moved toward the fence, ducking between the slats. "I will *drag* his ass back to bed if I have to."

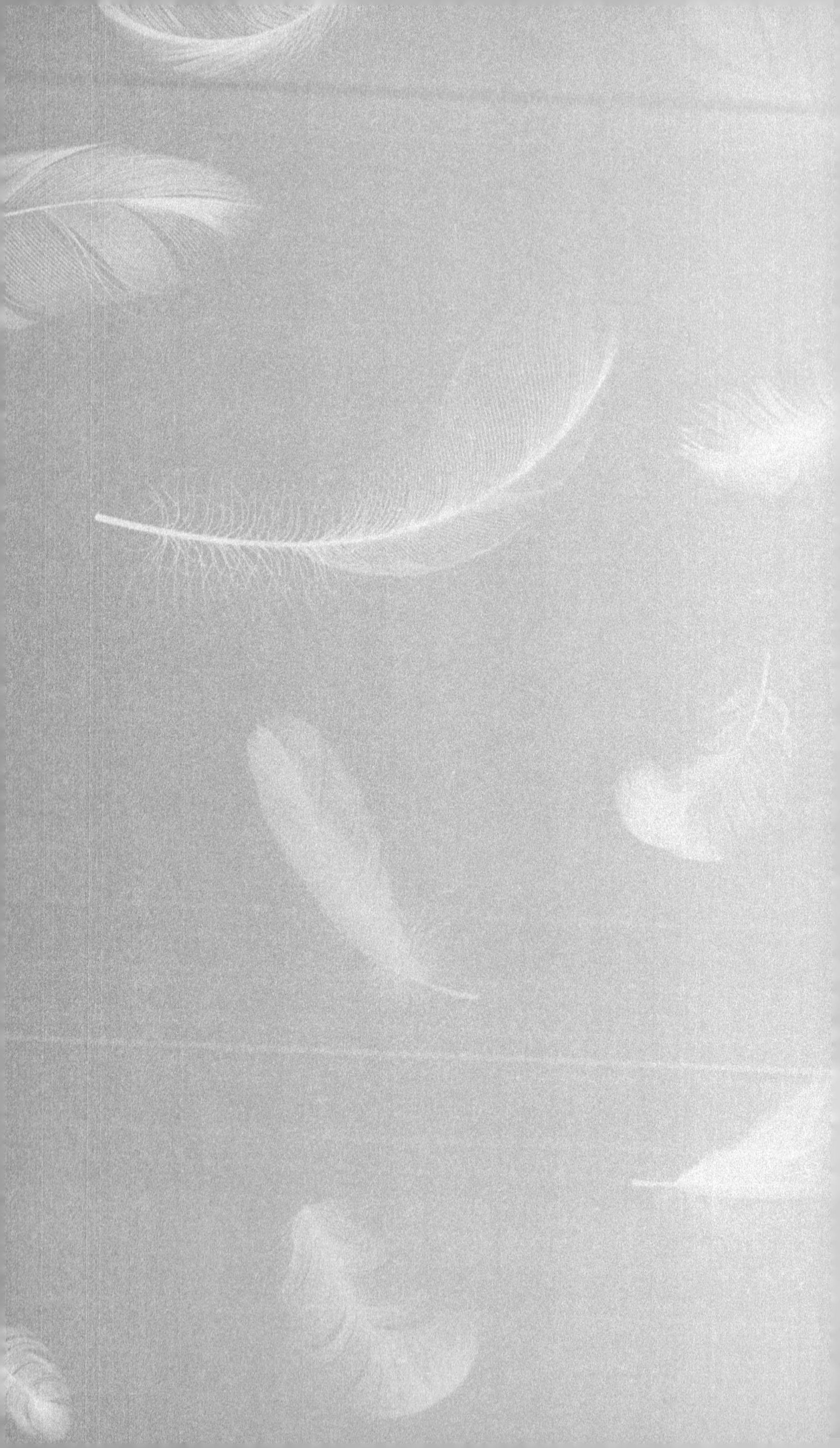

CHAPTER 5

SECRET SECRETS HURT SOMEONE

Look, there goes Godzilla!

Okay, I wasn't a three-hundred-and-fifty-five-foot radioactive sea monster. But I sure *felt* like one, ready to breathe nuclear fire and all, as I stormed through the stables.

That stubborn *bastard*.

"Ooooh, shit!" I hissed when I nearly collided with a pimple-faced kid and his beefy bay horse. "Sorry!" My voice sounded throaty and raspy...the kinda warbles the possessed Reagan had made in *The Exorcist*. And the horse sure looked at me like it thought I was in Pazuzu's clutches. It squealed (horse language for *oh, hell naw*) and bolted, dragging the poor kid down the aisle.

"Sorry!" I called again as I burst out the door. But I didn't look back to see if the boy had re-wrangled the horse. My gaze was focused on the rocky field that stretched alongside the castle, where Cheriour was not only teaching a training session, he was *participating* in it.

They were having some kind of knife throwing contest.

A group of twelve took turns chucking blades at straw targets. At least Cheriour wasn't doing hand-to-hand combat or sword fighting (small mercies), but he pivoted on his barely healed leg when he tossed his next knife. He hit the bullseye—because *of fucking course he did*—but the grating *creeee-pop* of his joints made half his trainees wince.

"Yo!" I yelled.

Several heads turned in my direction. One woman flinched mid-throw and missed her target by a mile.

Cheriour took his sweet old time swiveling to look at me —apparently, wiping an invisible patch of dirt off his knife took priority. When he finally deigned to grace me with his attention, he had a deadpan, almost bored expression on his face. But he couldn't fully hide his pain. Sweat trickled down his cheeks. He stood on a slant, keeping his left foot mostly off the ground. The jumbo toothpick rested against his hip.

I was definitely, *definitely* ready to breathe fire. Or cry hysterically.

Or both.

Or neither.

My emotions were so fucking loopy right now.

So I settled for yelling.

"You *idiot!*" I screeched as I reached his side. "Did you break your fucking head at Niall? Is that why you're being a dumbass?"

A few people sniggered. Quinn shimmied beside me but scooched sideways, giving me room. Y'know, in case I detonated.

Cheriour said nothing. Did nothing. Didn't even turn a hair.

I flicked a tear from my cheek and kept right on ranting. "*Your body is broken!* I barely—*barely*—kept you together long enough to get you out of Niall. And I've been *begging* you to take it easy. To give yourself a few goddamn days to *heal*. Why won't you listen to me?"

"Addie…" he drawled.

"You know what, no…don't even bother saying anything." I flung my arms through the air. "I was gonna try to convince you to come to your senses. *Again.* But you'll just ignore me. *Again.* And I'm too goddamn tired to deal with this bullshit. If you wanna break your stupid body, have at it." I turned, pinching the bridge of my nose as pain pulsed behind my eyeballs, and began my Godzilla stomp back through the stables.

Cheriour followed. His jumbo toothpick made an echoey *clink-clank-clink* against the slate rock covering the stable floor.

Anger raked its nails deep, *deep* inside me. Because Cheriour's gait was painfully uneven, his breathing danger-ously ragged, and it *should've* been common sense for him to go, "*Yeah, my body's wrecked. It hurts to move. I'm gonna stay in bed today.*"

Apparently, he had no common sense. Or he was too obstinate to pay attention to it.

And seeing him in pain? It hurt.

I *hated* that it hurt.

Hated that I cared about him enough to have that empathy.

I wanted to keep screaming. But I slowed down, giving him a chance to catch up. Because, y'know, I wasn't a *total* asshat.

Through the stables we went, me scaring people and horses shitless as I stormed by, and Cheriour garnering a very different type of reaction.

"Cheriour!" one bushy-browed man called jovially.

"How are you feeling?" another crooked-nosed guy asked.

"It's good to see you, Cheriour," a handsome woman gushed.

Cheriour grunted an acknowledgment to each of them but said nothing else. Probably because he was fighting to breathe.

Fucking mulish prick.

Why, why, *why* did I have to be so insanely attracted to a friggin' pighead?

I came to a stop outside Abby Normal's paddock and leaned against the fence, squeezing my eyes shut when the whiskey-crack in my skull throbbed.

Abby Normal nuzzled my arm, her hot breath fanning over my hand. But then she let out a warbled *mowow* when Cheriour caught up to me.

"Knock it off." I booped her nose.

She stilled but kept making threatening noises at Cheriour.

"Addie." My name wheezed out of Cheriour's mouth.

"I'm tired of this, Cheriour." I stroked a hand over Abby Normal's face. "Of watching people get hurt. Or sick. I'm *fed up*. And *you*..." I turned, forcing my eyes open even as the sun drove sizzling spikes into them.

Cheriour stood a few feet away, his shoulders bunching as he fought to control his breathing. Sweat sparkled on his chalk-white face.

"You've gotta stop," I whispered. "Before you drop dead of a heart attack. Because...because..."

"He'll join Gabriel before long...he suffers, dies, and rises. Again, and again, and again..."

I dug my fingers into my chest when that piercing mystery pain returned with a vengeance, twisting around in my insides until my stomach ached. Then the spasm loosened, leaving me sore. Winded. Hollow.

"Addie..." Cheriour took a limping step toward me.

I ground my teeth and gave him my best demonic "stay away or suffer the wrath of hell" face. Which was apparently pretty damn good, because he moved back.

Even Abby Normal reacted. She did more *mowowing* and started twerking from side-to-side.

"Abs, hey! It's...I'm not mad at you. Can you chill?" I reached through the fence and touched her shoulder.

She snorted, recoiled from me, and kept gyrating.

I must've conjured up a *helluva* demonic expression.

"I'm sorry. To *both* of you. It's just...I'm a fucking wreck right now." I plunked my forehead against the top of the fence and closed my eyes, inhaling deeply.

Slowly, Abby Normal stopped weaving. She hovered over me, smacking her lips. Her hot, metallic-scented breath puffed over the back of my head.

All the while, Cheriour had said nothing. Done nothing. But when I turned to face him, I found his gaze locked onto me. A rarity—normally he'd've been swiveling to monitor all the hustle and bustle around him.

"How unhinged do I look right now?" I swiped my hair over my shoulder, grimacing at the wonky state of my braid. Half the strands poked out of the twist in snarled, frizzy pufts.

Yeesh.

Cheriour said nothing. But he didn't look away either.

"That bad, huh?" My laugh sounded bitter. "I think I've ...I dunno. I've got too much crap in my head right now. Too many questions. And I *know* you can answer some of them, but...I mean..." *The potential answers scare the shit outta me, so I've been too spineless to ask.* I ground my teeth into my tongue, refusing to vocalize that last thought. "I didn't wanna bombard you while you were out of commission. But since you seem bound and determined to drive yourself into the grave, could we put some things to bed? *Before* you crap out? Like..." The questions raced through my mind faster than trains on a high-speed track. "If you *do* crap out on me, right here and now, what will happen? Will you come back as...as...as whatever Gabriel was?"

Cheriour fixed those dispassionate eyes on my face and droned a soft, "Yes."

"Huh. Shoot. Okay. And you realize that a week or so ago you were"—I pinched my pointer finger and thumb together—"this close to kicking the bucket."

"I'm aware."

"Then why *the fuck* are you trying to push yourself back to that point? Are you in a *hurry* to join Gabriel?"

"No."

"Then *why?*" But, before he could answer, I added, "And, y'know what, since we're on the topic of '*why*'...why didn't you tell me *anything?*"

Cheriour stared at me quietly a moment longer before murmuring, "I'm sorry, Addie. Truly. I should have..." His mouth twisted. And then he turned, his bones grinding out a loud *pop* as he shifted his weight and began walking.

"Where—?" I started in a huff.

"I'll answer what I can of your questions," he said. "But not here."

It was only after I rolled my eyes and ground out, "*Of course*...gotta build up that suspense first, huh?" that I realized people were watching. A lot of people—half the castle residents were scattered around the area, gawping at us. Including Mr. Shit Brick (aka, Quinn).

Well, okay. Cheriour was off the hook for the abrupt exit...*this time*.

I gave Abby Normal a goodbye pat and jogged to Cheriour's side. He stayed silent, even when I grasped his arm and let him use me as a human crutch. But I wasn't much sturdier than his toothpick. Because I couldn't stop shaking.

"D*UDE*..." I GROANED AS I STARED AROUND CHERIOUR'S ROOM.

All the rooms at Sanadrin were glorified shoeboxes: small, claustrophobic, windowless, and lit only by candles (which were *evil* inventions—no one would change my mind on that).

Cheriour's was a shoebox that had been reamed by a nuclear explosion. There was stuff *everywhere*: papers strewn across the floor, clothes piled in the corners, weapons leaning against every available inch of wall space. Cheriour's bed sat askew atop its wooden slats, with the sheets half on, half off. Two chairs butted against each other in the center of the room. You couldn't walk without stepping on or bumping into something.

"You've been here a week. A *week*!" I plucked a piece of paper off the floor. "How the heck do you mess up a room so fast?"

Cheriour limped over the debris and picked up a leather

flask that had been strung to the back of a chair. "Here." He handed it to me.

"I *know* that's not alcohol. Because you don't drink." Sure enough, it was water. Plain, gritty, Sakarian water.

I *hated* the water here. It hadn't made me sick (surprisingly), but it always had an earthy, mushroom-y taste. Unseasoned and unclean mushrooms, to be more accurate.

But I drank half the flask in several big gulps because it did soothe my raw throat.

Cheriour pushed a chair toward me. "Sit," he said as he lowered himself into the other chair, propping his bad leg in front of him. His shoulders rose and fell in shallow beats as he fought to keep his breathing controlled.

"I hope you're in *lots* of pain right now," I seethed. "Serves you right." I grasped the back of my chair, pulled it toward me, and then let it go. The front legs hit the floor with a clattering *thunk*. I did it again. And again, yanking the chair a little farther back each time.

"If you need to keep your hands busy, you can help me clean these..." Cheriour tilted his head toward a pile of leather in the corner of the room: an unholy mess of scabbards, vests, holsters...all the latest in Viking Weapon technology.

"Whoa-ho-ho. I'm surprised you know what the word '*clean*' means." But I walked over and snatched two vests out of the pile. Because why not? It was something to do.

"There's a tin there." Cheriour pointed to the edge of his bed. "And a few strips of cloth."

I snatched them as well, gagging at the odor seeping out of the closed tin. "Dear God...what's in here? Rat poison?"

"Cod oil." Cheriour took a vest and a rag from my hands. "Animal hide stiffens, especially when exposed to moisture."

He tapped his thumb against the splotchy bloodstain on the front of the vest. "Cod oil keeps it pliable. Prevents it from cracking."

"And makes it stink to high heaven?"

The ghost of a smile brushed Cheriour's lips. "There are worse smells. You're fortunate to have never worked in a tannery." He rested the tin against his good knee, popped the cap off, and dipped the edge of the cloth into the jiggly gloop inside.

Bleh...

Cheriour smeared the goo across the vest, massaging it into the leather. After a few passes, he glanced up at me, like *"Got it? Or do you need a 'Leatherworks for Dummies' manual?"*

I smashed my rag into the congealed oil, flopped into the chair across from Cheriour, and smacked the vest over my knee, giving it a deep-tissue rubdown.

"Don't scrub too vigorously," Cheriour cautioned.

I glowered at him as I lightened my strokes.

For a few minutes, we worked quietly while Cheriour's hitching breaths returned to normal. And then, shockingly, *he* broke the silence first.

"Most people"—he kept his eyes glued to his lap as he spoke—"are not aware I am Fallen."

My fingers faltered as ice rushed through my veins. "Oh...*crap*...did I blow your cover when I threw my tantrum?"

The corners of his eyes crinkled. "I doubt any were listening so closely."

"Okay. Well, that's good. But I'm *really* sorry. I was being an ass, stomping all over your old wounds..."

"No, Addie..."

"Because, I mean, *I get it*. Trust me. I get it. Some stuff's too murky to talk about."

"It's not..." His mouth contorted. "I don't mind you knowing, Addie." A short, breathy laugh escaped him. "It's *odd*. To acknowledge the life I've almost forgotten."

My heart tugged. "*Almost* forgotten? Was it traumatic? Were you *trying* to suppress it? Until I dredged the bad shit back up?"

Cheriour shook his head. "No. It wasn't traumatic. Not until the end."

That last bit was a fucking land mine. I steered around it. "Sooo...what was it like, then? Being a Celestial?" I prodded in the softest, sweetest customer service voice I had in my arsenal. And then I clamped my teeth over my tongue, giving him space to back out if he needed it.

"Not so very different from being mortal." Cheriour dipped his rag back into the cod oil, his jaw ticking as he wrestled the words into submission. "Sometimes I forget I *am* mortal. Until I need to move. Mortal limbs are not so swift."

"If mortal you is the slowpoke version, I'd hate to train with Celestial you." I grimaced.

"My thoughts tangle more," Cheriour continued, partially speaking over me. "My mind is limited now. More sluggish."

Which, yeah, that tracked. Definitely explained why he could multi-task like a dream but sometimes struggled to spit words out. There was too much data being pumped through that head of his and not enough bandwidth to accommodate it.

"So Celestial you had a high-tech brain and hyper-speed. But you had to have other things too, right? Super

Hulk strength? Titanium bones that felt no pain? Some Doctor Strange-level mastery over the multiverse? Or... *flying*! You had wings, right? I'm assuming? Sorry!" I added when he opened his mouth. "I'm bulleting a lot at you. But you don't have to answer if—"

"I don't mind, Addie." His lips tilted up. "You can ask. It's alright." He flipped the vest over, kneading the cod oil into the small fissures around the arm holes. "Yes. I had wings. And more strength. But I was not immune to pain— no Celestial is. If you injure a Celestial, they'll suffer. But they'll heal before the wound can claim them. As for the rest..." He paused. Frowned. "Celestials perceive things differently than humans. Their sight is vast. If I were still a Celestial, I would not simply see you as you are now. I'd see the entirety of your life. From your conception until your death. Your triumphs. And troubles. Illnesses you suffered. Losses you endured. The happiness you experienced. Time is complex..."

"But humans are too limited to see it," I echoed the statement he'd made to me months ago, when I'd first arrived at Sakar. "We think it's a linear line."

Cheriour glanced up, a surprised smile stretching over his mouth. "You remembered."

"Shocker, right? Occasionally I squeeze some actual information in between my pop culture tidbits," I laughed. "Not gonna lie, though...seeing a gazillion versions of a person while you're trying to have a conversation with them sounds like a massive headache."

"For a human, it would be. Mortal brains cannot conceive such imagery. When I Fell, those were the first memories I lost. I've forgotten other things as well. The sensation of traveling—or flying, as you called it. My home in the Celestial City..." He paused again. "The longer I'm mortal, the more the memories fade. Eventually, I may forget I was a Celestial. I'm not certain. Most Fallen don't live long enough to see their memories dwindle. They succumb quickly to hunger, dehydration, or disease." His hands roamed over the leather. "When I Fell, I was expected to die within a year."

Flip-flop went my nervous stomach. "But you—you've been alive longer than a year, right?"

Cheriour's mouth twisted. "I've been *mortal* for more than a decade."

I didn't miss the emphasis on the word *mortal*. The politically correct way of saying, *"I used to be im*mortal*, so I'm a fuck-ton older than ten years."* "Well." I cleared my throat. "Give it another decade and you'll be old enough to drink. I'll throw a twenty-first birthday bash for ya..."

Cheriour gave me a long, indecipherable look.

"Eh, we'll make the drinking age here eighteen," I amended. "That's the minimum for every other country back home. 'Cept America. We were behind the times..."

"Gabriel," Cheriour carried on, ignoring my tirade, "was the first of my brethren to Fall to Ramiel. Several decades ago." His cheek puckered as he bit the inside of it.

He was struggling. Whether he just couldn't find the right words or this topic was causing him anguish, despite his assurances otherwise, I didn't know.

I gnawed on my lower lip and rubbed the stinky rag in slow circles over the leather.

Wax on, wax off.

"You asked if I would share Gabriel's fate when I die," Cheriour finally continued. "I will. Although my appearance won't match his until I've perished dozens of times. Each time Gabriel rises, he loses more of himself." Cheriour stared unblinkingly down at his piece of leather.

That stoic but unsarcastically worried expression had my heart flipping upside down. "I'm sorry," I said.

But that, apparently, was the end of the Celestial/Fallen conversation. Because Cheriour rolled right to the next topic. "And you were right. In what you said before. I *should* have told you more." He inhaled as he draped the rag over his bad leg and ran his thumb over the vest, checking for dirt spots. "I knew...*suspected* who you were the moment you arrived. You have her eyes."

I swallowed as I thought back to the memory that had surfaced while Ramiel fondled my soul: that gaudy room with a gazillion hiding spots, and the girl who'd been ushering me into one of those hideaways.

A girl who had my eyes. Purple. *Vibrant* purple. A mutation so rare, most considered it an impossibility. Everyone back home had always assumed I wore colored contacts, and they all said the same stupid thing when they realized my eyes were 100 percent authentic: *"Wow. You won the genetic lottery. Maybe you should start playing the Powerball, huh?"*

"Her name was Lasair," Cheriour said.

"What?"

"The woman you saw." He lifted his gaze toward me. "And purple eyes are no less rare here."

"I was talking, wasn't I?"

"Always." His lips twitched. "The image you saw of her was likely a memory."

"A memory I didn't remember until a week ago?"

"Childhood memories are easy to suppress." Cheriour

shrugged. "You lived with Lasair. For a time. Until you were taken."

"I—*taken*? And I've *heard* that name before...Lasair..." I pressed the heels of my palms into my temples as my over-worked brain went *thimp-thwack* against my skull.

"I told you the name," Cheriour said. "When you first arrived at Niall."

My suddenly numb hands slid away from my face. "Shit, you're right! She—you said she was the former ruler of Netheridge, right? I stayed in her room?"

Cheriour inclined his head. "I thought you would recognize her name when I said it that night. But you didn't."

"How was I supposed to recognize a name I'd never heard before?"

"You *had* heard it before. You lived with her. As I said." Cheriour's mouth distorted again.

A nervous bubble rippled through my stomach.

I didn't *want* to know whatever explanation he was grappling with.

At the same time, I *needed* to know.

Secret secrets are no fun. Secret secrets hurt someone.

I was about to get a massive smackdown.

"Lasair had a child." Cheriour's voice was back to *sloth creepy-crawling up a tree* speed. "Six years ago, that child was taken from her."

Oh *hell* no. "I swear to freaking God, if you say that kid was me, I'm gonna shove this cod oil up your nose..."

"Then I won't say it." Cheriour gave me a pointed stare.

Fuck. "But you believe it?"

"Yes. I do now. But I was expecting a *child* to return. When you arrived, fully grown and seemingly powerless..." He bunched his shoulders beneath his ears. "I *suspected* you to be Lasair's daughter. But could not *confirm* it. Lasair's power was most volatile when her emotions were high." A huff escaped him. "As your emotions *always* seem to be."

I waggled my middle finger in the air.

"I thought you would loose your power eventually. *If* you were Lasair's daughter. I monitored you. Quinn kept you guarded. He also tried to *force* your power forward—"

"Wait...Quinn was in on this too?"

"—but you never lost control. So I doubted my assumption. Until you landed in the fire."

Heh. *Landed in the fire.* A graceful way to describe how I'd roly-polied around in the smoldering wood and rammed embers up a Wraith's ass.

That Wraith had died, singed and covered in blisters.

I'd emerged without a single burn.

"Lasair was a Firestarter." Cheriour enunciated *every. Single. Word.*

I started shaking my head, ignoring the ache that ripped up the back of my neck and seeped across my skull.

"These may not be the words you want to hear." Cheriour honed that intense gaze on my cheek. "But you *are* the child Lasair lost. I'm certain of it now."

"No. Impossible. Because not only did I have a mother— a *biological* one—"

"She wasn't."

The leather vest made a harsh, wet *plop* as it slid off my jiggling knee. "She definitely was. And even if she wasn't, this...*story*...is still impossible. You said this *Lasair* lost her kid six years ago? I'm thirty—er, maybe thirty-one at this point." I was a Sagittarius (December baby). And since I got abducted in *November*, my birthday had already come and gone. "The math doesn't add up."

"I thought the same at first. But time is not linear," Cheriour said.

I dropped my head into my hands, digging my nails into my scalp as white spots zig-zagged before my eyes. "Ugh, dude. My head was jumbled enough. Why did you have to make it *worse*?"

"I'm answering your questions," Cheriour droned.

"Yeah. Thanks, smartass. I guess I should've specified that I wanted answers that made *sense*! Not this twisted, *Interstellar* B.S."

"The right answers aren't always the most logical."

"Aaand now you're starting on the *philosophical* B.S." I raised my head to glare at him. "But riddle me this, Socrates...*Why*? Let's say everything you've told me is true...I have my doubts, but I'll roll with it for now. If I'm some, I dunno, a child lost to time, *why*? Why was I taken away? And why in ever-loving fuck was I brought back? Also...that red-headed bitch—Celestial—whatever—I *told* you about her," I snapped when Cheriour frowned. "I mean...you were kinda loopy that day, but I still told you. She's the one I saw at Niall, *and* she abducted me. Right in front of my pizza..."

"That," Cheriour said, "was likely Kylah."

"Okay. Who's she? The Pizza Burglar?"

"She's one of the Guardians of Time."

"Oh good. We jumped out of *Interstellar* and into a Marvel movie. Cool."

Cheriour's shoulders rose as he drew in a big breath. "I don't know *why* you were taken from Sakar. But I believe Kylah sent you back because of what happened to Lasair."

Nope. *Nopenopenopenope*. I didn't want to know.

But the question slipped out of my mouth anyway. "I'll bite...What happened to her?"

Cheriour's lips twisted. "She's gone."

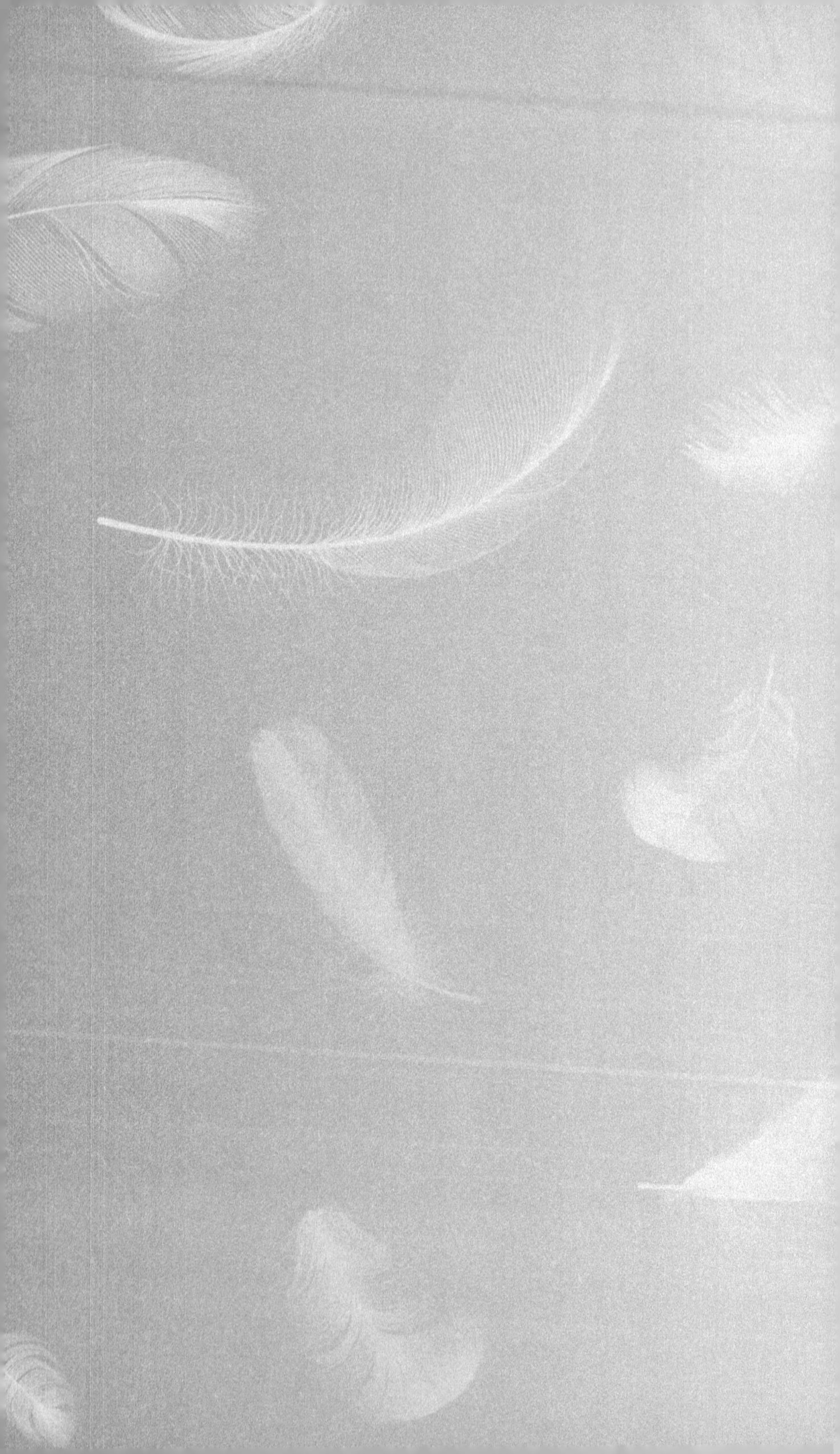

CHAPTER 6

TWO PEAS IN A FUCKED-UP POD

I stood so fast, the chair backflipped and clattered to the ground.

"Addie," Cheriour started.

"I...uh...." I wiped my sweaty hands on the seat of my pants as I walked across the room. My stomach did a viscid *squitch-squatch*.

"Addie." Cheriour's voice sounded different. Deeper. "You should—"

"I'm sorry. But I have to...go...do *something*." I scuttled out of the room, hoping the fresher air in the hallway would settle my riotous stomach.

It didn't.

Foul, battery-acid-tasting saliva pooled over my tongue.

"Addie!" Cheriour called again.

Before he got his broken legs under him, I bolted through Sanadrin's narrow halls, twining down the tight, oppressively dark stairways. I mean, these corridors had *some* lighting. A sconce hung every ten or so feet, but it was a crapshoot as to whether they'd be lit.

Smart people carried a candle with them when they traversed the castle.

I was not a smart person.

So I fumbled through the darkness, periodically whacking my elbows against random bump-outs in the walls and popping my ankle in funky divots in the floor. My rasping breaths, hissed curses, and occasional spatterings of word vomit ricocheted off the stone, filling the halls with my dulcet/echoey tenor.

My mother was a dental hygienist. My dad was a...a...well, I dunno what he did. But he worked in an office. Typical nine-to-five grind. I have pictures of them! And videos. I know what they looked like. Know what they sounded like. They were my parents.

But what if they weren't?

What if a big, fugly, angelic stork dropped me on their doorstep?

Or...oh God, what if they did *have a daughter and I replaced her? Like a—a changeling? Is that what evil elves are called?*

And why am I so upset about this?

Whether I descended from normal, red-blooded humans or a flyin' purple-eyed people eater, the end result was the same: my parents were long dead. And I was still Addie Collins, hairstylist extraordinaire, consumer of junk food and all things pop culture, and a badass nerd.

This news does not change who I am.

So why did it make me angry?

Out the castle doors I went (and I only got lost once on the way there...a new record for me), still breathing worse than Godzilla on a bender.

I wanted...

My *car.*

I wanted to slide behind the wheel and listen to the

familiar rumble and screech of the motor. I wanted to blast music until my ears bled. It would quiet my racing thoughts, at least for a few minutes.

I wanted to go...*somewhere.* A bar. Brewery. Winery. Restaurant. A grocery store. Somewhere I could be surrounded by regular people and listen to them bitch about their day jobs, swap spoilers about the latest TV show, spout conspiracy theories about some shady politician, or complain about stuff they saw on social media. As though those insignificant annoyances were the biggest tragedies mankind had ever faced.

Normal. I wanted something fucking *normal.*

A few months ago, I'd heard all that mindless chitchat every single day. Usually while grabbing my morning coffee.

And now, standing outside Sanadrin's black fortress, Cheriour's words churning in my head as the Sakarians around me went about their day...my past life seemed as distant as a dream. Something that had never actually existed.

Because it hadn't. Not really.

What if I was living in some *Twilight Zone*-esque nightmare and my memories were only dreams?

It was probably why I'd been feeling so odd lately. The dream had shattered. I couldn't pretend it was real anymore.

I shivered as a cool, moist breeze ruffled my hair.

"*Fuck!*" The scream fist-punched through my chest. It *hurt.* And it left me doubled over, my hands pressed against my knees.

To my right, Abby Normal *mowowed* softly. She stood against the fence, hanging her head over the rails, giving me a confuzzled look.

A few people stopped. Stared. I didn't recognize any of

them. And most were coated in grime and soil. Farmers... *maybe?*

I had no idea what kind of jobs people had here.

"Are you alright?" a tall, soot-covered woman asked.

"No," I grunted.

"Do you need me to get someone?"

"Definitely not." I pictured them flagging down Cheriour: *"Hey, y'know that looney lady you're always with? The chubby blond? She's being* extra *crazy today. You wanna go get her before she scares the kids?"* I sniffed and straightened. "Is-is there a bar around here?"

That question earned me a bunch of blank stares.

"A...what d'ya call them?" I amended. "Pubs? Taverns?"

"Aye," one of the men said. "There's the Snake and Spider Inn..."

"*Yeck.* Is that really the name?"

His weather-beaten face crinkled when he smiled. "It's in the city. On the main street. You can't miss it."

"Are you sure you're alright?" the first woman asked. "Because I can get—"

"I'm fine." I pivoted, throwing a tense, "Thanks, though!" over my shoulder before I darted off.

A few people stared as I galumphed unsteadily down the walkway. One kind, chubby-faced boy (he couldn't have been older than ten) helped me with the wooden gate that separated the castle from the city. I'd had to *push* the gate. Not *pull*. Thankfully, the saintly boy intervened before my thirty seconds of fruitless yanking caused another meltdown.

But no one else said or did anything as I escaped into the bustling city.

It was so, so, *so* overcrowded. I couldn't move without

jabbing elbows or ramming someone's foot or tripping over the young kids who gleefully treated the street as their playground, even as their frazzled parents screeched to, "Mind where you walk! I'll not be saving you if you get yourself trod on!"

It was a *madhouse*.

And this was apparently the central shopping hub for Sanadrin. Rickety market booths lined the packed-dirt street on both sides, jampacked with people selling cheeses, breads, fish, and clothes.

A Viking Walmart.

But instead of flashy signs, vendors squawked and yelled to advertise their prices and special deals.

And, let me tell ya, some of these sales were *too good* to pass up.

"Two coins! Only two! For five *fresh* rabbits." A woman twirled a spinner rack full of dead bunnies.

"One loaf, one coin," said the man holding baguettes that looked harder than...well, a cock. *Har, har.* Seriously, he white-knuckled those bad boys, and his fingers left no imprints. None.

"If ye give me three coins for this here dried goat, I'll give ye a fresh rat." This last bit was said as a yellow-toothed man thrust a cage of *very alive* rats in my face.

I yelped.

The mass of rats squeaked and undulated against the wooden bars of their mini prison. There were so many of them crammed into the tiny space. And one in particular, a teensy brown floofball, looked close to being smooshed to death. It was stuck in the corner, its bottomless black eyes wide, pink nose flaring as the rest of the rats stampeded over it.

"They're young. *Fresh.* What do ye say, hmmmm?" The man gave the cage a hard shake.

"Urrmm...*no*," I said. Those poor things looked *petrified*.

The man shrugged. "Three coins!" he bellowed in my ear before he turned on his heel, pedaling his shellshocked rodents to the next cluster of people.

"Jesus..." I scooted to the center of the street, *away* from the booths and their weirdo snacks. Because, *oh yes*, the rats were definitely meant to be snacks. Another guy sold dead rats on sticks...and people *were buying them*! Especially kids, who seemed *thrilled* to munch on their rodent corn dogs as they tottered behind their parents.

I got the appeal of shoving food in a kid's face to keep them occupied during a grocery run. Freda used to do it to me all the time. But *rats*?

I shuddered and then squeaked out a "sorry!" when I barrel-rammed into a tight cluster of people. They didn't even care. Probably because they were used to it.

Crowded cities were all the same: too many pushy-shovey people and not enough space.

I kept walking, the endless chatter, shouting, and jostling becoming a white noise. A very *soothing* white noise. Because, yeah, the ick food choices aside, this wasn't all that different from taking a stroll through NYC. So I felt a smidge calmer when I found the Snake and Spider. A distressed wooden sign hung over a crooked door depicting—*drumroll please*—a snake and a spider, locked in what was probably meant to be an epic battle between the two creepiest sons of bitches on Earth. But it looked like the snake was going down on the spider.

And that spider did *not* seem upset about it.

I snorted and swung the dilapidated door aside, beaming when a wall of noise rose to bitch-slap me. *Music.* And loud peals of laughter. This place was *packed.* A rippling wave of humans flooded the space. Some sat at the round wooden tables scattered throughout the room. Some had gotten lucky enough to nab a seat at the L-shaped bar. But most stood shoulder to shoulder, tucking their booze against their chests as they swayed to the music emanating from the far side of the room, where a band sat clustered against a wall, trilling away on their...flutes? Was that what the long pipe-looking things were called? And I knew those pear-shaped instruments weren't guitars, but they sure *resembled* rudimentary guitars. The music was *good* too. Old-fashioned Irish-style jigs. Perfect for dancing; a few people were even attempting to do a drunken waltz on the very few open spaces of floor.

It was barely noon. And the place smelled worse than a nightclub right before closing time: the succulent perfume of cheap beer, unwashed and sweaty bodies, cigarette smoke, and other lush bodily odors. Half the people in here were *smashed.*

And, oh, how I wished I could join this Boozy Brunch. But one glance at the bar squashed that hope. Everyone was tipping little silver coins toward the bartender in exchange for their beer.

And my pockets were emptier than my soul...

Har, har, har.

Seriously, I hadn't been making a steady paycheck since I arrived at Sakar. I hadn't even known money was a *thing* in this world before today. And I wasn't depressed enough to start begging for freebies. Yet.

But I walked up to the bar anyway, wedged myself into

the corner, and watched as the tall, balding man poured beer out of paunchy wooden barrels. He was a good bartender: quick, friendly, and he didn't miss a beat.

"Hello there!" He turned to me with a toothless smile. "What'll you have?" His eyes narrowed slightly as he studied my face. "Ah." He drummed his fingers against the bar. "You'll be that new arrival Cheriour found a few months ago, eh?"

"Guilty." I nodded. "What gave it away?"

He touched the corner of his left eye.

I sighed. "Of course." Those purple irises were more glaring than a neon sign.

"And your tunic," he added with a warm laugh. "Not many people'll come in here wearing something so fanciful."

I plucked at the collar of my dazzling blue/pink shirt. "Ah...yeah. I guess this sticks out like a sore thumb, eh?"

"A bit." The bartender tapped the counter. "Anyway, since you're new, I'll cut you a deal. One coin'll get you two mugs of ale and a bowl of stew. Or, if you prefer, I may have a little wine left..."

"Oh. Shoot. I didn't realize you were gonna give me the newbie special. Ummm, I don't have *any* coins. *Sorry*! I was planning to hang out and people-watch. But if this is paying customers only, I'll leave. I totally under—"

A coin clattered onto the counter in front of me.

I whipped my head around as Cheriour wedged himself into the narrow space on my right side.

"Cheriour!" The bartender grinned and swiped the coin off the counter. "*Hoi*! This is a surprise. I didn't think I'd *ever* see you in here."

"I didn't expect to find myself here." Cheriour leaned heavily against the bar, propping his toothpick against his legs.

"Well." The bartender cleared his throat. "Being as you *are* here, I've had some folk asking...is Netheridge still being evacuated?" His voice dropped, even as a few people turned to gawp at us.

Cheriour inclined his head.

"*All* of Netheridge?"

"Yes."

"Right. Well." The bartender turned the coin over in his hand. "I'm sure you're not here to talk about that, eh? What'll ye two prefer to drink? Ale? Wine?"

"I'll take whatever beer you've got on tap...er, *ale*," I amended at the bartender's befuddled look. "I'll take the ale."

"Water. Please," Cheriour said.

I waited until the bartender shuffled away before I whirled to face Cheriour. "Dude...how the *fuck* did you limp down here so fast?"

"I know the city better than you," he said.

"Hmm, well—" I cut myself off, teeth sinking into my tongue, when a name rose over the swell of chaotic noise.

"Seruf. I'm telling you, she was *there*!" a man cried.

I whipped my head around so fast, my neck cracked. But the bar was too crowded, and there were too many other people talking. I couldn't tell who'd said her name.

But I heard it again.

"Seruf went into Niall, yes? But she never came back out, did she?"

And again.

"Seruf's still in Sakar. Mark my words."

"Addie?"

I jumped when Cheriour touched my arm. And my vision fuzzed as I took a big gulp of air—apparently the first breath I'd taken in a while. The rush of oxygen sent another bout of pain ripping into my chest.

I leaned my elbows against the bar, hung my head, and fought the urge to scream.

Would this *ever* get better?

Cheriour's thumb rubbed circles into my bicep, calming me. A little.

"Hey, Cheriour..." I swallowed. "At Niall...I know you were kinda out of it that night. But do you remember any of it?"

"Some," he said.

"Do you remember what happened with Seruf? How we got away from her?"

He shook his head, frowning.

I nodded and ran my finger over a jagged, discolored crack in the burnished wood.

"I assume Kylah intervened?" he pressed.

"No." My thumbnail scraped over a moist section of the bar, leaving a pale scratch behind. "I...I did *something* to Seruf."

"Here we are!" *Of course* the bartender chose *that moment* to return. But he gave no indication he'd overheard my dirty little secret (thank *fuck*) as he slid two wooden mugs onto the counter and placed a bowl in front of me. "If you need anything else, wave."

"Alrighty." I forced myself to smile and waited until he turned away before I snatched the beer and took two big chugs. It was...piss. Not literally. But it *looked* like piss and tasted like cheap Natty Light. It hit my gut with an acidic *plllaappffff*.

Cheriour shoved his mug of water toward me.

I glared at him.

He stared unblinkingly back.

"If I wanted water, I'd've ordered water," I said.

He kept up the thousand-yard stare.

"Ugh, fine. *Stop* with that judgy look." I snatched the water, downed half of it in three too-big gulps that left a lingering ache in my trachea, and shoved the mug back at him. "There. Happy?"

"*Exceedingly.*"

"*Whoa, Nelly*! Look at you coming in with some snark." A strangled laugh fizzed out of me. Because I'd never, *ever* heard a spicy side to his voice. Even on the rare occasions he'd had to yell to get my attention or bellow a command, he'd never lost that slow, syrupy drawl. But the word he'd lashed at me ("*exceedingly*") was syrup with a healthy dusting of jalapenos. "You must be spending too much time with me." I gave his shoulder a gentle poke. "I like it."

He pushed the bowl of steaming stew toward me. "What happened with Seruf?"

Dang it. My mood had *just* lightened a smidge, but that bitch's name was an anchor, yanking my emotions down into a black abyss.

I cocked my head, making sure the people around us were well involved in their conversations before I wrapped my hands around the steaming bowl, steeling myself for what I was about to say. "I killed her. Somehow. I don't...*Something* happened. I don't really know what. But I—She started *glowing*. And when I touched her—I mean, my hand went *right through*. And I touched her *soul*. Or Essence. Or whatever. I saw her *memories*. Then she was taunting me, and I hit her, and..." I blew out a quivering breath. "She *disintegrated*. And I—Something happened to me too. I haven't been...*right* since."

Cheriour's face was a little too blank. As though he was utterly appalled by my scattered confession and trying his damnedest to hide it.

"See the kinda entertainment you miss out on when you get stubborn and don't listen to me when I say '*stay away*?'" I huffed. "Because I *tried* to warn you. You could've picked a comfy seat and seen Seruf blow away like 'Dust in the Wind'...God, I love that song. Think the band up there knows any Kansas?" I couldn't see the musicians through the throng of gyrating drunkards, but I jabbed my thumb in that general direction. "I remember the lyrics..."

"Addie." Cheriour touched my arm. "You—"

"I wasn't planning on *singing*. Don't worry. But I can write the song down for them to sing. You got paper?"

"No. Addie...be still." He shook my arm.

Er...well, no. *I* was the one shaking. Hard enough to make my teeth chatter. Cheriour was trying to hold me steady.

"You also missed out on seeing Ramiel," I added.

At that, Cheriour's grip turned bruising, even if his face remained unreadable.

"But that's when Kylah showed up. So you snoozed through the arrival of *three* Celestials."

An earth-shattering *bang* rocked the tavern as a guy did an ungraceful somersault over one of the tables and crashed to the floor, bringing the table with him. The band stuttered at the noise. The bartender yelled. People shrieked with laughter.

"Addie." Cheriour leaned his head close so I could hear him over the racket. I shuddered at the way his breath tickled my ear. "You said you haven't felt *right*. What do you mean?"

Welp, right now I felt kinda horny. He was standing so freaking close, his chest pressed against my arm and his lips almost grazing my cheek...

If I angled my head just a tad, I'd have my mouth on his.

Focus, Addie!

"I've been..." I blew out a breath. "Scrambled. Emotionally *and* mentally. Maybe a little physically too."

"Have you heard voices?" he asked.

"Voices?"

"Yes. As though someone is speaking to you."

"Uhhh. No. Unless you count my own voice. Which I guess some people would. Talking to yourself is a sign of insanity, right? But...*should* I be worried about hearing other voices?"

"No."

"Then *why* did you ask that question?"

He blinked slowly.

"Because now I'm paranoid! Is that a thing that happens?"

"No."

"Dude...you better stop with the one-word answers. Do you know what's wrong with me?"

"Likely nothing. Souls are fragile, Addie," he added when I hissed, "and slow to mend. Considering what you've told me, your soul has been damaged. You need to give it time to heal."

I pursed my lips. "Is that not *exactly* what I've been telling you to do? How 'bout this: I'll give my soul time to heal when you give your body time to heal."

He sighed, his jaw ticking as he whizzed his eyes around the room.

"I guess that's a no. So you'll be crippled for life, and I'll be a headcase. What a fun pair we make. Like two peas in a fucked-up pod." I took a swig of beer and then washed it down with a hearty gulp of stew. "*Ooooh!*" I smacked my lips. "This is *amazing*! Holy cannoli...it's *real* food. Not the bug guts schlock everyone's been pushing on me." I took another big gulp. And then another. It was like a watered-down version of Campbell's beef stew, so not the *best* thing I'd ever eaten but certainly the tastiest thing Sakar had offered so far. "You mean to tell me"—I flicked some excess broth off my lips—"that all I had to do to get real food was flash some coin? Which, I have questions about that. Because I didn't realize you guys knew what money was. Fuck, I might've had a dollar or two stuffed in the pocket of my dress—remember the dress I wore when I arrived here?"

"I remember," Cheriour said.

"It got *ruined*. Almost. I saved most of it, but...well, it probably poofed with the rest of Niall. Anyway, I always stuffed ones in my pockets and then forgot about them until I did the wash and all my stray change got waded into a massive spitball. If money is a thing here, and one lousy coin gets passable beer and a decent meal, what would a full *dollar* have gotten me? Ah, never mind. There's probably a currency difference, right? What is one coin worth here? Is it a cent? A dollar? More? How many hours does a person have to work to earn one coin? And...hey, do you want any of this? I've been hogging it like a greedy gremlin, but technically, this is *your* meal. It came out of your paycheck...Do you get a paycheck? If you do, how come I don't? Actually, I should bill all of you for trauma expenses. You wanna know how many years of therapy I'll probably need to undo the damage from the past two months?"

Cheriour wasn't even looking at me. *Typical.* But he made one of his strangled sounds—one I *used* to think was him biting back a scream. Now I recognized it as a laugh.

"You think my fractured mental health is *funny*?" I asked.

A smile unfurled across his lips as he took the bowl from me (because, y'know, I'd been ramming it against his knuckles). "I'm glad you're talking again," he murmured.

"*Pffft.* Did you forget to put your hearing aids in? I'm *always* talking."

"Not like this." Cheriour swallowed a generous bit of the stew, then passed the bowl back to me, giving my knuckles a brief caress before he drew his hand away.

"Food makes me happy." I shrugged and slurped some more.

In the middle of the bar, a sozzled, red-faced woman gave an almighty belch that rattled the support beams and then took a nosedive straight to the floor, making a pit stop to thwack her chin on one of the wooden tables. Roaring guffaws reverberated around the room (mine included), and the crowd shifted to give the woman space, which gave me my first clear view of the band.

There were a dozen men and women of varying ages playing instruments. The youngest looked to be about fifteen, the oldest about sixty. I scanned their group and damn near spat out my next mouthful of stew when my eyes caught on an all-too-familiar face.

The man sat smack in the middle of the band, his back resting against the wall, looking utterly relaxed even as his fingers feverishly plucked at one of the pear-shaped guitars.

A man with graying, sandy-colored hair and bright blue eyes.

"Holy moly." I stood on my tiptoes, craning for a better look. "Is that *Quinn*?"

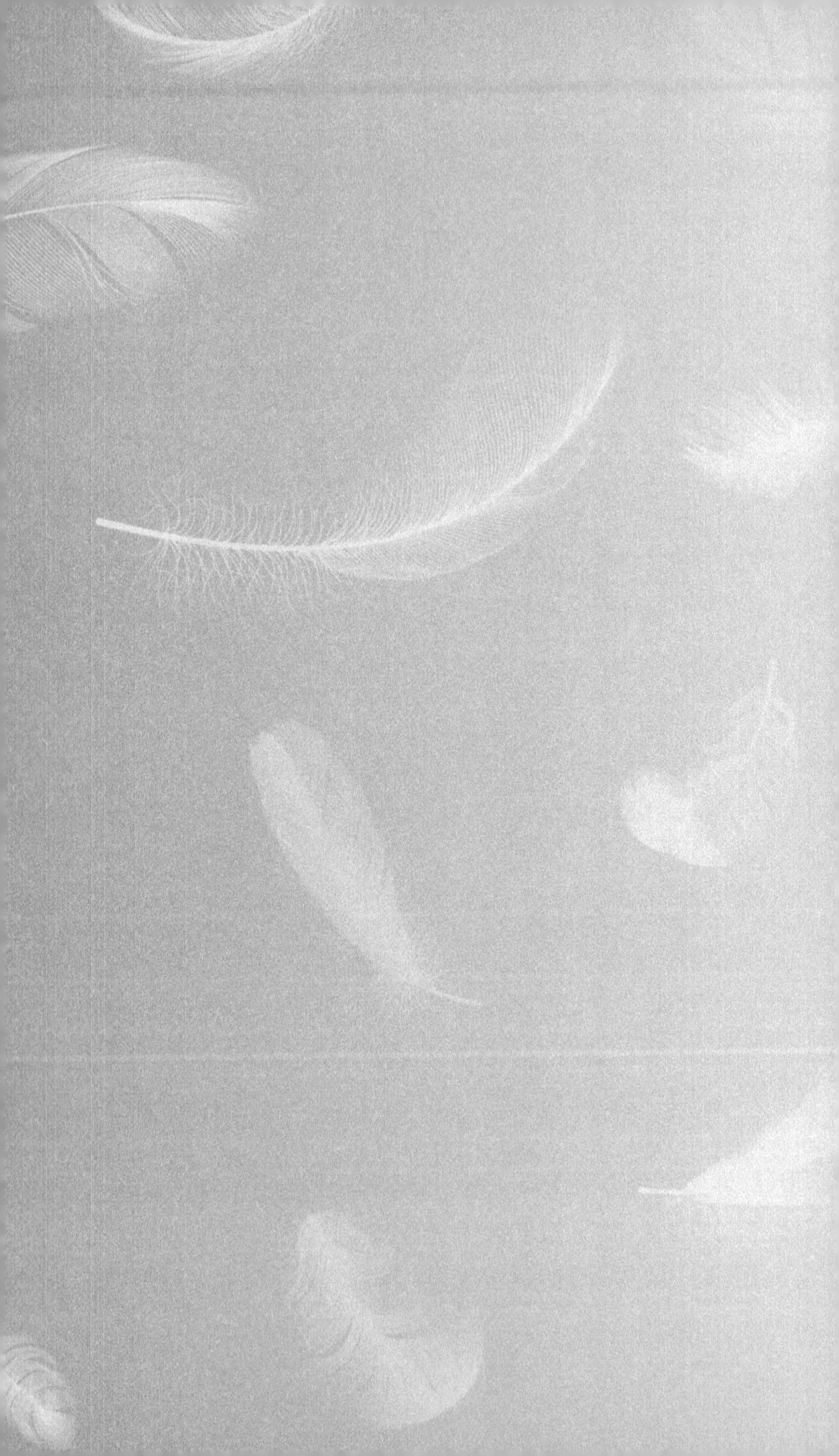

CHAPTER 7
RAT Z**OO**MIES

Cheriour stood so close to me, his chest pressed to my arm, that I felt his laugh rumble through him. "Yes. I knew Quinn would find his way down here." His warm, tea-scented breath ruffled my hair as he spoke.

Across the room, Quinn had his head bowed, his eyes focused on a spot on the floor. His fingers danced over the strings while his left foot tapped a beat. When the music swelled, Quinn leaned into his instrument, strumming with intense fervor, his head swinging in time. Then the song softened, fading away on a long, mournful note.

Quinn straightened, swiped his hair out of his eyes, and took a long pull from the cup resting on the ground by his chair.

Gosh, he was *really* young. I'd always pegged him as a middle-aged man, but seeing him now, without the hard-etched lines on his face and his hair flopping into his eyes... he looked almost boyish.

"He's thirty-three. I believe," Cheriour responded to the words I must've blurted.

Quinn bent over his instrument again as the band struck another chord. A smile danced at the corners of his mouth.

And it was so...*bizarre*, seeing that impish grin on his normally sourpuss face. Watching him go full rockstar...

I snorted. Then laughed. I guzzled beer, trying to hide the fact that I was starting to sound like a hyena on helium. But then I choked, drooled all down my front, and laughed even harder. "Oh fuck." I wiped a hand down my chest, giggling even more when the beer squeegeed off the shirt.

"Are you alright?" Cheriour touched my back. Probably trying to decide if he was going to have to do the Heimlich.

"*No*. I'm losing my fucking mind," I said with a guffaw-cough. "*Why am I laughing?*"

Cheriour raised a brow, his lips twitching. "I was hoping you'd tell me."

"I can't. Because I have no friggin' clue," I gasped, grasping the edge of the bar when my giddiness left me lightheaded. "*Phew*...that felt kinda good, though. Laughing over nothing. I guess that's why they say it's the best medicine. Anyway, I had *no idea* Quinn was a musician. And a damn good one. Like...*dang*."

This latest song was an ethereally romantic track. Quinn did most of the heavy lifting on this one, playing the main parts while the others softly strummed in the background. And his fingers pulled some soul-stirring sounds from those strings.

My heart swelled. He nearly, *nearly*, wrung a tear from me.

"How long has he been playing?" I asked.

"Most of his life," Cheriour said. "He prefers the harp. But he has a good ear for music and can play any instrument."

"The harp? Huh. You know, I've actually never seen the harp played before."

"Quinn is rather…" Cheriour paused, his lips pursed as he searched for the right descriptor. "*Enchanting* with it."

He was pretty dang enchanting with his guitar thing too.

Quinn brought the romantic song to its soft, sad close. And then he drummed his feet against the floor, beaming, as the rest of the band started another energetic tune.

"This is kinda nice." I bobbed my head with the beat. "Y'know…I get that you only came down here because I was having a meltdown. But are you cool with hanging out for a bit? To listen to the music?"

Cheriour's eyes brightened, the corners crinkling with a barely perceptible smile. "For a bit. Yes."

We ended up staying at the tavern for almost a full hour.

I snagged a couple of stools when a group of people vacated the bar and did the shitfaced shuffle up to the dance floor. Cheriour didn't even protest when I barked at him to sit. He sighed, tucked his jumbo toothpick under the bar, and hefted himself onto the stool. So I *knew* his leg was hurting. Mr. Macho wouldn't have sat for anything less than a fifteen on the pain scale.

But sitting there with him, gluing my side to his chest while he loosely twined his arm around my waist, listening to the music…

Everything else disappeared.

This was the appeal of a raucous bar: they were so chaotic and cheery, they made it easy to forget the shitstorm happening outside.

"Would you dance with me?" I asked Cheriour when the band began a lively jig that had half the patrons cheering and clamoring for a spot to dance. "Not right now, obviously," I added. "But when you're *not* broken, would you dance? If I asked you to?"

Cheriour winced, his eyes roaming over the sea of people mashing into each other. "Yes. I would," he said.

Which made my heart dip into a fluttery somersault. "I'll bet you're a graceful dancer. Way better than these idiots." And then I kissed his cheek.

Cheriour smiled, dragged those wandering eyes away from the crowd, and angled his head to meet my gaze. He kissed me back—a brief, tentative, and sinfully sweet peck on the lips—before he gave my hip a gentle squeeze.

And damn if I didn't get a titillating thrill outta seeing his big, work-roughened hand flexing around me. My belly did all kinds of tumbles and flips.

But then he ruined it.

"I have to return to the castle," he murmured in my ear as he slowly, almost wistfully, drew away.

"Ugh, *seriously?*"

"I've been away too long." A distant look skipped across his face. His brain had totally switched gears and was focused on whatever duty he'd remembered he'd neglected.

I glared at him. "You better not be going back to do training."

"No. I have other tasks that need my attention. Most of which I can do while seated. You can stay here..."

"Nah." I drained the last of my beer. The relaxing ambiance wouldn't be the same without him.

As we turned to leave, a guy with a blotchy red face strutted in. He was already sloshed and swaying sloppily to the music as he quaffed a rat on a stick.

Yeck, yeck, yeck!

I didn't even *like* rats. And I pitied the poor bastards. Especially after I'd seen that frightened cluster jammed into that cage. What an *awful* fate they had waiting for them, getting strapped to a spit and roasted over a fire until they were crispy.

I shuddered and turned to Cheriour. "Hey...you got more money on you?"

He blinked. "I do."

"Cool. You mind helping me with a rescue mission?"

"What?"

"Just...follow me." I grasped his arm and led him up the congested street, past all the vendors and people, until...

"Aha!"

The yellow-toothed peddler was still wandering around his booth, rattling the wooden cage. "Three coins!" he called to passersby. "Three coins'll get ye fresh goat and the rat! A hearty meal!"

"Hey!" I dropped Cheriour's arm and scuttled up to the vendor. "Hey there! Okay, serious question: Can I have just the rats?"

The man turned and gave me this incredulous *"Bitch, did you really inquire about the rats? Instead of my lovely, overcooked goat?"* look. But his face relaxed when Cheriour limped up behind me.

"Ah, Cheriour!" he chuckled. "So ye'll be wanting the goat, then, yes?"

"Just the rats," I said.

"And the goat," Cheriour sighed as he reached into his shirt pocket for the coins. "You can give her the rats."

"Excellent! It's good to see you, Cheriour! Now, I've only the one rat left, but he's a young, healthy fellow." The man ripped a rat out of the cage and thrust it into my hands.

I squealed as the rodent scrabbled around my palm, its claws scratching my skin.

"Would you like me to slaughter it for you?" the man asked.

"No! *Shit!*" The rat nearly took a swan dive off my knuckles.

"Hold him around the shoulders, Addie," Cheriour said. "It will keep him still."

I wrapped my fingers like a claw around the rat's torso. The animal stilled but quivered so hard, I swore its teeth rattled.

"Now then," the man clapped his hands together, "come pick your cut, Cheriour! This here is the freshest..." He said the last bit in a stage whisper, as though Cheriour was an ultra-special customer getting secret insider info.

As Cheriour limped to the booth, I raised the rat up to eye level.

It was the little brown one who'd almost gotten smooshed by his cage mates. And, Christ, he was fugly. His hair stood up in every direction, and his left ear had a big chunk missing. He reminded me of the derelict sewer rats who wandered city subways, usually high on junk food and nearly radioactive from the chemicals they slurped from the drains.

But he was really stinking cute, with that sniffy nose and those doleful eyes.

"Why did you need the rat?" Cheriour asked a few minutes later as we made our way back to the castle. He clutched a meticulously wrapped parcel in his free hand, one that smelled faintly like burnt oil at a BBQ truck.

"I dunno." I stared at the rat as it clung to my hand. "He seemed sad."

"He seemed sad?" Cheriour repeated slowly.

"I mean, they were gonna ram a stick up his ass and shove him in a fire. You'd be sad too. And scared, if you were in his shoes. No one deserves that. Y'know? And he's a cutie."

"I would *not* consider rats cute," Cheriour said.

"Hmm, they kinda are, though. Do you see his teeny pink nose?"

"They're vermin."

"And yet people around here *eat them*!"

"Because they're common." Cheriour shrugged. "Livestock perish easily. Rats endure. And many people have developed a taste for rat meat."

"Have you? Developed a taste for it?"

He said nothing.

"You *have*! Dude, I'm judging you *so fucking hard* right now. Wait...hold up..." I turned, gaping at him. "Have *I* eaten rat meat? Was that one of the dishes y'all served at Niall? Or here? OMG, it was, wasn't it?"

He huffed. "Would you like me to answer that question honestly?"

"*UGGH. No*! Definitely not. I think I'm gonna be sick..."

"You haven't eaten rat meat *recently*. If that helps."

"No, it doesn't freaking help. The fact that I ate it *at all* is skeeving me out."

"It didn't make you ill."

"That's not the point! You fed me rat! *Rat*! And didn't even have the decency to tell me what I was eating! Y'know, back home, we've traced a lot of diseases back to rats. They're nasty little fuckers with big hit lists."

Cheriour's right eyebrow rose. "And yet you're holding a rat."

Yup. I'd walked right into that one. "Well...yeah. But I'm gonna let him go. And then wash my hands. *Thoroughly*."

"If you release him, he'll be caught again."

"Not if I put him out in the woods."

"Then a bird will catch him."

"Wow, can you stop with the Debbie Downer shit? Why can't you let me save an innocent—*oooh*. Oh, you bastard." I'd pivoted to find Cheriour staring off at something in the distance, a smile tugging at his mouth.

He was *enjoying* this.

"You're teasing me, huh? *Jerk*. I'll keep him, then." I rubbed my thumb under the rat's soft belly. "And I'm naming him Splinter." Because...*duh*. How could I name a rat anything else? "Or...is it a her? It? Do you know how to determine a rat's sex?"

Cheriour briefly rolled his toneless eyes over me. "I'd imagine you'd check its underside."

"You'd *imagine*?"

"I've never desired to determine the sex of vermin."

"But what if he's a she?"

"Does it matter?"

"Not really. The name's still gonna be Splinter. But this guy...gal...whatever...it was in a cage with a dozen other rats, and I'm sure that dimwit vendor wasn't separating boys from girls. *Orgies* probably happened. Lots of 'em. So if he's a she...well, I wanna be prepared in case she pops out rat babies."

At that, Cheriour's huff turned into a full, deep belly laugh. The kind that sounded masculine and sexy and made my insides light up brighter than a Christmas tree. "Ask Braxton." Cheriour shifted his package under his arm and booped the rat's nose.

And I almost died from cuteness overload.

My giddy joy was almost enough to dispel the cloud of depression that hovered over Sanadrin's hulking black fortress.

Almost.

Because when we walked through the gate and a wild-eyed, pale-faced girl came swooping down on Cheriour saying Maddox needed him *urgently*, my joy withered and died.

It'd been a nice afternoon. Perfect, really. The best day I'd had in a long time. But it didn't change the fact that we were stuck in Sakar. And the world around us was crumbling.

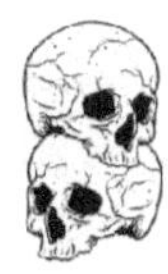

I DREAMED THAT NIGHT ABOUT A WEIRD, MURKY MUSIC VIDEO TO Michael Jackson's *Thriller*—one of my all-time faves. Except my nightmare was not campy and fun like the song. It was *horrifying*. Because the zombies springing from the graves were all people I knew. People from Sakar. People from back home.

And the lead singer—the man in the snazzy red suit—was Cheriour. Except he wasn't dancing. Oh no. His mangled corpse jerked and hitched in jiggy ways, sure. But only because of the bloodied ropes around his arms, legs, and throat.

No. Not ropes.

Those were *intestines* shackling him, forcing his normally graceful body into an awkward, rigid dance.

The dream faded. It didn't send me jerking awake in the throes of a wild scream—that never happened to me. Nightmares left me groggy and confused as I listened to my pulse pounding in my ears. Except this time, the pounding was accompanied by Michael Jackson's oh-so-smooth voice.

I *loved* that song.

And I kept singing it in my head as I rolled over, searching for a spot on my straw pillow that wasn't soaked with sweat.

When I caught flickering in the corner of my room, my grogginess vanished in a *whoosh* of panic.

Fire! The room is on fire!

My eyes sprang open.

And relief made every muscle in my body quiver. Because my room wasn't on fire. The dancing light came from a small candle on the wall, and Cheriour sat on the floor beneath it.

I exhaled, relaxing back into my pillow. The sleepy, fuzzy fog around my brain had lifted, but I didn't move. Not right away. Because Cheriour didn't seem to realize I was awake, and the scene before me was too precious to disturb.

He sat to the right side of the candle's light. His hair hung loose and damp upon his shoulders, as though he'd just stepped out of the shower. And those curls were extra springy, so he had at least finger-combed them. The fire cast a sparkly, almost mythical glow over the dark strands.

Beautiful.

His left leg stretched out in front of him, and his feet were bare. The ends of his breeches only came down to mid-calf, so I got a good gander of his puffy purple ankle. His other leg was curled up against his body in a half criss-cross. Splinter the rat sat in the cradle between Cheriour's calf and thigh, looking smug as fuck as he watched Cheriour fiddle with some cylinders of wood.

It took me a few seconds to figure out what Cheriour was doing. But, once it sank in, the scene before me became ten times more adorable.

He was building a home for Splinter.

And, by gosh, Splinter deserved this pampering. The poor guy's afternoon had been nothing short of traumatic.

After rescuing him, I'd given him a *thorough* bath. "This isn't a personal thing," I'd cooed as I dunked him in a bucket of water. "And it's not your fault if you have fleas. But I will *not* be happy if I wake up tomorrow and have creepy crawlies all over my room."

Splinter had spent the whole bath staring up at me with his bottomless black eyes like, *"Plllllleeeeaaassseee don't let me drown!"*

He was extremely tolerant and didn't bite or scratch, even with all the crap I put him through. Although, according to Braxton, *most* rats were gentle.

"Ach, rats are kind-hearted souls," Braxton had said when I'd shown him my new pet. "Ye got yerself a young lad, Addie."

"Thank fuck. I did *not* wanna play midwife to a rat," I'd muttered.

"And he's little more than a babe, this one." Braxton had nuzzled the rat. "He likes yer voice."

So I'd done a lot of talking to Splinter that afternoon, telling him about my home, regaling him with some of my favorite movies, and giving him the full rundown on his ninjutsu-fighting namesake. And I apologized profusely when I trapped him in an upended bucket for the night. I *hated* plonking that pail over the scared, sad-eyed rodent.

But what else was I supposed to do? I didn't want him to go gallivanting through the castle and end up as someone's morning shish kebab.

But now Splinter chilled in Cheriour's lap the way a king would recline in his throne, smugly supervising the construction of his new home.

Cheriour worked silently. Swiftly. He made almost no noise as he finished assembling the enclosure. Even when he set the wood pieces against the stone floor, he did it so gently, the little *click* was barely audible. His fingers never fumbled or faltered. He didn't work off a blueprint. He didn't use rulers or measuring tape. And he hadn't exactly taken a stroll to a hardware store and asked for a dozen pieces of the finest lumber, pre-cut to size. Naw. These were bits of firewood—old and weather-worn planks he'd eyeballed and cut to size with a hand saw.

It was incredible the way he could brainstorm some-thing and build it without *any* guides.

"No," Cheriour murmured.

I jolted and sank my teeth into my lip, figuring I'd said *something* out loud.

Until Cheriour tilted his chin down and wiggled his right knee, shifting Splinter back a few inches. Because Splinter, giddy with excitement about his new home, had started crawling. "Not yet." Cheriour turned the enclosure around, twisting an extra set of screws into the corners. "It's almost ready."

Oh Em Gee!

This was so freaking *adorable*! I couldn't take it. I *really* couldn't. My heart felt like a water balloon stuck at the end of a hose—filling and filling, until the latex screamed in pain from trying to hold back the inevitable burst.

I was *so* screwed.

Because this guy I'd known barely two months, and who was the *total opposite* of my type...*ooh, boy.* My head had gone right over my heels for him.

And these warm fuzzies? They were fun and comforting now, sure, but good emotions always had a flip side. Happiness was always shadowed by sadness, calm always tailed by anger.

And love? That motherfucker was *insidious*. Because when it had you in its delicate grasp, everything was sunshine and rose-painted glasses. But when it exposed its fugly backside, it pinned you down and violated you six ways to Sunday.

Heartbreak hurt like a S.O.B. and it was gonna wallop my ass sooner rather than later.

I couldn't keep Cheriour. Not while we were both living in this shithole world.

But if I'd met him back home, I wouldn't have given him the time of day. I would've been too shallow, too absorbed in my own life, to see how special he was.

It was so fucking unfair.

"Wood shavings will work best." This time, when Cheriour spoke, he looked at me.

"Huh?" I pushed myself onto my elbow, trying to ignore the way my heart went *"squeee!! How cuteeeee"* when Cheriour lifted Splinter off his lap and deposited him into his new home.

"Wood shavings. For bedding." Cheriour's words ended with a slight grunt as he stretched sideways, picking up the bowl of water I'd put under Splinter's bucket. "And you'll need to get him something else to chew. Rope, perhaps. Otherwise, he *will* eat the wood."

Splinter stuck his nose through the bars of his enclosure, his whiskers bouncing as he sniffed.

"The top slides." Cheriour moved a panel of wood back and forth across the top of the box, demonstrating how to open and close it.

I laughed. "'*Vermin*,' you said. '*Only good for eating.*' And then you built him a mini mansion?"

"I built the enclosure for you," Cheriour corrected. "Since you were adamant about keeping the rat."

"Uh-huh. If you say so. I'm sure that's why you were letting him snuggle on your lap too."

Cheriour tucked his chin down slightly. A barely notice-able reaction, but one that clearly said, "*Aw, shoot, I got caught.*"

"Did you even realize I was awake?" I chuckled.

Cheriour nodded.

"*Seriously?*"

"You sang. When you woke."

"Damn it. And I thought I was being quiet."

"You're rarely quiet." Cheriour turned, drawing his right leg to his chest and resting his elbow against his knee. "Addie...would you like to talk more?"

"About what?"

He pinned me with a long "*you know what*" look.

And I did. *Oh*, I did. "Nope."

His brow rose.

"Not tonight, at least. Maybe later. When my head's not so messed up."

He nodded. "Understood."

"Would *you* like to talk?" I asked. "About whatever happened this afternoon with Maddox? Or about anything else?"

"There isn't much to discuss," Cheriour murmured. "Hadleigh, a town in Netheridge, was attacked. It still stands, but it's ailing. Maddox wanted to send riders to aid them."

My skin bristled. "I hope to *God* you're not planning on strapping your busted ass to a saddle and tagging along with the rescue crew. I *will* smack that handsome face of yours. If only to knock some sense into you..."

"I told him not to send any more riders," Cheriour whispered.

My jaw snapped shut. "None?"

He smoothed his hand over his puffy leg, keeping his eyes focused on his fingers. "Too many cities are being attacked. We don't have enough riders. And those we already sent have failed to return. We can shelter survivors if they make it here. Otherwise"—his hand froze against a gnarly splotch of purple bruising on his calf—"we can't do anything to help them." A heavy sigh rattled his shoulders.

My heart twitched. I started to say something. Stopped. Tried again. Got stuck again. Managed a strangled, "I'm sorry," wanted to add more to it, but ended up repeating "I'm sorry" three more times.

Because what *could* I say to that? "*I'm sorry this world is falling apart. I'm sorry you get stuck having to make those kinda decisions,* knowing *people are gonna die whether you help or not. That's a heavy burden to carry. I'm sorry everyone's suffering. I'm sorry, I'm sorry, I'm sorry, I'm sorry...*"

The phrase passed through my head (and mouth) so many times, it turned into goop. A slushy stew of letters that meant nothing.

Cheriour lifted his head and gave me a soft half smile, acknowledging my ham-fisted apologies. But then we both flinched and grinned when Splinter emitted a blaring series of chirps and chitters and sprinted around his new home. Rat zoomies. They were pretty damn cute.

"Thank you for making that," I said. "Really. He's way happier in there than he was in the bucket."

Cheriour inclined his head.

"What time is it, though? I freaking *hate* that there are no windows in here...and I hope you didn't give up a full night's sleep to build that."

"It's likely an hour until dawn," Cheriour said. "Perhaps two. At most."

"So you *did* sacrifice sleep?" I gaped at him.

"I wouldn't have slept anyway." Cheriour pressed the back of his knuckles to the enclosure, letting Splinter sniff his hand.

"Well," I thumped my thin mattress, "you wanna try to sleep for a bit? This bed's not half bad. Definitely better than the pancake one I had at Niall. And I'll keep my hands to myself. Scout's honor. No feeling ya up. Unless you *want* me to. Because I'm game if you are. But you *should* wait...oh... okie-dokie."

Cheriour's bones crunched and popped as he pulled himself to his feet.

"I would've helped you get up!"

"I'm fine, Addie," he said.

"You are not *fine*." I said the last word in a deep, exaggerated drawl.

With an exhale, Cheriour grabbed the candle off the wall and limped to my bed.

"Wait, why are you bringing *that* over here?" I sat bolt upright as the dancing flame twisted and twerked its way closer to my bed. My *highly flammable*, straw-stuffed bed.

"I can't see without it," Cheriour said.

"Oh, right. Haha. See, I always blow it out and stumble around until I smack into the bed. I guess I can't ask you to do that, huh?" I scooted back a bit when Cheriour lowered himself onto the edge of the mattress, still holding the candle.

Why, why, *why* did candles always look so fucking cheery? They were *evil*. Pure, maniacal, evil.

Inky blackness consumed us once Cheriour blew the flame out. And a puft of waxy, smoky aroma wafted up my nostrils, almost making me sneeze.

Once the tickle in my nose passed, and I knew I wasn't gonna spray snot all over him, I turned to Cheriour and nuzzled the side of his neck, curving my arm around his belly. *Gingerly*. He did, after all, still have a wound healing at his ribcage.

But he didn't flinch when I trailed my fingers over his stomach. And his long, slow inhale sure didn't sound like a pain response.

"C'mon." I pulled away. "Let's get to sleeping. *Before* we start playing around. I'm still tired. And you shouldn't be pulling all-nighters during recovery time—uh-uh. That's not gonna work. *I* sleep on the right side of the bed."

Cheriour had sprawled across my spot. "So do I."

"Well, that's annoying. But since this is *my bed*, I'm booting you to the left side. Scoot over."

He gave a long-suffering sigh but moved.

Then he plonked his head in the center of the pillow, leaving me only a teensy sliver, and dumped all the blankets on me with a grunted, "I'm warm enough."

"You probably have a low-grade fever," I grumbled. "But

I'm sure you won't stay in bed and let the fever burn itself out, huh?"

"Hmmm."

"That's what I thought." And, yeah, he was obnoxiously warm. I shoved the blankets to the bottom of the bed and curled on top of him, burrowing my head against his shoulder (since he hogged the freaking pillow) while he rested his hand atop my hair. My palm splayed across his chest, tracing an idle, swirly pattern around his collarbone. Beneath my ear, his pulse strummed away. Strong and steady, even if it was a bit too fast.

It didn't take me long to get into that warm, fuzzy area between waking and sleeping. I was still alert enough to feel Cheriour's lips touching my brow, but my limbs had gotten heavy, as though I'd been encased in a vat of wet concrete, sinking down and down and...

Cheriour stiffened half a second before an almighty *bang* filled the room.

I jolted, accidentally whacking Cheriour across the throat and making him cough.

Quinn's face leered at us through the darkness, illuminated only by the candle in his hand.

"*Gah!*" I squawked. "Jesus! You could've at least knocked."

Quinn's eyes swept over Cheriour and me. But if he was surprised (or pissed) to find us cuddling in bed, he didn't show it. "Apologies," he said in the flattest fucking voice, "Calvin said he saw you coming up here, Cheriour, and I..." He puffed out a breath. "Emall has fallen. Its survivors are approaching the city."

CHAPTER 8

GREETING THE END OF THE WORLD HAPPY AND SHITFACED

The small group of survivors staggered into the city, ashen-faced and shell-shocked, as the sun speared through a bloodred sky.

Emall had been a decent-sized town, according to Cheriour, housing hundreds of people. And only *twenty* made it out alive.

Most of them sported grim injuries and were too traumatized to realize how fucked up they were. One man called a gaping abdominal wound a *stomachache*. Another guy had a massive hole in his thigh, but he slurred (multiple times) that he'd made it through the battle "with nary a scratch." Other people also insisted they were fit, even as they lurched around on broken bones or wobbled from severe blood loss.

One young-ish woman—hard to guestimate her age when half her face had been skinned, but she *seemed* young —somehow managed to stay aboard a horse despite missing her right arm. And she *carried the appendage* with her—kept it draped across her lap and muttered that she could suture it so long as we had thread.

This woman, apparently, had been mauled by a hell-hound while trying to evacuate Emall. That'd been six days ago, and she'd been wandering around like the Armless Horseman since.

And that detached arm was *mangled*. The skin near the top looked as though it'd been run through a shredder and had turned some funky colors.

"Alrighty, honey, let's get you down," I said as I helped her off the back of the horse.

She gave me a dazed, barely focused look. But she held her loose, pockmarked arm in an iron grip.

"Steady does it." I kept my arm around her waist, trying *really* hard not to stare at the yawning hole by her shoulder blade. Christ, it *stank*. Worse than a garbage can full of rotting food. Decay. Definitely. And it smeared pus *all over* my side. *Yum.*

Thank frick my snazzy shirt cleaned itself.

"Are you alright?" Cheriour asked me as we passed him. He sat in the grass along the walkway, talking to one of the survivors, a scrawny woman who was surprisingly lucid considering both her eyes had been ripped from their sockets.

"We're good. Right?" I gave the one-armed woman's hip a squeeze. "We're gonna find a spot to sit ya down while we wait for the doctors. Here we go...a nice cushy patch of grass. Just for you. This is a premium spot too. Because *look* at that sunrise." I pointed to the still-red sky. "Gorgeous, right? Although it might be a bad omen. What's the saying? 'Red sky at morning, sailors warning.' I think that's it. Or, if you're a *Lord of the Rings* fan, a red sun means blood has been spilled. But we'll go with the sailor's saying," I added when the woman gave a hacking cough. "It's probably more accurate. Means we might be in for some shitty weather, but we'll have you inside by then. Don't worry."

The woman said a few unintelligible words and slumped into me, crying out when her arm almost plopped off her lap.

"How 'bout I take that off your hands—er, hand?" I asked.

"No!" she hissed. "I need thre-duh. I can't looosh id. Ids me ssword-duh arm."

"Well…" I lifted the rotting arm off her lap. It was stiff and cold. Blood caked the cracking, purplish skin. "Listen, Jamie Lannister learned to be a master left-handed swordsman. I'm sure you will too. Give it a few weeks and you'll be trouncing everyone in training."

But she never would learn to use a sword in her left hand.

Eleven of that group of twenty died within three days, including my one-armed swordswoman. Quinn and Maddox did *everything*, pushing themselves to the brink of collapse to get people healed, but the survivors had lost too much blood, and infection already had them in its ruthless grasp.

And just when the remaining survivors seemed to have made it out of the woods, they were all stricken down again in the cruelest way possible:

Elion's disease.

THE TALE OF EMALL WAS A TRAGIC STORY THAT WOULD REPEAT itself over and over and fucking over again.

A week passed. Two. More survivors from doomed cities flocked to Sanadrin. Sometimes they came maimed and bloodied, like the poor bastards from Emall. Sometimes they arrived burnt and coated in a grimy layer of ash and soot.

Most couldn't, or *wouldn't*, talk. Those that did...well, they sure didn't have anything nice to say.

"Wraiths are *everywhere*."

"There were too many. We couldn't hold them back."

"This is all Seruf's doing. Mark me words."

"Aye, I never saw so many of those Wraith bastards. Not until Seruf claimed Niall."

Oh, yeah. I heard that bitch's name. *A lot.*

Nearly everyone thought she had parked her perky ass in Niall and was sending henchmen to slaughter us pesky human brats. And what was I supposed to say when people ranted about her? *"Erm, no. You see, Seruf took the highway straight to hell. How do I know? Well, I'm the one who sent her there. Because I can do this cool trick where I reach through people's chests and destroy their souls. Isn't that fun? Now, who wants me to tend their wounds?"*

That would go over like an erect priest in a nunnery. (Har, har, har.)

Not that I cared if people suddenly started looking at me like I was Ooogie Boogie. But I didn't understand that power, didn't know how to explain it, and *really* didn't want to advertise it.

When you didn't understand what worms were wriggling around in the can, sometimes it was best not to bust out the can opener.

And Cheriour, as far as I knew, hadn't told anyone my

dirty secret. So I blathered about other things instead. I spent every day with the sick, the injured, and the dying. Talking to them, trying to help them, and failing. No matter what I or anyone else did, people kept slipping away.

The gnawing pain in my chest returned when I watched the first wave of bodies being buried. And it grew. *Festered.* Nothing eased it. Cuddling with Splinter was about the only thing that *sometimes* helped—he was such a freaking snuggle bug. As soon as I picked him up, he'd nuzzle against my hands and stare at me with those wide, innocent, bottomless eyes, as though saying, *"I'm sorry you hurt. But pets me, and you'll feel better!"* And I did.

But the pain was always there, biting into my chest and driving me half up a wall with a constant urge to scream, cry, or bash my head into something until the lights went out. Or, y'know, have wild, headboard-banging sex. That *might've* helped. But Cheriour had become this elusive creature who could only be glimpsed for a fleeting second at dusk if the sun and the moon were aligned (aka, the poor guy was so busy dealing with the fallout of all these crumbling towns, I rarely saw him). Whenever we crossed paths, he looked utterly exhausted, with the racoon rings under his eyes becoming a permanent fixture. Twice, I coaxed him to sit still long enough for a shoulder massage. The dude had some big ole whopper knots jammed along his neck, but he didn't let me work them out all the way. The whole time, he fidgeted, his eyes and hands restless. He never relaxed.

But neither did I. Because how could we?

When survivors stopped coming to Sanadrin, and people began clamoring to send a search party, Cheriour reluctantly took the risk. He sent five riders to comb the ruined towns nearby.

The only update we got came from Braxton. Three days later, he declared two horses from the group were en route back to Sanadrin. He never found the other three.

And the two horses came back riderless.

LIFE MARCHES ON.

That was the saying, right?

No matter how many times your world got flipped upside down, kicked sideways, and bounced through the shit pile, life kept moving forward.

But sometimes, it left people behind.

I'd definitely been left to rot in a muddy rut on the side of the road. Because everyone else kept plugging along, living their lives. Thousands of people dead? That was sad and all, but the laundry wouldn't dry itself. Wraiths on the rampage? Yeah, it was scary. But a horse wearing a worn-down shoe was scarier. Sanadrin being the last human piece on the chessboard, primed to be overtaken? That really sucked. But the tavern had a special on ale tonight. "And you might as well greet the end of the world happy and shit-faced, right?"

The latter, of course, being something I'd flippantly said to the barista at my favorite coffee shop, back when I'd been living my cushy life in the twenty-first century and things like zombie apocalypses and angelic wars were *entertainment.*

I'd been a fucking idiot.

Because being here now, in a real-life apocalypse, seeing

the way people suffered and waited for the inevitable fatal blow to fall…I couldn't grab a beer and cheerily wait for it to be over.

But everyone else did.

And I was expected to do the same.

Over the next week, I was given two daily "tasks": combat training—this time with Kaelan as my instructor, since the Breakfast Club was mostly kaput and Cheriour had too much on his plate—and manners schooling with Abby Normal.

Working with Kaelan wasn't bad. The kid was so stinking sweet and adorably excited to lead his own training sessions. So I went through the motions, forcing myself to smile, crack jokes, and act normal. All the while, I bit my tongue—*hard*, usually until I drew blood—and kept thinking, *What is the fucking point?*

I'd *never* be a good fighter. Ever. And my poleaxe wasn't a magical, Excalibur-type weapon that could take down a Celestial. My old poleaxe (version 1.0) hadn't even survived the fires at Niall. Version 2.0 probably wouldn't do much better.

Training was pointless.

But not as pointless as Abby Normal's sessions. Especially since they were supervised by the rarely sober Braxton, and Abby Normal proved to be an *extremely* uncooperative student.

"Quinn wants her proper trained," Braxton hiccupped one dreary afternoon as he slumped outside her paddock, watching me with unfocused eyes. "Broken like a savvy old"—*hic*—"pony. Ach, she's a right bitch, that 'un," he slurred when Abby Normal ripped a rope halter out of my hands.

My heart skittered as her fang brushed against my knuckles, but there was no broken skin. Thank *frick*.

"Make sure ye don't wrap the line around yer hand. She'll break yer wrist if she bolts."

"She doesn't even have the halter on!" I said.

A few feet away, Abby Normal pummeled the halter into the ground.

"Ach, well, ye'll be needin' to do that first." Braxton swayed.

"How?"

"Pop it over 'er head."

Abby Normal gave a violent shudder and propped her forehooves on the noseband of the halter, clutching the headpiece between her teeth. A sickening *crrrrittccchhh* filled the air when she whipped her head back and tore the rope in half.

"'Pop it over her head,'" I grumbled. "*Sure.*"

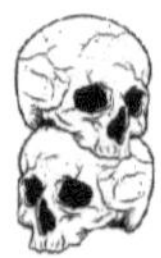

I LAY SIDEWAYS ON MY BED, MY FEET PROPPED ON THE FLOOR AND my back extended in an awkward angle that kind of hurt but also helped stretch the kinks out.

Splinter shuffled around on my chest, sniffing at my damp clothes. I'd gotten caught in a rainstorm. Why? Because Braxton had passed out by Abby Normal's paddock, and I'd had to drag his ass *alllll* the way back to the castle. He was freaking *heavy*. And I wasn't exactly Hercules. But if I'd left him there, Abby Normal would've broken down the fence to get to him. She'd already been eyeing his prone form and making long, hungry whuffles.

So I'd saved Braxton's miserable life. Whoo-hoo. Go me.

We were all gonna die soon, anyway. But at least he got one more day to drink himself into a blissful oblivion.

I sighed but smiled when Splinter curled himself on top of my left boob. "You little pervert," I laughed. "But that's the cushiest seat in the house, huh? Even if the girls aren't as boisterous as they were a few months ago."

I lay in silence for a while after that, staring at the quivering snatches of candlelight on the ceiling. Feeling Splinter breathe and shuffle against me. Wondering if the yawning ache in my chest would ever go away. Pondering what the fuck I was doing here.

There was a *reason* I'd been sent to Sakar, and it wasn't to entertain a dying population with shitty jokes and pop culture references. The Celestials must've wanted me to *do something*.

But what?

Not to use my weird Soul Stealing ability, apparently. The red-headed bitch (Kylah) had been adamant that power would lead me down the path to evil.

And being fireproof was cool, but what good did it really do? I could save people from burning buildings but not from any other attack.

Did I have a third power hiding dormant inside of me?

I sure hoped not.

But then, why was I here? If I couldn't help these people, *why did the Celestials send me?* To watch everyone die? Was this place actually hell? Had I suffered the wrath of God for all the times I'd drunk, fucked, cursed, and taken the Lord's name in vain?

Jeez, I sure had a lot of strikes against me, didn't I?

"Addie?"

I jolted and then puffed in relief when Cheriour lightly tapped on my door.

"Come in." I craned my head, watching as he pushed the door open and leaned his hip against the frame, swiping his damp hair over his shoulder. He'd gotten caught out in the storm too and looked no less miserable about being soaked to the bone.

But, my gosh, he made the drowned-rat style look *hot as fuck*.

My stomach fluttered as a bead of water dripped off his beard, trickled down his throat, and disappeared beneath the collar of his shirt. His very *wet* shirt, which clung sinfully to every dip and curve of his muscular pecs.

"Would you like to talk?" he asked as he closed the door behind him.

I jolted and dragged my eyes away from his (gorgeously muscled) chest. "Uhh, what?"

"Would you like to talk?" he repeated.

"Nah."

When he frowned, I blew out a breath. "Okay, I'll bite. How much did you hear? Before you walked in?"

"Nothing," he said.

"Huh. Really? These walls must be pretty soundproof."

"You weren't talking, Addie." He studied me, his eyes unreadable.

"Well," I laughed, "that's gotta be a first."

"Indeed."

I twisted to give him a good, long stare.

God, he was rip-roaringly attractive, especially right now. (There was *something* about wet men; they instantly became ten times more fuckable.) But he also looked exhausted, with those ever-darkening bags under his eyes, the tension hunching up his shoulders, and the hurt and grief buried deep, deep, *deep* into his hollow gaze.

"Do you wanna have sex?" I blurted. "It might make both of us feel better. Or it might not. I don't know. But I like you. And I *really* want to. Only if you do too, though, y'know?"

I did not, in a million years, think he'd take that bumbling and unsexy invitation.

But he shocked the hell out of me when he flashed a lopsided smile and stepped forward.

Fuck. Yes.

CHAPTER 9
TICKLE FETISH

Relief flooded me when I stood on shaky legs and put Splinter back in his enclosure. Relief, anticipation, and fear—fuck, I didn't even know *why* I was scared. But my stomach contorted with nerves, my heart walloped my breastbone in rapid, unsteady beats, and a morbid thought bounced around in my head, one that brought my teeth slamming onto my tongue before I could vocalize it: *Halle-freaking-lujah. I'm gonna get to see this man naked before one (or both) of us dies.*

For the past few weeks—*months*—death had been poised to drop an anvil on our heads at any second.

So could I be blamed for zooming to Cheriour's side and smacking my mouth against his? I had the green light. I was *going...*

He grasped my hands, stopping me.

Welp, that was the quickest light I'd ever seen.

"That, sir, is what we call a *tease*," I grumbled as I backed up and dropped my ass onto the bed.

Cheriour followed me down, wrapping his arm around my waist and pulling me flush against his body.

His *gloriously chiseled* body, fully recovered from the battering it'd taken a few weeks ago thanks to the extra dose of super special healing medicine he'd finally accepted from Quinn.

My mouth went dry as I ran my hand along his chest and traveled down, down, until I felt the hard, defined lines of those six-pack abs through his damp shirt. His stomach hitched when I twirled my thumb around his belly button. *Fuck me.* I wanted to get my hands on those muscles, skin to skin, so I could *really* feel them quiver. Especially when I started licking and biting them.

I tugged at his shirt, trying to free it from his pants.

With a breathy laugh, Cheriour batted my hands away.

"Dude..." My whine of complaint trailed off when he touched his mouth to mine in a languorously sweet kiss. His lips moved as slow as molasses, giving me time to feel him. To *savor* every facet of him. Like the sigh he made when I drew his bottom lip between my teeth. The earthy scent of rain still clinging to his skin. And the way his hands cupped my face, his fingers barely, *barely*, touching my skin, as though he was afraid his callouses would scratch me.

Little did he know, I *enjoyed* being scratched.

I gave his mouth a nip and reached for his shirt again.

He nipped me right back and nudged my hands away.

"Are you a little nervous?" I asked when he closed his palm over my wrists, holding them away from his shirt. "I'm not asking to be judgy. Honest. I just need to know so I don't bulldoze too hard and do something that's gonna make you uncomfortable."

"Addie." Cheriour's lips twitched. "I'm not nervous."

I looked down at my lightly bound wrists. "So what's with the shackles?"

His thumb caressed my forearm. "You move too quickly." He gave me another delicate kiss.

I exhaled around his lips. "I guess you're not into quick and dirty tumbles, huh?"

"No."

"Of course not. It figures you'd be all-in on this slow and sappy shit."

With a low laugh, Cheriour turned his head and touched his lips to the shell of my ear.

And his *beard*—I didn't even *like* beards, but when his brushed my skin...*goosebumps*. I got goosebumps *everywhere*. It tickled as it pricked against my suddenly overheated flesh. A short giggle bubbled out of me.

Cheriour, the overly observant bastard, zeroed in on that reaction. He paused and blew a puft of air against the side of my neck. And then he *bit* my earlobe! Not hard. Just enough for me to feel the rasp of his teeth. But a sharp, tingly *ziiing* zipped up my spine. I squirmed and grunted, fighting against the laugh fizzing in my throat.

Cheriour's mouth curled. He gave my ear another light graze and skated his hand along my ribcage, searching for more tickle spots.

The fucker was being *playful*.

Every time he licked, bit, sucked, or pressed his fingers to a spot that made me jerk, twitch, laugh, or utter gobbledy-gook, he smiled, thoroughly enjoying himself.

I did *not* enjoy it.

Okay, no, I totally did.

But I was a greedy and impatient bitch. I wanted to have

my fun. And I knew I could find some places that would have him speaking gibberish.

I turned my face into his neck, giving him a not-so-gentle bite.

His sharp inhale was *heavenly.*

He retaliated by skimming his fingers down my side from armpit to hip, doing a fancy twirl that made me writhe.

I clamped my lips together, but the laugh rose anyway and blew through my nose in an oinking snort. And that obscenely wet and ultra-unattractive noise was the last straw. Peals of uncontrollable, high-pitched giggling gushed from my mouth.

Cheriour didn't let up. Even when I flopped back onto the mattress, my legs flailing so hard, I accidentally drilled my heel into his thigh ("S-s-serves you right, ya jerk!!" I managed to say), he kept his torment going. He leaned over me, one hand braced beside my head while the other slid beneath my shirt, his fingers twirling in feather-light strokes that had my muscles spasming and my belly aching with mirth.

"I think you have a tickle fetish," I gasped when he finally paused, giving me a moment to breathe.

He gazed down at me, the normally taut line of his mouth curled into a lazy, lopsided grin. "I like your laugh."

Thimp-thump went my heart. Nerves weaved around my stomach again, pulling hard enough to hurt. Because I'd never seen him make an expression like this before. It was soft, almost boyish, and downright blissful. And it gave me *all* the warm fuzzies.

I cleared my throat. "Y'know, I think you're the first person to like my laugh. I've been told I sound like a hyena. Or a pig. Or an unholy cross of both."

"You don't sound like a hyena," Cheriour said. "The pig is more accurate."

I thwapped his shoulder. "Jerk!"

And I got rewarded with one of his rare belly chuckles. That gruff, masculine rumble had my brain fritzing and zaps of pleasure shooting into my belly.

"Now, *your* laugh"—I made the chef's kiss gesture—"is a divine sound. You should do it more often. A bit of laughter a day keeps the doctor away. Or something like that." I leaned up to kiss him.

He pulled away, that crooked smile still firmly in place.

"Dude, your laugh might be divine, but there's a special place in hell for people who tease."

"I'm not teasing." He traced a finger along my cheekbone, down the side of my neck, and across my throat, pausing when I swallowed, as though he got some kinda thrill out of feeling my throat bob.

My entire body locked into a shudder because I was *sure* he'd go farther south. But his hand traveled back up, touching my other cheek, tracing the shell of my ear, and combing my hair.

"How slow do you actually wanna go?" I asked. And, okay, my voice was a little (a lot) squeaky. I'd been holding my breath for the last few seconds (or minute), waiting. The anticipation did funny, thrilling things to my insides. But impatience also frothed inside me, making my fingers itch to feel his skin. To unbuckle that thick leather belt, rip the laces off his pants, and slip my hand inside.

My pulse roared. So loud, I almost didn't hear myself say the next words: "Are you planning to be done sometime this year?"

"Be still, Addie," Cheriour murmured.

"Can I at least take your shirt off? Please?"

The right side of his mouth tilted up in another slanted smile that *reeked* of smugness.

"You *are* teasing me." I pinched his shoulder. "Bastard. I'm taking your shirt off—hey!"

Before I could tug at the hem of his shirt, he pulled mine over my head. Which didn't exactly go smoothly. I got momentarily tangled in the material because I'd shot my hands up too quick, nearly whacking him across the face. But then it was off. Leaving me...*not* bare.

"Okay, well, this ain't exactly sexy lingerie, is it?" I said when Cheriour touched the fugly, stained bandaging wrapped around my chest. (I did *not* put the stains there. The cloth came that way.) "I *had* a bra. A nice one too, with padded cups. But the Wraiths killed it. And the girls are too boisterous to go free 24/7, so I'm bringing the mummy look back in style."

Cheriour tugged at the binding, unraveling the knot I'd tied on the right side.

"Oh, you're going for it, huh?" I pushed myself up onto my elbows, giving him easy access.

He took his sweet old time, meticulously unfurling each layer and pausing every two seconds to run his hands over my belly or draw a pattern on my collarbone. Or, infuriatingly, halting to dote on my (badass) pop culture sleeve tattoo.

When I wriggled, trying to slide his hands onto more fun areas, Cheriour chuffed, *scolding* me, and pressed his other hand to my belly, holding me down.

"Listen," I half growled when he swooshed his index finger over the T-Rex skull on my *Jurassic Park* logo, "I love this sleeve. It's my pride and fucking joy. I'll gladly walk you through every single pop culture icon I've got on there. But there are times you admire the tats and times you don't. *This is not the time to ogle my tattoos!*"

The corner of Cheriour's mouth quirked. "I like the colors against your skin." He bent and touched his lips to the tip of the J.

Boom.

Chills.

Chills *everywhere.*

This man was gonna be the death of me.

Cheriour's eyes followed the ripple of pebbled goose flesh spreading over my body and cocked his mouth into another smile.

"You bastard—oooh!" I shuddered when his hand slid away from my tattoo and slipped under my loosened bra, grazing the underside of my breast. "I hate you."

He huffed as he slowly, *sllllooooowwwwllllyyyyy,* unwrapped another layer.

This stupid binding had four layers. And he'd only undone two of them. *Two.* A fucking sloth could've gotten me undressed faster.

"By the time you get my bra off, my boobs are gonna be sagging with old age." That was *not* a breathless squeak in my voice. Nope. And I definitely, 100 percent did not make an embarrassingly loud *gu-ugghh* when Cheriour finally got my makeshift bra off and traced the outer edges of my boobs. Not even a full touch. Just a light tap that had my ab muscles tightening, bracing for more. Meanwhile, he lowered his head, his mouth working against mine in a series of barely there kisses that left me straining.

I grasped his shirt, hauling the hem up.

He nudged my hands away.

I reached for his pants, clawing at the belt.

That earned me a harder "no-no" nudge.

"Oh, you've got some kinks." I breathed harder than a winded rhinoceros. "You're a *sadist*. That's cool. I respect it. But it's not—ugh, *goddamn* you."

He cupped my breast *fully*, his thumb moving in painfully slow circles.

"This isn't *my* kink. And I wanna let you do you. But..." I jolted when he bent his head and nuzzled the side of my neck, his teeth scraping gently, so, *so* gently over my skin. "Can we kick this up a notch?"

That was *not* a whine in my voice.

Not yet.

In a few seconds, he'd have me whining, though. Especially if he kept nibbling my neck and fondling my breast, his touches and kisses so damn light, they were becoming a slow-burn torture. A tickle that never went away, no matter how I squirmed, grunted, and cursed.

I raked my fingers through his damp hair. "Payback's a bitch." I pulled his head down and gave his ear a sharp bite. "Remember that. If you torture me, I'm gonna torture you right back."

My ultra-vicious threat did jack-squat to intimidate him.

"Gah!" I squealed when he pressed a hot, wet, open-mouthed kiss to my boob.

His low, husky laugh vibrated right through me, and the way his breath danced over the damp mark he'd left on my skin...

My hips bucked as a stinging electric current rollicked through me.

"Okay...no...nope. You're done." I shimmied out from

under him. "You had your fun. But now I wanna play. Your shirt's coming off."

Cheriour grinned and sat back on his haunches, watching *intently* as I ripped his belt off and yanked the shirt free from the waistband of his pants. It took me one swift, albeit jerky, move to get it over his head. Then I smashed the offending garment into a ball and shot it across the room.

And for a second, two, three, I stared, admiring the long, lithe shape of his body. His rugged, moisture-slick skin shimmered in the faint candlelight. Shadows pooled in the dips of his muscles, making them pop, even as the soft sworls of dark hair spattered over his torso softened the harsh lines.

Christ, he was *beautiful.*

I laid my palm over those yummy, chiseled abs, reveling in his unsteady sigh. And my fingers immediately caught on the pale pink line that curved in a half U-shape down his sternum, stretching toward his belly button.

Other scars speckled his skin. Lots of them. Little nicks, mostly, with some other big slashes mixed in. A jagged lesion hooked around his left hip, curling down his stomach and into his dark-haired happy trail before disappearing under the waistband of his breeches.

My mouth watered.

Bad, brain. Bad.

Because I hadn't even inspected the scar I was most worried about yet: that large, angry-looking pucker splashed beneath his rib cage.

I tentatively traced my pointer finger over it.

"Addie." Cheriour's abs flittered as he laid his palm over mine. "Wait."

"Are you still in pain?" I flipped my hand over, threading my fingers through his.

"No," he said. But his fingers clenched around mine, betraying his calm words.

"Hmmm, that sounds like bullshit. And there's no *reason* to feed me bullshit. You don't gotta act tough, Cheriour. If it hurts, tell me. *Please.* So I know to keep my paws off—" I bit back an awkward peep when Cheriour raised our joined hands and brushed his knuckles against my breast.

"It doesn't hurt, Addie." And with that, he released my hand and spun himself around, exposing his back to me. "This would've startled you," he murmured. "I wanted you to see it first."

I fully expected his back to be as scarred as his front. It wasn't.

It was *worse.*

"Oh my God, Cheriour..." His *entire back* was a convoluted mess of wrinkled and discolored scar tissue. Dozens upon dozens of gnarled, leathery welts twined around his spine and fanned out along his shoulders. And at each shoulder blade, protruding maybe a quarter of an inch...

"That's *bone*!" I prodded his right shoulder, gasping when my fingers hit the brittle strip of white cartilage, which stretched the full length of his scapula. "You have *exposed bone* back here!"

"It's not human bone." He turned his head, jaw ticking. "It's the remnants of my wings." His muscles bunched as I gingerly rubbed the area.

"Does it hurt?" I asked.

"Sometimes. Not from you touching it, though."

Heat radiated from his wing stump. I cautiously laid my palm over it, wincing when the ragged edges scalded my skin. "I'm so sorry, Cheriour. Do you ever miss them? Or... *heh*, stupid question, huh? They were your wings..."

"They were. But the longer I'm mortal, the more I forget the sensation of having wings." He leaned back, nudging my palm, silently giving me permission to explore.

So I swept my hand along his spine—*gently*. Not pressing down with my fingers, just letting them glide over his skin.

I didn't even know it was possible for human skin to *feel* this way, all stiff and leathery, with deep, craggy bumps. The texture more resembled a cheapo crocodile pleather bag than human flesh.

I hated those scars. Because they looked so unbelievably painful, and I didn't even want to *imagine* the agony he'd been in when they were inflicted.

But I also loved those scars. Because they were a part of him, and I adored every part of Cheriour's lithe, muscular body.

My hand slid down to his hip, and I gave his (rock-hard) ass a pinch as I leaned in and kissed the center of his back.

Cheriour's muscles tightened beneath my lips. He laughed breathlessly and shimmied away, turning to face me again.

"You sure that didn't hurt?" I asked.

He shook his head.

"And you solemnly swear you're not pulling your macho act, right? I mean, back kisses make me squirmy too—*don't* even think about it," I snapped when he twined a hand around to my back. "Not right now, at least. We're talking about *you*. And working on your communication skills. Because I *know* you hide shit, and I need to know you'll be honest with me if you don't like something. Because I'll be honest with you. But it's gotta be a two-way street if we want this to work..."

"Addie..." Another lopsided smile lifted Cheriour's mouth. "I will tell you if I'm uncomfortable. I *promise*. But sometimes you'll need to stop talking"—he tapped his thumb to my lips—"if you'd like me to speak."

"Right...yeah...touché." I nuzzled my brow onto his. "Feel free to slap a hand over my mouth if you need to or... *ummphh*."

Cheriour kissed me. *Deeply*. A suckling smooch that had tingles shooting all the way to my toes.

I arched against him, shivering as our bare chests rubbed together.

He groaned and shifted, tilting me back onto the mattress.

"*Nope*." I tore my mouth away from his. "Uh-uh. You had your fun. Now it's my turn."

And I was gonna have *a lot* of fun.

He let out a soft "ugh" when I yanked him down and shoved him onto his back. I crawled on top of him, grinding my hips against his. *Hard*.

Cheriour's throat bobbed frantically around his caught breath. His body shifted beneath mine, rising into the friction.

A full body quake seized me, and I was sure my face had contorted into an ultra-attractive "oooh, that feels good" look. Because the friction was hitting just right. For both of us.

I ground down again and again, letting my hands roam up his chest. When he blew out an unsteady breath, his hands grasping fistfuls of my ass, I raked my nails into his left pec and captured his mouth in a long, greedy kiss.

Sadly, when I tried to tickle him, I didn't get much of a response.

But when I dragged my teeth along the chorded muscles of his neck while simultaneously pinching his nipple...

Cheriour grunted and dug his fingers into my ass as he rolled his hips into mine.

Yeah, buddy! Now we were cooking.

I teased him, alternating between harsh bites and soothing licks as I ground down on him—sometimes firmly, sometimes lightly. A pink flush blossomed over his cheeks as he writhed beneath me, his hands grappling against my skin.

It was the *perfect* time to slide off him.

After I scooted away, he lay still for a second, two, looking adorably flustered.

I stretched out and dragged my nails over his straining, sweat-slick stomach. "I told ya, payback's a bitch."

He flashed me another (ridiculously sexy) slanted smile and pivoted onto his side, drawing my leg over his hip. A sharp, warm *zap* of pleasure bulleted through my belly as he rocked lazily, hitting *the perfect freaking angle.*

"Oooh, damn!" I hissed.

He groaned—a low, barely audible sound that vibrated through my very core.

We weren't even at the good stuff yet. Our *pants* were still on. This was basically intense cuddling. But, fuck, it felt good to have him against me, his skin hot and firm beneath my hand. Those six-packy abs spasmed whenever I scraped my nails over them. And the look on his face: his eyes glazed and sleepy, his jaw relaxed, lips parted...

Gorgeous.

I kissed him, sucking that lower lip between my teeth,

basking in the scrape of his beard against my chin. He made a throaty "*hmmmm*" and kissed me right back.

God. This was so, so *good*.

But it wasn't enough.

I was stretched thinner than the girdle I once wore to a buffet-style wedding reception with an open bar. That girdle had stretched to its last thread and started screaming before the end of the night.

As I was now. The slow thrusting of Cheriour's hips and his leisurely pets were stretching me further and further, until the tension bordered on painful, and I was one hors d'oeuvre away from popping my stitches.

"I can't do this slow shit anymore." I scrabbled for his pants.

He chuckled, peppered my brow with light kisses, and nimbly undid my breeches.

Meanwhile, my hands stumbled on his, getting stuck on the laces.

"How many goddamn effing knots did you tie...*holy shit!*" A gasp tore out of me when his hand slipped into my unfastened waistband. His fingers were uncertain at first. Almost clumsy.

I abandoned his tight-laced pants and dug my nails into his side, holding on as I wriggled my ass, helping him slot his touch into the right spot.

Ziiiiing.

Deep, warm, electric heat sizzled low in my stomach, making me keen.

Cheriour's intense gaze burned a hole into my cheek. He shifted his fingers, exploring, prodding, all while studying the way I moved and the sounds I made, letting my reactions guide him.

His fingers lost their hesitancy *very* quickly. And he learned how to stroke and twirl in ways that left me panting.

"*Uggh, shi-ooo...*" I arched against him, babbling a steady stream of nonsense words. "Okay... no... you gotta stop." I batted his hand away and tried to cajole my pleasure-mush brain into focusing for two friggin' seconds so I could get his pants off. "I want a turn. Goddamn your laces...*ahh*," I sighed in relief when the knot came loose and I was able to rip the strings through the loops. "Now we're talking..."

I yanked his pants down and flailed until I was completely free of mine. And then I was on top of him, licking and kissing every inch of him I could get my mouth on. Salt and rain flavored his skin, and my tongue lavished over the varying textures of his body. His skin was coarse in most areas but downy soft in others, like the backs of his ears, the undersides of his arms, and his nipples.

"Hmmmm." Cheriour fidgeted when I ran my tongue over his left nipple. I dropped my mouth down farther, kissing his navel, which only earned me a low exhale. But biting his belly had a harsh groan rattling his chest. So I gave him lots of love bites. And each "*hmmmuggh*" I dragged from him made my heart skip.

And when I finally sent my mouth south and wrapped my lips around that luscious, rigid appendage...

The lack of noise there was actually more rewarding. He threw his head back, mouth gaping and stomach contracting as he fought for oxygen. All I had to do was suck a little and...

Ding, ding, ding!!

His breathy "*OH*" was the winner. The sound that made everything inside me light up.

But then he shakily pushed me away.

I chuckled. "Too much?"

He crawled back on top of me, settling himself between my thighs, and snatched my mouth in a desperate kiss. Molten heat coiled low, low, *low* in my belly when his hips lurched in a scattered thrust.

"Fuck." I ripped my lips from his and bonked my head back on the mattress, trying to settle my roaring emotions. We were both so on edge, neither of us was going to last long once he was inside of me.

And we had to get a not-so-fun discussion out of the way first.

"Hey..." I cupped his chin. He had his eyes closed, looking utterly relaxed, even as sweat trickled down the side of his face. "Cheriour, look at me."

Slowly, he opened his eyes. And that pleasure-induced haze was a sexy fucking look on him.

Focus, Addie!

"I know you guys don't have condoms here. And I've been off the pill for a few months now. And my period's been kinda whack...*the point...*" I stuttered when he kissed my palm. "You gotta pull out. Okay? There is no way in *hell* I wanna get pregnant here."

"I know, Addie." He rubbed his cheek against my hand. "I was already planning on it."

"Yeah, well..." I gulped, my hand falling away as his hips oscillated languidly against mine. "I didn't know if you knew the old pull-out method. I don't like it. At all. I also don't like relying on other people. Normally, I'm the one who supplies the condoms. I got burned once by putting too much faith in a guy and I *swore* I'd never let anyone burn me again. But I can't skip to the nearest drugstore and pick up a pack of Trojans. So...I'm trusting you. *Please* don't make me regret it."

His brow rumpled as he clutched my hands. "Addie..."

"Because I *will* castrate you if you knock me up. So help me—"

"Addie!" He huffed and dropped a kiss to my nose. "I would *never* betray your trust." He didn't say anything else, but he didn't *need* to. His fervent stare and the tender way he stroked my face spoke volumes.

"Alrighty, then." I twined my legs around his hips, pulling him closer.

He flecked kisses over my brow and cheeks and made a hollow grunt-mewl as he thrust inside of me.

Per-fucking-fection.

Absolute perfection.

His hands clenched mine so tight, I almost thought he was gonna break my fingers. He moved slowly at first, experimentally rolling his hips to search for the spots that stole the breath from my lungs. Then he writhed more erratically, his muscles spasming, and his breath coming out in short, quivering puffs as he reached the end of his tether.

All the while, I clung to him, my knees digging into his sides, and squeezed my eyes shut, savoring each pleasurable pulse zipping through my belly.

He pulled out, as he'd promised, and finished with a yell, a noise that shot another sharp *ziing* through my stomach.

Then he shifted, his trembling hands traveling down my body, slipping between my thighs.

"Dude..." I clawed at his hands, my eyes rolling to the back of my head when the slight curl of his fingers had fireworks exploding across my vision. "You don't have to... *oooh*...oh fucking...*shit!*"

I squealed, thumping my heels into the mattress as that pleasurable coil of heat exploded, sending shockwaves all throughout my body.

He held me as I stilled. Kissed me as I caught my breath. Nuzzled me as my brain came back online.

"Ho-ly *shit*." I laughed and gave him a sloppy smooch. "That was...I mean...*amazing*... Why in ever-loving fuck did we wait so long to do this?"

Cheriour didn't answer. But he had a big, dumb, shit-eating grin on his face.

CHAPTER 10

THREE WEEK BLACKOUT BENDER

"What am I going to do with you?" I slumped against the paddock fence when Abby Normal turned her back to me.

Another day, another failed attempt to get a halter on her. "Between you and Cheriour...how'd I get stuck with the two biggest pigheads in Sakar?" I asked.

Her tail twitched.

A nasally snore rumbled from behind me. Braxton. He sprawled on the ground in a drunken stupor that even the endless hustle and bustle of foot traffic didn't rouse him from. And his head was smack-dab in the middle of the walkway, so everyone had to step over him. A few people cursed and gave him dirty looks as they passed. Most shook their heads and muttered things like, "poor blighter."

I glanced at the wispy clouds rolling overhead. They didn't *seem* to be rain clouds. Not yet, at least. But it was freezing with them hogging the light.

Fall had officially...fallen.

And the days were getting short. It couldn't have been

later than two or three PM, but the sun already sat low in the sky. Once it set, it'd be too bitter for Braxton to sleep outside. I'd have to haul him back to the castle. *Again.*

"How long has he been sleeping?"

I turned when Quinn strolled down the walkway, coming to a stop beside Braxton.

"He zonked out about ten minutes ago," I said.

Quinn gave Braxton a not-so-gentle boot to the ribs. Braxton grunted, gagged on a mouthful of spit, and carried on sleeping.

"Lovely," I muttered. "He's so attractive when he's asleep, isn't he?"

Cursing under his breath, Quinn knelt and yanked the flask from Braxton's belt. After giving it a brisk shake, he popped the cork and dumped the contents over Braxton's face.

With a gurgley snort, Braxton sprang up. "Eh? Ach, Quinn! Ye bloody bastard." He sneezed once. Twice.

And Quinn was right in the splatter zone.

"Hahaha, *bullseye!*" I cackled.

Quinn made a long *urguuuh* of disgust and mopped the spittle and snot off his chin. "For feck's sake. Braxton, I *need* you to...Braxton! *Focus!*"

Braxton went cross-eyed watching an amber droplet slide off the tip of his nose. A sour look curdled over his face. "Ye"—*hic*—"wasted me drink."

"You've had quite enough." Quinn snapped his fingers. "Braxton...*look at me*...have you seen anything of Laewaes?"

"Bugger off." *Huck.* "Glenarm fell"—*hic*—"years ago."

"Then it's a good thing I didn't ask about Glenarm. We need to know the status of *Laewaes.*"

"'S all the fecking same."

Quinn sighed and tugged at the crest of his hair. "Go... eat something, Braxton. When's the last time you had a proper meal?"

Braxton pursed his lips as though deep in thought, even as his barely focused eyes fluttered closed. "I can't remember. Mayhap when we feasted by the waterfall...Mighty fine meal, that was. Remember, Quinn?" He flashed a loopy, lopsided smile. "Ye was all"—*hic*—"*smitten.*"

A neon-red blush bathed Quinn's cheeks. "Hardly."

"It's okay, Quinn," I sniggered. "I get smitten over food too."

"Ha!" Braxton chortled, although I didn't know if my words had registered in his alcohol-soaked brain or if he was reacting to Quinn's embarrassed scowl. But he burst out laughing all the same. And then he hiccupped, muttered a low *"feck,"* and gushed vomit all down his front.

Quinn scuttled away just in time to avoid the yuck.

Braxton swayed, almost flopping into the puddle of bile. Quinn grabbed him by the scruff of his neck, holding him upright.

A cluster of people passed by, all making identical *ick* faces as they skirted the steaming bile crawling along the walkway.

"Uggghh." Braxton spat and patted his belt. "Where's my feckin' drink?"

"Right here." Quinn pointed to the steaming pond of upchuck. "If you want it back, I'll let you go."

Braxton grumbled. "Ye feckin' cad...I'm no savage brute who'll drink his own sick. Oi, Addie." He turned his bleary eyes toward me when I choked on another guffaw. "Where'd you come from?"

"Seriously?" I shook my head. "You were *just* talking to me!"

"Ach, the last time I saw ye was when ye brought that wee rat...poor fellow..."

"That was *three weeks* ago!"

Braxton wrinkled his nose and looked panicked for a hot second, as though realizing he'd been on a three-week blackout bender. But then he burped, and his face slackened again. "Stop messing with me head, Addie."

"This is quite enough." With a deep grunt, Quinn hauled Braxton to his feet and gave him a rough slap on the cheek. "Go get yourself something to eat—*Braxton!*"

Braxton swayed, giggled, and started to timber. Quinn barely caught him in time.

"Wouldn't it be easier to Vulcan Mind Meld the drunk away?" I asked. "Heal him sober?"

"If it were that simple, I would have done so already." Quinn hoisted Braxton's arm onto his shoulder. "I can heal the aftereffects of drinking. But when whiskey is coursing through his blood, I can do nothing."

"Ah. Got it. So the next time I have a hangover, I should come to you for the cure?"

Quinn's face creased into a disgusted snarl. Like, *"Absolutely not. If you* dare *to disturb me for a hangover cure, I'll whack you upside the head."*

"Okie-dokie. I'll take that as a no. I'm sure Maddox would do it, though," I chirped.

"You will *not* use either of our powers for something as trivial as—"

A warbling roar cut him off.

Abby Normal, clearly not entertained by this drunken shitshow, pivoted and barreled into the fence. She snaked her head over the top rail and flashed her teeth at Quinn and Braxton.

"Abs..." I gave her nose a sharp tap.

Braxton belched in Quinn's ear and opened his eyes wide enough to get a good gander at Abby Normal's fangs.

He blinked once. Twice. And flew back with a booming "*arrrrgggggghhh!*" Down he went, his legs flipping over his head in a backward-flailing tumble-sault that somehow rotated him right back onto his feet.

"Bugger me." His shocked, red-rimmed eyes looked ready to bug out of his head.

"*Pfffffttt...*" I tried to contain the laugh. *Tried.* But it made a wet raspberry sound as it exploded from between my clenched lips.

Quinn turned away and covered his mouth with his hand, attempting to hold his miserable pout in place, but he was *totally* laughing.

"Cads!" Braxton shrieked. "Both of ye! Why in the feck—aw, feck it all—I think I wet me pants..."

Quinn choked.

The sight of Braxton glumly prodding the seat of his breeches, checking for moisture, had me doubled over, clutching the fence for dear life.

He might not've wet his pants. But I was about to.

"*Braxton.*" Quinn had to say the name three times before it came out as a coherent word and not a breathless, babbling snort. "Go to the castle and get something to eat."

"I'd rather have somethin' to drink."

"Did—did we not have this conversation five seconds ago?" I clutched at my aching stomach. "The rum is gone, Braxton."

"Eh?"

"Go eat a Snickers. You'll feel better."

"I never understand half of what ye say, Addie," Braxton grumbled.

"Likewise."

"Braxton...Cheriour, Maddox, and I will be meeting in an hour," Quinn added. "We'll need whatever information you can give us. And I need you alert enough to know the difference between Glenarm and Laewaes. We also need you to send birds to Hadleigh and Muirin—"

"What's the bloody point?" Braxton spat at his feet. "They'll all be fallen soon, aye?"

"But some may not be yet," Quinn said. "You're the only Speaker left. We *need* you."

A dark expression contorted Braxton's face. "Fine," he snapped. "And once ye've used my fecking powers, will ye let me drink in peace?"

Quinn lifted a hand to his head, clutching at a chunk of his hair. "You *know* I didn't mean it that—*Braxton!*"

Braxton spun and started a stompy, zig-zagging walk to the castle.

"Well." I bumped Abby Normal's muzzle when she whipped her head in Quinn's direction. "That went splendidly, huh?"

Quinn whirled on me. "Why is your Púca still charging the fence?"

I shrugged. "She's not a people person." This said as Abby Normal rolled her ravenous gaze over Quinn and smacked her lips.

"You were supposed to work with her!"

"Yeah. And Shitfaced Sam"—I nodded toward Braxton's tromping form—"was supposed to help me. Because I have no idea what I'm doing and need someone to teach me. But I'm sure you can guess how that's been going."

"How far have you gotten with her?"

"Uh...well...she's pretty tolerant with lots of stuff. See?" I pinched Abby Normal's upper lip between my forefinger and thumb. She flashed me an exasperated side-eye but stood still as I lifted her lip up over her fangs and muttered *"grrrr"* under my breath. "She's as sweet as can be. But God forbid I put a halter anywhere near her face."

"She's not halter broken?"

"Oh, she's broken *plenty* of halters."

"Unbelievable."

"I'm dead serious. Peek your head into her pasture...her latest victim is right by the gate post—"

Quinn ripped a knife from his belt.

"Whoa! The *hell?*" I flung my arm across Abby Normal's face, shielding her. "Don't you *dare* stab her. She's kinda bitchy, sure. But she hasn't hurt *anyone*. You don't get to kill—"

"Relax." Quinn flipped the blade, handing the hilt to me. "I'm going to fetch a halter. I want you to cut your arm."

"Excuse me?"

"She needs *incentive* to accept the halter," he said. "You can't merely throw it over her face. On horses, we use oats and mash. For her..." His lip curled in disgust as he eyed Abby Normal. "We'll use blood."

"I didn't realize I'd asked for your help," I grumbled. Sure, I *needed* the help. But Quinn was the last person I wanted teaching me. I'd never forgive him for chucking a knife at my head. Or for beating the snot out of me in those early "training sessions."

If holding grudges was an Olympic sport, I'd have more gold medals than Michael Phelps.

Spatters of laughter plumed toward the heavens as another cluster of people sauntered down the walkway, heading for the castle. Cheriour walked with them. He stayed at the back, his head down, silently listening to the rowdy conversations in front of him. Weapons and bags engulfed his shoulders, their weight forcing him to bow his back.

He stopped when he saw me and Quinn.

After last night and that *amazing* sex, the sight of him had my heart doing a jig.

Until he tilted his head and propped a hand on his hip. Very much a diva pose. I could practically hear him thinking, *Behave.*

Just like that, the warm fluffies vanished. I rolled my eyes.

He smiled and continued walking, hefting the baggage more securely onto his shoulders.

"Fine," I grumbled, both to his retreating back and to Quinn. "*Fine.*" I snatched Quinn's knife, rolled my sleeve up, and dragged the blade down the length of my forearm.

And, *ooof*, I should've thought this through more. Because a half a second before blood erupted from the wound, the pain hit. "Oooow," I hissed. "Oooh, mother-fucker, that stings!"

Quinn's brow shot up so high, it almost disappeared into his floppy hair. "A small cut would've sufficed."

"Yeah, well, I don't do shit halfway. Stop, Abs." I elbowed her when she leaned into my shoulder, whuffling and *mowowowing*. "So, what am I supposed to do with this?" I raised my heavily bleeding arm.

"Well, I wasn't expecting you to slice your arm in half," Quinn said.

"Oh, *pssh*, don't be so dramatic. *I'm* the Drama Queen around here, kay? And I'm not sharing my throne with you."

Something glinted across Quinn's face. A smile, or a shadow of one, at least. "I'll fetch you a halter. You'll use your blood to coax her into putting her head into it."

"That'll actually work?" I shoved Abby Normal's chin when she stuck her muzzle against my ear, giving me a wet willy.

"It should. Stay away from the Púca until I've returned." Quinn made a beeline for the stable, probably worried I'd bleed out.

I mean, *I* was starting to worry about that. Because thick ribbons of crimson were blobbing from the foot-long gash and plinking onto the grass.

Beside me, Abby Normal whickered and began her nervous weaving.

"Sorry, Abs." I stepped away from the fence, giving her space.

She bobbled back and forth, exuding thin, tense grunts as her eyes rolled in their sockets.

Quinn, thankfully, came dashing back as she started a new noise: a quivering *hurhururhur*.

"Here." Quinn chucked the halter at me. "Wipe your blood over the nose piece—that's the *headpiece*," he groaned when I anointed the rope with my blood.

"Is it?"

"Can you not tell the difference?"

"Between the two identical loops of rope? No, I can't tell the difference."

"One is *considerably* larger than the other."

"Says who?" But I smeared my bleeding arm over the *slightly smaller* loop. "Okay. Now what?"

"Now I'll heal your arm." Quinn grasped my wrist and tapped his fingers against the base of the wound. "*Before* you drive that Púca half mad."

My skin zipped itself shut. No more gash. There wasn't even a scar left to commemorate my dumbass slash.

"That power is so freaking cool. But so much for not wasting it on *trivial* things, huh?" I gibed.

Quinn's hand was clammy when he released my arm. "Go show the Púca the halter."

Abby Normal watched me as I ducked under her fence. When I held the halter out, she dove for it, nosily sucking the blood off the rope.

"Ha!" I squealed. "Look at that! This is the closest she's *ever* let me get with a halter."

"You should've done this from the start," Quinn said. "She would've been halter broken by now."

"Well...I can't do what I don't know. *Ooooh*! She put her nose right in there!"

Abby Normal, apparently not satisfied with guzzling on the rope, had shoved her nose through the loop, slithering her head toward my arm. The long, slimy length of her tongue dragged over my skin, slurping the tacky patches of blood.

"Gross, Abs," I said.

At the same time, Quinn shouted, "Addie! Back away from her! *Now!*"

"Chill. She's not gonna bite me. I hope," I added under my breath. But Abby Normal's eerily intelligent eyes were placid as they rolled toward me. She stuck her tongue out as far as it would go, careful to keep her teeth away from my skin. And she had the halter half over her face. So, on a whim, I grasped the headpiece with my free hand and pulled it over her ears.

She tensed briefly, her neck arching. But then she sighed and resumed her languid lapping of my blood.

"You put far too much trust in that creature." Quinn's cheeks puffed on an exhale.

"Abs has *never* tried to hurt me," I said. "And she's helped me out of some sticky situations. So she has my trust. All of it. She's earned it."

Quinn watched Abby Normal for a moment longer, his lips puckered. Then he glanced at the cloud-glazed sky, rubbed a hand over his hair, and asked, "Do you trust her enough to ride her?"

"I already have. Kinda. She carried me and Cheriour out of Niall, remember? I dunno that I trust *myself* to stay on her back, but that's a whole other issue..."

Quinn's hand moved back and forth through his hair until the gray-speckled strands stood straight up.

"You got something on your mind, huh?" I prodded.

Quinn grasped a chunk of his hair and gave it a harsh yank. "What happened with Seruf?" he asked.

My chest tightened. "Huh?"

"Seruf. She was there the night Niall fell but hasn't been seen since. Everyone fears she's lying in wait and will attack Sanadrin next. But Cheriour"—he dropped his hand and rubbed his jaw—"isn't concerned about her whereabouts. Which is unlike him."

I shrugged, hoping Quinn couldn't hear my galloping heart. "Guess he figures there's not much he can do."

Quinn's eyes narrowed. "You and Cheriour were the last to leave Niall that night. What happened?"

"You'll need to ask Cheriour."

"I have. Many times. He's not answered me. So, I'm asking you."

"I don't know."

He drummed his fingers against the top of the fence. "You're lying."

"Hmmm, I think you're just not happy with the response. *I don't know.* Okay? That's my final answer." No way in *hell* would I give him the full "I turned Seruf to dust" spiel. He'd tried to lop my head off before he knew I had powers. What would he do if he knew I could crush a Celestial's soul with my bare hands?

Quinn sighed. Tapped the toe of his boot against the fence. Lightly smacked his palms against the top slat...

"Whatever you're working up the nerve to say...spit it out," I snapped.

Brrrrrmmmmpppphhh went his fingers against the wood. "Has Cheriour told you of Muirin?"

Which was...*not* what I'd expected him to ask. "Uh, no? The name sounds familiar, though. Somewhat. It's a town, right?"

"It's a city in Vatra, a country that fell more than a decade ago."

"Oookay?"

"We believe there is a Celestial there. I'm *trying* to have Braxton confirm..."

"Wait...hang on..." *Now* I remembered where I'd first heard the name: back in the old Breakfast Club days at Niall. Garvin (God rest his poor, questioning soul) had mentioned it. And Belanna... "Belanna said no animals had provided confirmation."

"Braxton says that too, but I'm asking him to send as many animals as he can manage. We *need* confirmation." Quinn rhythmically smacked his other hand against his thigh. "Otherwise, Cheriour will ride out."

"*What*?!"

Quinn raised his palms in a "don't go full bitch on me, I'm just the messenger" pose.

"That man is gonna be the death of me," I hissed. "He's *suicidal.* Honestly. Does he think he can single-handedly fight a Celestial?"

"The Celestial may be from Raphael's army. If so, they can help us."

My mouth closed with a snap. "Oh."

"Yes. *Oh.*"

I stared at Abby Normal again. She'd dropped her head and slipped into a light, post-meal doze. But her eye opened when I touched her cheek.

Her slitted, vividly *red* eye.

"Everyone who's gone outside Sanadrin hasn't come back," I whispered.

"I'm well aware." There was an unspoken "*duh*" in Quinn's drizzling, sarcastic voice.

Abby Normal rolled her eye upward as I ran my palm over her scaly neck. She whuffled again and dropped back into her doze.

"*Do you trust her enough to ride her?*" he'd asked. Now I got why.

Everything outside Sanadrin was a wasteland overrun with Wraiths who would see a human coming on horseback a mile away.

But what if that human rode a Púca and wore all black? Would that human be able to camouflage themselves and blend in with the black-armored, Púca-mounted Wraiths?

I laughed. Bitterly. "Motherfucker. I should've known you weren't helping me out of the kindness of your heart."

CHAPTER II

WAKING THE FUCKING KRAKEN

I sat diagonally across Cheriour's bed, my right leg outstretched over the edge to keep Splinter confined to the mattress. As Splinter shuffled and snuffed around, I skimmed through the slew of sketches in my lap.

And, okay, I wasn't snooping. Not really. I'd asked this morning (admittedly, as Cheriour was getting dressed and I was eye-humping his ass) if I could clean his room a bit.

"It makes sense to share a room at this point. Right?" I'd questioned. At his nod, I'd added, "And it doesn't matter to me which one we pick. They both suck. But yours is a freaking pigsty. Mind if I go in later and straighten it up a bit? To make consolidating easier?"

He'd made a faint "eh." Which had sounded like a yes to me. Or at the very least, an "I don't care."

And I *had* done some cleaning—you could actually see the floor now! Kinda. A full hour of sorting and straightening had only cleared a narrow path from the door to the bed. And then I spied his drawings, piled haphazardly beneath a rock on his dingy mattress, and got distracted.

Cheriour was a freaking *amazing* artist.

The top sketch was a full landscape of the city and castle at Niall, but it could've been easily mistaken for a black-and-white photograph. He'd captured *every single* detail of the castle: the smooth, glass-like stones; the porthole-sized windows; the slanting steps outside the front door. People and horses scattered about the grounds, each one meticulously, *intricately* drawn. One of them was Belanna, leading her big black stallion. A mischievous, thousand-watt smile brightened her face.

Flipping through a few more pages revealed another picture of Belanna, this one a portrait of her holding a bird on her arm. Her devilish grin was firmly in place, and it was so realistic, I half expected her to come to life and whip that impish smile at me.

There were other portraits sprinkled in, but most of the people were unfamiliar. There were other landscapes too, mostly of places in Sakar, although he had a few that *might've* been locations from back home. One piece bore a *strong* resemblance to the Vatican, but it had clearly been drawn while he was bedridden. Not that it was *bad*. Naw. Just less detailed than some of the others.

"Ugh," I groaned when I turned the page and saw my own mug staring back at me. "Talk about a jump scare. I think this one can burn..."

"Don't."

I glanced up as Cheriour stepped into the room, dumping a jumble of weapons onto the floor. He didn't look at me—too busy staring at the heap of papers in his hands.

"Yo, can you put those away?" I jabbed my finger at the weapons. "I *just* got that part of the room cleaned."

He sighed and used the toe of his boot to nudge the

weapons off to the side, ramming them in with the rest of the mess.

"You're such a slob," I grumbled.

He flipped one of his papers over, his brow furrowing as he read. "Don't burn the drawing."

"It's my face. I'll do what I want with it." But I would never, *ever* destroy this picture. Because the more I looked at it, the more my stomach fluttered.

Drawing-me wore a big smile, so my chipmunk cheeks were out in full force, but my eyes *sparkled* with mirth. I had my left arm raised to comb my fingers through my hair, and he'd nailed every pop culture emblem on my tattoo, from the *Jurassic Park* logo to the sketch of Edward Scissorhands hugging Kim Boggs.

The detail was *astounding*. He'd been meticulous about capturing every dip, curve, wrinkle, nook, and cranny on my body. But he did so lovingly, showcasing even my worst imperfections in the most flattering way. Because he didn't see them as imperfections. They were simply a part of me, and he seemed to find all the parts of me beautiful.

"So, I have two questions for you..." I lifted my portrait and waved it through the air. "First of all, how dare you?" Heh. Unfortunately, *The Office* references were way funnier when people caught onto them and responded with their favorite quote. "Second of all, when were you planning to tell me about your little vacation to Mirror-in?"

"Muirin," he corrected.

"That's what I said."

"I have no plans to ride to Muirin," he said.

"Quinn made it sound like you were packing your bags."

"He and I both want to confirm the rumors. And he knows I would ride out if we had no other option. But I've not yet decided anything." He glanced up at me. "I wouldn't have left without telling you, Addie."

And his slightly morose look was all the proof I needed that he was being honest.

I exhaled as some of the tension ebbed from my shoulders. "Okay. Thanks."

He hummed gently and tossed a piece of paper onto the ground.

My eyes narrowed. "Y'know, there's this *magical* invention called the *trash can*. You chuck all your unwanted crap in there and...*voila*! No more garbage on your floor."

"Hmmm."

"I put one in the corner for ya. How 'bout you give it a whirl?"

He didn't answer. *Typical.*

I rolled my eyes. "You're lucky I like you. So...how important is this? The trip to Muirin?"

"It depends."

"On?"

Cheriour pulled his eyes away from his papers. "On who is there."

"So there is a Celestial hiding out there?"

He shrugged. "Perhaps. I'm not certain. Four months ago, Lasair—"

I flinched. That name had some *nasty* emotions tied to it.

Cheriour paused at my reaction and gave me a slow blink, waiting for me to dissolve into a manic meltdown. When I didn't, he kept going. "She believed Hurleigh—"

"Well, *that's* an unfortunate name," I chortled.

"—a Celestial in Raphael's army," Cheriour spoke over me, "may have maintained a home on the coast. Belanna tried, many times, to verify that claim. None of the birds she sent could confirm Hurleigh's presence. Braxton has also tried and said the same."

"Which means there's nobody home...I'd assume? But then, you wouldn't be considering riding out there if that was the case."

He inclined his head. "If Hurleigh does not wish to be seen, Braxton and Belanna's birds will not find him."

"Of course. He's a magical camouflaging Celestial. *Why not?* Uh—Splinter—uh-uh..." I scooped Splinter up when he meandered too close to the edge of the mattress.

"Why is the vermin on my bed?" Cheriour asked.

"Umm, you *love* this vermin. Don't even deny it. And with the state your sheets were in, Splinter is probably the *least* vermin-y thing crawling around on your bed. Anyway, if this Hurleigh guy is that good at hiding, how did Lasair know—or *suspect*—he was there?"

"Seruf told her..."

"*What?*"

"...which is why I remain skeptical."

"Okay...you gotta back up a bit. Lasair heard it from *Seruf?* How? *Why?* Seruf wasn't the type to cough up helpful information."

Cheriour pursed his lips.

"Ah, fuck. I *know* that look. You're gonna tell me something I don't wanna hear, aren't you?"

"Seruf," he said as he kept his eyes trained on me, "was the Celestial who created Lasair."

"I fucking *knew* it." And, yup, there was the pesky pain in my chest again, gleefully spearing my insides as my brain digested this new information.

Splinter, sensing my change in mood, ambled over my calf and curled onto my kneecap as though comforting me.

It didn't work. But it was adorable all the same.

"Okay...so..." I steepled my hands over my mouth, fighting to control my racing thoughts. "Seruf—wait, was that pedo my *grandmother*?"

"No," Cheriour said. "Seruf *created* Lasair. She did not birth her."

"There's a difference?"

"As for why she would divulge information to Lasair... I'm not certain." His brow crumpled again as he lowered his eyes back to the papers. "But riding to Muirin may be the only way to confirm."

"Won't Hurleigh keep hiding, though?"

"Perhaps." Cheriour tossed another piece of paper onto the floor.

"Your confidence in this half-baked scheme is inspiring. *Truly*. How long would it even take to get to Muirin?"

"Ordinarily, a month. Perhaps less. But the quickest route is through Niall. That is no longer a viable path. Now it may take longer."

A *month*?

Jeez. Maybe I had to rethink my plan. Because being on the back of a horse 24/7 for thirty or more days...*ouch*. Talk about a chapped ass. I'd need a whole *gallon* of Monistat by the end of that ride.

"But if this Hurleigh guy is there..." I started.

A red tinge burgeoned over Cheriour's cheeks.

Interesting.

"As I've told Quinn," he drawled, "even if Hurleigh is there, he's not likely to help. I know him."

"You *know* him?"

"Yes. I was a Celestial. Hurleigh was my kin. Once." Cheriour's mouth thinned.

Very interesting.

He rarely showed this much agitation.

This Hurleigh must've been a shitbag. Or maybe a Cousin Eddie type: the obnoxious wrecking ball of the family.

"Okay, but you were considering going out there. Right?" I asked. "So you must think there's a chance he can help, even if it's a slim one."

"I'm not optimistic."

"But what's the alternative?" I pressed. "You've got… how many humans are in Sanadrin? A few thousand, at least. Right? You don't gotta give me the exact number," I added when Cheriour opened his mouth. "The point is, we're all clustered in this one little corner of the world. And what's the plan? Hide here until everyone dies?"

"No—"

"I mean, I've been here barely three months and I've seen *two* countries fall. You realize how insane that is?"

"Are you going to let me speak?"

"No. Because I want you to hear me out first. Then you can have the floor. I wanna ride to Muirin. No, no. Don't dismiss the idea yet," I said when he rolled the remaining papers under his arm and dragged his eyes over me. "I've got a plan. It's not a *great* plan. But it's something. If I take Abby Normal and I dress in all black, *maybe* I can pass for a Wraith. At least from a distance. It'd give me a better shot of getting to Muirin alive, wouldn't it? I'm fireproof too, so no Wraith is gonna BBQ my ass. And, well…I…What happened with Seruf…I might be a crappy fighter, but I'm not entirely useless. And if Hurleigh's there…I dunno. Maybe I'll catch him on a good day, and he'll decide to help us."

Cheriour sighed and coiled his left hand through his

beard, tugging on the strands. "Keep looking through the drawings," he said.

"Seriously? I offer to sacrifice myself on a suicide mission, and *that's* your response?"

"The drawings," he repeated.

"I put a lot of thought into my plan," I grumbled as I flipped a page over. "A *whole* afternoon's worth of thought. And you tuned me out. Freaking jerk...Wait..."

After flipping several sketches over, I reached the page he'd clearly wanted me to see.

My chipmunk face stared up at me again. This time, Cheriour had sketched me in a full-body pose and swathed me in black armor. A breastplate hugged my torso, curved panels gripped my shoulders, tubes of metal encircled my arms and legs, and dark leather wreathed my thighs. A spiked helmet also rested against my left hip, tucked under my arm. This wasn't just a drawing, though. It was a blue-print, with scribbled notes on how to cut, melt, and turn the metal black.

"You're right," Cheriour said. "If you can make your Púca ridable, you have the best chance of getting to Muirin unde-tected. Turn the page."

"Holy shit," I murmured. Because the back of the paper featured a rearing Abby Normal, fully decked in a hulking black saddle and a chain bridle.

He'd put a *ton* of thought into this. Way more than my hastily brainstormed speech. "Why didn't you say anything to me before?" I asked.

"It was merely an idea I'd had." He lifted his right shoul-der. "And I'd not yet decided what to do about Muirin."

"Did Quinn know about this?" I waved the page through the air.

"No. Although I'm not surprised he arrived at the same conclusion. But before you commit, there are some things you need to consider." Cheriour walked to the bed, lowered himself down beside me, drew my leg into his lap—being extra careful not to disturb Splinter—and kneaded his knuckles into my calf.

And, oooh, fuck. It felt *amazing*. I didn't even realize you could get muscle knots in your calf, but Cheriour was working a big one loose.

He smiled when I groaned in reaction to his mini massage. "I can make this armor," he said. "But I don't have access to the metals Ramiel uses for his Wraiths. This"—he reached across my lap to tap the page—"will look the same but serve no functional purpose. A blade would cut through it."

As he drew back, he gave Splinter an affectionate bump on the head.

"Ha! I *knew* you liked him." I tapped the back of my hand against Cheriour's arm. "You big softie. But"—I flicked the sketched breastplate—"I take it you can't steal this metal off a dead Wraith?"

"It would be an ill fit. And too many modifications will expose you. Even this armor"—his (super strong) fingers pressed and stroked my calf—"will only be passable from a distance."

My hands twitched, both from my nerves and the delicious pain that accompanied the release of a muscle knot.

Cheriour's palm smoothed over my leg, rubbing the back of my knee. "You should depart before the weather turns for winter. That is less than a month to get yourself and Abby Normal prepared. You'd be safest traveling alone. The path will not be easy. And in Muirin, you will find only ruins. If Hurleigh is not there, or if he refuses to help, you'll need to choose whether to stay for winter and find shelter amongst the debris. Or risk the weather and attempt to return to Sanadrin. You would also need to consider Abby Normal's condition. Even if you want to return, she may not be fit enough to do so."

"Well." My throat made a weird *click-click* as I swallowed. "You paint a rosy picture, don't you?"

"You should understand the risks before you decide."

"I gotta know the pros too, though. If the best-case scenario happens and Hurleigh decides to help, what'll it mean for us?"

Cheriour squeezed my leg. "It could mean the difference between surviving the winter and not."

I turned the page back over, staring at the sketch of me wearing the armor. It was badass, turning me into a warrior queen, ready to hop aboard my dragon and toast King's Landing.

Or, y'know, *save it.*

But I'd be no better than a cosplayer posing as a warrior queen: decoration only. Like Cheriour's armor.

Cheriour reached for my hand, his fingers twining with mine. The warm rasp of his palm and the quiet rhythm of his breathing soothed me.

"Would you be able to draw me a map?" I asked. "A *detailed* one, showing me exactly how to get to this place. It's gotta be idiot proof too. I've never had to read a map before."

"I could. And I would make sure you could read it."

I nodded. Okay. One worry down, right? I wouldn't be wandering around aimlessly, hoping I'd stumble onto the place.

But there were dozens of other worries.

"Is there anything I should know about Hurleigh? Things I can use as bribery. Or anything guaranteed to piss him off...*Definitely* give me that info."

"Hurleigh is not temperamental," Cheriour said.

"Oh, good. So he's not gonna shoot laser beams out of his eyes if I disturb his slumber?"

"No. He's a Sea Guardian."

"A...*what*?"

"He has some measure of control over the sea. And he can use it to conceal himself. Muirin overlooks the sea."

"Aw man, this place is a *beach town*? You should've led with that. But..." I frowned. "What do you mean he has 'some measure of control over the sea'?"

"You saw what Seruf was able to do with fire," Cheriour said. "Hurleigh can do the same with water."

"Of course he can. Why not?" I blew out a breath. "And... I *know* I'm not gonna like this answer...but if he's using the ocean to *conceal* himself, does that mean he's lurking under the water somewhere?"

Cheriour inclined his head.

"O...kay." I squeezed his hand "So I'm not just gonna go poke some Average Joe Celestial out from behind a tree...I've gotta wake the fucking *kraken*? This should be fun, huh?"

CHAPTER 12

EXPLORERS ON THE ENTERPRISE

I had three weeks, maximum, to get my ass out the door. To make sure I was on the road before Jack Frost crawled out of hibernation.

My days became so jam-packed, I barely had time to breathe. I mean, I *liked* it. The busy days distracted me and helped keep my head screwed on straight. But it also meant time was fast-forwarding on me when I would've preferred to stay on pause for a bit.

My combat training sessions continued in the mornings. Because *of course* they did.

"You'll not have an easy road," Cheriour said as he dragged me out of bed at the ass crack of dawn.

"Which is why I should sleep while I can." I waved him away and tried to burrow back into my warm, Cheriour-scented blankets.

"You may find yourself in danger." He wrapped his arms around my waist and lifted me to my feet, ignoring me when I hissed. "As your combative skills are weaker than a child's—"

177

I flashed my middle finger in front of his face.

"—I will oversee your training again. You'll continue to train until you depart."

And the bastard made the sessions *harder*! I'd apparently been playing on beginner mode before. Now, I'd plummeted into hard mode, and I still didn't know how half the controls worked, so I winged it. *Badly*.

When I finished my daily boot camp, it was time to put Abby Normal through hers.

Braxton had been fired from Púca training—thank fuck. Instead, I spent half the time under Cheriour's supervision (which I did *not* mind, even if he was a hard-ass and I wanted to smack him upside the head sometimes) and the other half I fumed under Quinn's hostile stares.

In all fairness, Quinn was helpful. But he was still a Shit Brick who rebuffed any attempt I made at conversation... and not in the quiet, bemused way Cheriour used to. Quinn usually responded with lashing words.

"Your hair's getting kinda long, huh?" I asked on a blustery day when I turned away from Abby Normal and saw Quinn fighting to keep a flop of hair out of his eyes. "Want me to trim it back for ya?"

"No." He ground his teeth around the word.

"You sure? I'm not saying this to trick you into a crazy mullet. Although you *could* rock a mullet. But I won't be an ass. Scout's honor. I'd only trim enough to get the hair outta your eyes. I'm *good* at that. It was my job..."

"Perhaps if you'd had a less frivolous occupation, you wouldn't need assistance with *basic horsemanship*," Quinn said in his snide/haughty voice. "You are standing too close to her head. *Again*. Can't you see her falling in?"

I was *lunging* Abby Normal (and no, lunging was *not* a

leg exercise around these parts; Quinn's blood pressure had shot through the roof when I'd asked that). This was a training method meant to "increase her fitness" by strapping her to a line and making her run in small circles around me.

It seemed like a perfectly functional and efficient workout. *Not.*

I was surprised she didn't spin herself dizzy by the end of these sessions. Because *I* was usually dizzy, watching her go around and around and around and around. And Abby Normal spent the whole session either attempting to rip the line out of my hands or trying to duck into the center of the circle—as she was currently doing. The movement Quinn called "falling in."

I waved the line at her ass, as I'd been instructed, to get her to move back out.

Abby Normal flattened her ears and launched into a massive cat leap. She whipped her head to the side upon landing, nearly peeling the line out of my hands.

"Abs," I hissed when a few inches of rope slid away, leaving a burning welt on my palms. "You bitch."

She gave me a wicked side-eye, as though seething, *"That's the pot calling the kettle black, isn't it?"*

"You are unfocused, giving her unclear instructions and reprimanding her for not understanding," Quinn snapped.

"Oooh...so kinda like you did to me back at Niall?" I gave the end of the line a warning wiggle when Abby Normal cocked her head too far in my direction, trying to sneak into the center again. "At least I'm not standing out here wailing on her with a whip the way you smacked me around with that sword."

Quinn scowled and gave his hair a violent swipe when another gust of wind blew the locks in front of his eyes. "Had you but an ounce of skill or self-preservation, I would not have..." He shook his head. "Instead, you wasted your day on *millets*."

"Mullets!" I corrected. "And, dude, with the way you play that guitar—or whatever instrument you were playing at the bar—you'd look badass in a mullet."

"Are you...speaking of the lute?"

"Nah. I know what a flute is. I'm not *that* dumb."

"*Lute!*" Quinn stressed the L.

"Oh. Yeah. I guess? If that's what it's called. You were pretty damn good with that thing."

When I craned my head, I caught him in an odd pose: all straight-backed and high-chinned, puffing his chest out like an overly proud peacock.

Abby Normal immediately noticed my split attention. She dropped her shoulder, squealed, and zoomed to my side.

And, well...I kinda (definitely) deserved the scolding Quinn dished out.

Thankfully, Cheriour was the one who first boosted me onto Abby Normal's back (after we spent four days trying to convince her the saddle wasn't evil). Because I was a nervous fucking wreck while riding her.

She was so...*slippery*.

The two horses I'd ridden before had been fairly straightforward. *Literally.* They usually only went forward. Sometimes backward. Occasionally, they did some side steps. But they were too rigid, too *solid*, to pull off Abby Normal's weird footwork. Even on her forward gaits, her body felt too pliable, and her legs seemed to move in too many directions, as though she had no bones and could bend, twist, and wriggle her body however she pleased.

Very snakelike.

It was *really* hard to ride, like trying to straddle a slick and jiggly water balloon. I never went faster than a trot, even when Cheriour took me behind the castle, where we had acres of rocky fields to ride through. I white-knuckled the reins and muttered a steady stream of, "Slow...easy now...slow and steady wins the race, y'know?" And Abby Normal, probably sensing a quicker pace would've made me crap my pants, plodded along, her ears splayed, looking bored with life.

"You'll not make it to Muirin before winter if you trot the distance," Cheriour drawled when Abby Normal and I crawled past him on one of our laps.

"I know." My knees *ached* from gripping the saddle, but I was scared Abby Normal would slip out from under me if I didn't squeeze with all my might. "I'll get up to a faster pace. Eventually."

Cheriour said nothing. Didn't make a snide remark about how I'd have more confidence in the saddle if I hadn't wasted my time back home on frivolous pursuits (aka, working and paying the bills) and taken riding lessons instead. He just settled himself down on the browning grass, sharpening the swords he'd brought out with him. His eyes watched me, and he occasionally called out instructions like "don't lean," or "put your leg in front of you," but he otherwise let me trudge around at my own pace.

And every afternoon, it was off to the kitchen with Kaelan—but not to eat. *Unfortunately.* The kitchen, with its six candle chandeliers and behemoth hearth, was the most well-lit room in the castle. Which made it perfect for my Survival Skills and Map Reading 101 class.

As food simmered over the stove (aka, fireplace), teasing me with its tantalizing aromas, I sat at one of the rumpty booth tables in the back corner with my adorkable tutor. We poured over Cheriour's map while Kaelan fed me tips and tricks on how to live in the woods—how to build shelter, the best way to tie a knot, differences between edible and non-edible plants, the proper way to stack wood for a fire, ways to gauge direction if I got lost...

There was *so much information*. And not enough hours in the day to absorb it all. My brain felt like a crusty dish sponge that'd been stuffed with soap and left on the counter to dry out. And my body didn't fare much better; I had muscles in every crevice blasting S.O.S. signals at me.

But my heart? It'd never been so content.

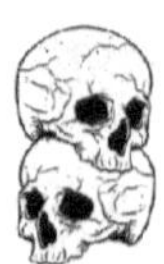

Over those three weeks, Cheriour and I fell into a blissful, domestic routine, one that felt *too* easy.

After we wrapped up for the day, we'd grab dinner together. Sometimes we'd only have the time or energy for a quick meal from the kitchen. But whenever we could, we ventured into the city and revisited the good ole Snake and Spider tavern for their stew special. Afterward, we'd peruse the city streets, usually hand in hand. And we talked. A lot.

I gabbed about places from back home: my favorite restaurants, the scenic views, the tourist traps that were too grungy to be worth the visit, and the under-the-radar places I'd refused to tell most people about lest they flock to it and ruin the aesthetic. Cheriour told me about the cities in Niall and how they'd thrived before Ramiel and the Dickhead Gang drove humans to near extinction. And he spoke of the cities he'd seen through time (the few he could remember, at least). Like Monschau, the German town I'd spied in one of his drawings back at Niall.

"Did you spend a lot of time in Monschau?" I asked him one night as we meandered through the streets.

He gave my hand a gentle squeeze. "Perhaps. I don't—" His mouth puckered. "You spoke of an omelet one morning. After you'd complained about the porridge."

"Porridge, my fucking ass. That shit was bug guts. Or worse, rat guts." I shuddered and gave Splinter, who'd made himself a cozy nest in the hollow between my shoulder and neck, a boop.

"It was porridge. Nothing more," Cheriour droned. "But after you spoke of the omelet, I saw the city. The image... *haunted* me. Until I drew it. I knew it was a place I'd been before. But..."

"You don't remember it?" I prompted when he trailed off.

"No. And the image has since faded. I remember what I drew. Nothing else."

"That's *horrifying*." I leaned into him, releasing his hand so I could twine my arms around his bicep. "Having memories disappear like that and *knowing* they're slipping away." I hugged him tightly. "I'm sorry."

His shoulder rose in a shrug. "It's not as bad as you're imagining."

"No?"

"No." He used his free hand to tuck a strand of hair behind my ear. "It's no different than forgetting a dream."

But he seemed afraid of his dreams.

Cheriour was a chronic insomniac. Every night, he joined me in bed (sometimes for sex, sometimes just for snuggles) but he rarely slept. And he put himself in deliberately awkward positions as though fighting to stay awake.

One night, I woke up to find him lying horizontally across the bed, his feet dangling over the edge, and his head pillowed on my stomach. His chin was cranked into his chest as he stared at a slip of paper, trying to read in the dim light.

He'd hummed contentedly when I stroked his hair but didn't move. And he didn't sleep.

Other nights, I found him sitting with his knees tucked up, furiously sketching on paper resting over his thighs, or crouched in the corner of the room, tinkering with some invention.

When he finally did sleep, he'd shimmy on top of me and black out. Then *I'd* be the one lying awake, sweltering under the dead weight of his slumber-heavy body.

But those nights were my favorite, watching him snooze as I petted his hair and brushed my knuckles over his cheeks. Sleep made him look younger. Vulnerable. *Beautiful.* And the sounds he made—those light snores and grunts— were freaking adorable.

"God, I am so fucked," I mumbled one time as I trailed my thumb over the leathery scar slashed across his eyelid.

I had those rose-colored, honeymoon-stage goggles *glued* to my eyes.

I liked him. A lot. Too much.

And I didn't want to leave him.

Because I'd miss this. The warmth. The flippy-floppy sensations I got in my stomach whenever I looked at him. This new relationship that was blooming.

At best, he and I would spend a few months apart.

At worst...well...*dead men tell no tales*. And they felt no loss.

But the loss would be there all the same: a love that got plucked before it had a chance to blossom.

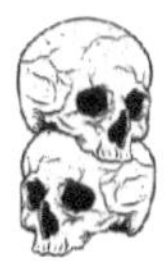

A FEW DAYS BEFORE I WAS SET TO DEPART, I GOT HOWLING NIGHT terrors that had me lurching awake, drenched in a cold sweat. And when I reached for Cheriour, seeking, *needing* his warmth, he wasn't there.

I brushed the fear quakes off as I dressed, got some food to settle my nervous stomach, and set off to search for him. But stepping outside had more cold sweat oozing across my skin. Because the sun cast a pink tinge on the puffy clouds, meaning Cheriour'd skipped out on waking me for training, and a crowd was gathered by the gate to the city, circling a burly black horse. A horse wearing the clunky, chain-link bridle we'd *just* gotten Abby Normal to grudgingly accept.

"Oh *no!*" I dropped my slightly moldy loaf of bread (aka, the breakfast of champions) and ran, hissing when the crowd shifted and blocked my view.

Had Abby Normal gotten loose? How?

And who the *fuck* had tried to bridle her?

An exclamation rippled through the group when the horse grunted and kicked out.

Don't hurt anyone, Abs. Please!

I rammed into people, tripped over feet, nearly bowled one man to the ground, but I made it to Abby Normal's side.

Except, this wasn't Abby Normal.

I froze, my fingers curling around the jingling metal reins as the horse spun and stared at me with a dark, deep brown eye. Then I pivoted and stood on my tiptoes, peering over people's heads. And, yup, there she was, still standing in her paddock, her lip curled in disgust as she watched the commotion.

My brain was so scrambled, I'd run right by Abby Normal and hadn't even noticed.

"Heh!" Braxton's voice boomed as he stepped out from the other side of the horse. "I said this would work, didn't I? Addie thought this was her Púca!" He smacked my arm. A tinkling *clang* reverberated on impact.

Shimmering black armor hugged him from head to toe.

"What are you—" I started.

"An uneducated eye is easily fooled," came Cheriour's drowsy voice. "A Wraith will not be. And the Púcas will scent your horse."

He stood a few feet away, the heel of his left boot propped against the stable wall. He was red-faced, and his extra-frizzy hair made a nice poof-halo around his head. A thick, stained leather apron draped over his front, and his fingers were nimbly sewing a patch over a jagged burn hole on the right side of it.

I'd never gotten fussed over work-roughened men in dirty clothes; it'd always looked too sweaty and stinky for my taste. But Cheriour wearing work-soiled clothes? *Good Lord.* My blood was *pumping.* And the urge, *the itch,* to free him of that grungy apron and lick the sweat off his skin was almost painful.

My brain was so consumed with horny imaginings, I didn't notice Kaelan perched on the wall beside Cheriour, clutching a spiked helmet in his left hand. Not until he giggled and said, "I've never seen you move so fast, Addie."

"Aye. Because she feared I was stealin' her Púca!" Braxton chortled.

Beside me, the horse snorted and shook his head. The reins tinged against each other, making a sound louder than most windchimes.

"So...wait..." I turned back to Braxton, who gave me a sloppy smile. "You're...*have you lost your damn mind?*"

"I'll be goin' to Muirin with ye." His breath *reeked* of whiskey. "Well, not *with* ye, mind. I'm leavin' now, and ye'll not be leavin' for a few days yet. Cheriour doesn't want me putting ye in danger..." He gave Cheriour a jaunty wave before he stage whispered, "He doesn't think my guise will work."

"I *know* it won't work," Cheriour said.

"Ach, see? He's a might testy this morn'." Braxton smacked my shoulder again. His horse shied away from the sound, spraying pebbles at the onlookers. "Sorry," Braxton chuckled as he steadied the animal. "He's not overly fond of the armor." He patted the horse's neck and winked at me. "I'll save us a wee bit of whiskey, so ye and I can toast our success when we get to Muirin."

"Braxton, I think you need to take the whiskey goggles *off*," I said.

"Eh?"

"Stop drinking for a few damn hours and actually *think* about what you're doing."

"Oh, aye," he chirped, "I've thought about it plenty. Ye and I, Addie"—he slung an arm over my shoulder—"we're pioneers..."

"Not the word I'd use. But...'kay."

"...going where none of these cads will dare to venture..."

"Now we sound like explorers on the Enterprise."

"And we'll be findin' that Celestial. Mark me words."

But he was the only one who looked confident.

Cheriour still wouldn't raise his gaze. Kaelan had a grin on his lips but kept shooting worried glances at Cheriour. The rest of the onlookers, an ever-swelling group of people who gawked and gawped, seemed kinda...disgusted? Maybe disappointed.

But Braxton hummed a lively tune under his breath as he checked his cinch, as though he was getting ready to head out for a sunny Sunday morning joyride.

His horse was *not* so cheery. With a piercing squeal, the animal zoomed sideways, his eye locked on the stables.

"Ach, come now, laddie," Braxton trilled. "I know the tack is might uncomfortable, eh? Think of how them Púcas feel, me lad. They have it worse than ye."

Cheriour stepped forward then, reaching out to stroke the horse's nose, steadying the animal. "Stay in the mountains," he said.

Braxton huffed.

"Braxton." Although still a slow drawl, Cheriour's voice had an edge to it now. "Do *not* venture from the mountain path."

"I'll consider it."

"There's *nothing* left at Niall," Cheriour continued.

"Aye. Perhaps." Braxton shrugged, patted his horse's neck, and mounted up.

I watched him, studying how the rippling metal shifted with his body. The plates clinked and clanked as he settled into the saddle but didn't seem to hamper his mobility. He swung his leg over with ease and popped his feet right into the stirrups.

"Huh." I tapped the plate covering his shin. "Y'know, I was worried this would be clunky to ride in. It doesn't look too bad, though."

"It's not so terrible. I'll be chaffed raw by day's end, mind." Braxton tapped at the sheet of metal that hung over his ass.

"Yeah, well, I get chaffed without the metal," I laughed.

"If you notice any problems..." Cheriour inspected Braxton's armor with a furrowed brow. "Come back. Immediately. I'll make the adjustments."

"Aye. I figured I'd give Larkin a good gallop to start. Take the silliness out of him." Braxton sat tall and still in the saddle while his horse skittered around in a small circle. "I'll be knowing right quick if something's not fitted correctly." He tapped his heels to his horse's side, sending him forward.

"Helmet, Braxton!" Cheriour called.

"Bloody hell." Braxton pulled his horse to a halt. "Oi, Kaelan—ah, yer a good lad." He clapped a hand against his thigh when Kaelan pranced forward, wagging the helmet through the air. "Ye've never seen Muirin, have ye?" Braxton took the helmet and crammed it over his head.

"No. But I've heard of it," Kaelan said.

"Ah. Ye were naught but a babe when it fell, eh? Damn shame. 'Twas a beauty to behold. When I'll get there, I'll send for ye."

"Braxton..." Cheriour sighed.

"Ye, me, and Addie can drink whiskey and soak in salt

water—feels mighty good on sore muscles, I'll tell ye." Braxton reached down, tapped Kaelan's golden head, and nudged his horse through the gates. "The rest of these cowardly sods can stay in this moshpit." And with that, he sent his nervously snorting horse on a springy trot through the city.

The people on main street screeched when they saw him.

"Ach, see! It works!" he bellowed. "I'm no Wraith," he added to the townspeople. "Oi there! You! What's in that wineskin?"

Kaelan laughed and dashed forward, leaning against the city gate to watch Braxton's departure.

Cheriour exhaled slowly and pinched the bridge of his nose.

"You look exhausted." I sidled up to him and grasped his hand, smiling when he twined his fingers through mine and gave me a gentle squeeze. "Were you up all night making his armor?"

"Hmmm."

"Well." I nudged my shoulder against his. "I'll make sure you get a good night's sleep tonight. How 'bout a massage? That'll loosen you up…"

His lips twitched, but his face hardened again when Braxton's jubilant, "Ha! Ye thought I was a Wraith, didn't ye?" drifted back toward us.

"So." I bit my lip. "What're the chances of him making it? Put it on a scale of one to ten. Ten meaning he'll be sipping margaritas on the beach by next week. One meaning he's dead as soon as he leaves the city."

Cheriour turned away, his restless eyes roaming over the dispersing group of people. "Three. *If* he avoids Niall."

"Even with his power? I mean, he's got a whole forest of animal spies at his disposal..."

"There are too many Wraiths. He can't avoid them," Cheriour said. "And they'll know he's riding a horse."

"Then why did you let him do this?"

"He was going to ride out regardless. I couldn't stop him. So I gave him a better chance of survival." Cheriour raised our joined hands so he could rub an itch on his cheek. And, y'know, sneak a kiss to my knuckles.

My heart clenched. God, I fucking *loved* the way he'd started slipping in these small, affectionate gestures. He was adorable. A big, warm-hearted softie with a grumpy-gills exterior.

He was making it *really* hard to leave.

Another sharp pang shot through my chest, followed by a flush of...*something* seeping through my veins. Sadness? Anger? Both? No idea. But a *grrrugh* of frustration fizzled out of me.

Cheriour's eyes crawled back toward me.

"Y'know you're getting old when you have heartburn 24/7, am I right?" I laughed and used my free hand to pound my chest until the pain eased.

He touched my cheek. "Are you alright?"

"Never been better."

A disbelieving "hmmm" rolled through him.

"Would it bug you? If I wasn't okay but refused to tell you what was wrong?"

He hummed again and inclined his head.

"Good." I stuck my tongue out at him. "Maybe now you'll understand why your macho acts drive me up a friggin' wall. But, anyway, let's get back on track...What're *my* chances of making it to Muirin? Using the same rating system."

Cheriour blinked. "Five," he said. With zero hesitation.

Yikes.

Not exactly the vote of confidence I'd been hoping for.

"Well." I gulped. "At least I'm fifty-fifty."

A gust of wind swooshed over us, carrying the last dregs of Braxton's boisterous voice. And I wondered if I'd ever see him again.

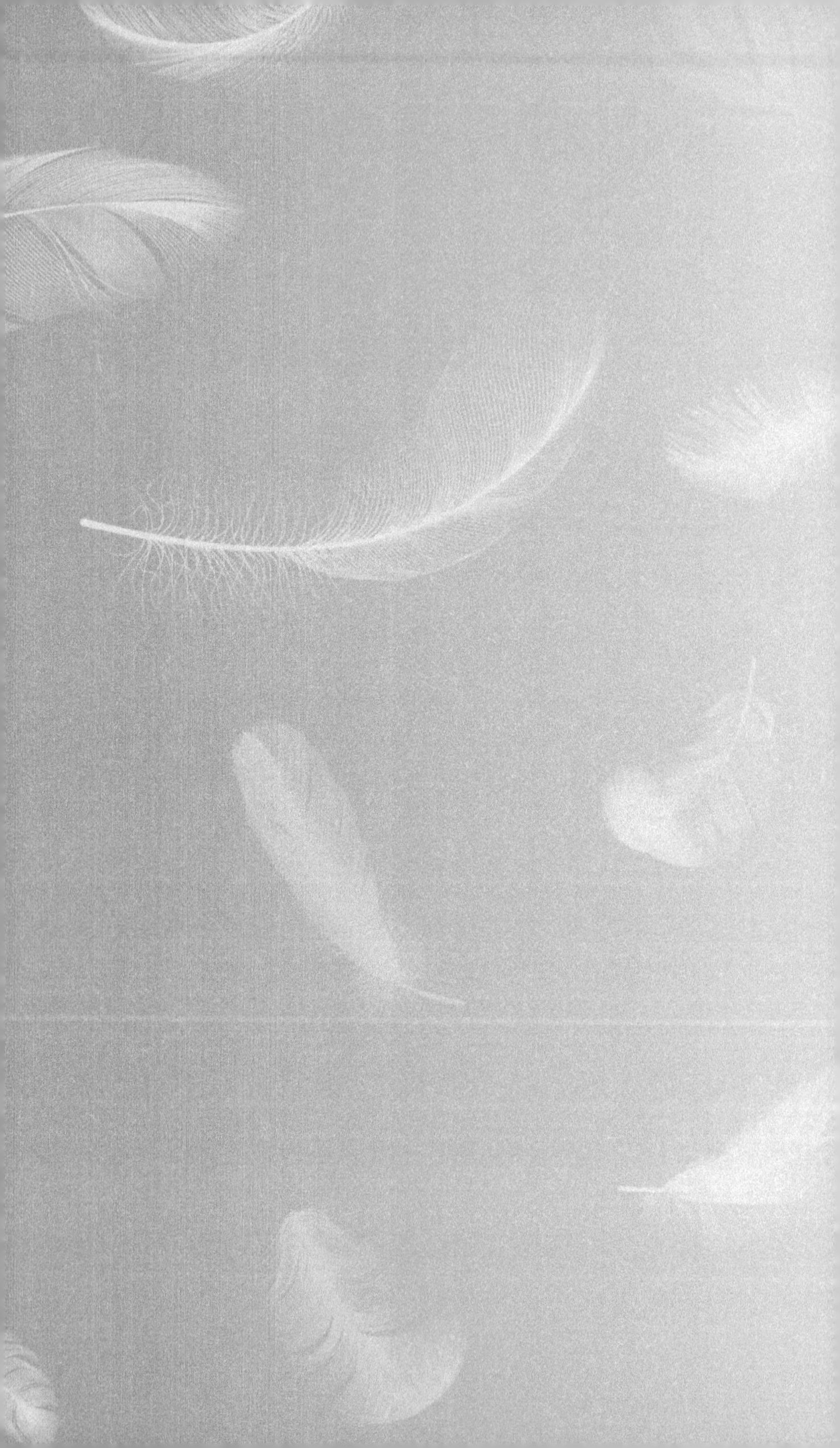

CHAPTER 13

THERE'S ALWAYS MOONLIGHT IN HALLOWEENTOWN

Compared to Braxton's clusterfuck of an exit, mine was boring.

I wasn't even nervous as Cheriour strapped me into the metal jumpsuit I'd be confined to for the next several weeks. I was...*resigned*. And not in a badass, *"I fear no darkness"* kinda way. My bone-weary emotions could only muster a disinterested, *"Another day. Another chance to die. What else is new?"*

"The objective," Cheriour said, "is *not* to die."

"Huh?"

"You were talking." He ran a hand over the glossy metal along my back. "How does this feel?"

"Meh." Truthfully, it wasn't terrible. The layers of razor-thin metal hugged my curves like a second skin. I could move, bend, and twist comfortably. Nothing chaffed or pinched in awkward places, even though I wore my blue/pink shirt and a thick set of leather leggings underneath. But it was...*odd*. Because although the armor didn't

195

hinder me, it didn't flow with my movements the way fabric would've. It left me a little stiff.

"It seems to fit well." Cheriour touched my left shoulder plate.

"I mean, yeah. It's *very* form-fitting. Highlights all my best *assets*. I think." I peered over my shoulder. "Damn, I can't really tell from this angle. How good does this getup make my butt look? Is the booty popping or getting lost in all the black?"

Cheriour sighed and shook his head, but I saw the coy smile tugging at his mouth.

And he *totally* peeked at my ass when I bent to gather my saddle bags.

He stayed close to me as we left the castle and walked through the pre-dawn smog to Abby Normal's pasture. Like, *glued to my side.* Our arms bumped and our hips occasionally banged. He held my helmet in his left hand, and he kept knocking it against his thigh, fidgeting.

He was nervous.

And I was calm.

It was fucking *bonkers*.

But he was a composed nervous. Unlike me, who bounced off the walls and spewed word vomit at everyone. Cheriour's face remained impassive, his eyes quiet. But he *fiddled* more, and he seemed lost without something to build, clean, or adjust. So, he recited instructions.

"The days are getting shorter, Addie," he said as I saddled Abby Normal. "Do *not* wait for the sunrise to begin each day. Ready yourself to ride before dawn. Do you have your map?"

"Yup." I tapped the small satchel wrapped around the pommel of my saddle.

"Be mindful of your landmarks," he reminded me. "If you see you've gone astray and are heading into Niall, turn back."

I nodded, checked Abby Normal's cinch to make sure it was tight, and picked up her bridle.

As usual, she stared at the heap of chains with her lips curled over her teeth in disdain. Then she went into giraffe mode, shooting her nose into the air, forcing me to teeter on my tiptoes to get the bridle over her head. She grudgingly softened her jaw to accept the bit, although she made a bunch of comical *"bleegh, it's icky!!"* faces as she twisted her head sideways and lolled her tongue out the side of her mouth.

My heart ached for her. This bit wasn't spiked like the barbaric torture devices the Wraiths used, but she was still bracing for pain. Still traumatized, even after being away from the Wraiths for weeks.

It really drove home how much they'd hurt her.

And now I was throwing her into the firing line again, potentially delivering her right back to her torturers.

I tried not to think about that. *Tried.*

By the time I swung into the saddle, the rising sun had turned the cloudless sky a bold palette of oranges, pinks, reds, and blues. A *perfect* autumn day: crisp and cold but clear and so saturated with color, it resembled a painting. Almost too pretty to be real.

The weather had been like this on the day I was taken away from home.

And that thought hit me harder than a sucker punch to the gut.

Because I'd *never* see home again. That picturesque autumn day would forever be my last memory of it.

My last memory of Sanadrin would probably be the same. Because there was no guarantee I'd ever see this place again.

So I tried to savor my last moments here as I headed out —in a way I hadn't been able to do before I left home. I absorbed *everything*: the clattering and clanging of the city coming to life for the day; the aroma of smoked meat wafting through the air and the human stench curdling over the streets; the rising babble of people talking and the way they looked at me as Abby Normal and I strolled by: worried but still hopeful.

Most of all, I watched Cheriour, committing every detail to memory: his messy bundle of curls fighting against the leather strap he'd confined them to; the way the sunlight dappled through the rows of buildings and cast a warm glow over his face, highlighting the crooked line of his nose, those deliciously high cheekbones, and his soft spattering of freckles. He drawled more instructions as he walked beside me, although most of his words mushed meaninglessly through my ears because I was hyper-focused on the syrupy sound of his voice, trying to tattoo it on my brain.

He glanced up at me at one point, letting me bask in his fierce green gaze, and sighed, realizing I wasn't paying attention to him. But he kept talking, even as he shifted closer and brushed his hand against my leg.

Although Abby Normal wasn't thrilled to have an off-limits human in snacking range, she tolerated his proximity. But she kept her ears flattened against her skull during the walk, silently sulking.

We trekked slowly through Sanadrin. But not slowly enough. Because after several minutes (although they seemed like only seconds), we were outside the walls and staring out at the vast, rocky terrain stretched before us.

Cheriour could accompany me no farther.

He handed me the helmet. "You must keep this on. At all times," he reminded me.

"Yeah, yeah." I *despised* wearing it, though. The narrow eye slits tanked my peripheral vision, and my every breath rattled through the thin mouth opening. I sounded like Darth Vader (*Hawwwww-pppeeerrrr*). "You better remember to take care of Splinter while I'm gone," I gave Cheriour his one and only reminder. "*Do not eat him*! I don't care how big of a rat craving you get. He's a pet. Not food."

"I will care for the rat," Cheriour said.

And I knew he would.

"Right, well..." I suppressed a burbly belch when my simmering anxiety abruptly cranked itself to high, setting my stomach on a rolling boil.

Abby Normal shifted and snuffled, sensing my sudden panic.

"Addie?" Cheriour asked.

My wavering exhale reverberated off the helmet, pinging a warm rush of air back onto me. And, phew, they really, *really* needed to invent toothpaste in this world. My morning breath was *rank*.

I blew out again, puckering my lips to get most of it through the helmet's blowhole, and stared across the stony field.

It was now or never. If I didn't go *right this second*, I'd lose my nerve.

"Under moonlight, he flies..." *Shoot.* Those weren't the right words. "Like a...vulture..." *Why* were song lyrics so hard to remember without the music?

"There is no moonlight," Cheriour said.

"There's always moonlight in Halloweentown."

I grinned when his mouth crumbled into the cutest confused frown and then tapped my heels against Abby Normal's sides.

We were off.

"Easy, Abs. Easy…don't go too fast…oooh, damn it, why you gotta *run* down the hill? Slow and steady wins the race. *This is not slow or steady!!*"

Abby Normal took the downward slope of a hill at a slithering canter. And she laid her ears against her skull when I loosed a banshee shriek and scrabbled for a bit of mane to clutch onto.

Three days into our trip, and she was probably (definitely) ready to dump me.

In my defense, the treacherous trails we'd spent the days traversing had thoroughly frayed my nerves.

Cheriour had marked those passages on the map as being *easy. Bull-fucking-shit.* They'd corkscrewed up and around the mountains, which meant Abby Normal and I climbed steep inclines and twined around the mountain on a *NARRROW* trail. My God, had it been narrow—the kinda slim space that made my asshole pucker and had me instinctively trying to suck my gut in. And whenever we hit a sharp curve that obscured the path ahead, my heart stopped. Because I was *waiting* for a jump scare. Like a stealthy Wraith. Or a blood thirsty Púca.

Thankfully, nothing awaited us on those jagged bends except my warped imagination.

It took half a day to reach the top of the first pinnacle—and *of course* I'd looked down once we got there. Morbid curiosity had me in a chokehold. As soon as my eyes wandered over the harsh typography of rocks and miniscule looking trees below us...*bam!* White spots everywhere.

But we made it up and over that first mountain in one piece (although my poor, abused heart had aged itself another decade) and plunked down for the night in a sloped valley. Which should've felt safe but was actually creepy AF. Sitting in near total darkness, surrounded by hulking hunks of stone, listening to the howling of the wind...it was the *perfect* setup for a slasher movie.

So, yeah, I didn't sleep much.

And the next morning, we awoke and repeated the whole freaking nightmare up the next mountain.

It was *not* a good start to this road trip. At all. Not even a little.

My anxiety left me dripping with sweat, which got tacky in some not-so-fun areas. And I couldn't pop this armor off and air out. Naw. I had to stay incognito. Even when I stank worse than a dead fish.

The Wraiths would probably smell me coming from miles away.

"You're lucky you don't sweat." I eyed Abby Normal's dry neck. "You don't...*eeeeeekkk!* Abs! Stop it!"

As she half sprinted, half slid down another incline, Abby Normal squealed and kicked her heels up, playing.

She'd been subdued through the mountain passages. Maybe she'd been worried about the footing or sensed my agitation. But now that we'd emerged on the other side of the mountains and our view was all long stretches of gentle slopes, she was having a freaking ball.

I was *not*.

By some miracle, I hadn't tumbled off her back. *Yet.* But Abby Normal's slippery stride, zigzagging down those hills, had me clutching the pommel of the saddle for dear life.

"Be *careful*, Abs. Plea—*what the fuck was that?*"

As Abby Normal skittered to the bottom of a slope, she kicked up a big cloud of pebbles, dust, and...

Bone.

A long, graying shard of bone pinwheeled into the air, bonking Abby Normal's nose.

"That—that—was that an arm?" I squealed. And then I glanced down. Baaaaad idea. "Oh God. Abs, stop!"

She was already slowing, her head swinging in agitation. Bones crunched beneath her hooves.

"Jesus..." I swung down from the saddle, wincing when my right foot trounced on a half-buried skull. Scraping my toe through the dirt revealed the rest of the body: a human, curled in a fetal position.

A bitter, artichoke-y taste blanketed my tongue as I stared out farther, finding more skeletons. Hundreds. Probably thousands. They crisscrossed over the stone and soil, stretching outward for at least a mile.

It was a graveyard. Or worse. Because bodies were *buried* in a graveyard. These bodies hadn't been buried. Hadn't been moved. They'd dropped dead here. Decomposed here. Mother nature had been kind enough to cover them in a sheet of windblown dirt and stone in an attempt to give them a "proper" resting place, one Abby Normal and I had been about to clomp all over.

"Where are we?" I turned to Abby Normal, asking the

question out loud even though I knew she couldn't answer me. The map could, though.

My hands trembled as I wrestled the map out of my satchel. Cheriour had folded the parchment into a tidy square. Because *of course* he had. He'd probably spent twenty minutes scrupulously bending each crease, only for me to rip into it like a kid tearing at their Christmas gifts. No way this sucker was going to be folded that neatly again.

"Okay…" I pressed the map against Abby Normal's shoulder, ignoring her annoyed side-eye, and tapped my finger over the miniature portrait of Sanadrin. "We're through these so-called *easy* passages here. And"—I glanced to the right and left, nodding at the mountain ranges on either side—"we came out right where we were supposed to. So…" I trailed my fingers over Cheriour's intricately drawn mountains, pausing when I came to the next minia-ture portrait. A city called Glenarm. Under the town name, Cheriour had added a note: "Fallen."

A soft breeze snaked through the area, shifting the dirt over the skeletons with an eerie *hisssssss*.

I twirled my thumb around the city Cheriour had drawn —the robust mass of houses and fields. A place that had once teemed with life. "There's *nothing* left." I shuddered as I stared at the desolate valley of bones before us.

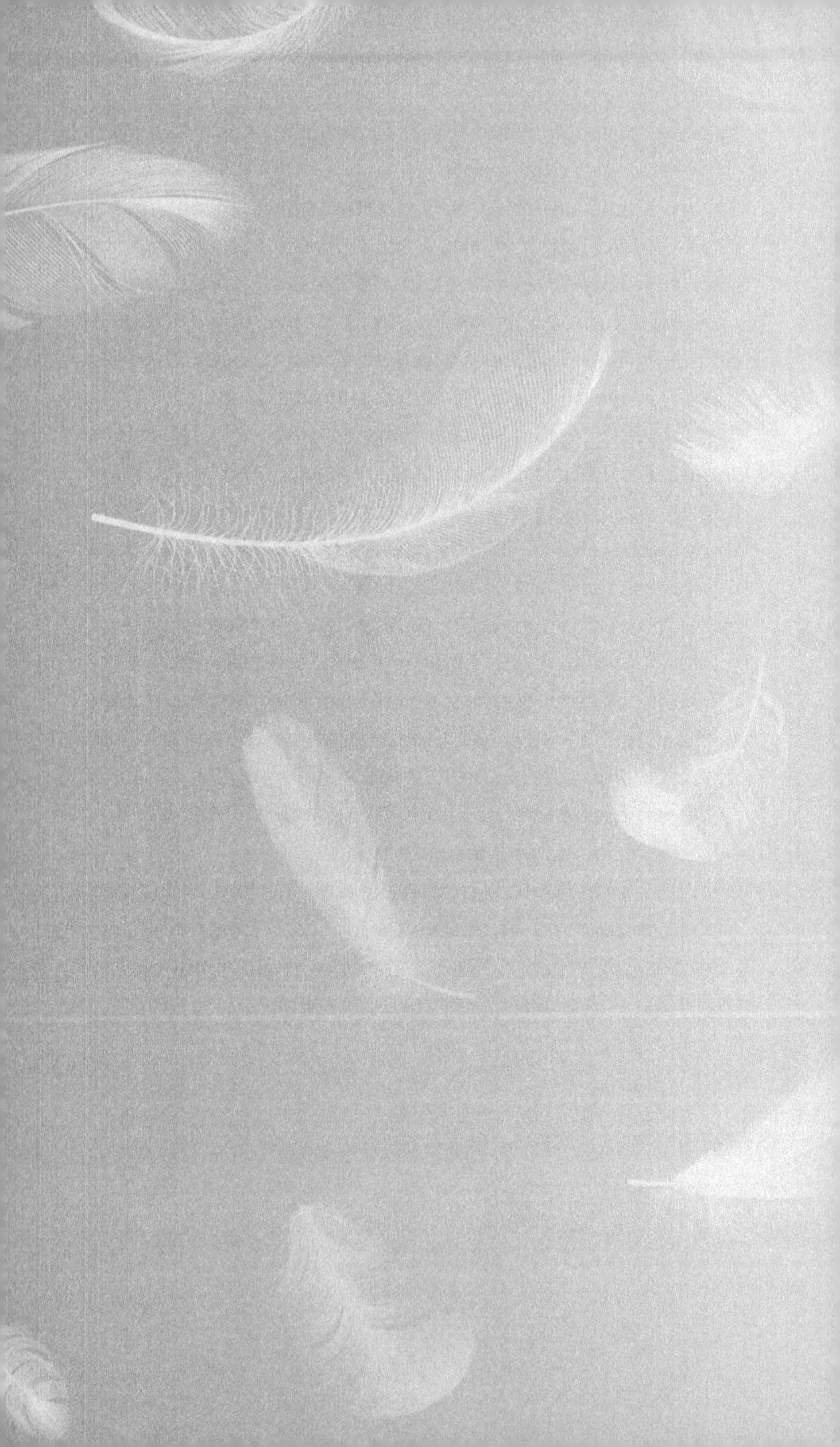

CHAPTER 14

EENIE, MEENIE, MINEY, MO

Mowow.

The warbled sound dragged me out of the first deep, dreamless slumber I'd had in the five days since I'd left Sanadrin. I cracked an eye open, saw Abby Normal's red irises peering through the near pitch-black darkness, and groaned. "Abs...I love you. But if you don't stop breathing in my fucking face, I'm gonna kill you."

Mowow. Snort.

She stood so close to me, her muzzle pressed against my helmet that spittle flew into my mouth.

"For fuck's sake, Abs," I choked. "I don't need to be kissed out of a sleeping curse. Even if I did, I sure as shit don't want a kiss from you." I batted her head away and rolled over onto my side. It took a few seconds to find a position where the metal armor wasn't cutting off my circulation and a rock, or root, or whatever else lay scattered on the forest floor wasn't drilling into my hip. And it took several more seconds to re-ignore the obnoxious babbling of the nearby stream. But once I got semi-comfy, my mind slipped into a fuzzy doze.

And I immediately started dreaming of lying in a cushy bed pressed against Cheriour's warm body as he peppered those languid kisses over my neck...

Mowowow. Huff. Stomp.

"Abs..." I mumbled when she glued her lips to my helmet again. Her repugnant, rust-scented breath (courtesy of the deer she'd sucked dry earlier) swished across my nostrils. "I'm going to strangle you. I swear to—"

A thin, frightened wail wavered in the air, followed by a sharp *crack.*

"What the fuck?" I sat bolt upright, swiping at the ribbon of drool trickling out of my helmet. Because, y'know, I was a *super* attractive waker. And I drooled rivers in my sleep.

Abby Normal made a low, worried *mowow.*

Another biting *crack* bounced off the trees. I couldn't tell where it was coming from, not when murky midnight darkness shrouded the forest.

Although, to be honest, having sunlight wouldn't have helped.

We were deep, deep, *deep* into the woods now, surrounded by a gazillion trees and bushes that all looked the freaking same. Which would've had me panicky—I'd watched way too many true crime horrors about the wilderness fucking up lost souls—if it hadn't been for one of Kaelan's pro tips:

"Follow the stream, and you won't be lost."

So I'd been sticking to the scrawny little stream that meandered through the shrubbery like stink on shit.

But now...

Zoooosh-crack!

"*Fuck!*" I scrambled to my feet. Wherever those sounds were coming from, they were getting closer.

We needed to skedaddle—and likely leave my watery lifeline behind.

"Alrighty, Abs, let's bounce." I sloppily saddled her and clambered onto her back.

Another thin cry rose into the air.

Beneath me, Abby Normal pivoted, her head cocking to the right and her ears pricking. "Is that where it's coming from?" I asked.

She remained motionless, staring off into the distance.

"Okay. I believe you. So let's go this way, yeah?" I tugged the left rein.

Abby Normal ripped it out of my hand.

"The fuck?" I grabbed the rein again.

Again, she wrenched it away from me.

"Abs! We don't know what this is! We need to *go!*" But no matter what I did, I couldn't get her to move. She went full "deer in headlights" while the snaps and wails drew closer and closer *and closer*.

A hulking, oblong shape weaved through the trees, just a shadow at first, until it got close enough for me to make out the details.

Humans.

A dozen of them, perhaps more, all shackled to a long, cumbersome chain that stretched between two black-armored Wraiths. The ringleader was mounted on a Púca. The trailer walked on foot, brandishing the biggest freaking whip I'd ever seen. Which he used *liberally*, based on the weeping gashes scattered across the humans' backs.

There were men and women of all ages in the group. The

oldest only looked to be about forty or fifty. The youngest was seven or eight—practically still a baby. They were bloodied and tired. Some cried or screamed obscenities and heaved fruitlessly at their chains. Most stared straight ahead, their faces pale, eyes blank.

My brain whirred, struggling to register what my eyes were seeing.

The Wraiths were...*transporting* humans?

Mowowow.

The Púca at the front of the group caught sight of Abby Normal and flashed her a demonic stare—ears flat, mouth gaping, eyes rolling—as it rose onto its hind legs.

Abby Normal lunged, walloping her forehooves into the ground, her head lowered like a viper poised to strike.

I squeezed my lips together, trying not to scream.

The enemy Púca darted forward. The chain was strapped to its saddle, so when it bolted, it dragged the whole line of humans.

My heart seized when people tumbled over each other, crying out helplessly, and my breath evaporated from my lungs when the Púca's fangs winked in the darkness, aiming for me.

It *knew* I was human.

The jig is up!

"Abs..." A barely audible whisper rasped out of me as my hands flew back. I had a stubby sword strapped to the saddle. *Somewhere.* Not that it'd do me any good even if I found it.

Abby Normal rose, pinwheeling her front legs through the air, nearly tipping me right over her back end, and loosed a roar.

"Enough!" The mounted Wraith seesawed on the reins, yanking his Púca to a halt and swinging it away from us.

I did the same with Abby Normal (except, y'know, more gently). She shook her head, clanking the bit between her fangs, and lurched into a marchy walk, steamrolling past the group.

The mounted Wraith didn't give two shits about us.

The one at the back gave me a cock-eyed glance but said nothing.

And the humans wouldn't even look at me. Why would they? To their eyes, I was just another Wraith.

Abby Normal kept walking.

I didn't breathe.

My lungs screamed with pain, and my vision fuzzed, but I held my breath until the group was several feet behind us. Then I choked on a shuddering gasp when another whip crack split the air, followed by a man's agonized moan.

I waited a heartbeat (two, three) for *something*. For one of the Wraiths to turn around, call out, or sound an alarm. They never did.

The cries and shouts eventually faded.

I flopped onto Abby Normal's neck, wrapping my arms around her. "Thank you, Abs. I would've made the wrong call if I'd run away, huh? But you knew, *and* you woke me up when you heard them. You saved my fucking ass..."

It was a relief. 100 percent. Because that had been a *close* call.

But a sour guilt came with the *"OMG, I'm still alive"* feeling.

I lived scot-free while those poor fuckers were strapped to that chain, going to...

Where? I mean, Wraiths *ate* humans. Why would they

chain that group and lead them around? Where were they leading them *to*? What were they going to do with them once they got there?

My hands shook.

I wanted to *do* something.

But I couldn't. Any attempted rescue mission would give me away. And I was a sucky fighter. I'd end up strapped to the chain alongside those people.

With a low, almost soothing series of *whuff-huffs*, Abby Normal weaved through the trees, her ears flicking back and forth. Back and forth. Like mini antennas.

I let her pick her own path, desperate to put as much distance between us and those humans as possible.

One last, distant *crack* disturbed the otherwise quiet wood.

And I let out a low *guggh* when that pesky pain raked its teeth through the inside of my chest.

TIME BECAME MEANINGLESS AS ABBY NORMAL AND I BUMPED around in the woods. Because the scenery *never freaking changed*.

Trees.

Big trees.

Little trees.

Leafless trees.

Leaf-spitting trees.

Big-ass plants pretending to be trees.

Scrawny trees pretending to be plants.

Trees, trees, trees, trees, trees...I was *so fucking sick* of looking at trees.

I was even *more* sick of the food. My pre-packed meals included crusty crackers (hardtack, Cheriour called them), leathery smoked meat, and nothing else. So I had plenty of carbs and protein but lacked anything that had taste. Abby Normal, however, made out like a freaking bandit. The forest gave her *plenty* of juicy critters to hunt.

Lucky bitch.

And the weather? As bland as the scenery and my snacks. Most days dawned cloudy and chilly and shot only pale snatches of sunlight to the forest floor. Sometimes it rained—and those stupid freaking trees made piss-poor umbrellas—but mostly it was...*bleh*. Dreary and depressing.

During one of those rainy days, moisture snuck between the slats of my armor and smeared wicked rashes over my lower back and the nooks of my knees. And the saddle had already chaffed my ass and crotch raw, so I was in *agony*, driven mad by all the burning itches I couldn't scratch. The only medicine I had was air. Cleaning the rashes and letting them breathe for an hour or so each day helped, but it was a scary freaking thing to do. Usually, I backed my butt against the fattest tree I could find and pulled Abby Normal in front of me so I had *something* to block the Wraiths from seeing my pasty white legs and bare ass.

And we had more close encounters with the Wraiths. Lots more. Thankfully never while my ass was exposed, but hardly a day went by without us spotting at least one of those skeletal bastards. Sometimes they carted more chained humans around. Sometimes they patrolled the lands alone. But they never looked at us. If their Púcas raised an alarm, it went ignored.

Those brief flashes of danger, and my answering bouts of panic, became...*routine.*

I would've lost count of the days if it hadn't been for another of Kaelan's tips:

"Time moves differently when you're alone in the wilderness, but you can track your progress by notching a piece of wood each day!"

So I found a stick and used the stubby sword to strike a line in it every night—I had to put that sword to work doing *something*, after all.

Five notches.

Eight.

Twenty.

Abby Normal and I slunk through the lands unnoticed for *twenty days*. And somehow, *miraculously*, we emerged from the endless ocean of trees exactly where we were supposed to: near the (also fallen) town of Hadleigh.

But the problem with reaching our next big landmark?

Wraiths. Wraiths *everywhere.*

Abby Normal and I walked along the tree line, roughly a half mile away from the town. The terrain was flat here, and the sunlight marbled the cloud-hewn sky, so I saw *everything.*

The Wraiths had made themselves snug as bugs in a rug in this town. They strolled up and down the streets, mostly sans armor, munching on meat (*human* meat) or slurping from wooden mugs. The beaming sunlight high-lighted all the juts and dips in their gaunt faces and made their pale, gray skin appear more of a sickly off-white.

They truly, *genuinely* resembled Jack Skellington. But an R-rated horror movie version of him, replacing his derpy smile and hyper obsession with Christmas with a sinister scowl and an appetite for human flesh.

I mean, why settle for a twiggy chicken leg when you could mow down on a chonky human thigh instead, right?

And humans still wandered the town. Several dozen, at least, maybe as many as a hundred—I sucked at eyeballing counts. But they were a sorry sight to behold as they trudged around, completing menial tasks while covered in blood, wrapped in grungy clothes, and confined to shackles.

Shackles!

They had those humans in *fucking chains*!

Fricking hell.

Púcas were scattered about the city streets as well, chains wrapped around the nose bands of their halters, securing them to posts or walls. Wickedly thick shackles encircled their ankles, hobbling them. The poor things couldn't move. Probably couldn't breathe properly with how tightly their muzzles were confined.

I stroked Abby Normal's neck, thanking every lucky star in the sky that she was out here with me instead of in that town with the other Púcas. "Poor things. Someone needs to bind and gag those Wraiths with their fucking chains. Give 'em a taste of their own—"

My tongue turned cottony when a rawboned human man strolled up to a gaggle of Wraiths, hefting a platter of steaming, freshly fried human limbs.

He was *serving* them!

What the actual fuck was this perverted hell?

The Wraiths laughed, snagged their snacks, bashed the empty platter over the man's balding head—for funsies, apparently—and shoved him away. He staggered, his feet tangling around each other, and skirted too close to a Púca.

Upon catching a whiff of the walking blood bag, the Púca whined and thrashed against its bindings. When it failed to break free, it lowered its head and bashed it against the fence post it'd been imprisoned with. Violently and repeatedly, until its brow burst open with a gush of blood.

As the Púca wobbled and cried, Wraiths dumped their food and rushed over. They seized the man, who babbled a stream of frightened, incoherent responses, and gave him a *sound* punishment.

Fifteen whiplashes.

I counted every single one, watched the way specks of blood glittered in the air each time the whip came whistling down, and I listened to the way the man moaned.

The Púca remained in its chains, screaming, while two other Wraiths attempted to patch its wound.

And, suddenly, Braxton's voice echoed in my head.

"We don't have enough people to be fillin' those houses. And I'd rather see it burn to the ground than watch Wraiths settle here."

I'd been hollow when I watched them destroy the disease-stricken town of Lamex all those months ago. Hollow and...*disbelieving*. Braxton's statement had hit me hard, but I hadn't fully grasped the meaning of it.

Until now.

My breathing turned unsteady as the Wraiths left the man to bleed in the streets. Rapid *hawww-peeerrr* sounds pinged off the inside of my helmet, mercifully drowning out the other noises coming from the town.

I half expected the Wraiths to hear me.

They didn't.

THREE DAYS LATER, WE WERE FUCKING LOST.

The open terrain was a breath of fresh air, but it provided *zero* reliable landmarks. There were no streams to follow. No mountains to use as a guide. Just long stretches of dying grass, occasional clusters of red-and-yellow-stained trees, and the open sky.

It was *gorgeous* out here, with the sun peeking out from behind the fluffy clouds and amplifying the fall colors on the trees. Absolutely picturesque, even if the weather was nipply (aka, freezing).

But I wished I knew where the freak I was.

I pulled out the map. Put it away. Pulled it out again. Put it away again. It wasn't fucking helping.

"Cheriour said to skirt to the right of Hadleigh," I mumbled on the fifth (or sixth, or seventh, or tenth) time I'd referenced the map. "And we did that. I *think*."

Abby Normal snorted, fed up with our jerky stop-and-go trek. She'd laid her ears back when I'd halted. Like, "*Bitch, you touch those reins one more time, and I'm gonna dump your ass on the ground.*" Now she stood, sulking, as the whisking wind made her mane stand on end.

"So where the eff are we?" I traced the map again, swiping my finger over the patch of flat terrain Cheriour had marked between Hadleigh and Swindon.

"Swindon is two day's ride from Hadleigh," Cheriour had told me when he'd drawn the map.

It'd been *more* than two days since we'd passed Hadleigh. And Swindon was nowhere to be seen.

"I suck, Abs," I sighed. "I must've taken a wrong turn somewhere. But *where*?" I glanced at the rolling fields of browning grass. Birds zoomed and cawed through the air. Two red-and-yellow-leafed trees swayed on my right side. "It all looks the same." My sigh poofed out of my helmet in thin, white clouds. "God, I miss having a GPS..."

Kaelan had shown me a way to navigate by shoving a stick into the ground and watching the shadows, but I must've been half snoozing through that class, because the memory was foggy. Even if I managed to un-fog it and make myself a DIY compass, it would only show me the big four (north, south, east, and west). If I was reading Cheriour's map right (that was a big if), Swindon was northwest...*ish*.

How the fuck was I supposed to calculate northwest-ish? Go north and hang a left halfway through?

Did it need to be a sharp left or a soft left?

Or a U-turn?

Or a roundabout?

"I'm getting a headache." I shoved the map into my satchel again. "Fuck it. We're gonna use my trusty foolproof method to get un-lost. 'Kay?"

Clink-clank went Abby Normal's teeth against the bit.

I closed my eyes, shivering when the icy wind snuck its spindly fingers through the slats in my armor, and did eenie, meenie, miney, mo to pick a direction.

And, color me fucking surprised, it *worked*.

Not two hours later, we trotted to the top of a gentle hill and found ourselves staring at a town.

Or, well, it *had* been a town at some point. Now it was little more than a charred skeleton. Rubble blanketed the streets. The few houses still standing were blackened and dilapidated.

"Friggin' hell," I mumbled. "Is there any place in this cesspit world that isn't fallen or infested with—hey! Abs!"

Abby Normal made a high-pitched *mowow* and did a weird, bouncy cat leap.

"*Woah!*" The saddle almost disappeared out from under me. "Goddamn, slippery—Abs! *What're ya doing?*"

She reared straight into the air, going fully vertical. I squealed and clung to her neck. My hips ached as I dug my knees into the saddle, squeezing with all the force I possessed to keep my legs from sliding back. Before me, all I saw was the slope of Abby Normal's neck and the flashes of black as her forelegs beat the air.

After several seconds, she crashed back down onto all four legs, nearly pitching me over her shoulder. And then she cat-leapt sideways, screaming when I panic-snatched her reins.

"Abs, you're killing me here!" I hissed. My leg had almost, *almost*, slipped up and over the saddle.

Abby Normal whipped her head toward me. Her eyes rolled in their sockets, looking wild. Angry. *Pained.*

"Abs, what—?" I started.

But then I saw them: the Wraiths emerging from the rubble and ruin of Swindon. There were a half dozen of them, all fully armored and armed.

And they were staring right at us.

CHAPTER 15
HUNGRY-HUNGRY HIPPO

"Fuck. Fuckfuckfuckfuck fuckity fuck."

When life gave you the middle finger, it was best to hurdle a few (dozen) F-bombs in its face. They did jack squat, but they sure felt good to say.

And there wasn't much else I could do. We were stuck. Turning and hightailing it the other way would've looked suspicious.

So I nudged Abby Normal into Swindon.

She gave me one last lingering look, her eyes rolling as though she was in misery, before she lurched into an uneven, high-headed trot.

"Oi!" the female Wraith at the head of the group called.

As my heart cartwheeled into my throat, Abby Normal snorted and cat-leapt again. "Urrgh!" My head whipped back with a crunchy *crrrittch-crraaaaackkkk*.

"Only one rider, eh?" The Wraith shook her head and turned to the others. "*One* rider. For this lot?"

Okay...well...*phew*, at least the disguise was still working. For now.

I tried to swallow once. Twice. Three times. A big ole lump of cotton sat at the back of my throat, choking me.

We clunked onto the rubble-decorated streets, past the first wave of cockeyed, half-burnt structures, and Abby Normal shot into another leap.

I snatched the reins with numb fingers that felt limper than a flaccid cock (har, har, har) and barely hung onto her.

"Abs," I growled under my breath.

She pirouetted with a worried *mowow*.

Then I saw them, shoved off to the side of the street, staring at us through the warped slats of rinky-dink fences.

Humans. Dozens of them. Corralled into two tiny pens, chained down, and smashed together like *fucking livestock*. And the odor rising into the blistery air was—*phew*. Worse than a porta-pot that had baked in the summer sun during a jampacked weekend-long music festival.

Which, considering the Wraiths likely weren't generous with handing out bathroom passes, those pens were probably *rife* with ick that would've made even the stankiest porta-pot seem sanitary.

"Is Oran sending other riders?"

I nearly jumped out of my skin when the female Wraith sauntered to my side, munching noisily on...on...

An *arm*.

As she waited for me to answer, she sank her teeth into the meaty bicep and *rrrrrrripped*. The flesh crunched (crispier than fried chicken) while juice spurted from the meat.

Blegh. OMFG. I was going to be sick.

And turning my head away didn't help.

Five other Wraiths sat in the center of the street, clustered around a small fire, cutting slivers off a woman—a dead and thoroughly roasted human woman. Their Púcas stood between the two pens. The poor beasts had shackles around their feet, their reins tied to those shackles.

Something bubbled in my chest. I didn't know if it was a cry or word vomit. Or, y'know, *actual* vomit. So I gnashed my teeth into my lip until the metallic tang of blood flooded my mouth.

Mowowow! Abby Normal rose into a half rear. Thick plumes of white vapor puffed from her billowing nostrils.

"Oi!" The Wraith at my side sprayed bits of half-chewed human when she spoke. "Are you deaf or daft? Is Oran sending other riders?"

Okay, so my disguise was *clearly* working. This Wraith was a few feet away, standing in broad daylight, and hadn't pegged me as a human. But I had to say something! She was *waiting* for an answer.

"Erm...*no*." I garbled the words into a guttural rasp that tore at my throat.

It must've sounded close enough to their gravelly way of speaking because the Wraith shrugged and gobbled another heaping mouthful of human. "'Nd eee doudt u cud bing dis dodt buk do Dial alune?"

Was that even in fucking English?

Swallow before you speak, lady!

I ground my teeth into my sore, bleeding lip. Sweat pooled in my pits, trickled down my back, and puddled under my boobs, lighting my barely healed rashes ablaze with a molten itch.

"Sure he did." Another Wraith stepped away from the BBQ, slurping from a beer mug. "Because Oran didn't read the report, did he? Were you expecting this many?" He gestured to the two overstuffed pens and then looked back at me.

Thank frick this was a question I could answer without opening my mouth.

"See?" The Wraith banged his mug against his thigh when I shook my head. "So, do us a favor, eh? Go back to Oran and tell him there's twenty-three—"

"Twenty-one." The female Wraith plucked a stringy bit of tendon out of her teeth.

"Oi, yes." Beer Mug jabbed his finger at the extra-crispy hunk of woman dangling over the fire. "I suppose we can't count the ones we ate, eh?"

My stomach curdled. And I must've made a noise because Beer Mug shrugged and said, "I'll take no reprimanding from you. We rounded this lot up *days* ago and waited here—with no food, mind—for Oran's riders. We got hungry."

"And we'll be hungry again," another Wraith chimed in. "I've already got my eye on the twitchy one." He leered at a middle-aged blond man who was, indeed, jittering in the chains.

"Bah," the female Wraith grunted. "That one will be tough, with all that shaking..."

"Should add flavor."

"He'll be a hard one to keep over the fire..."

"Should ease the boredom then, eh?"

"And he's old."

"I always did like me meat well aged."

"No. We'll be eating the imposter next. As I already said." Beer Mug pointed at the left pen, and then turned to me with a conspiratorial snigger. "We caught this blighter wearing *our* armor."

My stomach dropped to my toes.

I tilted my head, focusing on the aforementioned pen. Sure enough, sitting in the middle, still wearing the black armor (minus the helmet) was Braxton. Blood caked his carroty hair, and his left eye was nearly swollen shut. But his other eye was clear and filled to the brim with rage.

Fuck.

I went rigid, my knees digging into the saddle, shooting pain up my hips.

Braxton stared back at me, his chin raised in a defiant, bitter expression.

Abby Normal whuffed and dragged her forehoof across the ground, reacting to my tension.

Braxton's eyes dropped to her. Rose back to me. Dropped to her again. His forehead crinkled.

"I'm telling ye," Beer Mug said, "the fecking meat bags are getting smart. So *why* were you the only rider sent?"

Ah, there it was. My mortal enemy: suspicion.

Beer Mug's milk-white eyes narrowed. His head tilted. "It don't make sense, eh? Oran sent *six* of us to this shite part of the country to gather humans. But only *one* to bring the humans to Niall? What were you told?" he pressed as he stepped forward. "Did he think our hunt unsuccessful?"

I kept my gaze focused on Braxton, begging, *pleading* for him to realize it was me. And he was starting to. His jaw slackened. His eyes darted between me and the other Wraiths as his mouth moved silently.

Yes! Yes, it's me!

"That is no Celestial metal." A gangly, gray-skinned hand touched my thigh, fingers tracing the curves in my armor.

I flinched. Gasped.

Abby Normal screamed and scuttled backward.

"Say, I know that Púca!" Another Wraith stepped away from the fire. "It's Ramiel's bitch."

"No." The female Wraith moved closer, eyeing Abby Normal speculatively. "Can't be."

"That's her! I'm certain of it. Look at the build...that bitch had the longest legs."

Clink-clink-clink.

Beer Mug had chucked his drink aside and snatched a chain off one of the Púcas.

"Abs..." I croaked and dug my heels into her sides.

But it was too late.

As she coiled, preparing to run, the Wraith lunged and lassoed the chain around her nose, pulling the noose tight.

Abby Normal bellowed and threw herself backward, her head twisting. Beer Mug hauled at the chain until she stilled with a low whimper.

I touched her quivering neck and fought the urge to scream.

Beer Mug's eyes rolled up toward my face. "You're no Wraith," he hissed.

Fuckfuckfuck.

Behind him, the Púcas, maybe sensing shit was about to hit the fan, screamed and thrashed, choking themselves on the chains and gouging the shackles into their ankles. Three Wraiths dashed over, snatched whips from their saddles, and cracked them over the animals until they stilled.

Abby Normal warbled, her hooves clattering against the stones as she reared again and again and again. But no matter how hard she fought, Beer Mug held fast, squeezing the chain around her nose.

We were *so* fucked.

Beer Mug sneered, showing off a full row of pointy teeth. "Clever, stealing the rogue Púca. But not clever enough. We'll be taking this mare. Ramiel will be most pleased to see her again." He had a demented cartoon-villain laugh: *he-he-heeeze, he-he-heeeze.* "And you'll be joining the rest of the humans here..."

A yell pierced the air when the female Wraith snatched the blond man out of the pen, brutally wrenching his fists through the shackles.

"But we won't kill *you.*" Beer Mug *he-he-heezed.* "Oh no. You'll go into the pen and watch them burn. When Oran asks, we'll say Ramiel's Púca"—he jerked Abby Normal's chain, *he-he-heezing* some more when she flung her head up —"killed them. And we wasn't about to let the bodies go to waste."

My heart felt wet and squishy as it flopped around in my chest.

Beer Mug hawed at Abby Normal's nose, as though trying to saw it off, and reached for me with his other hand, intent on pulling me out of the saddle.

We had to go. Run, run, *run!* It was our only chance at this point.

"Get your fucking hands *off* her!" Blood pooled in my mouth when I wrenched my teeth out of my tongue. And the sound of my voice—my *real* voice—startled Beer Mug. He glanced up.

I jabbed my thumb into his eye.

He stumbled back with a hissing curse, momentarily loosening his grip on the chain.

"Abs!" I pummeled my heels into her sides. "GO!"

With a snarling Mufasa-esque roar, Abby Normal rose onto her hind legs, whipped her head around, and snatched

Beer Mug's arm. Her fangs made a tinny *thi-ung* as they punched through the metal plate on his bicep.

His cursing morphed into a wail of pain.

Abby Normal gave her head another violent shake and bolted, dragging him beneath her. There was a *whomp-thump-whomp* as her hooves pummeled his body. His bones broke. Midnight-blue blood sprayed into the air, splattering Abby Normal's shoulder and my left thigh. But she held onto him.

Until his arm came off with a wet pop.

"Jesus, Abs," I muttered when she spat the appendage out. But I gave her a big, thumping pat on the neck. She was a disgusting and violent bitch, sure. But she was the *BEST* disgusting and violent bitch.

Abby Normal tore down the street, walloping her hooves against the cobblestones.

A swell of shouts swarmed after us.

"OI!"

"Mount up!"

"Where's my bloody bow...?"

"Do *not* let that Púca escape!"

"Mount up *now*! GO!"

I glanced over my shoulder.

Three Wraiths were already mounted and driving their Púcas into a gallop.

"Aw fucking hell." I spun back around, crouching over Abby Normal's neck. Her mane flapped in the breeze, the ends pinging off my helmet. "We need to pick up the—"

Whizzzzzsssh.

Zooooossssshhh.

A barrage of black-tipped arrows careened past me.

"Motherfu—"

Whoosh.

Thunk.

One of the arrows punched into my left shoulder, blowing right through my flimsy armor. A fizzing tingle shot down my arm, stealing some of the sensation from the tips of my fingers, but there was no pain.

Was that a bad thing? Did that mean I'd punctured an artery—or, God forbid, my heart? Was I *dying*?

Mowow.

Abby Normal's head snapped up, nearly whacking my chin.

I gulped and raised my eyes, watching the world bounce between her ears for a second, until the oncoming shape registered in my brain.

A dilapidated building loomed before us. Its roof was M.I.A., and the remaining walls were only three, maybe four feet high but made of solid stone.

And it was too damn late to turn away.

With a strained grunt, Abby Normal threw herself into the air. Her front legs paddled wildly, straining to clear the wall, and her back hooves cracked against the stone.

"Holy frick!" I lost my balance as we landed in the building, flopped onto her neck, and smashed my crotch against the pommel of the saddle (*ooouch!*). And the party wasn't over yet. After three fumbling strides, during which the burnt remnants of furnishings tried their darndest to ensnare Abby Normal's feet, we had to exit the building.

"Jesus!" I clutched her mane for dear life as she did another desperate, crazy-legged leap through the air. Her back legs *thunked* the wall again. *Hard.* Her breath hitched when she touched down on the other side. Her stride broke.

Behind us, all three Wraiths made the same jump. I

angled my head and caught sight of them as they sailed over the exit wall. Those Púcas tucked their legs up, made a graceful arch through the air, and cleared the stone by a foot.

It figured I'd have the defective Púca who couldn't jump for shit.

And this stupid town was an obstacle course from hell. Chunks of buildings, old carts, obnoxiously big heaps of wood, and random knickknacks crisscrossed the road. Abby Normal had to keep jumping, and she kept whacking her legs on the debris, no matter how hard she tried to clear them. And I wasn't much help.

Because, y'know, she had a defective owner who couldn't ride for shit.

"Sorry, sorry, sorry!" I squealed every time Abby Normal's legs bashed into something. And I veered her in every direction, trying to find clear areas to run. All I did was throw her deeper into the shit pile.

The Wraiths zigged and zagged and leapt along with us. And they were right up Abby Normal's ass.

We had to get out of this stupid town.

A patch of dead grass peek-a-booed between two rows of crumbled buildings on my right side.

Bingo!

I tugged on the right rein. "This way, Abs!"

Her hooves skidded over the ashy terrain, but she made the turn, and her ears pricked, eyeing the open space that stretched before us. But this was like the final level in a video game, where everything and the kitchen sink was thrown at the player. The alleyway was uncomfortably narrow, and hordes of random knickknacks lay scattered across our path. Abby Normal scrabbled over one cart.

Another. Her foot got caught in a bucket and, for a few terrifying strides, she teetered. Until the bucket shattered, shooting shards of wood into the air. One of them spiraled up and belted her nose. She grunted.

"You're doing good, Abs!" I tried to assure her, even as my chest went *hic-hic-hic* around my labored breaths.

Why was I out of breath? I wasn't the one jumping!

Oh, har, har. I forgot about the *fucking arrow* in my shoulder.

It still didn't hurt, but my fingers were totally numb. When Abby Normal leapt over the skeletal remnants of an old booth, I couldn't even fist that hand into her mane.

My breath *heezed* when Abby Normal staggered into a rubbish pile and ran out with a bit of rope coiled around her front ankle. She squealed, kicked, and the rope flew off. "Good job," I muttered in her ear. "I'm gonna get you out of here, Abs. 'Kay? Hang tight."

Abby Normal keened. Her sides heaved, and her nostrils made an echoey noise as she exhaled panting breaths. Kinda like the rumble of waves hitting the shore.

Pfffpt.

Pfffpt.

Pfffpt.

And then finally, *finally*, the rattle of her hooves striking stone changed, morphing into the rolling sound of thunder as we hit the grass.

But the three Púcas were right behind us.

"Go, Abs!" I shrieked. "Go—too fast! *Too fast!*"

Abby Normal's hooves hungrily gobbled the ground. The sheer speed of her gallop had the wind bitch-slapping my face, stealing the breath from my lungs, and nearly knocking me off the saddle. In a scrambling attempt to grasp the pommel, I lost the reins. They flapped uselessly around her neck and were too damn slithery for me to grab onto. Even her mane, billowing across my face, didn't stay still long enough for me to get a good handhold. Every time I tried, I only succeeded in ripping a few errant strands from their roots.

My right foot slipped out of the stirrup, and the iron banged against my shin, sending pain rocketing up to my knee. My left foot held on, but only barely. The stirrup slid all the way to my tippy-toe.

"*Eeeeek!*" I squealed.

Bushes, trees, stones, and tall stalks of grass whizzed by us too fast for me to get a good look at.

I'm gonna fall!

She was too goddamn quick.

But at the same time, she wasn't quick enough.

The three Púcas drew alongside us: two on my left, one on my right.

Abby Normal's ears flattened, and she surged forward, finding another gear.

The Púcas stayed with her.

She couldn't outrun them.

Before us stretched a wide expanse of hilly fields. A forest smudged the horizon several miles away. Even if we could make it to the woods, what then? Keep running until we hit kingdom come?

Chriiiiippppp, chrip, chirp...

I squawked when something small, feathery, and chittery whisked over my left shoulder.

A bird.

Chrrriiippp!

The brown sparrow flew forward a few feet before it

turned itself around, looked me in the eye, and dive-bombed off the top of my helmet.

With another chittering *chriiiip*, the bird rushed back toward Swindon.

Braxton.

That was his doing, right? It had to be. Birds didn't voluntarily race alongside galloping horses, right?

Right??

Was he telling me to turn back?

Could we turn back?

Mowowowow.

The Púca on my left oscillated inward and bared its fangs at Abby Normal.

She snapped, her teeth clinking threateningly.

The Púca on her right snaked its head around, poised to give her a whopping hickey.

"Buzz off, pervert!" I thwacked my hand across his brow, hissing when my palm collided with the solid bone of his skull.

Whack!

The Púca's rider clubbed me across the face.

Pain mushroomed over my cheek, turning my vision white. I teetered, felt the saddle slipping out from under me and made a panic-snatch for the pommel. My right hand gripped the hard leather. My left slid uselessly to my side.

Abby Normal cried out, her ears flicking back toward me.

"You irksome meat bag," the Wraith called to me. "You'll burn for this. *Slowly*. We'll start with your legs...leave you alive as we devour you." He licked his lips.

Fucking hell.

We had to do something. And *stat*.

But what?

Maybe the old "turn and burn" would work. *Maybe.*

Probably not.

But we had to try.

Abby Normal's ear flipped back as I leaned over her neck, fumbling for the reins. The suckers were slimier and wrigglier than snakes, but I captured one in my right hand. The fingers on my left weren't working anymore. I couldn't bend them. Couldn't *feel* them.

The Wraith on my left side stretched his arm out. My heart stopped when his fingertips brushed my rein...

His horse, mercifully, wobbled off course *just enough* to put distance between us.

I tried again to grab the flinging rein.

Again, it evaded me.

"Abs..." My voice was a gasp. Weak.

Abby Normal lifted her head. Her muscles bunched as though she knew exactly what I was gonna ask.

"Abs...STOP!"

She hit the brakes so hard, her ass scraped the ground.

I braced my good hand against her neck, holding on for dear freaking life as momentum shoved at my backside and tried to pitch me over her shoulder.

The other Púcas kept on galloping. Their riders screamed and seesawed the reins, but the creatures were slow to respond.

Well, two of them were.

One whipped his head around, his red eye locked onto me.

Or, to be more accurate, locked onto the arrow lodged in my shoulder: the tap holding all the juicy goodness at bay.

"Abs." I gathered both reins in my right hand. "We have

to go. Back..." Almost every word I spoke was punctuated by an *eeeeee* gasp. "The town. Braxton."

She turned when I laid the reins against her neck and struck up a gallop when I tapped my heels on her sides. But she was tired. Sore. Her stride had a slight hitch.

"Hang in there, Abs!" I called, even as the wind ripped my voice away.

As the stone streets of the town came back into view, she sucked back with a long, strained grunt. Almost as if to say, *"Bitch, you're putting me through this again?"*

But then her ears snapped back as hoofbeats approached.

That one damn Púca—Mr. Hungry-Hungry Hippo—was only a few feet away. And closing *fast*.

With another roar, Abby Normal rocketed forward and clumsily hopped over the first of a metric *shit ton* of obstacles.

Hungry-Hungry Hippo stayed right at her tail.

"Sorry!" I called over each jump and swerve. I tried to stay with her, tried not to jerk on the reins or land too far back in the saddle. But most of the time, I struggled to hold on.

And to breathe.

And to *see*.

I didn't even know if half the obstacles were real or part of the mass of black spots that had appeared before my eyes. I damn near missed my turn coming off the dinky alley. Thankfully, Abby Normal was already leaning that way as though she knew to turn.

She cut the corner, bucking to get rid of the tangle of partially singed cloths snagging her back legs. As she touched back down, I caught a flash of red on my right.

"Oh *fuck*!" I swung my leg forward over her shoulder, and barely, *barely* avoided the other Púca's snapping teeth. And then I abandoned the reins again, snatching Abby Normal's mane when my ass scooched partway off the saddle.

Abby Normal's head shot up, her ears flicking back.

"Go!" I screamed.

The other Púca was right at her flank, his red eye still glued to my left shoulder. Blood dribbled from the corners of his mouth.

My blood?

Had the fucker gotten his teeth in me??

My eyes flew to my leg.

The Púca's gaze followed, and his downward glance sent him weebling off course.

"*Focus*!" The Wraith sawed the spiked bit into the Púca's mouth, savaging the poor animal's tongue and gums.

A bigger, foamier vat of crimson bubbled from between the Púca's lips.

Oh, thank *fuck*. It wasn't my blood after all.

But it would be. If we didn't get away from him.

Abby Normal howled and kicked out with both hind legs, swiping the other Púca in the chest. It fell back but gained on us again when Abby Normal blundered over a cart.

Abby Normal's breaths fluttered out in shrill wheezes.

Or maybe that was mine.

Or maybe it was both of ours.

But she sucked in a big, fluttery gasp of air before her next jump. "Hold on, Abs," I murmured.

Over a ruined house Abby Normal went, her stride

faltering on the landing. Only for a split second, but it was too long.

The other Púca touched down alongside her.

His teeth snapped, digging first into her neck, which made her *mowow* in pain, before his eyes zeroed in on me.

I didn't even *think* before I snatched the Púca's bridle, right above its bit, and ripped. The bit clanked against his teeth. He whined, tasting more of his own blood and feeling the sting of another laceration to his poor, abused mouth.

The Wraith seized the back of my neck, hauling me half out of the saddle.

My legs flailed, tangling in my stirrup, which proved to be the *only* thing that kept me attached to Abby Normal's back.

The Wraith dug his claws into my neck. "Where were you going?" he laughed. "Who did you think was going to help you?" He wrenched my head back, almost reclining me into his lap.

My ass smooshed in the narrow gap between the Púcas' rolling bodies, and the stirrup leather squeezed the everloving shit out of my ankle, cutting off my circulation.

The Púca *mauled* Abby Normal. His teeth raked her neck, drawing oodles of blood. And she could do *nothing* to defend herself, not while I was stuck half in and half out of her saddle.

"Hold on, Abs!" I ground my teeth.

The Wraith scoffed. "When will you *learn*? Sakar is dead…"

"*Not. Fucking. Yet.*" I rammed the heel of my palm up, up, up, until the Wraith's nose squished beneath my hand.

He gave an almost comical *sqqqquuuueeee*, like a fart balloon deflating, and loosened his hold.

"Always wear a helmet." I flung myself back into my saddle. "You only get one head—"

Ziiiing. Hungry-Hungry Hippo's teeth scrapped against my elbow, denting the metal but not piercing it. "Freaking—*arrrghh!*"

The Wraith rebounded with a snarling, "Cow!" and bonked my helmet off my head.

Stars erupted before my eyes.

He nabbed the end of my braid and dragged it back, tearing a few strands from the roots.

"*Addie!*"

Dimly, I heard Braxton's shout.

Through the blotches of white and black shrouding my eyes, I saw them. Six humans. Freed from the pens. Crouched low to the ground behind the chain they'd strung over our path.

Each person had a plank of wood in front of them.

I blinked. Counted. Four strides...three...*two* away from the chain.

"Abs!" I yelled. "STOP!"

Again, she did that ass-scraping halt. Again, the Púca beside us kept going, gathering himself up for the jump.

I screamed when the Wraith stole a chunk of my hair, then I saw the exact moment he realized what was about to happen. He threw both hands back onto the reins and pulled with all his might, but it was too late.

The Púca leapt over the chain.

The humans snatched their planks, thrusting them upward into the Púca's belly.

He made a horrible squall as he tumbled in a full ass-over-head somersault, body-slamming the Wraith into the ground. Crushing him.

And then the Púca quieted, his legs twitching as blood spouted from the holes punched along his underside.

Beneath me, Abby Normal's belly heaved. Her muscles trembled.

My breath *hic-hic-hic-hiced*. Hot, sticky blood trickled down the side of my face from where the Wraith had torn off a piece of my scalp. More blood oozed from the fresh cuts on Abby Normal's neck.

I put my hand over one of her wounds, trying to stem the bleeding.

Or, well, that was what I *wanted* to do.

But I leaned. And leaned. And kept leaning until my chin smacked against the stone street.

Abby Normal stood over me, screaming.

I blacked out before I could comfort her.

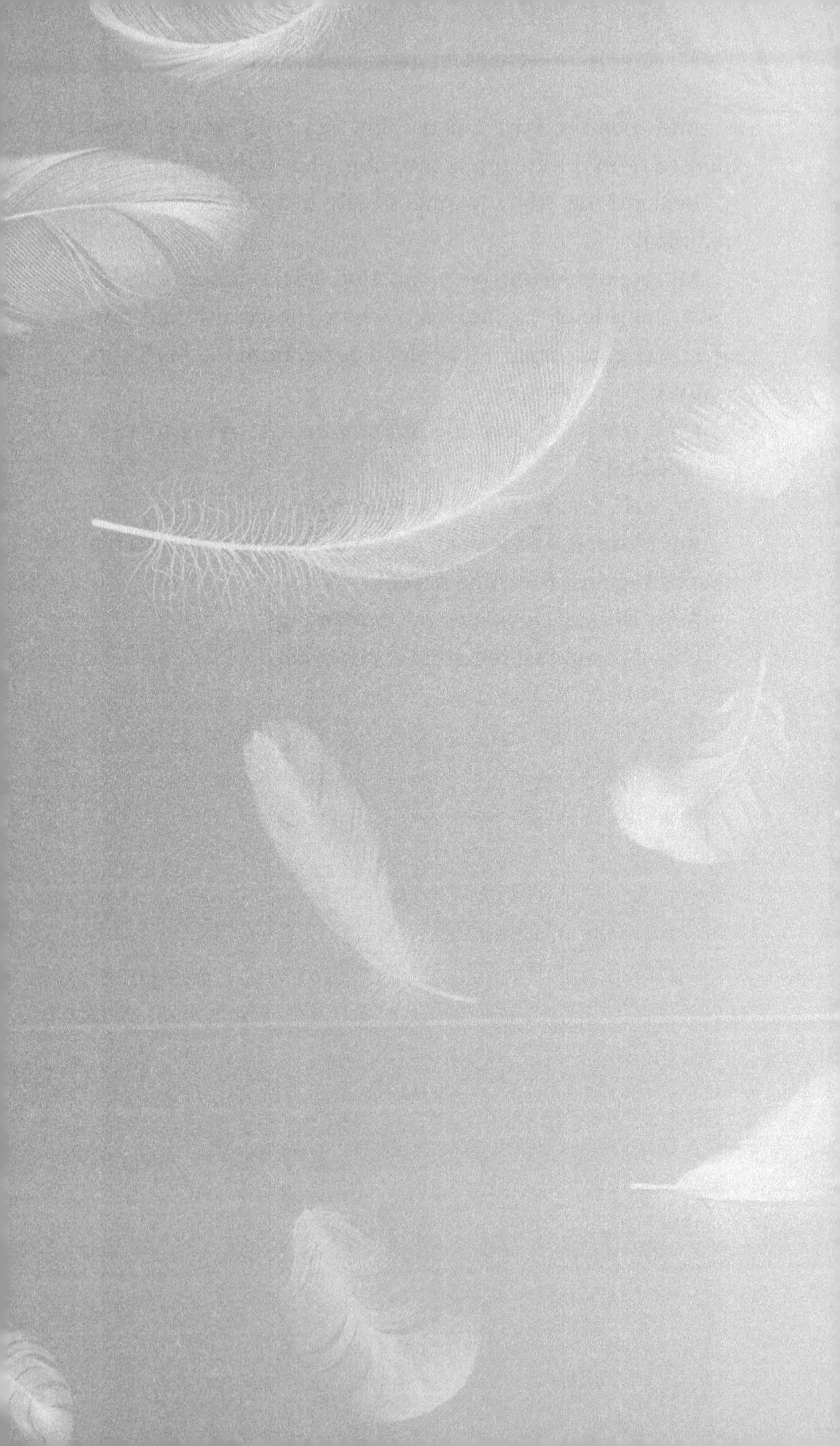

CHAPTER 16

WHAT'S A LITTLE E. COLI BETWEEN FRIENDS?

I awoke with a scream. Why? I dunno. Maybe because it felt like my shoulder was being methodically sawed off.

"Addie...be *quiet*." Braxton's voice was right at my left ear. "We finally got yer Púca to settle."

Somewhere in the distance, Abby Normal wailed.

Pain ricocheted around my shoulder again.

"Ooh, damn," I grumbled as I fought the lead weights holding my eyes closed. "That *hurts!*"

"We have to get the arrow out."

"*What?*" I wrenched my eyes open, gasping as the hazy late-afternoon sun drove needles into my eyeballs.

I was sitting up, surrounded by a half circle of people. All of them were strangers, except Braxton, who knelt in front of me, one hand holding my good shoulder to keep me upright while the other curled around the arrow.

His pinky finger twitched. Pain zipped through my veins and...*whoosh*, black-and-white checkered spots exploded before my eyes.

"*Ouch!* Ow, *fuck.* I'm gonna die, aren't I?" Fear left a zesty taste in my mouth.

"No, yer—" Braxton started.

"Why the *fuck* did I wake up just to kick the bucket? *Ouch!* You fucking bastard!" I squealed when Braxton wrapped his fingers more firmly around the arrow.

"We'll be needin' to take this out." A vein pulsed at his temple as he pressed his lips together.

"Don't you *dare* laugh at me."

"I'm not." But he couldn't even finish his sentence. He pressed his knuckles to his mouth, making a throaty *cheech-cheech-cheech.*

"Bastard." I tilted my chin up. Over his bouncing shoulder, I saw the cluster of humans milling about. Half of them were still shackled and waiting for the unchained people to bust them outta jail. And that process looked *painful.* It involved stretching the chains taut and wailing on the rivet with a sharp object until it loosened.

Jaysus. There were gonna be lots of broken bones in this crew.

Abby Normal walked several yards away, pivoting in a slow circle, flanked by a salt-and-pepper haired man and a sallow-faced woman. The guy held her reins, and the woman had a rope attached to the bit. Both were armed with chonky planks of wood and moved like stiff-legged robots, never taking their eyes off Abby Normal. But she was docile. Her sides still heaved, her nostrils flared, and she made a strained, fluttering *ffffpt, ffffpt* when she breathed. Blood ran in lazy rivers down her neck and dribbled down her right foreleg and left hind. She moved sluggishly, her head down, her ears splayed out to the side. She was tired. And hurting.

But she kept rolling her red eyes toward me.

"She'll be alright." Braxton followed my gaze. "Her wounds are shallow. Marcus and Aria will keep her walkin' 'til her breathin' slows. But ye, Addie...if ye keep yellin', ye'll be upsettin' her."

"Well, stop trying to rip the arrow through my heart, and I'll stop yelling," I said through gritted teeth.

"The arrow's not near your heart." A woman with tawny skin and luscious (if slightly matted) mocha-colored hair crouched beside me, surveying my wound.

"It's close enough." I squinted at her. "Who are you?"

She waved her arm dismissively. "It's not even in the bone. And the name's Deborah," she added as she tapped her thumb against the injection site.

A *ziiing* of pain shot up my arm, followed by tingling in my fingers. I hissed a long curse.

Braxton's strangled guffaws deepened.

"Fuck you," I snapped. "I-I'm not...stop laughing! And *stop touching it*! For fuck's sake. It *hurts*! And I'm not great with pain."

"Ye don't say?" Braxton sputtered.

I used my working hand to flash him the middle finger.

"It won't hurt as much once we remove the arrow," Deborah said.

"Like hell it won't—"

"It's in the muscle—"

"I don't *have* any muscle! I'm all flub."

"—so it'll heal quickly."

"Not if you blindly yank it out. And tear my flubber and tendons and...whatever else."

"If ye stay still." Braxton cleared his throat. "It's not

likely to hurt." He touched the arrow again and broke off laughing when I yelped.

A tall beanstalk of a man walked by at that moment, scouring caked blood off his hands. He paused when he saw me and chortled. "She's a brave one, eh?"

"I've got an idea," I gasped. "Why don't I shove this arrow up your ass? See how *brave* you are then?"

"If ye want to do that, it's best to have this arrow out. Yer arm'll work better, eh?" Braxton gave me a playful wink. "Aidan, can ye hold her right side?"

"Sure thing," chirped the beanstalk dude.

"Deborah, could you stay on her left?"

"Yes."

"Wait—oh, you two *suck*!" They both grabbed me at the same time. Aidan clutched my bicep while Deborah pinned my left arm to my side.

"Braxton..." I swallowed as he approached me, still laughing. And I *swore* that chuckle had gotten more maniacal. "Listen, I will do *whatever* you ask if you leave that arrow alone. Doesn't matter how weird or kinky it—"

Braxton reached over my shoulder and snapped the back half of the arrow off.

"Ow, ow, OW!" More neon-bright checkered spots flashed before my eyes. "Stop! Okay? *Stop*! You don't have the right tools. And *infection*...always a concern...and...." I gasped when Braxton waved the newly freed arrow in front of my eyes. A smug-as-shit grin stretched over his face.

I hadn't felt him pull the arrow out.

"There," he said. "If ye'd spent less time belly-achin', we could've had this done several minutes ago."

Blood dribbled from the arrow shaft.

I cocked my head to the side, wincing when the yawning hole in my shoulder hawked a big blood loogie.

"Heh." I blew out a breath. "Look at that. I'm not dead."

Deborah slapped a crusty, yellow-stained rag over the wound.

A piss rag. *Fantastic.*

"As we said," Braxton chuckled, "it was in yer shoulder. Clean through the muscle. Ye might have some trouble movin' yer arm for a few days, but ye'll have no problems healin'. Oi!" he bellowed over his shoulder. "Nathan! Have ye found anything?"

"Yes! I had a Neem seed. But I'll need a few more minutes to let it grow." This response came from somewhere behind me.

"Good," Braxton said. "Once ye have the leaves ready, can ye bring them here?"

"Of course."

"And collect as many as ye can before we leave. Now, Addie." Braxton idly waved the blood-soaked arrow around, sending blood droplets cascading into the air. "We're goin' to bind yer shoulder. Then I need ye to be helpin' me with yer Púca. I have some poultice for her legs. And—" He cut himself off as a bird careened overhead, tittering up a storm.

A blank expression washed over his face. He looked like a space cadet high on crack.

"Er...earth to Braxton," I said after several seconds. "Are you okay?"

He shook his head, clearing the vacant expression away.

"How long do we have?" Deborah asked him.

"They'll be here before dawn," he said.

"*They*? Who..." I gulped. "Wraiths?"

"Aye. Comin' to *collect* us." Braxton's face puckered in disgust as he spat those last words.

"Collect us for *what*?" I asked. "Seriously, why were they holding you guys here? And where are they taking all these people they're transporting?"

"We were bound for Niall." A puckered V formed between Deborah's eyes. "To serve that vile swine, *Oran*. He wants to turn Sakar into Uchen. And he's doing a mighty fine job of it."

Which totally answered my question...*not*. "What's—"

"We'll need to be gettin' ye and yer Púca fit to leave," Braxton cut me off. "*Quickly*."

"Have you anything under this armor?" Deborah asked me.

"Urmmm, yeah. My shirt. But it hasn't been aired out in a while, so it probably—oh, snap. Heh. This shirt is friggin' amazing. It doesn't even *stink*."

Deborah had unclipped my breastplate and stripped it off, baring my dazzling blue/pink shirt, which looked fresh and wrinkle free, as though it'd just finished a wash cycle and had hung on the line to dry. There were no splotchy pit stains. No under-boob sweat streaks. No funky gym bag odor. *I* stank, but the liquidy fabric hadn't absorbed any of my juicy body odors.

The blood bubbling from my wound didn't even stick to the shirt.

"That—that's a Celestial garment." Deborah went all googly-eyed.

The other man, Aiden, pulled a slack-jawed *"huuuhh?"* face as he fingered one of the gold tassels.

"Sure is. I love this freaking shirt. You'd have to pry it out of my *cold, dead hands*." I aimed that last bit at Aiden. He grinned sheepishly, raised his hands in an *"I'm innocent, I swear"* gesture, and walked away. I frowned at Braxton. "So... back up...you're gonna have to explain things slowly to me. My near-death experience fried my brain—"

"You were *not* near death," Deborah said.

"Let's start off easy. What do you mean 'you and your Púca?'" I continued. "What about the rest of you?"

Braxton turned his head away.

But before I could bitch at him for ignoring my question, a wiry, pale-haired man slid to a kneeling stop in front of me and plunked a branch of thin, spike-edged leaves onto my lap. "You'll need to grind these," he said breathlessly. And then he popped back to his feet, staggered a few steps to the right and vomited over a Púca's carcass.

The same Púca who'd tried to gun me down. Mr. Hungry-Hungry Hippo.

"Excellent aim," I said.

The man flashed me a lively smile and *took a freaking bow* before he scurried off.

"Let me guess," I asked, "he's a hybrid?"

"Sure is," Deborah answered. "Nathan might be one of the last Gardeners left."

"Yer right lucky he was here," Braxton added, "and with the Neem seed." He snatched the branch and waggled it in front of my face. "These'll be helping that wound of yers heal."

"I don't think a bunch of leaves are gonna help." I grimaced when Deborah pulled the seeping, blood-soaked rag from my wound. She tossed it aside and replaced it with a grimy, brown-stained one.

"Are you using *toilet paper?*" I trilled.

"Eh?" Deborah pressed down until my shoulder pounded with pain.

"*Ouch!* The rag." I jutted my chin at the oblong skid mark splotched over the fabric. "Did someone wipe their ass with that?"

"Perhaps." She shrugged.

"Ugh. *Wonderful.* Why not? What's a little E. coli between friends?"

"She only needs it to stop the bleedin'. Then we'll pack these on." Braxton whistled a chirpy tune as he plucked the leaves off the branch, gathering them into a neat pile on the ground. Then he smashed them with a rock and spewed a big wad of spit over them.

"Oh, yes. Because that'll be *so much* more hygienic," I said.

Braxton spat over the leaves again.

"Yup. Just keep spitting. The more germs you get on them, the better," I grumbled.

"Stop yer belly-achin', Addie," Braxton giggled as he ground the leaves down to a paste. "These will help." With that, he glooped the leaf mush into my wound.

"That's good. *Real* good." I braced against the pain. "The blood loss wasn't enough to kill me, so we'll let infection take a crack at it. *Perfect.*"

Both he and Deborah ignored my snide commentary.

"I'll not tie your arm down." Deborah wound strips of fabric around my shoulder, yanking on each layer like she was trying to tight-lace a corset. "*Don't* use this arm unless you've no choice."

"Well." I hissed when she wrapped a layer of bandage around my chest, giving the girls a good smoosh. "It's a good thing I'm a rightie."

Braxton skirted off while I was getting mummified and strolled back a moment later, tossing a small flask between his hands.

"Oh, thank *God*...you've brought alcohol!" I said.

"Ach. No." His face pinched. "Sorry to be disappointin' ye, Addie. But them bastards drank me whiskey." He jabbed a thumb to the right, where the Wraith's arm poked out from beneath his fallen Púca. "This is for yer Púca." He shook the flask. "Ye see, old Larkin—me stallion—well, he was a good old chap with old injuries that swelled in the morn'." Braxton swallowed. "But he won't be needin' this anymore. And yer Púca struck her legs a few times. This'll keep them from swellin'. But ye'll need to hold her head..." He cast a wary glance at Abby Normal, who still walked between Marcus and Aria. She'd thankfully stopped breathing like an asthmatic T-rex, but she had started to ogle her companions the way I sometimes eyed up a juicy double hamburger.

"Right...okay..." I gathered my rickety legs under me and stood.

Bam!

Black and white squares. That was all I saw. A heavy pulse pounded through my wound, and each deep *whomp-whomp-whomp* carried sharp licks of fire.

I staggered, having a brief second where my stomach army-crawled up my throat and I was sure I was going to puke all over myself. And then the checkerspots faded. My stomach settled. Although I still shook worse than a junk food junkie in an off-limits candy store.

"Ye alright?" Braxton asked.

"No." I stumbled forward. "But let's get this over with before I pass out."

Abby Normal made an affectionate *whuff-huff* when I took the reins off Marcus and unhooked Aria's rope from the bit. "Thanks, guys. I've got her from here."

I didn't need to tell them twice. They *booked it* away from her.

"Don't pay attention to them, Abs." I patted her brow as she loosed a long exhale. "You're still the bestest bitch, no matter what these yahoos think."

Aria cast me an incredulous look over her shoulder.

"They just don't know you yet." I touched Abby Normal's neck, where the zig-zaggy teeth marks still lazily seeped blood. "One of these days, Abs, I'll repay you for all the times you've saved my ass."

She billowed gently, but then pinned her ears when Braxton crouched by her left hindleg.

"Be nice, Abs. He's trying to help," I chided.

Her ears relaxed. But apparently, she and I had the same pain tolerance (aka, none). Because when Braxton prodded her puffy ankle, she kicked out with a squeal, nearly drilling her hoof into his face.

"OI!" he boomed.

She snaked her head around, fangs making a *crrrrink* as she ground them against each other.

All the color rushed from Braxton's face. "Feck, Addie. Hold her head steady! I don't need the bloody bitch to be bitin' me."

"She won't bite. Will ya, Abs?"

Abby Normal snapped her teeth.

"See?" I cackled at the *"you've gotta be shitting me"* look on Braxton's face. "Perfectly safe."

Braxton shook his head. Huffed. Used his shoulder to

swipe a bead of sweat off his brow. And then uncorked his poultice flask. "I need a fecking drink."

"You and me both."

Braxton grumbled and trailed a hand along Abby Normal's leg, slathering it in goopy/chunky poultice. It was *rancid*, reminding me of the cheapo New York City pizza joints that bathed their pizza in garlic to mask the nastiness of their grainy dough and ketchupy sauce.

Abby Normal slanted her head sideways, reacting to the odor, the slimy feel of the goop against her legs, or both. Her mouth gaped as her tongue slurped obscenely over the bit. "Knock it off, Abs," I said.

She stilled her tongue and stiffened when Braxton poked another cut on her ankle.

"Poor thing. C'mere." To keep her still and offer some comfort, I wrapped my arm around her head, drew her into my chest, and rested my sweaty cheek against her brow.

Because, y'know, hugs were awesome. Hugs made things better.

"Hugs are dangerous when yer lettin' a bloody Púca put her teeth that close to yer skin," Braxton said.

"Oh, shush. You wanted me to hold her head. I'm holding it. And she *loves* hugs. See?"

Abby Normal exhaled in a long, relaxed snort.

As Braxton grouched and shimmied around her, inspecting her cuts and spreading his garlicy sludge over her bumps and bruises, I embraced her, watching the hubbub around me to distract myself from the pulse of pain *whomp-whomp-whomping* away in my wound. There were so many people (twenty-one, if the Wraith's count had been accurate). And now that I was looking at them, *really* looking, I despaired at their battered state. They were all hollow cheeked and gaunt. Most nursed broken bones or open wounds. But they still cracked jokes as they warmed themselves by the fire. Some had made a contest out of pissing and/or spitting on the Wraith corpses—evidently, they'd speared the other two Púcas and clubbed their Wraiths to a pulp while I'd been K.O.'d. And on the very outskirts of town, the Gardner, Nathan, merrily tended to a fugly little tree that slanted sideways, brushing its toothed leaves against the ground. His smile never faded, even when he doubled over and vomited again.

These people *amazed* me. They'd barely escaped being turned into KFH (Kentucky Fried Human), their entire world was in the shitter, and they chirped and chuckled as though it was an average Thursday on the job.

A pang shot through my chest, tearing the breath out of my lungs.

Abby Normal flinched when I let out a long, strained grunt.

"Ye alright, Addie?" Braxton asked.

"No." I squeezed my eyes shut.

"If yer shoulder's in that bad a state, we can try to tie it..."

"It's not my shoulder," I said a little too snappishly. And then I let out a wavering breath when the spasm loosened.

"Are ye hurt elsewhere?"

"No. Well, I mean..." I drew my tongue between my teeth before I could vocalize the next bit. *My insides are fucked. Have been since I vaporized Seruf's soul. But I'm sure it's no biggie. The bitch just gave me a record-breaking case of indigestion. That's all.*

"I'm as healthy as a horse." I patted Abby Normal's cheeks as I opened my eyes...right in time to catch Nathan puking. *Again.* He still had that thousand-watt smile on his face, though. And he was flirting it up with a handsome, square-jawed man. The vomit seemed to have punctuated his sentence. "I really like you" *bleggghh.* "Wanna go get dinner tonight?"

"Do all hybrids get sick when they use their powers? Or do they go a little...y'know..." I raised my finger to my temple, making a twirling motion.

"Curly-haired?" Braxton asked.

"Cuckoo," I finished. "Unhinged."

He shrugged as he stood and swiped his greasy hands over his black armor, making it all streaky. "It's different for all of us. But...yes. We all suffer from our powers."

Well, I'd *definitely* crossed over to the dark side when I snatched Seruf's soul. I'd embraced my hybrid power and was now doomed to suffer for the rest of my miserable existence...

"And ye'll be countin' yerself as one of us now, eh?" Braxton winked.

My heart stopped.

"Don't think I've forgotten what happened at Niall."

Oh. *Fuck.*

"Can ye start fires? Or are ye merely immune to them?"

Oh. *Oh! Thank fucking Christ.* He was talking about me being fireproof. Not whatever that other friggin' power was.

"No. Or...I dunno. Maybe? I have *zero* interest in testing it, though." I never thought I'd be *relieved* to discuss my flame-retardant skin.

"Ach, I don't suppose I blame ye there. Ye ken, we had a Firestarter in the army. Once."

"So I've heard."

"She had yer eyes."

"I've heard that too."

"And yer temper. Although she lacked yer charm." He beamed at me.

I batted my eyelashes at him.

"But I'm bein' unfair." Braxton chuckled. "I knew Lasair when she was a wee girl, and she was plenty charmin' then."

My chest tightened. "You knew her?"

"Aye. When we were youngins." He grinned. "She had a goat who used to escape and run into the market. She never knew 'twas Belanna and me that taught him to open gates."

"Oh jeez. I don't even *wanna* picture you and Belanna as kids. You were probably the twins from hell."

"Nothin' wrong with havin' a spot of fun—"

"Your poor mother. I'm sure she earned a sainthood after raising you two."

"—and Lasair's goat was always happy to oblige. Mischievous little blighter, he was. Lasair used to get so angry—never with the goat, mind. More with the market vendors who'd fuss about his escape. And she wasn't afraid to voice her opinion, even to the adults. 'Don't leave yer wares hangin' in the open and ye'll not have to worry about them being eaten.'" He said this in a high-pitched falsetto that made Abby Normal jump and kick sideways.

"That was 100 percent your fault," I told him when he gave Abby Normal a wary glower.

"Ach." He waved his arm and then sighed. "Lasair loved those goats of hers. And she was *good* with the animals. A cryin' shame she couldn't have been made into a Speaker instead of a Firestarter. This town might have survived..." He drummed his fingers against his breastplate. "We all used to

live here, ye ken? In Swindon. Me and Belanna and Lasair...
we dwelled a stone's throw from where we're standin' now.
The houses are gone, mind. And the bookshop—"

"*Bookshop?*"

"Oh, aye. Lasair's father...well, he wasn't *truly* her father.
Much like me mam wasn't truly me mam. But they raised
us. And Terrick, Lasair's pa, had one of the last bookshops in
Sakar. I've never been much for readin', but me mam loved
Terrick's store. So did Belanna."

Ding-ding-ding! There went the lightbulb in my head.

"*There's no place like home, eh?*"

The last words Belanna said to me, a quote from *The
Wizard of* freaking *Oz*. I assumed she'd pulled that from the
movie. But what if she'd gotten it from the *book*?

And what if that book had been at *Lasair's freaking
bookshop*?

Had that Terrick guy been abducted and sent to Sakar
with a copy of *The Wizard of Oz* in his back pocket? Was that
book *here*?

But before I could ask, Braxton snapped his eyes to the
sky, getting that "*space cadet high on crack*" look again.

A bird soared overhead.

"Shite..." He dashed away and snatched my breastplate
off the ground. "Ye need to go, Addie. They're movin' faster
than I thought."

"The Wraiths?"

"Aye. Ye need to be well away from here before they
arrive."

"What about you guys?"

Braxton's nose scrunched. "Don't ye be worryin' about
us. Ye focus on gettin' to Muirin. We'll take care of the
Wraiths."

"Hmmm...here's a pro tip for ya, Braxton: Never play poker."

"Eh?"

"You're a *terrible* liar. You're gonna lose this fight, aren't you?"

"Well." He shuffled his feet, kicking a small stone. "I was *tryin'* to be calm and reassurin' like. I didn't want ye fussin' about us. There's nothin' for it, Addie. We have nowhere to go. But ye..." He waved the breastplate in front of my face. "Ye were in front of a Wraith, and she didn't know ye were human! Ye *can* make it to Muirin."

"And leave you all here to die?"

He shrugged. "Ye'd save a lot more lives if ye found that Celestial."

I shook my head, the twinge tightening in my chest again. No. No. Nope. Absolutely the fuck not.

But what else could we do? They couldn't go back to Sanadrin—not with the major Wraith infestation spreading across Sakar—and they couldn't go to Muirin with me because they'd blow my cover.

Unless, y'know, I strapped chains on them and called them my meat bag bitches...

"Feck...*Addie!*" Braxton's jaw dropped. "That's brilliant!"

"What is—oh, wait. Did I say any of what I just thought out loud?"

He gave me a toothy smile. "The guise will work. We'll need to be findin' ye a whip and seein' what supplies we can collect..."

"No. Uh-uh. That was a half-baked, spur-of-the-moment thought. And it was meant to be *private*, Braxton."

"But methinks ye said it out loud because ye knew it was a good idea." He winked.

Acid bubbled in my gut. "I blurted it out because my brain's fucking broken and I have no censor. It is *not* a good idea. If the Wraiths catch us, I'd be handing you to them on a silver platter. We're *not* doing it. Hell will have to freeze over first."

THE ABBY NORMAL EXPRESS

Apparently, hell had frozen over.

A coiled bullwhip encircled the front of my saddle, and a long length of chain wrapped around the back, one the humans had *voluntarily* strapped themselves back into.

I mean, the shackles weren't *fully* hammered shut; everyone'd left gaps on their wrists so they could, in theory, bust out in an emergency.

I did *not* hold much stock in that B.S. theory.

"For the record"—I nudged my heels into Abby Normal's sides—"I think this is a bad idea."

"Ye didn't have a better one, though, did ye?" Braxton gloated.

I glanced over my shoulder and caught him doing a skippy jig in the chains, looking happier than a pig in poop.

"I think I liked you better when you were drinking, Braxton," I said.

He waved cheerily.

Beneath me, Abby Normal lurched into a walk. She moved sluggishly. *Stiffly.*

Braxton had sworn up and down that she was fine, but I didn't like the way she felt under the saddle.

I didn't like the way I felt *in* the saddle. My left arm was useless. Trying to grip something? Pain. Raising my arm? Double pain. Reaching forward? Triple pain. The swinging of Abby Normal's walk? Crippling pain.

Life lesson learned: Never be without ibuprofen. Keep that shit stashed in your bra. Because you never knew when some maniacal Celestial was gonna drop-kick you into a world where people thought *plants* cured your wounds.

The fucking plants didn't do *shit.*

I rested my pulsating arm against my left thigh and tried to keep my upper body still. Which made my back ache. Because, y'know, I was *old* and had a creaky back, rickety hips, and shoddy knees.

More reasons why I needed ibuprofen.

"Stop belly achin', Addie," Braxton called.

At the same time, Deborah and Nathan both said to, "Give the leaves time to work."

I dropped the reins and used my working hand to flip them all off.

As we exited Swindon, miles of heavy, metallic-gray skies stretched overhead. The clouds hung low, seeming close enough to touch, and they puffed a mist of rain-scented perfume over us. We had roughly an hour of daylight left, so we'd soon be traveling in the dark. Likely in a thunderstorm.

Fan-fucking-tastic.

Behind me, someone sneezed.

Abby Normal jerked her head and kicked out with her left hind.

"Bless you," I snapped at whoever had sneezed.

Abby Normal's ears flicked back and forth. Back and forth. Uncertain. Cautious. Listening to me, the people behind her, and the oppressive silence out in front.

I rubbed my knuckles against her mane. One ear turned back toward me, staying there a moment, while the other kept swiveling.

"Right." I drew in a deep breath, steeling myself before I called, "Well, welcome to the Abby Normal Express. It's gonna be a bumpy ride. I'd tell y'all to strap in but...you kinda already are. There are no complimentary meals. No toilets, either...Although, for the *love of God*, tell me when you need a potty break. I don't need any of y'all trying to aim while walking. No one likes to get pissed on. That smell lingers."

Someone gave a chuckle that sounded downright devious.

Probably Braxton. He was the type to have a pissing war with someone. *"Har, har, whip it out, boys! Let's see who can hit the rock first!"*

"Estimated time of arrival is a few days," I continued. "Or a week. Or...whenever. *Assuming* we don't get lost."

"Ah, we shouldn't lose our way so easily," Deborah said. "Muirin looked to be almost straight north from Swindon."

"And you know how to figure out which way north is?"

"Of course." This said almost like a question. *"Of course I know the barest basics of navigation...Why don't you?"*

"Okay, well, *good*. Because I don't know north from my left hand. So, if Abs and I start going off course, let me know.

'Kay?" I stroked Abby Normal's neck. "We'll do what we can to get ya there in one piece. But no promises."

The last leg of a road trip was always the *worst*.

Especially since this one took us through some *loooonnngggg* stretches of wide-open space. The trees, as much as I loathed them, would've at least given us cover and places to hide if we sensed trouble brewing. But we spent less than a half a day tramping through a dinky half-acre wood and emerged onto the vast slopes of dead grass that would be our view for the remainder of the journey. The terrain left us exposed. When it rained? We all got soaked. When the day dawned blustery and cold? We all gave our muscles a good workout by shivering.

And if any Wraiths lurked nearby, they would've been able to spot us from *miles* away.

I *waited* for that to happen. Every time I spotted a shadow, even if it was only a dappled pall from the clouds, or heard a distant noise, even if it was only the screeching of wind, my heart stopped.

Braxton's power made him a handy lookout, but it wasn't perfect. He had blind spots in areas where animals were scarce (like the flatlands). And animals missed things.

"They're no' different from us," Braxton said one day. "They get absorbed in their comins and goins and don't always notice when somethin's afoot."

"Is that how you got caught?" I asked. "Because the animals were daydreaming?"

"No. I *knew* the Wraiths were there that day. Wasn't much I could do given they had me surrounded. And their Púcas scented Larkin. Poor old chap," he muttered glumly.

Which was...*not* reassuring.

Because then I imagined an ambush scenario where hordes of Púca-mounted Wraiths descended upon us, cackling and squealing as they stared at the lavish buffet laid out before them.

The ache in my chest turned cold. Slithery. And it *never* went away.

Neither did the pain in my shoulder. The skin never got red or puffy; the few times I changed the bandages, the discharge was always a light pink or a totally clear fluid. No pus. No muss. (Har, har). It seemed I'd dodged the infection bullet. But goddamn, it *hurt*.

Days passed.

Our progress was *excruciatingly* slow. If I saw a straggly little shit tree a few miles away in the morning, it would *still* be a few miles away by the afternoon. I swore either the ground was moving, stretching things farther and farther away, or we were walking backward.

The weather was cold. And damp. And the sky always seemed to be deciding whether it wanted to piss on us or hold it in another day. I'd never, *ever* seen so many low, dark clouds.

Abby Normal eventually got some pep back in her step, but her right hind ankle kept puffing up.

"It's bruisin'," Braxton assured me on the third (or fourth, or fifth—I hadn't kept up with my stick calendar) day. "Nothin' more. The walkin' will do her good. Keeps the blood from poolin', ye see."

Walking might've done her good. But walking while carrying a saddle, equipment, and a floppy sack of potatoes (aka, me) probably made the injury worse. I dismounted and strolled beside her for chunks of the day, giving her as many breaks as I could without running the risk of looking suspicious. "Wraiths are not so considerate to their beasts," Deborah kept reminding me. And Abby Normal never protested when I cinched up the saddle and mounted. But I *hated* the way her back leg occasionally hitched. Hated that the only reason she had that puffy ankle was because she'd been scrabbling to save my ass. But all I could do was pat her neck and give her nose boops and hugs, hoping her weird "Abby Normal" brain understood how grateful I was.

The people behind me sported some gnarly injuries too. More than half walked with jerking limps. Most were ashen-faced and shaky, and sometimes needed to lean against others for support. But they remained in good spirits. Like... *really* good spirits.

After several incident-free days, their low, deep laughter became my constant background music.

After a full week, crude jokes and obscene tales flew through the air.

I didn't yet know all these people. There were twenty-one of them. The four at the head of the chain were Braxton, Deborah, Nathan, and Marcus—whose quiet nature balanced out the other three goofballs. The rest? They'd given me their names, multiple times, but my mind was too warped with paranoia and pain. Trying to retain them was harder than holding water in my cupped palm.

On one late afternoon, a little more than a week after

we'd left Swindon, *certain* members of the group (aka, Braxton) got a little more rambunctious than usual.

The rippling, cloud-laden sky had developed a hazy orange glow: a sign of the impending sunset. Beneath me, Abby Normal plodded along, her ears splayed as though half snoozing. But each time one of Braxton's maniacal laughs punctured the air, she jerked.

"Ye know wee Kaelan?" Braxton boomed, no doubt trying to make sure everyone at the back of the line heard him.

The people at freaking *Niall* had probably also heard him. My God. His voice could rupture eardrums.

I stroked Abby Normal's neck, soothing her when she flinched.

"Is that Cheriour's boy?" asked a deep-voiced man named Hugo (or Harry, or Henry...something that began with an H).

My stomach did a swoop-swoop. *Cheriour's boy.*

Kaelan wasn't Cheriour's biological kid (obviously), but the two were close. And I'd never asked them how that relationship formed.

I needed to make that a priority when I got back.

If.

"Aye," Braxton continued. "Oh, I have a yarn to spin about him. Kaelan fancied this lass—ugh, I can't remember her name. I suppose it doesn't matter. He saw her in Sanadrin and became *smitten.* So I says to her, 'Have some heart and give the poor lad a good rut. He's a wee bit nervous. And too shy to ask himself.' And she agrees, but I also says to 'scream real loud; make the lad feel good.' So when we celebrated after the fight, I made sure Kaelan was well in his cups and then let her take him to her dwellin'.

The wee lad was *beside* himself with excitement. But then" —Braxton choked on a giggle—"he started ruttin', got near to finishin', and she screamed for him. The poor bastard near shite himself thinkin' he'd done somethin' wrong. He ran back to the castle in naught but his bare arse. Cheriour had to go get his clothes."

I had to join in on the sniggering. *Had to.* Even though my heart broke a little for Kaelan. But that scene reminded me of an '80s-era teen sex movie, and I had a soft spot for those awful 80s raunch fests.

"That's kinda awful, Braxton," I said, once I'd stopped chuckling.

"Ach, 'twas only a wee spot of fun. He laughs about it now. Ye ask him. And Cheriour...I've got a story about him too. Ye ken she and Cheriour rutted," he stage-whispered to the group.

"Nice, Braxton." I rolled my eyes. "*Super* classy. Thanks for making us sound like animals in heat."

"Really? Cheriour?" Deborah asked. "I wouldn't have thought him interested. I tried. *Years* ago—before I met Isaac, mind."

"So did I," a sprightly, middle-aged man named Shay said. "He looked at me uncomprehending like."

"He did the same with me!" Deborah laughed. "And ye remember Pippa...rest her soul. She took her tunic off and sat beside him for an hour. Said he didn't even look at her."

"I took my pants off," Shay cackled.

Okay...*gross.* "Can y'all stop talking about how you tried to fuck my—er—Cheriour?"

Deborah tutted affectionately. "We only wanted to get a rise out of him. It was harmless fun—"

"Apparently, I have a different definition of '*harmless.*'"

"—but he's not an easy one to get a reaction out of. Or to get close to. He must like something about you."

"I've got a banging body. And a nice ass." I wiggled my booty in the saddle.

"Aye, ye do have that, Addie," Braxton said.

At the same time, Deborah commented, "I don't think it's anything particular on your body that drew him. Not to say your body isn't a draw," she added when I *humphed*. "But he always seemed the sort who wouldn't fuss about that."

Thimp-thump went my heart.

Because Deborah was absolutely right.

Cheriour *enjoyed* sex, sure. But he wasn't driven by it. There'd been plenty of nights he'd been perfectly content with cuddling. And when we did shuck the clothes off, he valued intimacy, the languid, sweet, sappy stuff. He had no interest in bing-bang-booming straight to the finale like every other guy I'd slept with.

Maybe his brain worked differently because he'd been a Celestial once. Maybe it was just...*him*. But he truly saw a lot more than curves and skin, even during sexy times.

That thought made me all tingly. And a smidge uncomfortable. Because I'd gotten attached to a deep, compassionate romantic, while I was a freaking horndog who constantly eye-humped his nice, lithe, rugged body.

"As I *started to say*." Braxton cleared his throat to get my attention. "Has Cheriour told ye of the time he drank himself off his feet?"

Nathan burst out laughing. "I remember!"

"Cheriour doesn't drink," I said.

"He doesn't drink *now*," Braxton corrected. "He did once. Traumatized him, it did."

Interesting. "Do tell."

"Ach, 'twas...five years ago?"

"Six," Nathan supplied.

"Aye, anyway...there we was, celebratin' our great victory."

"You kept Wraiths out of the city. Hardly a victory," Deborah rebuffed playfully.

"'Twas a victory in my eyes," Braxton argued. "And Jane—ah, ye would've loved her, Addie. She had the best ale in all of Sakar."

"As good as your whiskey?" I asked.

"Better."

"Oh, I'm sure her ale was *delicious* then." *Not.*

"She gave free drinks to the soldiers. As many as we wanted. Mighty generous of her. And Cheriour came to the pub because he wanted to 'ask Quinn questions.'"

"Questions?"

"Somethin' practical that had no business being in the pub that night," Braxton harumphed. "So, Quinn says, 'Have a drink,' and Cheriour says he doesn't care for the taste. But Jane had given him her best ale, one of the few barrels she *wasn't* givin' us for free. And I suppose he didn't want to hurt her feelin's. So he drank it. And she brought him another, and another again. And he was drinkin' them fast, tryin' to leave."

"Oooh noooo..." I cringed on Cheriour's behalf. "He chugged them?"

"Aye."

"Had he eaten anything that night?"

"Likely not. Anyway, she brings him a fourth ale. But now, he's not lookin' like he has his sea legs anymore..."

Braxton guffawed. "He's still tryin' to have a conversation with Quinn, but he's not makin' a lick of sense."

"Wait, wait, wait...hang on..." A dark, depressing thought crossed my mind and sent ice cubes jangling in my stomach. "If someone did something messed up to him, I don't wanna know."

"Ach, it was nothin' like that," Braxton laughed. "He fell."

"Fell?"

"Aye. He was gettin' frustrated that his body wasn't workin' right, so he tried to walk away. But he couldn't get his legs sorted, so he fell. *Very* graceful like. He only hit one chair. Right well broke his nose, though."

It was *horrible*.

But *hysterical*. Picturing smooth, nimble Cheriour taking a nosedive onto the bar floor.

My skin prickled with secondhand embarrassment.

But a short, barking laugh burst out of me.

"Quinn tried but couldn't get him back to his room, so Cheriour slept in the pub. *Alone*, Addie. No one did anythin' to him. But he woke in a mighty uncomfortable state," Braxton cackled. "He hasn't had a drop to drink since. Couldn't handle the pain, I reckon."

No.

Cheriour would've shrugged that hangover right off— the dude had a *crazy* high pain tolerance. But having his brain get fuzzy and his body uncoordinated...*that* would've bothered him.

The alcohol had made him vulnerable.

And he resisted things that made him vulnerable. Like sleeping, or resting to allow his body to heal, or admitting when he was in a crap ton of pain.

It was sad to think about. The dude was always on edge, never able to relax, and he'd developed a resentment (or a fear) of the one thing that had *forced* him to loosen up for a hot minute.

No wonder he had knots the size of watermelons in his muscles.

Mowowow.

Abby Normal hit the brakes and popped her head up.

"You okay, Abs?" I asked.

She made another warbled *mowow* and scuttled back a step, her tail flicking.

A reaction I knew well by now.

"Something's wrong." My mouth got that dry, cottony sensation as I twisted around, searching the expansive field. But there was *nothing* out there. No Wraiths. Or Púcas. Just the sparse trees speckling the area and the low-hanging sky.

"I don't see anything in front of us," Braxton said.

"The coast looks clear to me too." I frowned.

"I believe we're still some distance from the coast," Deborah said.

"It's...never mind. I'm wondering if she sees something we don't? Or smells something?" I touched Abby Normal's neck.

Her front hooves struck the ground.

A warning.

But of what?

"She might have something under her saddle," Deborah supplied. "My mare used to fuss like that. One little twig would drive her mad."

Abby Normal's head cocked sideways, her ears planted forward.

"No." An icy sheen of sweat prickled over my skin. "She's picking up on something. God fucking damn it, I *knew* this was a bad idea. How fast can you guys get out of those—"

I saw it before I heard it.

A mountain loomed large in the distance, one that appeared to be a glimmering turquoise in the dim sunlight and whose white caps frothed and churned, cascading in a graceful arc toward the ground.

That mountain had *not* been there thirty seconds ago.

As Abby Normal emitted a long, frightened wail, a great *whooosh* rumbled the earth.

A wave.

It was a *mother flipping tidal wave.*

And it had sprung right out of dry land.

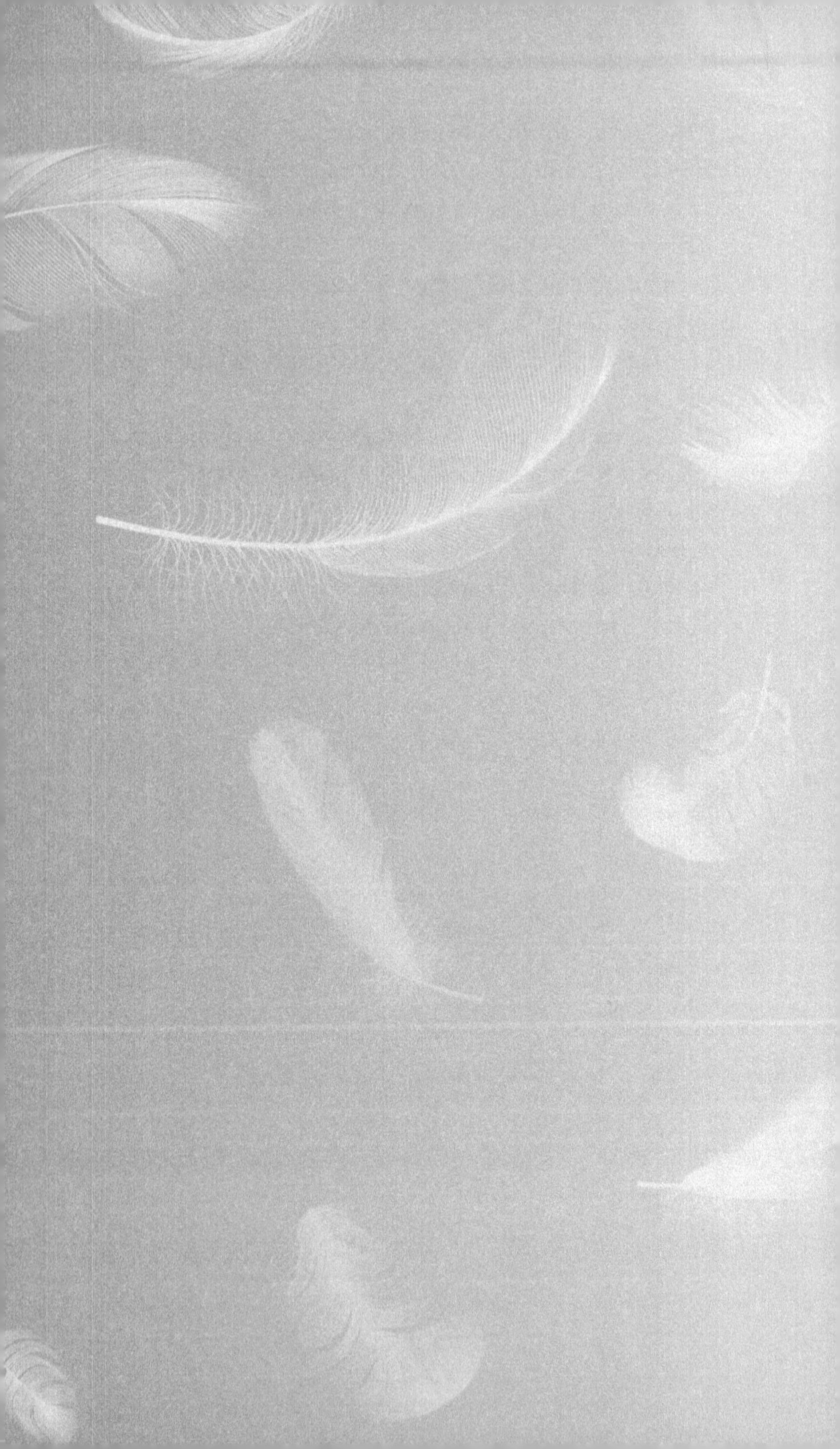

CHAPTER 18

AN ALIEN, ALL DAPPERED UP IN HUMAN SKIN

I squeezed my eyes shut. Opened them.

The wall of water was still there. It was *colossal*—nearly the size of a high-rise. Fluffy vats of white foam curled over the top as it hurtled toward us.

What. In. Ever. Loving. Fuck??

Behind me, multiple people shared my sentiment. The word "feck" plumed into the air, almost muffling the deep, droning *rrrrrrrrrrooooooooaaaaaarrrrrr* of the wave.

Almost.

I turned and loosed a vinegar-flavored hiccup as I studied the long line of people behind me, all shackled to that stupid goddamn chain.

"Get out of the—*what the hell?*" I screeched when a man suddenly *materialized* on my right side. Literally. One second, I had nothing but air and grass on that side; the next, a jittery blond dude stood two inches from my knee, free of the shackles and looking poised to heave chunks all over my lap.

"How in the—y'know what, don't even answer that.

Fucking hybrids. Just...help me get the rest of them out of the shackles."

I swung my leg over the saddle.

Abby Normal made a low, strangled series of *mowows* and bolted sideways.

"Accch!" My left foot caught in the stirrup, traveling with her, while my right leg hit the ground several inches away. My hip popped. I was too old to be doing splits.

"Addie!"

"Oi!"

"Fecking buggard!"

People cried out when Abby Normal's sideways leap rattled the chain and knocked half of them on their asses.

"Abs! Whoa!" I snatched her reins. She halted and allowed me to detangle my leg, but she screamed bloody murder the whole time, emitting high-pitched trills I'd never heard her make before. "I know, Abs. I'm doing what I can. And you..." I whirled at the blond-haired guy. That bastard had done *nothing* to help. He was too busy ogling the wave and doing a weird seesaw walk backward. "The fuck are you doing?" I yelled. "Can you help? Guess not..."

The man tripped over his own feet and *thunked* to the ground, where he sat like a lump on a log, watching the doomsday tsunami thunder closer. And closer. And...

Jesus, that thing was right on top of us! I could *smell* the sea salt now.

"*Get out of the chains!*" I bellowed at the group.

Abby Normal *mowowowowed* and swung her ass sideways again, jangling the chain.

"Hang on, Abs. I'm gonna get this off you." My breath rattled out of my mouth in a sputtering *urk-urk-urk* as I reached for her saddle. I couldn't get the cinch loosened!

Not one-handed. Not while Abby Normal weaved, bobbed, and shivered.

Rrrrrroooooaaaaarrrrr!

Cold, misty air assaulted my face. The roaring rattled my eardrums and had the earth shuddering beneath my feet.

We were gonna be crushed! Shattered! Broken into a million pieces!

I scrabbled at the cinch, accidentally clawing Abby Normal's belly. "God-fucking...*finally*!" The strap came loose with a low *cling*.

I shoved at the saddle, letting it and all my supplies crash to the ground.

Shadowy darkness enveloped us.

Everyone screamed.

The wave, only feet away now, was tall enough to *block the freaking sun.*

It was like something from a cheesy popcorn disaster flick: a scene too preposterous to be real.

But it *was* real. In T-minus five seconds, we'd be underwater.

And more than half the group were still in their shackles, struggling to break free.

"GET OUT OF THE CHAINS!" I bellowed again.

There was nothing else I could do.

As the wave rushed toward us, I wrapped my arms around Abby Normal's neck, burrowing my face into her mane and clinging onto her with every ounce of strength I had.

Icy water *pinged* off my armor and soaked through the cracks to bite at my skin. I howled, bracing for impact.

It never came.

The *rrrrooooooarrrr* still battered my ears. Small droplets continued to *plonk* off my armor. But there was no pain. No pressure. No broken bones.

Was I already dead? Bim, bam, pulverized Addie?

"My word," Deborah breathed.

"It...it...*stopped*," Nathan stuttered.

I cracked an eye open, glimpsed the rolling turquoise wall two inches from my face, and shrieked, *"Holy mother-fucking shit!"*

My lovely falsetto juddered the wall.

Abby Normal jumped. Several other people cursed at me.

"Bloody hell, Addie," Deborah snapped.

"Ye cad...were ye tryin' to stop me heart?" Braxton hollered.

"Sorry! It's...that's...it..." In front of me, the monstrously high wave had...*frozen*. Water still churned. It still rumbled and frothed. But it stayed in one spot, as though it'd been encased in glass, doomed to tumble around in an endless stationary loop. "It *stopped*?"

"Looks like it," Deborah said.

I turned to the group, saw the sea of pale, dumfounded faces staring back at me, and laughed nervously. "I'm assuming this is a first for y'all too, right?"

To which I received a babble of scoffs, curses, and a dismissive, "What do you think?"

"Thought so," I mumbled.

In front of me, the stagnant wave gave a particularly unhappy grumble and spewed fizzy white foam on me and Abby Normal. She trembled when the water globbed over her rump. "It's alright, Abs." I stroked her neck. "It's...I mean, it's freaky as fuck. But it's kinda pretty."

She billowed and flashed me an incredulous side-eye.

But the wave *was* stunning, with the way the aquamarine water glimmered and rolled. And, because I was me, I had to touch it, if only to confirm this off-the-wall-bonkers sight was real.

I gingerly prodded the wall. The rushing water zipped over my fingers with a *bzzzt*. "Heh. That's cool!"

I poked it again. And again. And a third time.

Bzzzt. Bzzzt. Bzzzt.

"Damn, this is *trippy*. A regular psychedelic nightmare. Think there are fish stuck in there?" I poked my whole pointer finger into the water, squealing when the pressure damn near bent the digit backward.

Abby Normal pinned her ears back.

"Because if there *are* fish, the poor bastards are probably —*gaaaaaahhhhh!*"

A figure *poofed* out of the wave.

Not a fish. A tall, studly hunk of a man.

No. Worse. A tall, studly hunk of a *Celestial*.

Was this Hurleigh?

Or did another Celestial have the power to call in a biblical wave?

I staggered back.

Behind me, people screamed.

Abby Normal was *done*. She roared and curled her lips over her fangs. The pupils of her eyes were so dilated, nearly all the red had vanished. And her ears laid so flat, they seemed to have sunk into her skull.

As the Celestial raised his head, sweeping a glistening curtain of chocolate-brown hair over his bare (and very muscular) shoulders, Abby Normal lunged.

"No! Abs!" I snatched at the reins.

She ripped them out of my hands and bulldozed

forward.

My blood turned to ice as she lowered her head and sank her fangs into the Celestial's thigh.

He didn't flinch. Just unfurled his glistering wings and used the left one to bash Abby Normal across the face.

She flew back with a pained wail.

"Abs! *Stop*!" I grabbed her bit when she coiled, readying herself to strike again.

At my intrusion, she screamed and rammed her shoulder into me, sending me spiraling sideways, where my feet collided with my discarded saddle. Down I went, my ass *thwapping* against the dead grass and my neck cracking as my head snapped back. "*Urrrrghh*, fuck! Ouch!"

The saddle flopped over my calves, the bullwhip unraveling and draping across my lap. I snagged it, my fingers digging into the handle as I hauled myself back to my feet.

"*Abs*!" I cried when Abby Normal charged at the Celestial, fangs blazing.

"*Enough*!" The Celestial pummeled her with his wing again, hard enough to open a jagged wound on her brow.

She sucked back, shaking her head, looking dazed.

The Celestial swiped at his ass-hugging black pants, stuck his fingers through the holes she'd gouged into the fabric, and shot Abby Normal a disdainful stare.

I scooted in front of her, raising the bullwhip.

The Celestial rolled his crystal-blue eyes over me. "That will not harm me," he said. "And your hands are unpracticed in the art of weapon wielding."

As if to prove his point, he flicked his wing at me.

Instinct had me cracking that bullwhip. It made an awful *zooosh-snap* as it wailed on the wing, knocking a bunch of feathers loose—then the tip of the whip bounced back and *clinked* off my torso. "Son of a *bitch*." The impact rattled my armor and had my bum shoulder cursing up a blue streak in protest.

The Celestial still didn't flinch, even when a tuft of colorful feathers fluttered to my feet.

Royal blue. Olive green. Sienna brown.

Peacock-colored feathers.

They were *stunning*.

As was he. Finely chiseled muscles rippled across his broad, bare chest. He had the kinda face that made poets weep, with his perfectly squared jaw, cleft chin, and sky-blue eyes. And the *hair...hmm*. The things I could *do* with that hair. Those chocolatey strands sopped with water, but they looked like they'd dry into artfully tousled waves.

Why were the Celestials so flipping gorgeous?

"You." The Celestial glowered at me. "Remove your helmet."

To which I responded, very maturely, "Make me— *oooofff*."

His wing trounced my head, cracking my neck back and knocking the helmet off.

"Oi! You bloody bastard!" Deborah shouted.

"Addie! Get down!" Braxton yelled.

I flinched and ducked half a second before a knife whooshed over my shoulder, followed immediately by a whizzing rock. They'd both gotten very, *very* close to clocking me in the head.

The Celestial sloped backward, gracefully avoiding both objects. They hurtled into the water, making that *bzzzt* sound as they punctured the wave.

He didn't look surprised by the sudden attack, or angered, as he rolled his wing in a shrug. "Should you wish to impersonate a Wraith," he said, keeping his baby blues locked on me, "you should not show such outward care toward your beast." He jutted his chin toward Abby Normal, who screamed and walloped her forehooves into the ground.

"We were about to get flattened by a wave," I snarled. "I didn't see the point in pretending anymore."

"Had you not traveled under the guise of a Wraith, I would not have created the wave." The Celestial did a full-on *Matrix* move, twisting his spine into a U-shape to avoid another oncoming knife. "Peace, humans!" He raised his hands, palms flat. "I mean you no harm."

"And why should we believe that?" I snapped.

"If I wanted you dead, I would've let the water finish its work."

I glanced at the behemoth wave. "Touché. But, y'know, the last Celestial I met wrecked an entire city for the heck of it. So forgive me if I don't buy your '*I come in peace*' spiel."

The Celestial gave a slow, bored shrug. "It matters not if you believe or disbelieve my words. You'll not be harmed either way. I have no liking for humans but no qualms against them, either."

Excitement suddenly swilled in my belly, duking it out with the anxiety that had reigned supreme for the last few weeks. Because this *was* him. It had to be. "So, you're Hurleigh, huh?" I asked.

The Celestial narrowed his eyes, studying me. "I am," he drawled.

I wasn't sure if my gurgling burp was due to my acidic stomach, or if saying the name had tickled my funny bone. Hurleigh. Like *hurling*. Like what I felt pretty damn close to doing right now. *Har, har, har.*

"Hurleigh?" Shay, one of the few people who'd shimmied out of the chains, stumbled forward.

I moved over, blocking him from Hurleigh's view.

"I-I know the name," Shay said dazedly. "During the first war, you took the humans from Daigh and Idril and brought them to Sakar. My ma was with child with me. She would've died if she'd stayed in Keld. You saved her. And me."

Hurleigh inclined his head but never took his eyes off me.

"Hang on...God, there are *so many* freaking names...Are those places or people?" I asked.

"Places," Shay supplied.

At the same time, Hurleigh said, "They are the kingdoms and cities of Uchen."

"Okay. And what is Uken?"

"Uchen," Shay corrected.

"Whatever."

"It is the last of the old world," Hurleigh said, "and the future that awaits Sakar."

Which explained exactly nothing. Until he added the next juicy tidbit...

"It is also the home of Ramiel."

"Oooh, so it's enemy territory?"

Hurleigh said nothing for a beat. Just studied me, his eyes burning a hole into my cheeks.

"There was once a time," he finally said, "when we were able to keep Ramiel and his zealot followers contained in Uchen." He stepped forward, letting his colorful, water-logged wings trail on the ground behind him. "We were ordered to bring what humans we could to Sakar, and my brethren were commanded to guard each coastal city. Ellard at Darfield. Me at Muirin. Gula at Ilragorn. And Zaphyr at Laewaes."

Hurleigh stepped forward again. And again. Closer to me. He seemed to not give a fuck about anyone else; he hadn't even looked at them.

My ears made that *whomp-whomp-whomp* noise again. The way Hurleigh looked, moved, spoke...it was eerie. Too fluid, graceful, and painfully beautiful. He was artificial; an alien, all dappered up in human skin.

My hands shook, but I forced my feet to be still, refusing to back away from him.

Hurleigh slunk closer, continuing his rambling history lesson. "When Ellard fell, we remained steadfast, as Raphael bid us to. Then he abandoned us. Upon realizing Raphael would not return to these lands, Gula and Zaphyr fled. I am the last of my brethren to maintain my post, although I was not able to prevent Muirin's destruction." He said this in a blasé tone. Like, *"A city fell and thousands died. But, y'know, oops."*

His nose crinkled as though he'd caught a whiff of something putrid.

Behind me, several people gave pointed coughs—the kind I sometimes got when something stupid or snarky tumbled out of my mouth.

Fuck.

I ground my teeth into my tongue.

This goddamn world needed to invent duct tape. Or Ativan. Or both.

"Before you," Hurleigh continued after a prolonged pause, "there are only ruins."

"We, uh..." A craggy ball of fear rolled down my throat. "We know, but we were heading this way to look for *you*. And then you found us! So that's convenient, right?"

He blinked owlishly and crept forward again, fully invading my personal space now. "My role may have been reduced to mere folly," he said, "but I will perform my duties until I have been recalled to the city. No Celestial or Wraith will pass from Uchen through Muirin. And no Wraith will ferry humans to Uchen through my post. I apologize for threatening your lives..."

"Dude, who are you kidding? You don't sound *sorry*."

"But I initially believed you to be a Wraith. And I reacted accordingly." He tapped a cold and slimy finger against my chin in an (almost) affectionate boop.

I snapped my head back.

He cocked his head as though confused, even though his face showed zero emotion.

"So, let me get this straight," I said. "You sent this big-ass wave to take out *one* Wraith? It's a bit overdramatic, don't ya think?"

"I must return to my post." Hurleigh turned, ignoring my snide question. "Should you still wish to enter the ruins of Muirin, you will have safe passage from here on. But be warned: you will find no solace there."

He raised his wings, flicked more water off his feathers, and *poofed*.

There one second. Gone the next.

His wave gave a trumpeting roar that left my hair standing on end and had several people behind me shrieking in panic. But then it retreated and shrank. The white caps steamed toward the darkening clouds, while the water seeped into the ground until there was nothing but a long stretch of dewy grass and a few sodden bushes. No flooding, puddles, or miles of wreckage. The elephantine body of water had vanished into thin air.

For a few seconds, or minutes, we all stood there gawping.

I was about 80 percent sure I'd pissed myself...maybe 90 percent. Thank *God* my armor wouldn't show any wet marks.

And a few others were probably in the same boat. Braxton wobbled and hit the deck. Shay started hurling (like Hurleigh...har, har, har). A whole cluster of people cursed and made these weird *eeeeeee* sounds, as though trying to suck air through a straw. Mr. Lump-on-a-log (aka, the useless cad who'd teleported out of the chains and left everyone else to die) had a vacant *"hurrr, who am I?"* look on his face as he watched the rolling clouds.

Even Abby Normal, standing several feet behind me, her head raised so high that she probably couldn't see anything over the flaring tip of her nostrils, trembled and made soft, scared coos.

Surprisingly, I was *not* the first one to speak.

That award went to Braxton.

"I told ye the guise was brilliant." His cackle would have put the Wicked Witch of the West to shame. "We fooled a feckin' *Celestial!*"

CHAPTER 19

LET'S GO TO THE BEACH

Braxton laughed. And *laughed.* He sounded like the Mad Hatter on an acid trip.

"What the *fuck*, Braxton?" I whirled to him but stopped short as a tight, slithery sensation fizzled in my throat. A trapped scream. Or a bubble of gas. Or puke. I legitimately didn't know what would come out of my mouth if I opened it. So, I clamped it shut, then smacked my hand over it for good measure.

Braxton kept cackling.

A man with bushy brown eyebrows (named Royce, or Reece, or something close to that) gave Braxton an irritated shove. "There's naught *funny* about this. I near soiled my trousers."

"I shite mine." Braxton flopped onto his side with another burst of hysterical giggling.

A few other people, who all looked queasy and shell-shocked, gave him wild *"dude, are you on crack?"* kinda side-eyes.

I swallowed once. Twice. Three times. The rising feeling

slowly subsided, but I kept my hand clamped over my mouth as I spoke. "Stop laughing, Braxton. You're scaring everyone."

"Ach." Braxton wiped at his teary eyes. "Belanna would've been *tickled* to have seen this."

And then he started bawling.

"Right...well..." I cautiously lowered my hand from my mouth so I could be heard over his blubbering. "I think we can give up the gimmick now. The Wraiths won't come this way. Not if they know they'd be flattened by Poseidon's wave."

"The Celestial is named Hurleigh," Nathan pointed out.

I scrubbed both hands over my face. "Never mind. Just... get rid of the chain, okay? Y'all sucked at the emergency release, and I'm not taking that chance again. Does anyone need help busting out?"

"I do," said an older woman with sophisticatedly grayed caramel hair. Seriously, she had perfectly placed gray streaks that more resembled stylish highlights than the dreaded old lady wisps. "Older," of course, was a relative term. She was a spry and fit woman in her fifties, but that was basically Methuselah age in Sakar.

"It's...Natalie? Right?" I asked as I walked to her side.

"Natalia," she corrected.

"Right. Sorry. I used to be a lot better with names. Before Sakar broke my brain. Anyway, let's see where you're stuck."

For Natalia, and eight others, it was all about the angles. The half opening in the shackle was so narrow, they could only slide their wrists out if they twisted them *just right* through the slot.

Which was not a good thing when people were in sloppy panic mode.

Thank Christ no one had gotten hurt.

"That was a close call, huh?" I prattled to a beefy man named Hugo. Who, despite his Herculean six-foot-seven frame, trembled harder than a dead leaf. I had to work to get his wobbly wrists through the opening.

He said nothing to me. And, once his hands were free, he smacked them over his chest as though trying to contain his racing heart.

I knew that gesture well.

"You okay there?" I asked.

He loosed a wheezing cough.

"Hmmm...'kay. You're definitely *not* okay. How 'bout you sit down for a bit? Or...yeah. I mean, I guess that works," I muttered when Hugo did a painful looking back-flop that left him lying spread-eagle across the grass. "You didn't hurt yourself falling like that, though, did you?"

He shook his head and closed his eyes, drawing slow, measured breaths through his puckered lips.

"Alrighty, then." I rubbed the back of my neck, made sure everyone else was safely out of the shackles, and then I pivoted to Mr. Lump-on-a-log, who was still lumping on his proverbial log (aka, sitting and looking miserable AF with his head between his knees). "Hey! You!" I called as I strode to him. "I've got a bone to pick with you, pal. You can *fucking teleport*? And you didn't think to beam anyone else outta here?"

The man raised his head, looked at me, and...

Yeah, I immediately felt crappy for yelling at him. Because he *looked* crappy. His amber-colored eyes were all red and puffy, and he kept taking these uneven *heee-hurrr* breaths. "I'm not much of a Traveler—" *heee* "anymore. The older I get—" *hurrr* "the harder—" *heee* "it is to stabilize."

His hands shook as he ran them through his gray-speckled blond hair.

Welp. Now I felt *extra* lousy. "Getting old sucks, don't it?"

He nodded glumly.

"Well...look, I'm sorry I snapped at you...er...what's your name again?"

"Darragh." He shook so hard, his teeth clanked.

"Darragh. Got it. For now, anyway. Can't guarantee I won't forget. But one of these days, I *will* remember all your names. Scout's honor. Are you gonna be okay to walk?"

"Yes." But he made no immediate move to stand.

"Well, if you need help, shout," I said. "We made it this far. I don't want any of you dropping dead in the home stretch. Got it?" Once he made an affirmative *hmmm-hurrr*, I called out to Abby Normal, who stood a few feet away, warily watching the horizon. At my beckon, she trotted over to me but never pulled her gaze away from where the wave had disappeared.

"Abs, you badass bitch. You took a good piece out of that Celestial, huh?" My fingers quivered as I stroked the shallow slice on her brow. The yawning hollow in my chest deepened. *Darkened.* A black hole, ready to swallow me up. But I forced myself to put on a chipper front as I trilled, "Alright, y'all, let's go to the beach."

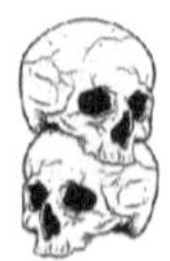

WHEN WE FINALLY ARRIVED AT MUIRIN TWO DAYS LATER, WE found ourselves crossing the border into a cheery little seaside town. Cozy Victorian style homes lined the streets. Cute shops sold overpriced T-shirts and the same ten decorations you saw in *every single beach house* ("Life is better at the shore!"). And a golden beach encircled the city. It was a nice, relaxing place to rest after riding the highway to Hell.

Bahaha. *As-fucking-if.*

Muirin—the *real* Muirin, not my imagined paradise—felt and looked like the last precipice at the end of the world.

Long rows of blackened and bedraggled buildings greeted us at the end of our journey. Surprisingly, most of them still stood erect, despite having been pretty thoroughly fucked (har, har), but they were a sorry sight as their gnarled walls creaked and groaned in the wind. Pieces of charred wood scattered across the ground, jutting from beneath the sandy soil. And clusters of skeletal trees decorated the area, their gray, spindly limbs looking like bony fingers stretching toward the heavens.

"I mean...." I cringed as I stood between Abby Normal and Braxton, watching the rest of our group solemnly survey the shit-pile town. "There is still some real estate value here, y'know? The ocean views are stunning."

Braxton made a noncommittal *hmmph.*

But the view was genuinely *gorgeous.*

Muirin sat atop a cliff overlooking a shoreline. There were no golden waves of sand here, though. A gray, gritty blanket of stone covered the beach, and the boulders zigzagging beneath the cliffs seemed almost malevolent—as though great, hulking monsters were lying in wait, eager to consume us piddly humans.

But the *ocean*...my God, the ocean.

Beneath a cloud-heavy sky, the deep-turquoise sea churned furiously, sending house-sized waves to pummel the shore. Plumes of white foam glittered in the air when-ever the sea collided with the land.

Wooooosh, smack, rooooaaarrrr.

It sounded like an angry beast.

It was as beautiful as it was terrifying.

"Looks like high tide," Braxton commented.

"I sure hope so," I mumbled. "If this was *low* tide, I'd've hated to see what the next level up looked like."

Wooooooshhhh. Roooaaaarrr.

A titanic wave body-slammed the rocks, spitting hissing foam into the air.

And then the wind whistled from the ocean, slicing its bitter cold right down to my bones. I shivered and hissed when the quakes sent fresh pulses of pain shooting along my bum shoulder.

I'd shed my fake armor as soon as we waltzed into this ghost town. And my blue/pink shirt was very well insulated. Better, even, than the jacket I'd worn when I crash-landed in Sakar.

But I would've almost, *almost*, been willing to trade this shirt for a parka. It was *that* cold.

*Whoooooooo...*another gust of wind wailed in our ears.

Beside me, Braxton grunted and rubbed at his arms.

The rest of our crew, pale and tired from the trauma they'd been through, stiffened. Some huffed into their hands to keep their fingers warm. Some started picking up pieces of wood and popping them into piles, like they were trying to tidy the place. Their efforts were pretty well wasted, but it kept them moving. Kept them from thinking about how fucking freezing it was, being this close to the coast at the start of winter.

They'd bundled in whatever clothing we'd been able to

scavenge from Swindon. Most wore two heavy wool shirts. A few lucky ducks had cloaks wrapped around their shoulders. It wasn't enough. Not really.

The only one *not* bothered by the cold was Abby Normal. She stood beside me on the edge of the cliff, her mane waving like a flag, her ears pricked and eyes bright as she watched the ocean. She didn't even flinch when I pressed my cold hands to her shoulder. Unfortunately, her scaly skin didn't emanate much warmth. But I leaned against her anyway, listening to the steady *whuff* of her breaths and trying to ignore the ache in my shoulder and the too-full feeling in the back of my throat, as though I'd ingested a rock that got lodged in my windpipe.

"It'll be dark soon." Braxton turned his head to the dreary, cloud-laden sky. "And rain's comin'...likely not tonight, mind. But tomorrow for certain. Mayhap we should work on securin' one of these buildings."

"What about Hurleigh?" I watched as a beefy wave impaled itself on the rocks, splattering its innards into the air. "Should we, I dunno, call for him?" Would he even hear us?

Or was he chilling down on that seabed below our cliffs, staring at us, trying to decide if we were worthy of his presence?

"He likely knows we're here," Braxton said. "I suppose he'll show himself when he's ready."

"*If* he's ready," I mumbled.

"Aye."

I gulped once. Twice. No amount of spit would budge the lump hanging out at the back of my throat.

Here we were. Trapped in these bleak, unlivable ruins.

We had nowhere to go, few supplies, and barely any protection against the elements.

And Hurleigh was ignoring us.

"If Hurleigh is not there, or if he refuses to help, you'll need to choose whether to stay for winter and find shelter amongst the debris..."

Cheriour had known this would happen.

He'd been visibly agitated when he told me about Hurleigh and Muirin and had fretted over me leaving because he *knew* I wasn't likely to return. But he'd hoped (as had I) this Hail Mary would work.

I missed him. So, *so* fucking much. Every time I dozed off, I dreamed of him. Not wet dreams—although a few got pretty spicy. Most were...*sweet*. And simple. I'd dream of holding his hand as we walked through a town, sitting in a field beside him, my head resting against his shoulder as he sketched, or lying next to him in bed, watching him sleep.

Some of these scenes were fragments of memories. Some were hopes of a future I didn't dare to wish for. They were all torturous.

Because I'd never see him again.

I wouldn't be riding the wave of success back to Sanadrin and declaring everyone saved. The mission had failed.

And the worst part?

I'd dragged these people here to die with me. Out on this cold, dreary, desolate cliff.

Tears slid down my cheeks.

The wind ripped them away.

CHAPTER 20
GLISTERING SEX CURLS

I hoped Hurleigh would prove me wrong. That he'd descend from the heavens the next morning, in all his bare-chested glory, and go, *"Humans! Bow down and pray, for I have come to free thee from thy tribulations."*

(No idea where the weirdly religious "lord and savior" monikers were coming from.)

He didn't.

He didn't arrive the next day, either. Or the day after. Or the day after that.

I even leaned into my odd "religious text" imaginings and tried praying to him. "Oh hail the mighty peacock-feathered Celestial. I beseech you to get your head out of your divine ass and come talk to me. Please?" This usually got shouted over the cliff's edge.

I couldn't *imagine* why it didn't work.

And my blood boiled whenever I pictured him chilling... wherever Celestials chilled (The clouds? The ocean?) and watching us panic-scramble to build a shelter. All while he kept his prayer phone on silent.

295

This was probably *entertainment* for him. Reality TV. *Extreme Makeover: Equipmentless Sakarian Edition.*

Seriously, we had *nothing*. No tools. Very few weapons. No food. Animals were scarce out here. We had no nets for fishing. And our resident Gardner only had Neem, hibiscus, and chamomile seeds left, which were edible but, woof, the gas pains from wolfing down raw flowers were *rough*.

To make matters worse, mother nature was PMSing. Big Time. Each day dawned gray, cold, and windy. Rain fell intermittently, sometimes spitting flecks of cold water on us, sometimes dumping buckets over our heads.

Our first order of business was getting shelter ASAP.

Deborah, thankfully, turned out to have some architectural knowledge. Because, as she'd seethed more than once, "I built my house with my own hands. Placed every stone and plank myself. Raised my children there. Until the Wraiths drove us out."

She didn't talk much about her kids and never went into detail about what had happened to her family. But the steely look in her eye spoke volumes.

She picked a roofless, rectangular barn to salvage for shelter.

"It's still strong." She smacked the timber walls to emphasize her point. "But we'll need to get it covered."

So, for three days, we tore half-burnt wood from the other buildings, scavenged for bits of rope, built hammers out of stones and sticks, and started building.

Well...everyone else did the building. With my bum shoulder, I was only good for holding down planks of wood while someone else hammered.

And we made progress. Solemn, quiet progress. No one had the heart to joke or exchange crass stories. Not even me.

Because arriving at our destination and realizing Hurleigh had *no* interest in helping us…it'd puffed the happy-go-lucky wind out of everyone's sails.

We were doomed.

Sakar was almost kaput.

None of us could fix that.

So we focused on what we *could* fix.

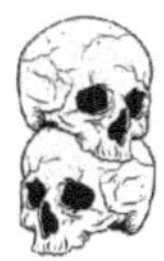

THE STORM CAME IN LIKE A WRECKING BALL (HAR, HAR, HAR) AND blindsided us.

Ten minutes before, the sun had been shining as we mashed the last few shingles over our newly formed barn roof.

Then a gust of wind came through, blew a bunch of dark clouds over us, and *bam*.

Thunder *exploded*. Like a firecracker going off over our heads.

"Fuck me!" I hissed when the loud clap made my ears ring. "We finished this in the nick of freaking time, huh?"

I'd been working atop the roof with the golden-eyed Darragh, who was nice enough, even if I didn't love having him wielding a rock hammer near my hands—not when he constantly had to fight to keep himself from *poofing* (or Traveling, as he called it). Because whenever he lost that fight, he tended to drop whatever he was holding.

My fingers had already had several close calls with that hammer.

This poor guy had definitely gotten the short end of the hybrid stick. His power seemed *awful*. And *painful*.

As lightning sizzled across the sky, Darragh flinched and contorted his upper body, like he was trying to slither out of a tight-bound rope. "I suppose we'll find out if this'll hold." His leg jerked, driving the heel of his boot into the roof.

Boom-crack-zzzzaaaapppp.

My hair stood on end as another jagged bolt zig-zagged across the sky. I *felt* the electricity rising off that sucker.

Darragh jumped about a foot into the air and...

Kerthunk.

His hammer clattered to the roof, *centimeters* away from my hands, as he *poofed* to the ground.

It was a freaking miracle I still had ten fingers.

"Thanks for waiting, bud," I called.

I immediately regretted the snark when he threw an ashen-faced grimace in my direction and muttered, "Apologies."

"Right...well..." I pressed my bum arm more securely to my chest as I shimmied toward the edge of the roof. "We should *all* go inside. Before we get three million volts straight to the heart." *Whoosh*...I slid off the slanted edge, hopping when my feet hit the ground too hard, and crashed into Braxton.

"'Lo there, Addie." He grabbed my good shoulder to steady me. "This'll be a bad one—"

Shhhhhiiiisssssshhhh. Another frizzing bout of lightning careened overhead. And the sky looked *really* funky, with big purplish clouds corkscrewing over the ocean.

My stomach tightened.

The howling wind ripped my hair out of its braid and

whipped the strands across my face. "We might end up in Oz by the end of this storm," I said.

"Eh?" Braxton mumbled.

Clearly, he was not as well read as his sister had been. "Never mind. Just...we've gotta bunker down."

With another rumbling bout of thunder, the purple-painted heavens opened, and sweeping curtains of rain cascaded down. The frigid droplets felt more like prickly needles of ice than globs of water.

"*Now*," I added. "We've gotta bunker down now! Yo!" I cupped my hands around my mouth so the people scattered around the town could hear my shout. "Get inside!"

"I'm nearly finished!" Aria complained. She'd been in the middle of hacking at a log with a serrated piece of rock.

The wind screamed and barreled into me, making my shoulder *pound* with pain. "You can finish it later!" I called. "I don't want anyone getting fried by the lightning."

A bolt vroomed across the sky, punctuating my words. And another roar of thunder rumbled the earth.

That got people moving.

"Where's Abs?" I turned, squinting against the lashing rain. "*Abs*! Oh...thank God," I said when she trotted through the deluge. "I didn't want you to blow away."

"For feck's sake," Braxton snarled, "does yer Púca have to bring *that*?"

Abby Normal came to a halt beside me, holding a rigid seagull by the foot. Its wings were draped over its head, stiffly wobbling back and forth in the wind.

"She's gotta eat," I said. "And we killed a seagull the other day..."

"Aye. We *killed* it. That one's still *alive*. If ye had to hear that animal's pain…" Braxton smacked his hands against his temple, trying to quiet the voices in his head.

My coping method for Abby Normal's hunting had always been "out of sight, out of mind." I looked away when she hunted and pretended she killed the animals she caught.

Poor Braxton didn't have that luxury.

I touched Abby Normal's waterlogged mane as I walked with her to the barn. "Eat that thing fast, Abs," I muttered. "Or Braxton might eat you."

The slanted barn door barely hung on its misaligned hinges. The first people to go inside had to open the door *very gingerly* and hold it tightly to keep the wind from kidnapping it. And the doorway, despite the wide expanse of the barn, was a narrow squeeze. Abby Normal dinged her hip on the frame when I led her through.

"Be proud of those hips, girlfriend," I laughed when she loosed an indignant squeal.

Once through the tight threshold, she had more room to maneuver. Not much, though. In the center, where the raftered ceiling arched to its highest point, Abby Normal only had a few inches of clearance. But the twelve people already inside were jamming up the center, and the interior décor (aka, the jumbled stacks of rubble) made it hard for me to pick a clear path to skirt around everyone. *Especially* since I couldn't see for shit inside the dark building.

"Sorry, Abs," I mumbled when I veered too far off course and thumped her head against one of the rafters.

"You brought the Púca in here?" Marcus walked in behind us, pinching his fingers over his nostrils to blow the rainwater (and big clods of snot) out of his sinuses.

"Yup," I said. "I'm not leaving her out in that storm."

As if emphasizing my point, Abby Normal grunted and shook the water out of her mane, spraying Hugo in the face as he tried to sidle past us.

"Isn't it a bit tempting?" Hugo warily eyed Abby Normal as he swiped the water off his chin. "To put her in an enclosed space with us?"

"She's got her snack." I jabbed a finger at the stiff seagull.

"Still...I'd restrain her," he said. "As a precaution."

A few other people hummed and nodded.

"I agree." This came from the sprightly Shay, who'd popped a squat against the right-side wall. "For her safety too. Horses can be jumpy in these storms."

A clap of thunder echoed overhead.

Shay jolted. So did several others.

Abby Normal didn't even flinch.

"Oh, yeah." I rolled my eyes. "*She's* the jumpy one. But... fine...*whatever*." I pinched the bridge of my nose. "I'll tie her up for tonight if that makes you all happy. Although you guys are getting worked up about the wrong thing. You know how much her poop stinks? Yeah. Imagine how toxic it's gonna be when she fires off in an enclosed space."

Abby Normal twisted her head in a "*Bitch...wtf? My poo don't stink, I'm a lady*" kinda look.

Then she blew big blood bubbles out the corner of her mouth.

As everyone else filed into the barn, I led Abby Normal to the back of the building, weaving her through support beams, clusters of people, heaps of debris, and around the stone firepit, where Deborah crouched, chaffing two sticks together.

A single spark flashed in the darkness, and a cold sweat prickled down my back, but the flame gagged on the damp wood and snuffed out.

Deborah cursed.

I fought the urge to emit a *phew* of relief.

We needed the fire to chase some of the frigidness away. I knew that. But I had zero faith the dinky hole in the ceiling (aka, our chimney) would properly vent the smoke out of the barn.

So I kept my gaze turned away from the firepit as I shuffled Abby Normal against the farthest pillar. "Alrighty." I uncoiled her bridle from where it had been lying in a tangled heap over my hastily discarded saddle. "Welcome to the Craptastic Hotel, Abs. Now, if you'll allow me to remove your jacket"—I wriggled the stiff seagull out of her mouth—"I'll slip ya into something cozy."

If looks could kill...*whew, man.* I'd've been six feet under from the one she flashed at me as I pulled her bridle over her head.

"Yeah, the accommodations are shitty, huh?" I tied the reins to the knobbly wooden pillar. "It's only for tonight, Abs. Feel free to one-star us tomorrow."

She angrily snatched the seagull off the ground and shimmied sideways, angling her head away from me.

Outside, the wind screamed. Around us, the walls groaned and shuddered. Cold, wet air seeped through the slats where warped pieces of wood didn't quite butt against each other.

Christ. And we were *all* crammed into this flimsy building. When the storm bowled it over, it'd wipe us all out at once.

Even if the walls held, Deborah's fire could still smoke-bomb the inside.

Maybe we would've been safer outside...

Deborah *tskked* and wagged her finger at me, very Dennis from *Jurassic Park* style (*"Uh-uh-uh, you didn't say the magic word."*) "Don't be thinking that way," she scolded.

Another explosion burst overhead, this one so loud, so close, it shook the ground. The walls made a strangled *uuuurrrggghhh.*

"Yeah," I said. "How silly of me to worry. This place is made of iron. It will not bend, burn, or break..."

"Parts of it may break." Deborah shrugged, even as she cast her eyes toward the ceiling, her hands flexing around her kindling stick. "But I chose a sturdy building, Addie. It will hold."

"Say that again...but *without* the hand-wringing and worried side-eyes," I said.

"It will hold." She repeated the words. *And* all her nervous twitches.

"Sure." My voice oozed sarcasm.

Thunder struck again. And again. And again.

Abby Normal snorted. A few people jumped or made low, frightened sounds, but no one spoke.

Boom. Boom. Boom.

God, why was there so much thunder? I'd *never* heard a storm like this before. The sky barely got a breath in between its explosive shouts. The rain pelted the barn so hard, it sounded more like hail. It was too loud. Too close.

Boom. Boom. Thunk!

My head whipped toward the left wall.

That last sound had *not* been thunder. Had not been rain.

Something had hit the side of the barn.

A wave?

No. It was too sharp to be a wave. Too *precise*. It sounded almost like...

Thunk!

With a great, wet squeak, the rickety door at the other end burst open, sending a rush of frigid air into the barn.

And there he was: our lord and savior in the flesh, his dewy bare chest and gleaming washboard abs shining through the darkness. "You've done admirable work." Hurleigh closed the door behind him and gave his wings a vigorous shake, blasting everyone within a six-foot radius with water. "Especially given the *limited capabilities* of your species."

"You've gotta be kidding me," I grumbled.

Behind me, Abby Normal spat out her seagull and screamed. But she didn't thrash or lunge for him this time. Instead, she stood statue-still, her head brushing the rafters as her breath roared through her nostrils.

"Dude, do you own a shirt?" I snapped at Hurleigh.

Deborah turned to me with a raised brow and smacked her stick against her thigh. A warning.

"I find human clothing restrictive," Hurleigh deadpanned.

"I'm sure ya do. With all those bulging muscles of yours," I said.

Boom. Boom. Boom.

The thunder almost banged in time with my racing heart.

Hurleigh strolled in a lazy half circle around the first cluster of people, his nose wrinkling when they scuttled away from him. And then he surveyed the walls, making long *hmmmmmsss.*

Oh, he and Cheriour were *definitely* related.

Except Cheriour's *hmmms* were sexy (most of the time). Hurleigh's were pretentious.

"Y'know…we could've rebuilt this *a lot* better with your help. I'm sure your capabilities aren't as *limited* as ours," I snapped.

Deborah cracked her stick again.

Hurleigh's head swiveled around with an odd, loose-lipped grin, the kinda face a baby made when it shat in its diaper. "You misunderstand me," he said. "I *admire* what your species can accomplish in such a short time. It's rudimentary, yes, but commendable all the same." He turned away from the walls, slicked his Sex Curls (aka, his glistering hair) off his shoulders, and strolled right up the center of the room, heading my way. Because *of fucking course* he would.

"Come with me," he said when he stopped.

His voice was polite, but the words had weight. The voice a trainer would use on a dog. *"Addie! Sit! Stay! Come!"*

Abby Normal billowed and flashed her fangs at him. "Stop, Abs." I pinched her shoulder. "Come with you… outside?" I asked Hurleigh.

He nodded.

"You're joking. Right? Do you *see* what's happening out there? It's…"

I let the rumble of thunder finish my sentence.

"It is the perfect time to speak," Hurleigh said. "For we shall not be seen."

And with that, he fluttered his wings, spraying water in my face, and *poofed* back to the door.

"Jerk." I swiped my sleeve over my chin.

"The storm shall not harm you." Hurleigh jerked his head, motioning for me to follow him, then stepped outside, sending another blast of glacial wind and rain into the barn.

"*God fucking damn it all to the fucking seventh circle of fucking hell!*"

Twenty-one sets of eyes followed me as I stomped up the barn aisle, muttering obscenities the whole way, and slipped out into the hurricane.

CHAPTER 21

JACK SPARROW SAUNTER

Outside was pure chaos.

Rain came down too hard and too fast. Water ran in rivers down my throat, flumed into the back of my nostrils, and flooded my sinuses. I sneezed once. Twice.

The downpour washed my snot away. Which was handy. No tissues needed.

Wind lashed and roared, pressing hard against my chest and shoving me backward. I couldn't see. Even when the gale shifted and my eyes weren't being pelted with rain, it was too damn dark. Sure, the flashes of lightning put everything in technicolor, but only for a second. It was like a strobe light: disorienting and blinding.

Hurleigh walked in front of me, his wings outstretched, as though basking in the torrent. He had no problem cutting through the storm.

I, on the other hand, pinged into *everything*. Rocks? I mashed my toes on them. Rubble? My knees bounced off it. Within seconds, my toes were throbbing, my right knee had developed a heady pulse, and I was *soaked*. The kinda wet that made you feel cold, slimy, and icky.

And I had no idea where I was walking *to*. Until lightning sizzled again, and I saw the mountainous waves of the ocean beyond the cliff's edge.

Oh, no. *Heck naw.*

Hurleigh stopped, turned, and gave an impatient jerk of his head.

A wave breeched the shore, its white caps spuming several feet into the air. "Absolutely not," I said, although the wind was so horrendous, it ripped the words out of my throat.

"I control the ocean." Hurleigh's voice was steady. The wind didn't have the power to silence him. "She does not control me."

"Well, whoop-de-doo for you!" I shouted. "But I ain't surviving if I get hit with one of those waves."

The next bolt of lightning zagged over the sea. In that split second, with the roiling waters turning a murky, angry green, and the blue of Hurleigh's eyes looking unnaturally bright against his otherwise shadowed face, I felt...

Small.

The ocean was so damn big. Hurleigh was so inhuman, so *powerful*. Next to the two of them, I was an ant, one that talked big game but was ultimately an insignificant pest that could be wiped out of existence with the barest flick of a finger.

"You do not need to fear the ocean whilst you are with me." Hurleigh turned and stepped off the edge of the cliff, dropping onto the flooded beach below. "The storm will not last all night," he called back up to me. "Don't dawdle."

I shimmied closer to the edge, squealing when a pop of

thunder and an incoming wave hit at the same time. The *roooooaaaaarrr-boooooom* rattled my insides.

That wave bludgeoned the shore, munched its way to the cliffs, and scarfed Hurleigh right up. But then it retreated, and he...*stood there*. As still as a fucking statue. The tide didn't move him. The onslaught of water hadn't fazed him. He merely glanced up at me with his head tilted and mouth pursed. Not impatient. Not yet. But getting there.

I spat out a mouthful of water before I spoke. "Can't we do this when the ocean isn't trying to Pac Man the entire goddamn town?"

"No."

"Why?"

"We are less likely to be seen this way," he said.

Another wave drummed against the beach. Hurleigh, his eyes never leaving my face, fluttered his wings and braced his bare feet against the top of the swell.

Literally *on top* of it.

The dude stood *on top of the water*!

He didn't sink. Didn't swim. Just stood in a casual crouch reminiscent of a surfer perched atop a board and allowed the receding tide to take him out to sea.

"What the—" The words jumbled in my throat.

Hurleigh, now a small spec out in the middle of a roiling ocean, back-stepped up the next surge. He rose, up and up and *up*, riding the swell of the surf as it shot toward land. When it crested and shattered against the shore, he rippled his wings again and gracefully levitated to the top of the cliff beside me. He got a brief *Little Mermaid* moment when lightning flashed and water plumed behind him.

"Erm...ahhh...you...*what?*" I sputtered.

The dude had *walked on water*.

Jesus Christ...pun *absolutely* intended.

I'd seen too much weird shit in Sakar. There wasn't any awe or disbelief left inside my cold, bitter, jaded soul. Only exasperation.

"Fuck this." I threw my hands over my head and turned. "I'm out."

"You'll die here," Hurleigh called. There was no hint of malice in his matter-of-fact voice.

But it felt like he'd slapped me.

"Excuse me?" I spun back around, spitting out another mouthful of water.

"You've not the provisions to last the winter here," he said. "My observations suggest humans need feedings three times a day..."

"*Feedings?* We're not livestock!"

"And you lack supplies to adequately feed once a day."

"We'll figure it out," I snapped.

"Winter is a mere breath away. There will be no foraging until spring. Many animals left this place long ago, and those that remain will soon flee to seek more favorable conditions. You'll die here," he repeated.

"Well, how sweet of you to worry." I tried to ignore the sticky, foul taste that curdled on my tongue at his words. *Tried.* "Are you gonna volunteer to help us out?"

"I *am* helping."

"Bringing me out here to drown or freeze to death in the middle of a hurricane is *not* helping. *Helping* would be using your Jesus skills to catch us some fish. Or putting those muscles to work and getting these ruined buildings back on their feet."

Hurleigh scoffed. Apparently, such menial tasks were beneath him.

My palm itched. I suddenly *really* wanted to smack that gorgeous face of his to kingdom come. But I ground my teeth until my jaw clicked and pain shot up the sides of my neck.

"The storm will end within the hour," Hurleigh continued, either not sensing my anger or not giving a fuck. "If you wish me to help you, we must move quickly."

He slid off the cliff's edge and landed on top of the water. *Again.* The surface wriggled slightly beneath his feet, as though he'd jumped onto a big, inflatable moon bounce.

I was 90 percent sure (maybe 100 percent) the only "help" I'd get tonight would be a quick death. But his words had hurt. *"You'll not survive the winter."* He was spot-on. I knew it. Everyone else did too. But we didn't talk about it.

Maybe a quick death was the best help any of us could get.

I peered down, my stomach sloshing in time with the waters below.

"You will not sink," Hurleigh said.

My toe skittered over the rocky edge, knocking a few pebbles loose. They spiraled over the cliff and straight into the barmy mouth of another ravenous wave.

Needles of fear pricked the inside of my stomach.

This was *fucking crazy!*

Those waves would eat me alive.

Hurleigh might've spritzed magical water-resistant pixie dust over the bottoms of his feet, but I hadn't. As soon as my feet touched that water, I'd sink. And get mashed against those rocks. And dragged out to sea...

"The storm will not wait for you to find the courage," Hurleigh droned as he bobbed innocuously on top of the wave.

"Fuck it all to fucking hell." I grit my teeth, swallowed against the sting of bile in my throat, and jumped.

"*Fuuuu—shooooo!*" My stomach lurched into my mouth as the ground vanished beneath my feet, and I plummeted straight into another spumy wave.

I screamed.

The fizzing water rose to meet me.

I squeezed my eyes shut, bracing to get dunked beneath the tide...

Instead, I bounced.

My ass hit first (the heaviest items *always* hit first) and I made an *ooo-uggh* when the surface beneath me wobbled and flicked me back into the air.

"Eeeeeeeeek!" I wailed on the ascent, pinwheeling my arms until pain jackhammered into my shoulder.

Down I went again, landing more softly this time and jouncing only a smidge before the surface settled.

Or, well, it settled as much as a storm-ravished ocean was capable of.

"What...the...*frick?*"

The water *bounced.*

Water is not supposed to fucking bounce!

But it did.

And the way it *felt* beneath my hands...

Yeech.

It reminded me of those clear stress balls, with a squishy, pliable outer membrane that kept the liquidy beads contained, even when you gave it a violent smoosh.

When I stood, the membrane dipped beneath the heel of my boot and snapped right back into place once I lifted my foot. "Whoa. This is...*oof.*" The tide rolled back out, swashing the water beneath me. The membrane still didn't give, but it weebled pretty good, and jiggling surfaces didn't help my shoddy balance. I tumbled and laughed when I bounced a half foot in the air. "Ha! Okay. This is really badass." I craned my neck toward Hurleigh, who'd been watching my (admittedly immature) display. "You, sir, have the coolest power in the land. Congratulations. But...*oooh* fuck...why is this getting higher?"

The water beneath me had swelled into a towering wave. Too high. *Fuck.* I could almost see over the top of the cliff...which was a few *dozen* yards away.

When had we gotten so far from shore?

How?

The water shifted, driving forward, ready to smash headlong into the cliffside.

So, it wouldn't be death by drowning after all. Naw. This was gonna be twice as painful. Death by clobbering.

"You will not die," Hurleigh droned.

"Wha—oooh, wait! You bastard!" I shouted when he did a jiggy slide down the other side of the wave, *away* from the shore, and *abandoned* me!

"Follow me," he called.

He didn't need to say it twice.

I wriggled down the other side of the wave and screamed when I landed in an uncoordinated heap at the bottom. "God-frigging-damn!" Pain fried my bad shoulder.

"We'll need to move quickly," Hurleigh said, padding his way across the water, not even bothering to help me up or look in my direction. "The ocean does not tolerate idleness on nights such as this."

"No shit," I grunted. Because, once again, water furled out as the ocean sucked in its breath, readying for another massive wave. I got to my feet, doing a weaving saunter that would've put Jack Sparrow to shame, and lurched after Hurleigh.

Up and up and up we went over the sea.

And down we slid on the other side, Hurleigh poised like a surfer balanced over his board, while I rolled like a pudgy panda. In between, we got a few seconds of somewhat steady terrain before the next wave began forming.

All the while, rain hammered us. Thunder never stopped rumbling. And the streaks of lightning got bigger.

The novelty of walking on water wore off pretty damn quick. Because it was exhausting. My thighs *burned*. The ache in my shoulder had sharpened into spindly teeth that gnawed at my nerve endings. And I had so much water up my nose, I couldn't stop sneezing.

We trudged along for hours. Days. *Weeks.*

It was probably only minutes.

But *seemed* like weeks.

"I shoulda taken the quick death..." I gasped at one point.

The waves changed as we moved farther, toward the center of the ocean. They were no longer towering monstrosities but rather (slightly) smaller, herky-jerky lumps.

Hurleigh stopped—not completely, but he wasn't gliding forward anymore, just shifting his feet up and down with the waves to keep them from pulling him back to shore.

He made it look so freaking effortless.

Meanwhile, I fell. Again. Almost got yanked back to shore with the tide. Caught back up to him. Tried to stand. Fell. Got hauled back. Lather. Rinse. Repeat.

"Can I hold your hand or something?" I seethed on the

fourth (or fifth, or sixth) time I fought to walk back to his side.

Hurleigh had watched me flounder and had said nothing. No offer of help. No *"hehe, stupid weak human, hehe"* remarks. Just that totally unreadable stare.

Like Cheriour's.

But worse.

Because Cheriour would've reached out a hand by now.

Hurleigh seemed content to watch me fail.

But when I snapped at him, he held out his hand. *Barely*. And he made *me* come to *him*. But, y'know, small mercies.

I clutched at his hot and slimy fingers until I was sure my knuckles would pop. But using him as an anchor didn't make things easier. I kept blundering as my feet skidded over the constantly shifting surface.

"You're struggling because you fight the ocean," Hurleigh said. "And she fights you back."

"Yeah, well," I wheezed, "she's a fucking bitch. And so am I."

His gaze remained on my face, even when I got into an almighty sneezing fit that threw me to my knees and had me white-knuckling his hand. "You realize that thousand-yard stare is creepy, right?" I sniffled.

But he didn't break his gaze. "Look to your left." He tilted his head. "What do you see?"

A tingle of fear tip-toed down my spine. "Is there a shark heading for us?"

"What do you see?" he repeated.

I didn't wanna look. Nope. We were out in the middle of the *ocean*. There were sharks, whales, squids, and...

Monsters?

What if the Loch Ness monster existed here? Or the Kraken?

"What do you see?" Hurleigh pressed.

Slowly, the low *dun-dun, dun-dun* of the *Jaws* theme jangling around in my brain, I turned and saw…

Roiling waters. And a shit ton of blackness. Nothing else. "Erm, there's nothing there…*oh*!" Lightning forked the sky, illuminating the jagged peaks of distant mountains.

Land.

There was *land* out there. Miles and miles of it.

"That," Hurleigh said, "is Uchen."

"*That's* enemy territory?"

This time, when lightning struck, I squinted and tried to suckle in every detail about that strip of land. But it was so shrunken by the distance, it might as well have been a piece of driftwood bobbing above the surface. And it was impossible to tell exactly how far away it was. It might've been a few yards or a few miles. It didn't really matter. The point was: enemy territory was *really* close to Muirin, separated only by a relatively narrow strip of ocean. And with the way the Celestials could *poof* anywhere they wanted…

"Ramiel and his ilk will not traverse the ocean," Hurleigh said. "Not anymore."

"Huh?"

"Earth weakens a Celestial's wings. The longer we remain here, the more their strength wanes."

"What does—"

"There was once a time when Ramiel and his ilk would have flown over the sea, but no more. My brethren may not drown as humans do, but they have an aversion to the sea and will not risk being plunged into her depths." There was almost a smidge of humor in his voice. Almost. A teensy, *teensy* smidge.

Zwooosh!

The next bolt of lightning hit *scarily* close. My hair stood on end as the bolt cut its way down to the ocean, leaving the air buzzing.

I shivered so hard, I almost knocked myself down again. This was *dangerous*, being out here, exposed to the storm. Hurleigh would probably have been A-okay if he got struck by lightning. I would *not* be. Even if my fireproof skin didn't fry, my brain would.

Whatever weird plan Hurleigh had up his figurative sleeve needed to be wrapped up. And stat.

"Why did you bring me here?" I asked. "It couldn't have been to show me how close Uchen was. You coulda told me that."

For a few seconds, my ears were filled only with the rumbling of thunder and churning of water. Hurleigh stood still, his eyes focused on the island, which gave me a second to blow some water out of my nose. Not that I would've cared if he'd been looking at me, but the privacy was appreciated nonetheless.

"Uchen is the last relic of an old world," he finally said. "A world that was forever changed when my brethren arrived. They have things your people desperately need but can no longer access in Sakar."

"Such as...?"

"Weaponry. Medicines. *Humans*."

"Humans? There's...there's people over there?"

"My earlier statement was not merely directed at those of you in Muirin." Hurleigh shuffled his feet and spread his wings, keeping himself (and me) stabilized when a series of big, choppy waves punched out of the ocean. "All of Sakar will soon perish. Wraiths vastly outnumber humans, your hybrids are a dying breed, and your food supplies and defenses continue to dwindle. Your very existence teeters on a precipice, poised to fall."

"So...wait..." I glanced at the shadowy mountains in the distance. "You're telling me the answer to all our problems lies in Uchen? Huh. Should we send Ramiel a telegram? '*911! People dying. Send help.*'"

"I would *not* advise contacting Ramiel."

"Well...*duh*," I snorted. "Do Celestials understand snark? Or is that a foreign language to you guys?"

"Ramiel," Hurleigh spoke over me, "*gifted* Sakar to his Wraiths after Raphael forsook it. He claimed it was their reward for serving him. It was a lie. Ramiel had no interest in these lands and has no fondness for his Wraiths. He kept only as many as he needed to preserve the way of life he and his ilk have grown accustomed to. The rest were banished to Sakar."

"Jeez. He sounds like a bang-up guy to work for..."

"This is why your lands are dying. With no one to govern them, the Wraiths have turned feral. They will ravage Sakar until there is nothing left for them to destroy. Ramiel will not rein them in. He cares so little for humans that it matters not to him if your people live or die. That apathy also extends to the mortals dwelling on his lands. There-fore"—Hurleigh turned his gaze to Uchen—"you may have a chance to take what you need from him."

"Take what we—*wait*. Is this what we're doing tonight? Going on a heist?"

"*No!*" Hurleigh's voice cracked around the word. "This is as close as I get to Uchen."

Beneath my hand, his fingers twitched in a brief spasm, and then his muscles went rigid as he forced himself to be still. He gave no other indication of fear. Aside from the one word, his voice remained blasé, his eyes fathomless, and his posture in full surfer boy chillaxation.

But I knew fear when I saw it. Like called to like, after all.

Ding-ding-ding! Those lightbulbs were going off in my head again.

"You're scared of Ramiel, aren't you?" I asked.

Hurleigh's head snapped around. "I am *not* afraid."

"Like hell you aren't. That's why we're out here in the middle of a goddamn hurricane, right? Visibility is crap right now. Your brethren won't peep out their windows and see you. It's probably also why you sent a tsunami to flatten what you *thought* was a Wraith. One measly little Wraith. But I'm gonna guess you haven't seen Wraiths in this part of Sakar since Ramiel dumped them here. So you saw me pretending to traffic people and had an "*oh shit*" moment, huh? Maybe thinking The Dark Lord was gathering his forces again."

Hurleigh's hand twitched.

Bingo!

"You're fucking terrified. And you're getting all huffy," I added when he opened his mouth, "because I'm right. Right?"

He clamped his jaw and drew his shoulders back, standing a little straighter, towering over me. The next flash of lightning highlighted the hard planes of his face, which were far too chiseled and perfect. Too *inhuman.*

"You should take more care with what you say, Adelaide," he rumbled.

Gah! My full name hit my ears like nails on a chalkboard.

And so did those words: *"take more care with what you say."* Because they were so very close to what Cheriour had once said to me.

Except Cheriour had been justified in saying it. Hurleigh was not.

A fresh wash of anger speared my chest. "It's *Addie.* And in my experience, people get pissy when they hear a truth about themselves they don't wanna admit. So I'm hitting the nail on the head here, huh?"

Hurleigh did this slow, inhuman blink as his left eyebrow crawled into an elegant arch. "Very well, Adelaide—"

"*Addie.*"

"—as you seem determined to expose me, let us both admit our truths. Yes, I am wary of my brethren. Raphael barred all entrances to the City, so I am as stranded as Ramiel and his ilk. And, should Ramiel find me, my fate would be far worse than any torment you could imagine."

"So, you hide?"

"So, I hide," he echoed.

"Why did you stay in Sakar?"

"I have bared a truth to you." Hurleigh's wings rose over his head. Like a peacock, trying to fluff himself up. "Now it is time for you to bare yours. Tell me, Adelaide—"

"*Addie!*"

"—how did you kill Seruf?"

"Err...huh?" My gut twisted. "Who-who says I did?"

"Seruf and Ramiel departed from Keld three months ago," Hurleigh said.

"You *saw* them heading for Sakar? And *didn't* try to pancake them with a wave?" I snapped.

Hurleigh ignored me. "Ramiel returned. Seruf did not."

"And you immediately jumped to the conclusion that *I* killed her? Based on what evidence? How do you know she's not vacationing somewhere in Sakar?"

"Am I to assume your avoidance," Hurleigh's eyebrow rose again, "and irritation are because you've heard a truth you do not wish to admit?"

My mouth snapped shut, and I choked when a glob of rainwater *wrooshed* down my throat. I sputtered. Spat. Sneezed (again). And stared right into Hurleigh's baby blues. "Look at you, fancy pants, using my own psycho-analysis mumbo-jumbo against me. Okay. Yeah, I killed Seruf. Dusted her real good. Happy?"

"I believe I asked *how* you killed her."

"I believe I asked you what evidence you're basing this off of. Because how in the fuck did you know?"

Hurleigh blinked. Once. Twice. "How did you kill Seruf?"

"*Jesus*, you're a broken record. I don't know. 'Kay?"

He blinked a third time. "How—"

"For fuck's sake! Are you really about to ask that question again? *Really*? Do you think if you keep annoying me, you'll get a different answer? *I don't know how I killed Seruf!* But I sure wish I *did* know, because I'd *love* to gear that power up and smash your soul to smithereens. You *useless sack of—*"

"You destroyed her Essence?"

"Holy moly! He speaks some different words! *Yes.* Apparently. But before you start asking 'how did you destroy her Essence?' fifteen million times, the answer is still, '*I don't know.*'"

Thankfully, he asked a different question. "Could you do it again?"

"Gee, I dunno. Maybe I'll do it again the day you get ballsy enough to take me shopping in enemy territory."

Hurleigh turned away from me, gazing toward the mountains of Uchen. "I will help you, Adelaide."

"*Addie*. Ad-dee. Two syllables. That's it. And...wait! Help with what?"

"The ocean will take you back to Muirin's shores," he said.

"Okay...but *what* are you helping with? You realize I was joking about—"

Hurleigh shook his hand free of mine and sank into a wave, leaving me stranded, alone, in the middle of the fucking ocean.

CHAPTER 22

GULPING JUICE FROM A RANCID PIECE OF PORK

The waves towed me back to Muirin, bashing me into some rocks along the way, and belched me over three boulders that protected a narrow strip of beach from the ocean.

My chin smacked the stony sand, and I tasted blood when my teeth gnashed my tongue. "Aw, heck." I pulled myself up to my hands and knees. The gritty soil beneath me was *gloriously* still and solid, but my brain still slish-sloshed in time with the raging sea.

I dug my fingers into the sand, trying to force my wobbly vision and tilting stomach to still.

Lightning cracked overhead. Then a frantic yell rose over the banging bout of thunder. "She's returned! OI! *She's returned!*"

I blinked, clearing the rainwater out of my eyes, as a dozen people descended the labyrinthine path along the cliff face and dashed toward me, spit-firing questions as they ran.

"Did you fly over the water?" Nathan asked.

"Will Hurleigh defend Sanadrin?" Shay questioned.

"Will he help us?" This quiet query came from Deborah, who'd also been merciful enough to rub my arm when she noticed me shivering.

The hope and excitement in their eyes broke my damn heart.

"He—" I started.

"Haha, Addie!" Braxton swooped in and smooched my cheek.

A very, *very* sloppy smooch.

I *swore* he swirled his tongue against my skin.

"Braxton." I wiped my wet sleeve against my face. "If you do that again, so help me, I will cut your tongue off."

"Apologies." He thwacked my bad shoulder.

"Ouch!" I yelped.

"Ach, apologies again." He laughed. "I *knew* ye'd get that Celestial on our side, Addie! So...what are we doin' now?"

"Does he want us to stay here? Or return to Sanadrin?" Deborah clarified.

"Ermmm...he said he'd get back to me later." *Not true.* But close enough. Maybe? I hoped. "So, we'll wait here, I guess. And we'll know something more soon."

"*I will help you, Adelaide.*"

Hurleigh must've gotten his definition of "help" from a different dictionary. Likely some special edition that only existed in the Celestial City: *How to Twist Words to Confuse the Ever-Loving Shit Outta Your Mortal Minions.*

A part of me was terrified he'd roll back into town and drag us all to Uchen.

Another part of me hoped he'd go to Uchen himself and come back bearing gifts.

He did neither.

I didn't see him again. Not in the days that followed, or the weeks. The weather turned *bitter*. Rolling thunderstorms came and went. The clouds sagged above us, so waterlogged and droopy, they looked almost low enough to touch. No matter how much rain they dropped, they were never emptied.

It rained. And rained. *And rained*. Occasionally, there were torrents of *freezing* rain. Or fat flakes of snow.

Hurleigh never showed.

And everyone very quickly lost hope. Because we were *barely* surviving.

"We have supper for tonight, Addie," Braxton said miserably one balmy afternoon when he found me sitting on the edge of the cliff, watching the beach below.

Or, to be more accurate, watching Abby Normal as she dug her hooves into the sand, searching for worms and other creepy crawlies.

I glanced up when Braxton spoke, then grimaced when I saw the Kentucky Fried Rodent he clutched in his hand. "*Ugh*. No thank you."

"Ach, it's not so bad." He sat beside me, tore a strip of meat from the rat's hide, and munched noisily. "Try it. It may be a while yet before we have meat again. These were all the rats nearby, ye see. The poor buggards were only young too..." He frowned and picked a piece of skin out of his teeth. "And there are no other animals. Most have ventured inland for winter. It'll be warmer there. And yer

Púca"—he jabbed a finger at Abby Normal—"terrorized the wee birds. They won't land here anymore."

"She has to eat too, Braxton," I pointed out. Poor Abby Normal had starved as much as the rest of us. Except she had the misfortune of having big, greasy slices of pizza (aka, humans) dangling in front of her face 24/7. And she reacted about the same way I would've if I was constantly being teased by scrumptious, off-limits food: she got cranky and had started isolating herself to the beach.

"I know." Braxton shoved another bite of rat meat into his mouth. "It's not that I fault yer Púca. But I—I don't know what to *do*. Belanna..." He swallowed and clenched his fists against his thighs. "Ach, but if only she were here, eh? Animals listened to her better than me..."

He looked so sad and defeated.

"All you can do is try, Braxton." I scooted closer to him, slipped my arm around his trembling shoulders, and pulled him into the tightest hug I could manage. "For the record, I'm really glad you're here."

He sniffled, laughed, and shoved the rest of the rat meat onto my lap. "Ye can finish that. Eat, Addie," he added when I started to push it away. "Ye'll regret it if ye don't."

"It's *rat*." I shuddered.

"It's meat," he pointed out. "Nothin' more."

"Ugh...*fine*." I raised the half-eaten rodent to my mouth, angling its shriveled face away from mine so I wouldn't have to stare into its crisped eyes as I mowed down on its flesh.

Hot juice spurted into the back of my throat as I took the first bite. Really *savory* juice. And the meat itself, which was so tender that it practically melted on my tongue, reminded me of a Thanksgiving turkey.

It was good.

Really good.

Delicious.

I'd die before I ever admitted that to Cheriour, though.

Assuming, of course, I ever saw him again.

THE FIRST HACKING COUGH ROLLED THROUGH MUIRIN ON OUR three-week arrival anniversary. Its victim was Natalia. And once that cough snuck into our pathetic city, it made itself nice and cozy inside the lungs of...well...*everyone.*

For days, a litany of squishy barks, rumbly gags, wheezing *hurk-hurks*, and deep, throaty *aaaarrrrguuughs* swirled around Muirin.

Phlegm. There was fucking phlegm everywhere.

And this flu (or whatever icky virus it was) hit everyone differently. Braxton spent most of his days doubled over and red-faced as he coughed up big lobs of mucus. Nathan got the stuffy sinus syndrome. Marcus's nose had turned into a leaky snot faucet—and he was gross about it, always swiping the runoff on his hands or blowing booger bubbles out of his nostrils.

Blegh.

Poor Deborah fared worst of all. Her lungs were totally submerged in the ick, and she was way too goddamn stubborn to take it easy. Kinda like someone else I cared about. Apparently, I was a magnet for pigheaded people.

"Whoa! Hands up!" I called, jogging to Deborah's side as she wheezed out another bout of coughing and almost dropped a stack of wood on her toes.

I took the stack out of her arms and motioned for her to sit. "Here. Chill for a sec before you zonk out."

She huffed, lowered herself onto her haunches, and spent a few seconds inhaling shallowly, as though trying to suck air through a straw.

Around us, a few other people shuffled by, all choking, sneezing, or doing a snotty combo. And all still working on refurbishing a second barn. To use as *storage*. Y'know...for all the food we *didn't have*.

"Addie..." Deborah sputtered. Choked. "How are you not"—*huuuuhhhzzzeeee* went her rattly breaths—"suffering with the rest of us?"

Oooh, I was suffering alright. But the virus hadn't wriggled into my lungs. Yet.

"I dunno. Maybe the magic of vaccines?"

"Id dad a pland?" asked the poor, stuffy-nosed Nathan as he tottered by. "Vadc-een?"

"Oh yeah," I said. "The *best* kinda plant. Can cure illness and polarize an entire society, all with one—"

Aaaaaaachoooo!

With a thunderous sneeze, Darragh teleported from where he'd been repairing our rock tools next to the barn and body-slammed poor Nathan.

"Apologies." Darragh wiped at his Rudolph-red nose.

"Ids aright." Nathan took a staggering step, blinked, and got this brief, blearily confused look on his face.

"You okay?" I asked both men.

Nathan nodded.

Darragh scowled and wiped his nose again. "*No.* I can't keep my fecking feet—" Panic seized his face when his nose did that telltale twitch.

"Try pressing your finger—never mind." I grimaced on Darragh's behalf when he lost the battle against the sneeze.

Poof.

Off he went again, this time crumbling in a heap on the ground several feet away.

"Poor bastard," I muttered.

Nathan started to say something, but then he swayed. His eyes glazed over.

"Nathan, you are *not* okay. How 'bout you take a seat too? Actually"—I glanced at the gloomy gray sky—"everyone should take it easy for a—*what the fuck?!*"

It happened so fast.

One second, the group was coughing their way through the building process.

The next, screams, snarls, and gushy gargles filled the air.

I pivoted and had half a second to absorb the sight of Marcus sprawled on the ground, howling as a rangy hellhound ripped into his stomach. The hound slurped on a juicy mouthful of intestines the way most people gobbled angel hair pasta.

"Where—what—" I started.

But then Deborah screamed.

More hellhounds bounded into the town. A lot more. At *least* a dozen.

One of them charged right for Deborah.

And there was no time. I had no weapon. I couldn't do *anything*. Except throw myself in front of her and take the hit head-on.

The hound leapt.

I flung one of the wood planks up to protect my face.

"*Oooomph.*" The hellhound's full weight smashed into my chest, sending me spiraling into Deborah's lap. "*Gaaaaahhhh...*" I screamed, white-knuckling that piece of wood with both hands as the hound chawed its *foot-long teeth* into it. Saliva dripped from its white-boned muzzle and plopped into my mouth. And, *phewwwww buddy*, that was about as pleasant as gulping juice from a rancid piece of pork. The taste...the *smell*...

I dry-heaved, gagging so hard, I stopped breathing for a hot second. Stars erupted before my eyes.

The hound reared its head back, gathering momentum, then snapped forward, its teeth chomping around the plank.

Crrrrkk.

The wood splintered. Right down the middle. Leaving me holding two jagged stubs.

The hound's fangs zoomed toward my jugular.

"*Aarrrgh!*" I felt the prick of teeth against my skin, the warm wash of blood trickling down my throat...

Sqqquuattch.

My hands instinctively slammed inward. And holy fuck, if I didn't catch the luckiest fucking break in fucking history. Because those barbed wood shards caught the hound in the squishy patch of skin between its jaw and throat.

The hellhound howled. Hot, sticky bursts of blood fountained from the two holes punched into its neck and splashed over my face, getting in my eyes, up my nose, and in my freaking mouth.

The hound contorted, its paws scrabbling over me as it tried to get control of its failing body. Then it collapsed on top of my chest, giving the girls another good bruising.

"Oh, shoo...*bleegggghhh...*" A watery burp burst out of me.

"Addie..." Deborah squirmed, wriggled, and managed to worm herself free of my bulbous ass before she doubled over, her body wracked with a cough that had her bringing up clods of mucus and bile. She weakly gave the hellhound a shove, trying to push it off me.

"I've got it, Deborah..." I shimmied out from under the hound, flipped over onto my hands and knees, and threw my guts up.

Stop! I told my body as it heaved. *Stopstopstop. STOP!*

I did *not* have time for this puking bullshit.

Because Nathan was about to be turned into chop suey. One hound had Nathan's hand clutched in its teeth, another was doing some fancy footwork to avoid the wood plank Nathan was trying to nail it with.

"Nathan!" I grabbed one of the wooden shards and lurched to my feet. Another deep, painful belch bubbled out of my chest as I lunged and rammed my stick up the hound's ass. The hound yelped and dropped Nathan's hand, which gave him room to pivot and drive his plank into the other hound's stomach.

"Whad—*accch-chooo*!" Nathan blew out a monstrous sneeze that left snot strings hanging from his nose. "Ugh." He sniffled and mopped up the mucusy mess. "Whad id happedind?"

"I don't know." I swiped a hand over the (thankfully shallow) punctures on my throat to stem the bleeding. "Just try to get inside. I don't think you're in any condition to—oh no...oh *fuck*!"

Shay was doubled over a few yards away, his face pale and streaked with blood. A hellhound had his left forearm by the teeth and was whipping its head from side to side, trying to tear the limb off. Shay bellowed and pummeled the creature's hairless skin with one of our DIY rock hammers. The hound barely flinched.

A second hound closed in on Shay's left.

He had no idea what was about to hit him.

"Shay! *Look out!*" I bolted, shoving away from the ground so hard, my right leg moved a patch of dirt out from under me. I bobbled, almost fell, and then got my footing sorted.

But my yelling had pulled a hound onto my tail. It bulldozed up to my right side, getting close enough for me to see the chunks of human stuck in its teeth.

I swerved with a shriek and dug in, coaxing more speed out of my legs. But it felt like I was running through quicksand, pedaling my feet as fast as they would go and getting nowhere.

The hound's paws pounded against the sandy soil. Its short barks and huffing breaths filled my ears.

I wasn't going to make it.

I begged my feet to take me a little farther. Pleaded my stride to stretch a little longer.

"Shay!" I screamed. "Look—*oof.*"

The hound's teeth clamped around my right ankle, yanking my leg out from under me.

In that split second, as my butt flew up into the air and my head pitched down, I saw the other hellhound close in on Shay. Heard the clink of its teeth as it bit his throat.

And then I crashed, face-first, into the ground. My nose broke with a sharp *crunch*, and hot globs of blood squirted into my mouth.

I screeched like a horny banshee.

Partially because Shay had collapsed inches away from me. His eyes glistened, wild and scared, and his mouth gaped around a silent cry as the hound ripped a chunk of flesh from his neck.

But my yell had also been one of agony. The other hellhound had its teeth buried in my ankle. The canines had punctured my boot, tore through the skin, and were now scraping several layers of marrow off my bones.

White streaks flashed before my eyes as red-hot tendrils of pain shot up my leg.

The hound shook its head, deepening his punctures, and pulled, dragging me a few inches over the ground.

"Fugly asshat!" I bashed my left foot against the hound's head, wailing when my heel bounced off unyielding bone. *"Get off!"* I twisted my upper body around, the air rushing out of my lungs when my oblique muscle popped, and jabbed my fingers into the hound's ear. "Take that, you fugly sack of—*thank you.*"

As cartilage crunched beneath my fingers, the hound loosed a pitiful whine, dropped my leg, and whipped its head back.

My fingers, when they came loose with a wet pop, were coated in gunky brown ear wax.

OMFG...Blegh!!

Just as I was sure the peanut-buttery scent of the ear juices would have me hurling again, I heard Abby Normal's frenzied *mowow*.

No! I flipped myself over. "Abs! *Don't!*"

But she charged up from behind me and ripped the hellhound away, savaging its throat with her teeth and crushing its body with her hooves.

"Abs! Get out of here!" I screamed.

One hellhound streaked across the soil. And then another. And another. All three had those hollow, bottomless black eye sockets locked on Abby Normal.

"GET OUT OF HERE!" I waved my arms, trying to get her to move.

But it was too late.

They swarmed her. Three at first. Then four. Then *six*. They jumped onto her back and bit at her legs to keep her from spinning and pivoting away.

She stumbled sideways, trampling Shay beneath her flailing hooves, and *whimpered*.

"Abs!" I drew my legs under me, letting out a strained, "God-fucking-damn...this fucking *hurts*!" when I put weight on my maimed ankle. "Hang on, Abs!"

I couldn't run. Not with my ankle spewing wads of blood and my entire leg getting zapped with an invisible cattle prod.

I took a step. Two.

My ankle said, "fuck you, bitch," and buckled, sending me back to my ass.

"Abs! *ABS*!"

She trilled at me, her eyes blown wide with panic.

I stood again.

Fell again.

And the hounds tore into Abby Normal.

One had her hind leg in its teeth; three more were on her back, clawing at her skin. The other two orbited her, nipping at her ankles. She leapt with a frightened screech, doing some impressive aerial gymnastics in a desperate attempt to shake them off. But she landed awkwardly on three legs, and her knees folded. She sank right to the ground.

"*Abs!*"

For a second—two, three—all I could do was lie there. And stare.

This was pure bedlam.

Beyond Abby Normal's flailing body, there were the dead. Five people, at least, all strewn across the ruins of

Muirin in several large, meaty chunks. More than a dozen hounds raced around Muirin, all visibly emaciated and ravenous. Their furless, mottled flesh wrapped tight around their bones. Ribs protruded along their sides, the ridges of their spines jutted along their backs, and their hips looked sunken.

Then there were the people left alive: weaponless, sick, weak, and fighting with everything they had to keep breathing. Braxton had wedged a plank of wood between a hound's jaws, blocking it from closing its mouth around his jugular. Aria lay on the ground, still alive and jabbing a hound's flank with a knife, but one of her legs was busted wide open, the skin torn away from the bone. The other leg was gone, bitten off at the knee. Nathan, Deborah, and a few others had run inside the barn. Three hellhounds smashed through the jerry-rigged door and merrily trotted out a few seconds later, each clutching stringy chunks of...*someone.*

It was a fucking bloodbath.

And Abby Normal...

My bodyguard, friend, and confidante...she was hurt. Badly.

Strained, throaty grunts rumbled out of her. Sounds I'd *never* heard her make before. Her legs thrashed, sending fat droplets of blood into the air.

Fear, anger, despair...one of those strong emotions grabbed my gut in an iron fist and *ripped* my stomach through my throat.

This isn't happening. It has *to be a nightmare.*

I blinked.

The chaos remained.

I smacked my hands against my ears.

The sharp howls and keens still filled the air.

They're all going to die.

I had to do something. *Anything.* Even if all I could realistically do was act as bait and give other people time to run.

I pulled my legs under me again, bellowing when my ankle cricked and vomited blood.

Abby Normal keened.

"Hold on...Abs..." I grasped onto my wood shard and forced my busted leg to hold my weight.

The pain was *blinding* and made my vision go all glowy. Abby Normal's trickling blood draped artfully across her body like neon light strips. The hounds left long streaks behind them when they moved, like headlights on a rainy night. And people were LED lightbulbs of varying watts.

I blinked, trying—and failing—to clear my vision before I swiped at the blood spuming from my broken nose and charged, raising my shard over my head.

Swing batter, batter!

Wham!

I pummeled the first hound so hard, it spiraled away from Abby Normal with an indignant squeak, which made my ears ring.

The hound cocked its head, giving me the best "*the audacity of this bitch*" look it could muster with its fleshless face before it dropped to its haunches.

I drew my shard back again. "Let's go, fugly."

It leapt.

I swung my shard around, screaming, "Yippee-ki-yay motherfuc—"

Acccccc-chooo!

With an ear-splitting sneeze, Darragh *poofed* in front of me, plastering my face with snot rockets.

His skin gleamed brighter than a forty-watt bulb.

"*Gaggguhgh!*" I couldn't stop my swing. I tried. But my arms were zooming on momentum, and the brakes didn't work. So I opened my hands, letting the plank slide through my fingers, and drilled my knuckles into Darragh's chest.

Or, well, I *should've* drilled them into his chest.

But my hands slid right through his left pec.

Whooosh. The scenery around me was whipped away faster than sand blowing in the wind. I plunged down, down, *down.* Into Darragh's memories.

No. Nonononono.

A colorful, confusing kaleidoscope of faces waterfalled around me.

Not again!

Voices bubbled in my ears—too many, talking too fast. I couldn't pick out more than a few random words or phrases.

No! Darragh isn't a Celestial!

Why had I ham-fisted his soul?

Darragh's memories were not *nearly* as violent as Seruf's had been. Not as bright or as loud, either. It was the difference between watching a movie in an old-fashioned theatre with a geriatric screen vs Seruf's 3D, 4DX experience. But Darragh's memories still whipped me around a loop-de-loop at top speed, and I had no idea how to stop the ride.

People sashayed above me. More undulated beneath my feet. Even more gyrated around me. Some I recognized. Quinn hung suspended like a bat—a *young* Quinn, likely in his early twenties. And, y'know what, he was a good-looking dude when he wasn't being a miserable sourpuss. His smile was relaxed, carefree, and his eyes twinkled with mischief.

But then he folded himself up and rocketed away.

Other people replaced him. *Dozens* of faces. Swirling. Sliding. Twirling...

My stomach heaved.

"*Gaaaaaahhhhhhh!*" Darragh's wail boinged around my ears, even as a blanket of disembodied voices swathed me.

"*Ye'll need to stun 'er, Darragh!*"

"*What the feck did you do to her?*"

"*She may be workin' with Seruf...*"

"*The girl killed more than a dozen...*"

"*She was a* child*!*"

Lasair rippled beneath my feet, her purple eyes peering up at me from her equally purple face.

Seriously, she was *covered* in bruises. Big, splotchy lesions blossomed across her cheeks and twined around her temples. And she was a *kid*, though it was impossible to pin her exact age with as marred as her face was. She might've been as young as twelve or as old as eighteen. But she was *young*.

And someone had beat the snot outta her.

Defiance smoldered in her eyes, even as her jaw trembled with fear.

And then she was gone, whisked away down the memory tunnel. Never to be seen again.

How the fuck do I get out of here??

Pain spiked its barbed fingers through my chest. Then it climbed up. *Up*. Punching small holes in the back of my neck as it crawled over my head, where it wrapped its arms around me in a loving embrace and skewered my brain.

The agony was *blinding*.

I cried and threw myself backward, desperate, *desperate* to get off this ride.

And then it exploded.

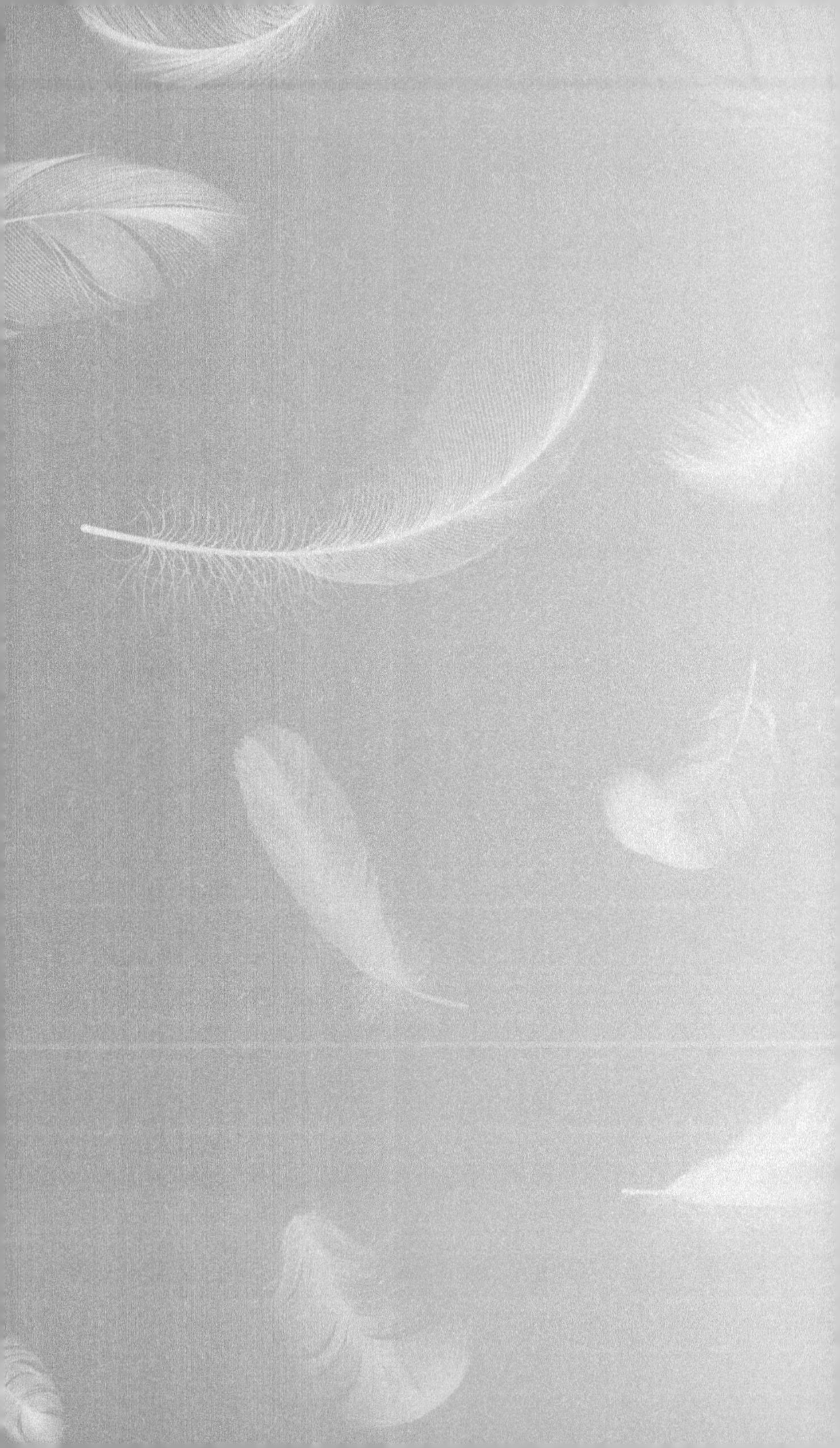

CHAPTER 23
SIX-PACKED MESSIAH

White.

It was all I saw, as though I had a bright-ass flashlight beaming into my eyes. And the pain in my skull *erupted*, sending searing lava all along my neck, my shoulders, my back, my chest...*everywhere*.

I was dead. Had to be. I'd been nuked. Blown to smithereens.

With a *pop*, the flashlight vanished.

I shivered when the pain gave my insides one last vicious rake before it retreated. And I blinked once, twice, clearing the spots out of my vision.

I stared up at the gunmetal-gray sky as I laid on my back. Darragh was draped over me, his weight crushing my lungs. Blood serpentined down his neck and pooled in my mouth.

"*Hmmm...guuuuhh.*" I choked. Spat. Fought for a trickle of air. Wound up inhaling more blood. Choked again.

A hellhound straddled Darragh's ass, its paws bracketed over my thighs. Its head was lowered, and it made obscene *shhhuck-shhhuck* sounds as it glugged juices from the spongy bit of exposed muscle on Darragh's shoulder.

Darragh wasn't moving. Wasn't glowing anymore, either. His skin looked flat. Dull. *Lifeless.*

"*Noooo.*" A low moan punched through my chest. "No!"

The hellhound snapped its head up. A fleshy string of—something (Muscle? Tendon? Fat? Veins?) swung from its lower jaw as it turned its unfathomable black eye sockets toward me.

The hound still glowed faintly—a pair of headlights behind a dirty, smudgy casing.

With a snarl, it lashed toward me.

"Gaaah!" I wrenched my left hand free and drove it up, fisting the hound's open mouth.

I had a split second to feel the coarse brush of its tongue and the scrape of its teeth before the world around me vanished. *Again.* But the hound's memories, what little I saw of them, were all shadows. Dark, indiscernible shapes loomed in the peripherals of my vision. Muffled, water-logged sounds strummed through my ears.

I didn't stay in that shadowy place for long.

The hound's teeth clamped down on my arm, puncturing right to the bone, and I zapped back to reality with a bloodcurdling cry.

The hound also keened and scuttled backward, its head swinging from side to side, trying to shake off the aftereffects of my soul fondling.

My arm *burned,* as though I'd been flayed with a red-hot meat skewer.

"*Goddamn it!*" I bellowed as I shoved at Darragh's limp, heavy body. He moved only an inch, despite me pushing at him with all my strength.

"Dude..." I sniffled when his head flopped across my boobs in a way that *would've* been obscene. If, y'know, his eyes weren't so dim and lifeless. "I know the girls are squishy, but they are not a fucking pillow. Get. *Off!*" I gave one last thrust and sighed when he slid sideways and slouched on the ground beside me. "I'm sorry," I added as I flipped onto my stomach. "So, so, so sorry." Tears scorched my eyes.

A gentle, fluttering breeze caressed my wet cheeks, drying them.

A breeze that also carried the soft flapping of beating wings.

I blinked to clear my vision and turned as Hurleigh bent and scooped the whimpering hound up with one hand, as though the German Shepard-sized creature was no bigger than a piddly house cat. With a long-suffering sigh, Hurleigh pinched the hound's chin between his forefinger and thumb and tugged.

The hound's neck broke with an echoing *crack*.

"What the—" I started.

"Evidently, you *do* know how you killed Seruf." Hurleigh locked baby blues onto me as he dropped the dead hound and snagged another away from Abby Normal. "And you are capable of doing so again." *Crunch* went the second hellhound's neck.

"Are you—was this—*what the fuck?*" As the gears whirred inside my head, hatred boiled in my chest. I was pissed. *Beyond* pissed. So angry, I had fire palpitating through my insides in time with the erratic thumping of my heart.

"You—you—sack of shit platter—absolute bastard—

fucking cheapo Jesus knockoff!" Nonsense words blubbered out of my mouth.

Hurleigh ignored my sputtering and took a casual stroll around the town, snapping hellhound bones. No matter how the hounds snarled and seethed and fought, they were helpless against his superhuman strength. He crushed them as easily as I would smoosh a gnat.

A stark and terrifying reminder of how powerful he was.

He could've stopped this massacre before it started.

He'd *chosen* not to.

My rage detonated. A bouncy red haze covered my vision as Hurleigh stepped around mangled body parts and trounced through trickling streams of blood.

Fucking useless sack of shit!

But everyone else fell over their feet to thank him—as though he was their six-packed messiah, sent from the heavens to free them from bondage.

"Don't fucking thank him," I snarled at Braxton, who'd gotten this sappy, dewy-eyed look on his face.

"Eh?" Braxton's brow furrowed.

"Don't thank him." I glued my eyes to the slick muscles that rippled along Hurleigh's bare chest while he killed the final hound. "He didn't *help* us. He staged this attack. Didn't you, Hurleigh?"

Hurleigh's head cocked sideways, pouring a shining curtain of chocolate waves over his right shoulder. "These are Ramiel's creations." He plonked the hound to the ground. "Made to assist his Wraiths."

"Way to deflect the question, asshole," I seethed.

"I do not keep hounds under my command."

"Okay, fine. You don't keep the hellhounds as pets. But

you *knew* they were heading this way. Didn't you? And you didn't stop them or warn us."

He inclined his head and arched his shoulders back, giving his wings a good stretch. A peacock preening and parading in front of a captivated audience.

And people *were* captivated. Most gaped at him, utterly awe-stricken. Those who didn't were too busy globing up mucus or blood to pay attention to much else.

Meanwhile, I breathed harder than a hippo in heat. Red still stained my vision. Big ole blobs of it splashed around the outer edges.

"*You said you would help!*" I shrieked.

Several people pivoted in my direction.

"I believe"—Hurleigh casually folded his wings along his back—"I said I would help *you*, Adelaide. And I have."

Now people spun to stare at Hurleigh.

They were like Wimbledon spectators, swinging their gazes between the players.

"*How did this fucking help me?*" I waved my arms at the steaming bodies and puddles of blood that now decorated the town. "It *didn't*! That's how. You didn't *help* at all. That would've required you to get off your lazy ass and—*eeeek!*"

Hurleigh *poofed* in front of me.

I stumbled back and cursed as I rolled my lacerated ankle. My leg buckled beneath the hot flash of pain.

Hurleigh grasped my arm—my *bleeding* arm—and held me upright. "I helped you," he said in a gravelly murmur, "by forcing you to use an ability you were frightened of."

"I was *not* frightened of it." My jaw clenched around the words.

His lip quirked. "'*People get pissy when they hear a truth about themselves they don't want to admit.*'"

"Ooooh, you—I can't believe—*Fuck you!*" I wrestled my arm back, whimpering when he clenched his fist, digging his fingers into my wounds, and held me in place. "You cock-sucking bastard piece of shit! What if I hadn't used that power? Huh? What if I *couldn't?* Would you have sat on your ass, drinking scotch or whiskey—or whatever you pompous pricks drink when you're being judgmental dick-heads—and watched us all *die?*"

He tilted his head. In a very "*umm, duh*" kinda way.

"*Un-fucking-believable.*"

Hurleigh pulled me closer, dropping his mouth near my ear as he murmured, "Considering you wastefully expend energy worrying over your humans, I did not doubt you would find the strength to use your ability. I am, however, surprised you—"

Whack.

My palm stung as I walloped his face.

I poured *every* ounce of strength I had left into that slap.

He didn't even flinch.

But I was 99 percent sure I broke at least one bone in my hand.

With a slow, owlish blink, Hurleigh snagged my wayward wrist in his other hand and pinned both my arms to my side. "I would not advise doing that again."

"Fine," I said. And then I spat in his eye.

That, at least, got a reaction out of him: he scrunched his nose. "I see you're upset—"

"*No shit, Sherlock!*"

"You have less than four days to compose yourself," he drawled. "There is a storm traveling along the coast. This may be your only opportunity to travel to Uchen. I will *not* take you there without the storm's cover."

"Yeah, because no matter how tough and mighty you *act*, you're chickenshit against other Celestials—"

"Know this, Adelaide..." Hurleigh's stern *"I'm about to dish some wisdom"* stare was a little less impactful with my spittle running down his cheek. "If you want to kill Celestials, you'll need to accept that some humans will die."

"I don't want to kill Celestials! And I *am* human. Stop talking about us like we're insignificant pests."

"They *are* naught more than pests. And you"—he released my hands and stepped back— "are *not* human." Then he *poofed* away, probably retreating into the ocean to get away from us "insignificant pests."

"Stupid, fugly, sack of...BASTARD!" I trumpeted after him.

Every single person was staring at me now, open-mouthed and wide-eyed, their injuries and illnesses temporarily forgotten.

"Addie?" Braxton stepped toward me. Blood trickled along the right side of his neck, oozing from his partially hacked ear.

I pivoted away from him, and my legs abruptly gassed out. I slid bonelessly to the ground, nearly landing on top of poor Abby Normal, who was still sprawled on her side, her mangled legs curled tight against her body. But her head was up. She watched me, the pupils in her eyes so dilated, I could barely see her red irises. And she trembled as I wrapped my arm around her face, pulling her in for the tightest hug I could manage.

"ADDIE...FECK...WHY THE *FECK* DO YE HAVE TO PLAY IN HIM?" Braxton turned away from me with a dry retch.

"I'm not *playing*." I jabbed my finger into Hugo's eye socket. Thorns of nausea twined around my own stomach when my digit disappeared into the hole with a soft *squelk*. "I'm trying to open the tap."

I mean, Hugo didn't really care that I was finger-fucking his eye.

Because Hugo's eyes were gone.

He'd died this morning, bringing our death toll to seven.

Unlike the other poor fuckers who'd lost their lives in yesterday's attack, Hugo hadn't been ripped apart and strewn in fifteen different places. But his face had been thoroughly, *disturbingly*, chewed off. The craggy, red-painted flesh more resembled ground beef than human skin. And he'd lingered for far too long like that, drawing thin patches of air through the squishy and misshapen holes where his mouth and nostrils used to be, before his heart finally stopped beating.

Because he was freshly dead, he still had blood. Lots of it. Crimson liquid gushed from his eye socket when I wriggled my finger in it.

"*Bleggghh...*"

Braxton and I both gagged at the same time. He faced the cliff's edge, his hands interlocked behind his head. "Why didn't ye slit his throat if ye were tryin' to make him bleed?" he groaned.

"Because...other people are using my sword right now."

"Ye could've asked me to fetch it for ye!"

"I didn't think of it!"

He harrumphed, coughed a few times, spat up a mucus

nugget, and dropped his hands to his hips, still facing the ocean.

I remained sitting, half cross-legged, in front of Abby Normal. The damp, icy ground seeped through my pants and made me feel like I had a wet ass. A very *cold* wet ass. If I stood up, I'd probably have icicles hanging from my butt cheeks.

This frozen ground *should've* made a great ice pack for my busted leg. But when I stretched my bare ankle and pressed it to the dirt, the cold didn't do anything to numb the fiery pain flickering from my six gaping punctures. My constant shivering wasn't helping, either. Although, the deep, bone-rattling vibrations were more pain quakes than cold shivers.

My chest was raw, my stomach chafed, and I still had an ice pick hanging out between my eyes. Combo this inward pain with the outward pain from my multiple wounds and...

Yeah. I was miserable AF.

It'd been a full day since the hellhound attack—maybe close to a day and a half now, since the overcast sky was getting dark and dusky.

Abby Normal had not moved.

Well, I mean, that wasn't *entirely* true. She'd gotten to her feet last night. But that was only after Braxton *insisted* she needed to stand.

"Lyin' down isn't natural for horses, Addie," he'd said. "She'll be havin' trouble breathin' soon."

So we'd poked, prodded, pulled, and annoyed the crap outta her until she'd clumsily drew three of her legs under her and stood. Her left hind was so shredded and swollen, it wouldn't hold her weight. Even now, she kept it cocked, the toe of her hoof ever-so-gingerly brushing the ground. The skin along her cannon bone was torn in three places, and the wounds were deep enough to expose quaggy bits of muscle and tendon.

"'Kay, Abs...here ya go." I rocked Hugo's body, nudging it against her muzzle.

Her head hung so low, her lower lip chilled in the dirt. She grunted when Hugo's body smacked her nose, and her nostrils fluttered around a long breath, but she didn't move. Didn't open her mouth. Didn't sniff or suckle the blood bubbling from his face.

The thorns tightened inside my stomach. "Pain really puts a damper on your appetite, huh? But you gotta eat, Abs."

Her strained sigh was whisked away by an oncoming gust of wind.

That breeze brought other noises with it: little pufts of conversation from three members of my crew—a woman with walnut-colored hair named Zara, the bushy-eyebrowed Reece, and the beanstalk-framed Aidan.

"Darragh..."

"...power...did she use one?"

"...*something* happened..."

"...not human..."

The three of them sat in a cluster nearby, huddling around a prissy fire as they used my sword to sharpen wooden stakes (aka, our ultra-advanced weaponry for if (when) we were attacked again).

"Hey, guys," I called to them.

They jolted.

"I have ears, y'know. And they work just fine. So can you do me a favor and take your shit-talking somewhere else?"

"We weren't..." Zara started weakly. But she trailed off when I cocked my head and glared at her.

"Like hell you weren't," I said. "And, listen, I don't care if you talk. I really don't. I'm weirded out too, so I get it. *Trust me*. And I wish I had better answers for you. I don't. And I'm sorry. But, please, if you're gonna run the rumor mill, do it somewhere I can't here you. 'Kay?"

At that, all three of them hung their heads, muttered half-assed apologies, and collected their supplies. As they left, they took turns exchanging furrowed "do we think this bitch is safe to be around?" looks.

Everyone had looked at me that way today. Even Braxton.

They'd all whispered. Not that I blamed them.

They'd heard Hurleigh call me inhuman and rant about me going on a Celestial killing spree. Speculation was to be expected. But no one had the gall to say anything to my face or the balls to ask me to clarify what had happened. They were probably afraid I'd shoot laser beams from my eyes if they *dared* to ask the wrong question.

I inhaled, closing my eyes, trying to slow my breathing so my pistoning heart would stop punching holes through my chest.

Through all this, Abby Normal still hadn't moved.

"C'mon, Abs." I opened my eyes and stroked her face with the backs of my knuckles. "Please? Just take a few mouthfuls."

Deborah and Natalia shuffled by, carrying a dead hellhound by its legs.

"See?" I said. "There goes my dinner."

God, the hellhound meat...*urrrggggghh*. I'd taken one bite of it this morning—barely a nibble. The meat was so stringy, gamey, and *bitter*. My unsteady stomach had gone, "aw fuck no," and chucked it right back up.

"This hound is a little plumper. I think. The meat may not be so stringy." Natalia's face turned a sickly shade of green as she stared at Hugo's body, sprawled between my legs. And her eyes were hooded. Wary.

"You should put some blood on your Púca's lips." Deborah's lungs crackled when she spoke. "If you can…without her biting you. I did that with my son"—she broke off as a deep cough shook her—"when he was sick. Sometimes getting the taste of food into their mouths brings their appetite back."

"It's worth a shot. Thanks!" I dipped my fingers back into Hugo's eye socket and swirled them until they were coated in slimy crimson.

Abby Normal didn't even blink when I waved my bloody hand in front of her face.

"You want me to do the choo-choo train?" I asked. And then I did it anyway. "*Chug-a-lugga, chug-a-lugga*, here comes the choo-choo train. *Whoosh!*"

I meant to stick my fingers into her mouth, but my hands were shaking so bad, I missed the mark and rammed them into her nostril.

"Sorry, Abs," I chuckled when she grunted.

Was I being super immature right now? Yep. But treating my gravely injured venomous horse like a stubborn toddler took my mind off my pain and helped to slow the other thoughts tumbling around in my bruised brain. Thoughts that were too big, too exhausting, and too depressing to dwell on right now.

So, I focused on something simpler (but equally important): getting Abby Normal to eat.

(I just, y'know, tried not to dwell on the fact that I was spoon-feeding her blood from a dead man.)

"C'mon, Abs…" I trailed my sticky, bloody fingers over her muzzle and dipped them between her lips.

She gave a big, tired exhale.

So I smeared more blood over her, giving her some zig-zaggy lipstick. "You look like a painted whore," I snorted, but the laugh sounded bitter, hollow, even to my ears.

I kept globbing the blood on, taking it to the corners of her mouth and stretching it up to her jowls, giving her a beaming clown smile. *"Do you wanna know how I got these scars?"* I crooned in the best Heath Ledger-as-the-Joker voice I could muster.

Which must've sounded zany as fuck because it made Braxton chortle.

"Addie." He walked over to me, a disgusted but bemused smile tugging at his lips. "What are ye—"

He froze, his eyes bugging.

"Oh shit. I don't like that look," I mumbled. "Braxton what's—"

But I heard it then, rising over the near-constant swishing wind.

Thunder.

But *not* thunder.

Hoofbeats.

Lots of hoofbeats. A horde of them. A *stampede*.

"Braxton…" His name burst out of my mouth in a high-pitched squeak. I wrapped my hand around Abby Normal's chin, holding myself steady as tremors exploded up my spine, twisting that ice pick deeper into my skull.

"No…no…it's alright…" Braxton threw both of his hands up, raking them through his hair. "It's alright, Addie…" He dropped his arms and let loose a villainous cackle that had goosebumps prickling my skin.

"You're scaring me, Braxton."

"It's not Wraiths." He whooped and then doubled over with an "Ach, feck," when a coughing fit seized him. "It's not..." *Arrrghh-spaaaat.* He hocked up a big ole loogie. "It's not Wraiths! I couldn't *hear* them—the ocean's a might loud, eh? They're humans, Addie. *Human.*"

He slapped his hands against his knees, did a weird power-punch thing, and skipped merrily through the town, bellowing, "OOOOIIIII! HUMANS APPROACHING!"

Abby Normal flinched and smacked her red-painted lips together. The tip of her tongue darted out, licking the blood from the corners of her mouth.

"There ya go, Abs." I stroked the underside of her cheek, feeling her throat convulse as she swallowed.

Her tongue slithered out again.

I rocked the body toward her. This time, she sluggishly sniffed the blood trickling down Hugo's chin.

"It's all yours, girlfriend. *Bon appétit!*" I said. "Now, I gotta get off my lazy ass and see what's going on. Oooh, fuck, shit, *ouch!*" As soon as I put even the teeniest bit of weight on my ankle, its rapidly throbbing pulse sparked pain *everywhere.*

But then I saw them, cantering toward Muirin, and the pain momentarily whooshed away.

A herd of horses. Bay horses. Chestnuts. Grays. Dark browns. Very, very few black horses. And none with red eyes.

The riders sitting astride their backs were, indeed, human, wearing brown leather armor—no black Wraith metal. And not every horse had a rider. Some were being ponied along, their saddles stuffed with pouchy bags.

There were a dozen...two dozen...*three*. I couldn't count fast enough. My eyes were too busy swinging back and forth, trying to absorb the scene and make my brain believe what I was seeing.

"HUMANS!" Braxton cawed in his raspy cough-ravaged voice.

A few people emerged from the building. And they all stared, looking every bit as confused, shellshocked, and awestruck as I felt.

The horses slowed to a trot and then to a walk as they breached the town.

The first one to stroll my way was a brown and white mare. A man with sandy-colored hair and bright blue eyes sat on her back.

Quinn! Christ almighty, I never thought I'd be relieved to see his sourpuss face.

"What happened here?" His cheeks puffed as he gazed around the city.

The question wasn't aimed at me. So I, for once, stayed silent and let other people answer.

My eyes roamed over the confusing mass of horses and people, and my heart stopped when my gaze caught on the final rider, who entered the town at a brisk walk.

Cheriour.

He sat astride a big bay horse and ponied a smaller bay —one with a familiar, crooked stripe: my old bitchy friend, Sacrifice.

The blustery, sea-salt laden air had crafted a nice frizzy halo around Cheriour's head, and the icy cold had daubed a pink rouge over his cheeks. But, gosh, I'd never seen him look so dashing.

My hands flew to my face.

Cheriour didn't talk or ask questions as he entered Muirin the way all the other riders were.

"*Hellhounds?*"

"We haven't seen hide nor tail of a hellhound in weeks."

"And there were no Wraiths?"

"Hurleigh was *here?*"

Cheriour silently drew his horses to a halt and patted both his mount's neck and Sacrifice's nose. His eyes wandered, scanning the crowd and assessing the condition of the town, the people, the corpses, the ruins, the sky...all the things his busy brain could absorb in a split second.

Then his eyes landed on me.

And I started crying.

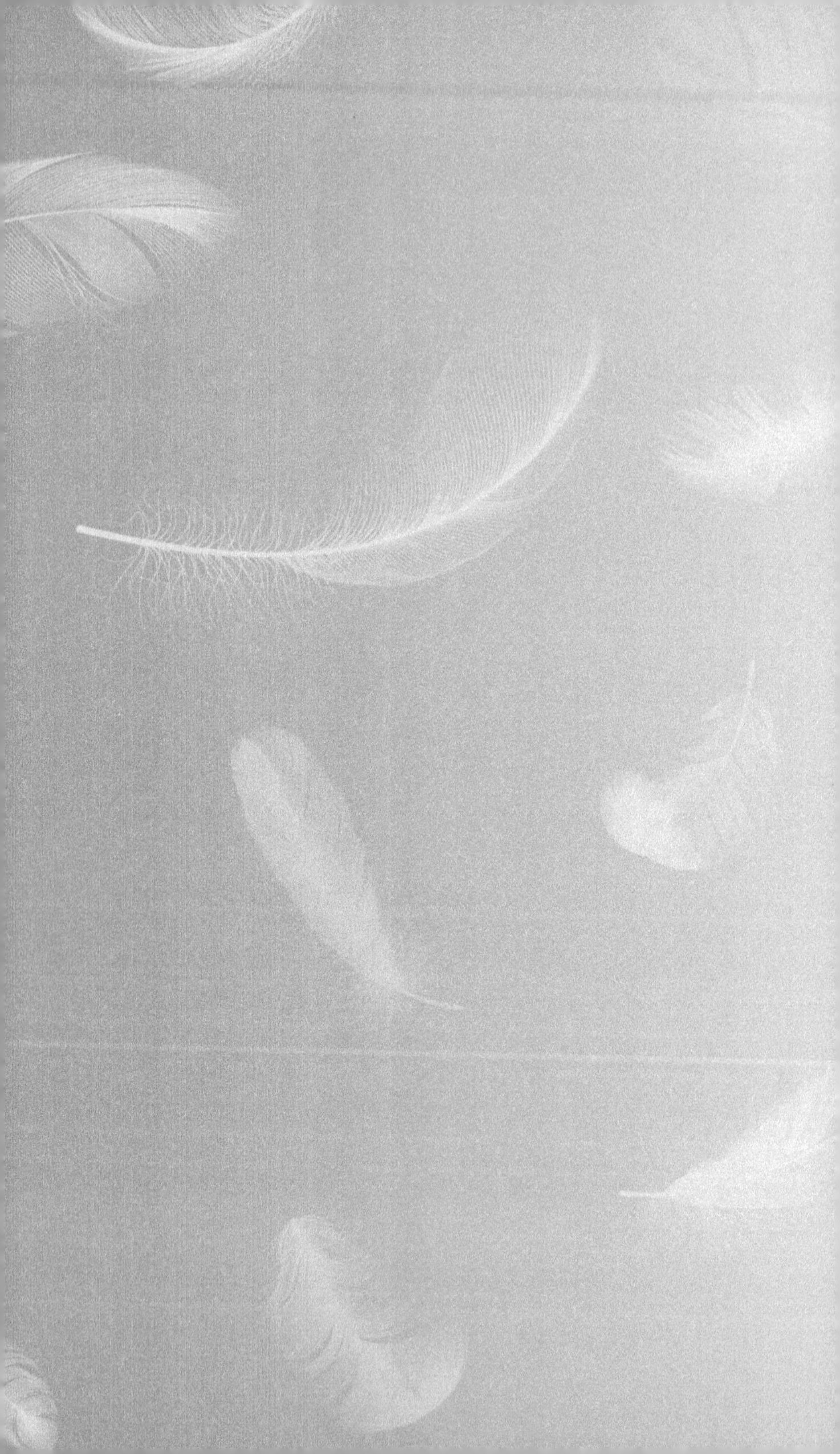

CHAPTER 24
THE WALL

I turned away, huffing shakily into my cupped hands as my vision bounced and wriggled. A hot tear, two, three, slid down my cheek.

Why was I crying?

I should've been happy. *Ecstatic.*

But my heart felt like it had been paralyzed by Púca venom and torn apart by a hellhound's teeth.

I dug my fingers into my cheeks. My hands were so jittery, I sliced my own skin with my nails.

Around me, people talked, laughed, or made unintelligible exclamations. Horses snorted, whuffled, and stomped. It was all white noise—loud, buzzy, and not making a lick of sense. The warm scents of hay, manure, and good ole Au Naturel B.O. musk filled my nostrils.

Talk about sensory overload.

"Rhona!" Cheriour's familiar drawl rose above the hubbub. "The cloths are in Shade's saddlebags. Sort through them and see what we have for bandaging. Nathan, are you well enough to Garden?"

"Yed," Came Nathan's stuffy response.

"The seeds are in Oak's saddle," Cheriour said. "Tessa will show you—"

"Addie?"

I winced and whipped around when a gentle voice sounded by my left ear.

"Kaelan!" I wheezed a thin laugh when I saw him standing next to me, holding the reins of a bulky gray mare. "My God. You have a beard!"

It was exactly the sort of beard you'd expect from a teenager: a little patchy and super adorkable.

He gave me this slow, sideways grin and rubbed at his stubbly chin. "I haven't had a chance to shear it." His smile faded as he dropped his hand. "Are you alright, Addie?"

"I'm fine." *Lies.* The world teetered sideways on me, and I saw two Kaelans instead of one. But, y'know, *totally* fine.

"And your Púca?"

Abby Normal was still dazedly lapping blood from Hugo's face. Even though she was surrounded by people, and Kaelan's nervously snorting mare was only a few feet away, she hadn't lifted her head.

"She's not fine." I wrapped my arms around my midsection when a deep, agonizing pang shot through my wounded heart. "I—"

"Kaelan!" Cheriour called. "Can you unsaddle my horses? Please?"

"Yes!" Kaelan said over his shoulder, and then he turned back to me, whispering, "He wants to see you."

I squeezed my eyes shut, my breath hitching when Kaelan pressed his palm against my shoulder. "Your Púca will be alright, Addie," he added. "We'll get her mended."

I kept my eyes closed. Even as he walked away. Even

when Braxton bellowed, "Oi! Addie! They brought *whiskey*!" Or when Deborah rasped, "There's smoked meat here, Addie. Why don't you sit and have a bite with us?"

I didn't answer them. Didn't look at them. I couldn't. Because my damaged heart was lodged in my throat now, and a foul, metallic tang enveloped my tongue—as though my heart was *hemorrhaging*, pooling blood into my mouth.

"Addie?"

Cheriour's droning voice, so close to me after *months* apart, made my stomach flip. Goosebumps erupted over my skin.

I wanted to throw myself at him.

But I also wanted to throw myself *away* from him.

There were so many emotions thundering inside me. Relief. Anger. Love. Fear. Exhaustion. Restlessness. I didn't know what was what anymore.

A bitter hiccup fizzed out of me. "Dude," I muttered, "you *suck* at making an entrance. I *reek*, and I haven't combed my hair in *days*. Haven't washed it in *at least* a week. You coulda given me a heads-up so I had time to make myself presentable. I'm a hot fucking mess right now. Y'know?"

Cheriour's rough, sand-papery fingers brushed my cheek and touched the end of my snarled braid. "There's nothing wrong with your hair," he murmured.

I snorted. "You *would* say that." I cracked an eye open, intending to eyeball his rat-nest hair and make an affectionally snide remark about how he hadn't combed it since I left. But then I saw the little wooden box at his feet and the whiskered nose poking between the bars. A set of bottomless black eyes gazed up at us, as though saying, "Pleeze don't step on me. I'm smul."

"You brought Splinter?" I choked.

Cheriour glanced at the brown rat, who had gotten *very* pleasantly plump over the last few months. "You asked me to care for it." And the slight crinkling at the corners of his eyes as he said this—like, "Duh, of course I brought the rat with me. I can't give him snacks if I'm not there."—had a laugh tumbling out of my mouth.

But it quickly morphed into a keening cry as the ground beneath my feet bucked.

I pitched forward.

Cheriour caught me.

His arms encircled my torso as he pulled me into his chest, holding me steady while the rest of the world dipped and twerked.

I clutched the sleeves of his jacket and buried my face into the crook of his neck, inhaling his pungent, earthy scent. His chest rose and fell in a steady rhythm beneath me, and his hands were warm as they soothingly massaged my back.

But nothing was grounding me. The world kept rushing in chaotic circles, as though I were trapped on an out-of-control Scrambler ride.

"I'm gonna...fuck, I'm gonna pass out..." I mumbled into Cheriour's throat.

He shifted his hold, dropping his hands to my waist and lowering me down. Down. *Down.*

Where was the ground?

*Oooff...*there it was. My ass bounced off it. The impact was so, so light, Cheriour hadn't let me plop, but tears *immediately* clawed at my eyeballs and tore at my throat.

"I am helping you, Adelaide..."

"It leaves a residue. One that will damage your soul..."

"You are not human."

Thoughts swirled around and around and around inside my head, like turds in a toilet. Except the toilet was clogged, so nothing ever went down. It kept churning, building, rising, until it eventually sloshed over the seat and drooled all over the floor.

This was my messy overflow.

"Addie…" Cheriour threaded his fingers through my hair, kneading my scalp, as I bawled. The kinda tears that hurt. More than hurt, they *ravaged.*

"I'm not much of a Traveler anymore."

"If you want to kill Celestials, you'll need to accept that some humans will die."

The black hole that had been brewing inside my chest opened, taking more of me. Trying to drag the rest of me into the abyss. The *only* thing I had left to hold onto was Cheriour.

And he held me as tightly as I clutched onto him.

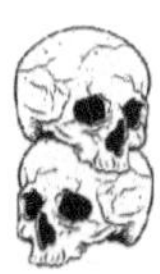

THE THING WITH THOSE KINDA TEARS? THEY DIDN'T ALWAYS MAKE you feel better. At least not right away.

Instead, they sent my mind careening through the stratosphere and soaring amongst the solar system, while keeping my heavy, wounded body strapped to the earth.

I was *completely* checked out the rest of the night.

Things happened. I remembered some of them. But it all seemed murky. Every memory was covered in a soft, blurry haze.

Quinn mended my ankle at some point while I was crying my eyes out. It wasn't a full healing job, only enough to close the large punctures. Apparently, I'd had a broken bone in there, and some small fractures in my hand too. Who'd've thunk it?

But Quinn repaired those as well.

The rest of my nicks, scrapes, bruises, and pulled muscles would have to heal on their own.

Later, as the sky above us turned inky, I held Abby Normal's head while Cheriour, Kaelan, and Rhona (my old "stick up her ass" guard) cleaned her wounds and tight-wrapped her legs. And then I limped alongside her, keeping her muzzle against my hip, while Cheriour and Kaelan linked their hands under her belly and half pushed, half lifted her into the barn, where she stood, listless and miserable, in the center. I sat beside her for the rest of the night. Both of us spaced out together.

People roamed around me, swimming in and out of my unfocused vision. They talked. I might've responded. Or maybe I didn't. I couldn't tell.

I had a brief moment of clear-headedness when Cheriour handed me a flask I'd expected to contain water. A fiery vat of gasoline sloshed over my tongue instead. *Whiskey*. It burned my mouth, my throat, my stomach...and fuck if that flame didn't feel good. Better than sinking into a scalding bubble bath after a stressful day.

But my knotted stomach wouldn't tolerate more than three gulps.

Cheriour also handed me food at some point. Smoked meat. I couldn't eat it.

After a while, I fell asleep, then woke from a nightmare

with a panicked lurch. Darragh's wails still echoed in my ears.

"Be still, Addie." Cheriour ran a hand down my back in a lingering caress.

I blinked. And the world, for the first time that night, came into focus.

I was lying in the corner of the barn, directly across from Abby Normal. Cheriour had balled up his jacket for me to use as a pillow—the tang of leather combined with Cheriour's musk was *fucking divine*—and an itchy wool blanket was draped over my shoulders. Splinter was curled into a pudgy ball at the crook of my neck. He squeaked when I reached up and lifted him off, but then he nuzzled into my hand and zonked out again.

A cacophony of wet snores and hacking coughs filled my ears as everyone else slept. Mostly everyone, at least. Quinn reclined at the back of the building, his eyes very much open as he fiddled with a bit of paper. Rhona leaned against a nearby wall, flashing that unblinking creeper stare. And my chronic insomniac (aka, Cheriour) knelt behind me, idly stroking my sides even as I sat up.

A sharp twinge bulleted between my eyes. It eased after a few seconds but didn't go away. Not completely.

Then again, the chest pains from my encounter with Seruf had never disappeared, even months later.

"If you use this power too often, you will change."

"Addie?" Cheriour murmured.

"C-can I talk to you?" I sniffed, using my free hand to wipe the sleep grit out of my eyes. "*Alone?* Maybe outside?"

He nodded and let his hand slide away from me as he reached for his jacket. I gave Splinter an affectionate nuzzle before I put him back in his enclosure. And the bleary-eyed look he gave me as I got to my feet...*damn*. I didn't know rats were capable of such murderous stares.

Quinn and Rhona's eyes followed us as we headed for the door—Cheriour shrugging into his coat, me with the blanket wrapped around my shoulders like a cape—but they said nothing.

It was pitch black outside. Darker than the depths of Satan's soul. The sky was so clogged with clouds, moonlight couldn't sneak through. And Muirin's streets weren't exactly well paved and freshly swept. Plus, there were horses milling about, nearly invisible with the way the darkness blanketed them. So I clutched Cheriour's hand as we walked, both for comfort and support, since my ankle was still weak and achy, and he was more sure-footed.

We stopped near the outer edge of the town and tucked ourselves into one of the half-crumbled buildings. This one had three walls and part of the roof still standing, so it offered some protection from the lashing wind.

As my eyes somewhat adjusted to the dark, I looked at him, *really* looked at him, for the first time since he'd arrived. His frizzy mass of curls rested in a sloppy ponytail over his right shoulder. The gloomy darkness shadowed all the right areas of his face, making his cheekbones pop and his emerald eyes glow. And his outfit was fucking *sinful*. Aside from his gray shirt and black breeches, he wore almost all leather: the form-fitting army vest, knee-high boots, and a perfectly distressed brown hide jacket. Which... *hmmm*...guys in leather jackets were always hot AF. But Cheriour in this jacket, with the way it hugged his lean frame...

My mouth watered as a spike of arousal pricked low in my belly.

Ermm...yeah. This conversation was gonna have to wait a minute.

And Cheriour seemed to be having the same line of thought (although I had no freaking clue what he found attractive about my sloppy, stinky self). Because when I dropped my blanket and leaned up to kiss him, he was already angling down to kiss me. Our mouths smacked ungracefully together. He huffed, the small laugh ghosting over my lips in a warm puff, while I made a weird half growl, half whimper.

The second attempt was a lot smoother. But he snagged the driver's seat, capturing my lower lip in a warm, tender suckle and touching my face in a sweeping stroke.

Absolutely the fuck not.

I liked that he was sweet. And teasing. And considerate. And compassionate. I loved *all* that about him.

But right now, I wanted—*needed*—something different.

And with as intuitive and observant as he was, Cheriour must've sensed that. When I splayed my hand against his chest, pushing him into the wall, he went willingly. When I fumbled with the ties at his vest, *desperate* to feel his skin, he helped me. His warm, steady hands guided my cold, trembling ones. All the while, his eyes never left my face.

With the vest undone, I yanked at his shirt, untucking it and slipping my hand underneath. His abs twitched beneath my prodding fingers. His chest did a hitchy stutter. And when I moved my lips to his neck, biting at the chorded muscle, he made that low "*hmmm...*"

Fuck. *Fuckfuckfuck.*

My pulse roared in my ears as a hot, pleasant zing frolicked around in my belly, the first *good* sensation I'd felt in so, so, so long.

I needed more. All the sounds. All the sensations.

My hand palmed the taut expanse of his chest, occasionally giving his nipples a tug or twist. All while I kissed and licked and sucked and bit his neck, his collarbone, his earlobe...any bit of skin I could get my mouth on.

But he was still too composed. Sure, he reacted with those deep hums and grunts. But he was still idly petting my hair and stroking my back. Still sneaking little kisses to my cheeks or brow. I wanted him *un*composed. I wanted to break his fucking brain, to have him lose himself so I could lose myself in him.

My hand dropped to the front of his pants, rubbing. *Hard.* Enough to have him sucking a long breath. But the laces on these breeches always tripped me up. Especially since he double knotted them—I guess to make sure he never got a case of plumber's crack mid-battle.

Again, he had to help me, but his hands were not quite so steady this time.

"Can y'all invent some fucking zippers already?" I mumbled when we finally, *finally*, got the waistband loosened. "This is such a pain in the friggin' ass." I dipped my hand inside.

His hips rocked right into my palm.

Ooh, yes! This was gonna be fun.

Five long, twisty strokes later, his stoic expression crumbled. He leaned back against the wall, one hand grasping my ass, the other rising to his own head, curling around the strands of his hair as his eyes closed.

Glorious. Absolutely *glorious*.

But I wanted more.

I teased, alternating between petting his chest and fondling his cock. Sometimes raking my teeth over his skin. Sometimes drawing his mouth to mine for a gentle kiss. And I *reveled* in how unsteady his breathing had become.

Warm shocks of electricity shot through me when Cheriour's forehead scrunched and his mouth parted around a deep, "*oh.*"

Hot. Hot. Hot. So fucking hot.

His legs shifted, stance widening to balance himself, as his hips began to roll more earnestly. I almost dropped to my knees then, because this position, with him against the wall, was better suited for a BJ than a handsy. My wrist was starting to cramp.

But he'd cradled my chin and pressed his now sweat-slick brow to mine. It was so dang tender. And, honestly, it was a major turn on. Watching the waves of pleasure wash over his face. Kissing him and swallowing every low, desperate sound he made. Holding him as he writhed and bucked and, at the very end, when his overstimulated body couldn't take any more teasing, trembled.

He finished on a guttural, almost pained groan that sent licks of fire dancing around in my stomach.

Afterward, he pressed unsteady, sloppy kisses to my forehead. Then he flipped me around, drawing my back against his now-heaving chest (his legs were probably too rubbery to leave the wall) and teased me as mercilessly as I'd tormented him. His calloused hands swept under my shirt, kneading my belly and loosening my makeshift bra so he could skim my breasts.

Fuck if it didn't feel good. His fingers roamed over me, touching all the places he knew would have electricity zipping through my veins. His mouth suckled on my heated skin—sometimes soothingly, sometimes more harshly—in carefully placed love bites that dragged knives through the already frayed ropes holding my nerves.

"Oooh, fuck you," I hissed, elbowing his side lightly when he inched the tips of his fingers into my waistband only to immediately pull them back out.

His chuckle rumbled through me as he gave my earlobe a soft nip.

When he finally did get his hands in my pants several agonizing minutes later...yeah, I wasn't doing much thinking then. Just feeling.

He alternated between feather-light touches and firm strokes, which drove me *insane*. Because every time I found a rhythm and started that climb, he stopped and pulled me back. *Deliberately*. And I *knew* it was deliberate because when I snapped, "Can you pick a fucking gear and stay in it?" he nuzzled the side of my neck and laughed.

It took several torturous minutes of cursing and clawing at him before he finally showed mercy and gave me what I needed. Shocks of pleasure zipped along my spine, forcing me to arch my back. Aching, heady emotions seized my body, locking my muscles and making my toes curl. I babbled and saw some big ole stars flashing for a hot second.

He had to hold me up when my legs turned to goo. I sighed. Panted. Laughed. *A lot*. "Fuck me," I wheezed between bouts of body-shaking giggles. "You and I need to stay away from walls."

Cheriour's lips curled as he kissed the shell of my ear. "I missed you," he murmured.

CHAPTER 25

COURAGE THE COWARDLY DOG

"Y'know, I actually did want to talk," I said. "I didn't bring you out here *just* for a hand job."

Cheriour's chest, pressed firmly against my back, rumbled around a nearly inaudible laugh.

It felt like he was purring.

We sat on the ground, him leaning against the wall where he'd gotten one of the best orgasms of his life (not to toot my own horn, but he'd made some faces I hadn't seen him make before), me tucked in the cozy cradle between his thighs. Both of us bundled under the scratchy wool blanket.

"I'm sure you're not complaining, though." I lightly pinched his knee.

"No." This said with a *very* self-satisfied drawl as he moved his hands to my shoulders and began kneading. Which felt achingly good, until his thumb hit my left shoulder.

I stiffened, bracing against the stab of pain.

Cheriour paused. His fingers flexed. Then he prodded—

gently—tracing the outer edge of the puckered wound through my shirt.

"That was an arrow," I mumbled. "Thankfully, it's 80 percent of the way healed. I'm sure it'll scar, though. And it won't even be a *cool* scar. Just this stupid, crooked line you'll only see if I wear a halter top."

Cheriour let his palm rest over the wound for a second before he moved his hands inward, turning his ministrations to the back of my neck. "What happened?"

"I said I got impaled by an arrow."

"Since you left Sanadrin," he clarified. "What happened?"

I shook my head with a scoff. "What *hasn't* happened? Hellhounds attacking the village. Wraiths shooting at me. Púcas chasing Abby Normal—which, how in *the frick* did you all make it here in one piece? Because I barely went a day without bumping into Wraiths and their meals on wheels—*humans*," I amended, because I knew without even looking at his face that he'd crumpled his brow. "They had humans in *chains*, Cheriour. If it hadn't been for Abby Normal, I would've joined them. We had *so many* close calls. And Braxton didn't make it. I found him at Swindon. His disguise had already been blown. So how did all of you sneak by unnoticed?"

"Hurleigh." Cheriour coiled a lock of my hair around his finger. "He—"

"Oh, hell, don't even get me *started* on him. That pompous peacock...y'know what *really* chaps my ass? The dude summoned a *tsunami sized wave* because he thought I was a Wraith. You realize all he has to do is flood Sakar to wipe out the Wraiths, and *bam*...our problems would be over."

"It's not that simple."

"Kinda is. Noah zoomed away from a corrupt society on his ark."

"That," Cheriour chuckled, "is a children's story."

My jaw dropped. "Holy cow! You know that one?"

"Slaughtering Wraiths would help. I'll not deny that," he spoke over me. "But a flood would not kill Ramiel. Or the other Celestials."

"Well, yeah. Okay. I guess you're right. And Courage the Cowardly Dog—Hurleigh," I clarified, "will split as soon as he sees another Celestial. Fucking spineless sack of shit. And, look, I get the irony here," I added when Cheriour started to speak. "Me calling him a coward is the pot calling the kettle black. But...God, Cheriour, the things he can do. He *controls the ocean*! And what does he use that for? *Nothing*. He doesn't help us. He didn't lift a goddamn finger when Niall was attacked, or those other places...Cynerik and...?"

"Jabbart."

"Right. Jabberjaws. I can't with these freaking names. But my point...he was here this whole time. Those places didn't have to fall. People didn't have to die. He could've stopped some of it. But he did nothing. And the shit he pulled with the hellhounds? He *knew* we'd be attacked, Cheriour. I still think he orchestrated it. And he was going to let *everyone* die because..." The words caught in the back of my throat. I dropped my head into my hands. "God, everything is so fucked up right now. I can't—"

Cheriour drew me closer, tilting my head back until it rested against the slope of his shoulder. He wrapped his arms around my midsection, took my shaking hands in his, and gave my whole body a comforting squeeze as he kissed my brow.

He was so affectionate.

And these little moments where he bucked the whole *"I'm a scary Viking here to steal your shit and rape your women"* vibe his outer appearance gave off and turned into a squishy, cuddly bear sawed at my heartstrings.

I angled my head, giving him a soft peck on the cheek. His crooked smile had my stomach jittering like a caged bird.

"There was a reason I was hesitant to reach out to Hurleigh." Cheriour kissed the top of my head and left his lips there, so I could feel their caress when he spoke. "He's not as powerful as you believe him to be, Addie. He only seems that way to you because you have limited experience with Celestials. And he *is* afraid. He knows Ramiel's strength. And he's seen what happens to Celestials who contest it. He'll not do anything to risk Ramiel's wrath. It's why he wouldn't help us before. He has only agreed to help now because things have changed."

"*'Things have changed.'* Like me killing Seruf?" I whispered.

Cheriour nodded.

"Is that why he's pushing me to go to Uchen?"

"We're all going to Uchen, Addie."

My brow shot up. "Seriously? *That's* why he brought you here?"

"Yes. Seruf ruled Daigh—a country in Uchen. As she's no longer living"—he traced his thumb over my knuckles—"no Celestials occupy those shores. This presents an opportunity we've never had. To breach Uchen and take what we need from it."

"You *really* think it's a good idea to go poking around over there?"

He exhaled. "I would prefer *not* to take people there. But our choices are limited. Sakar is dying, Addie. The *land* is dying. These attacks haven't only destroyed people and cities. Crops were eradicated. The autumn harvest was slim. Spring's will be slimmer. Nathan may be the last Gardner left. He cannot single-handedly harvest all of Sakar. Animals have perished as well. The Wraiths have no need for them but know we depend on them. They butcher herds for sport." Cheriour's chest expanded with a heavy breath.

"So, you wanna raid Daigh for supplies?"

Cheriour's chin dipped against the top of my head— a nod.

"That's a helluva of a big risk. And even if we pull it off... it would only buy us a few months. If that. It won't save Sakar."

"I know."

And he didn't have to elaborate. I got the memo.

It was why I'd ridden all the way out here on nothing but a wing and a prayer. Because sitting idly by, watching everything around you get chopped to bits and knowing your ass was heading to the guillotine next—*that* was torture. But fighting with everything you had to keep your head on your shoulders took away some of the anxiety. It gave you hope, even when you *knew* that blade would dice you up eventually.

Death was better served with a healthy serving of hope. It was less depressing that way.

But still...

"I'm scared, Cheriour." I scooted my ass back, getting as close to him as I could without crawling into his skin. "Not of going to Uchen. Not really. I think I've gotten desensitized to the battle bullshit. It doesn't pack the same fearmongering punch as it did a few months ago. But I'm scared of..." I dug my nails into Cheriour's knuckles when Darragh's phantom scream ricocheted around my head. "I'm scared of *myself*. I haven't been right since I killed Seruf. It...fuck, I dunno how to describe it. It's like there's this festering wound inside of me, and it doesn't heal. It just keeps growing. And my emotions are *permanently* out of whack. Half the time, I don't know what I'm feeling. I keep telling myself it's stress or PTSD or both. With some high-fructose corn syrup withdrawal thrown in. And they're probably all contributing, but I can *feel*, deep down, that there's something wrong." I gnawed on my lower lip until I tasted blood. "And whenever I get upset, this wound...*flares up*. Or something. It *hurts*. Like now..." I squeezed my eyes shut when another spasm speared my chest.

Cheriour shifted, cradled my quivering hands between his, and tucked my head under his chin, holding me through the worst of the pain.

"Kylah told me this power would damage my soul." I shuddered when the ache eased. "But Hurleigh wants me to use it—he practically *forced* me to. And...I *know* I didn't kill Darragh. The hound did. But I used that...soul-stealing power on him by accident. I couldn't stop it. I don't know what turns this thing on or off. It just *appears* and takes over. And it hurt him. I heard him *screaming*. It hurt me too. And I...what if this power *does* destroy my soul? What if it already has? Do you know when your soul's gone? Do you *feel* it? Or do you wake up one day and become a cold-hearted, murderous asshat? Will I lose my memories? If I don't have a soul, will I even care that the memories are gone? I'm...this is *terrifying* to think about. So I've been *not* thinking about it. But..." My chest tightened again. I jolted, and my voice cracked around the next words. "I can't stop thinking of it now. It won't *go away*."

Cheriour dropped his head, rubbing his cheek against mine. "I...I'm sorry." He sighed and kissed my ear. "You haven't lost your soul, Addie. I promise. But I don't know how your power works or what damage it does. I wish I could offer you assurance. Or train you to control it. I can't. But the fear you've described...I...I..." His throat made an audible click when he swallowed.

Ice clinked and clanked inside my stomach. I turned slightly to look at his face. It was expressionless, his mouth in a neutral line, his eyes focused on something by his right knee. But I felt the pain, the uncertainty, radiating from him. In the way his shoulders had bunched up around his ears. The way his jaw ticked.

He was traumatized by the same fears.

Because he had that damn Fallen curse hanging over his head.

"Cheriour..." I untangled our hands and stroked his cheek.

His eyes closed as he leaned into my touch.

"We really are two peas in a fucked-up pod, aren't we? I'm sorry." I cupped his face and gave him a hard, deep kiss, suckling on his lip and stroking his tongue until one of those soft hums vibrated through him and the tension ebbed from his shoulders.

Seruf had hit the nail on the head with our romance. *Tragic love stories*. We really were living in one, but we faced something worse than death.

Losing ourselves.

Losing our memories, our emotions, our annoying little quirks—everything that made us who we were—and morphing into soulless monsters who could, feasibly, be weaponized against the people we cared about.

Cheriour flinched.

"Oh, crap. Did I say any of what I was thinking out loud? If so, I'm sorry. Maybe it's a sign we should keep kissing, huh? To keep my mouth occupied?"

His lips twitched. "It's dawn, Addie."

I blinked and noticed the grayish light enveloping us. "So?"

"I've brought your poleaxe. You'll train with me this morning."

"You're kidding, right?"

"I need to assess what you remember."

"Apparently, I need to assess *your* fucking memory," I grumbled. "I'm injured. Did you forget that?"

A smile touched his lips. "You're healed."

"Not fully—*urgh*, hey!" I grunted when he scooted out from under me and climbed to his feet. "You bastard!"

He petted my hair.

I whacked his hand away. "Don't get all touchy-feely and try to coddle me. The moment's over. I'm mad at you now."

He laughed and gave my braid a playful tug.

And I had to chuckle as well. Because how was I supposed to stay mad at him?

CHAPTER 26

METEOROLOGIST CHERIOUR

It was as cold as a witch's tit, especially since we stood near the cliff's edge, where the wind wailed like a jilted lover on a rampage to wreak havoc upon those who'd wronged it. Thick furls of pewter-green clouds revolved lazily over the sea. A zingy aroma of salt, moisture, and seaweed wafted through the air. Everything was damp. My hair was plastered to the back of my neck, and Cheriour's curls poofed into a big frizz halo—that was the downside to coarse hair. Didn't quite hold the moisture as well as other hair types.

And the brutal bastard had me in training for *two hours* in these conditions.

I used my fully sharpened poleaxe. He had a weedy stick. And he still beat the snot out of me. (Not literally. He was considerate and kept his hits light. But he hit me an awful freaking lot.)

And when he wasn't smacking my ass around, he orbited me, barking commands.

"Straighten your back."

"Raise your elbow. The poleaxe will do you no good if you hold it there."

"*Move your feet.* You cannot be idle in battle."

Apparently, I'd forgotten 75 percent of what he taught me, and he seemed damned determined to make sure I regained every ounce of memory before the end of the day.

And of course, my blunderbuss show was performed in front of a live studio audience. Everyone popped a squat on the ruins to watch the training—and to caw playfully at me every time I fumbled.

"Ach, get yer head out of the way, Addie! It's too big a target!" Braxton hooted.

I turned, started to roll my eyes at him, and then hissed when Cheriour drilled my ribcage.

"*Focus*, Addie," Cheriour chided.

"How come you're not tormenting any of them with this training bullshit?" I jabbed a thumb at my captivated audience, and then ducked with an "*eeeeek!*" when Cheriour slashed his stick near my bum shoulder.

"They"—a smile crawled over his face—"are competent fighters. You are not." He tapped my hip in a way that almost could've been considered playful—if he hadn't then immediately tried to drive his elbow into my chin.

"You almost had him there!" Natalia called a little while later when I winged my poleaxe at Cheriour's head, only to have him smoothly duck and rebound with a cross-body swipe.

"You're better than I thought you'd be, Addie," Deborah laughed at one point.

When I turned to flip her off, Cheriour thwacked me across the back of the legs.

"I hate you," I snarled at him when the end of our

session left me winded and wheezy, with swamp ass and big ole pools of sweat under my boobs. Drying sweat and cold air did *not* mix well. I had steam coming off my body.

Cheriour collected the poleaxe from my cramped hands and gave my upper arm an affectionate squeeze.

Over the ocean, thunder rumbled. Not a big, earth-shattering boom, but a long, slow roll that lasted nearly a minute before it finally tapered off.

My hair stood on end.

Everyone quieted. Stared.

Cheriour closed his warm, sweat-slick palm over my hand, steadying me.

"Is that it?" Deborah asked.

"You daid we would deave wid de dorm, yed?" Nathan's still-stuffy voice wavered.

Cheriour cast his eyes to the waterlogged clouds above, then lowered his gaze to the foamy waves battering the shore. "We likely have another day," he said, even as a harsh gust of wind snagged the damp curls off his forehead and made them dance artfully in the air.

"Do we know yet how we're getting across?" This came from Quinn, who'd been reclined against a nearby rock for most of my training session, watching me with bleary, red-rimmed eyes. Beads of sweat crowned his forehead. His hands quaked around the piece of paper he kept fiddling with. A night and morning of healing had left him sicker than a dog. I actually felt bad for him.

"Addie said Hurleigh took her over the ocean before. Eh, Addie?" Deborah looked at me for clarification. "But I doubt he'd be able to fly all of us..."

"He didn't fly me," I said.

Quinn's glassy eyes snapped to my face. "Then how did he get you across?"

"We walked. Literally. *Over* the ocean. On the water. It was the trippiest experience of my life, let me tell ya. Cool as shit, though."

Quinn blinked. Several other people gave me googly-eyed, incredulous looks. Cheriour, of course, stared at the ocean, seemingly ignoring me, but I could practically hear the gears grinding in his head. "Braxton," he called. "Are all the horses acclimated to the ocean?"

"Ehhhh." Braxton sniffed and thumped his heel against the rickety U-shaped wall he sat on. "A few are a might unsure of it. The rest aren't so fussed...but...Addie, what d'ye mean ye walked on the water?"

"Exactly that," I said. "Hurleigh made the water solid... ish. And we walked on it."

"What d'ye mean by solid-ish?"

"It was jello-y. Which means nothing to you," I added when he flashed me a sideways "speak English, lady!" look. "Okay, let me think of a better descriptor. Ummm...so, I guess it was kinda like mud? Just with more...*bounce*."

"*Mud?* Feck me." Braxton cupped his hands around his head. "There's naught I can do to prepare them for that."

"Can you make certain they're relaxed around the waves?" Cheriour didn't look away from the ocean. "Work with them now. *Before* the waters worsen."

"Aye." Braxton sighed, raised his fingers to his lips, and whistled, summoning the herd. Then he grumbled under his breath, "Bloody fecking...they're *horses*. They want naught to do with the sea. Poor fecking bloody blighters..."

As his grouchy form walked away, I sidled up to

Cheriour's side. "Are you sure it's a good idea to bring the horses?"

"We need them." Cheriour dragged the end of my poleaxe against his boot, watching the blade dig a long, white line into the leather.

"Yeah, but…" I dropped my voice to a whisper, allowing it to be muffled beneath the stampede of hooves from the horses responding to Braxton's whistle; I didn't wanna scare the shit out of our eavesdropping spectators. "Cheriour, I was out on that ocean during a storm. It is *terrifying*. And, yeah, I know I'm a scaredy cat. But *everyone* will flip when they're bouncing around on twenty-foot waves. Guarantee it. You'll have a hard time getting the two-legged landlubbers across. I can't *imagine* the horses are gonna cooperate."

"We have Braxton," Cheriour said. "He will keep them calm."

Sure. We had Braxton, who currently resembled a preening Disney Princess as he walked along the cliff's edge, followed by the entire herd of horses. But those horses were awfully spooked. Half of them jittered and cackled whenever the wind blew. The other half peered down at the PMSing ocean with big bug-eyes.

I blew out a breath. "He's gonna have his work cut out for him."

"Braxton will keep them calm," Cheriour repeated. "And the riders will keep their mounts on course. We will make it to Daigh on the horses." He said this with an ultra-bored drawl. Like a teacher explaining the homework assignment for the fifteenth time to a blank-faced kid who'd mentally checked out around third period.

"This is such a bad idea." I pinched the bridge of my

nose, although it didn't vanquish my constant headache. "But, whatever. *Into the ocean of death, rode the five hundred!*"

"There will be only forty-six of us," Cheriour said.

"Yeah, I get that. Smartass. It's a poe—"

"And the poem references *six* hundred. Not five hundred."

"*You fucking know that?*"

His lips twitched.

"How...*how*...do you know *The Charge of the Light Brigade* and *Noah's Ark*, but you don't get all the other references I make?"

"Some stories return when you mention them." He tapped his temple. "Others don't. I suppose some tales are more timeless than others."

"Umm, these stories are timeless too..." I lifted my sleeve, flashing the bottom part of my tattoo, which had the Marvel medley, *IT*'s red balloon, the *Ghostbusters* logo, and the mountain from *A Nightmare Before Christmas*. "And so are my other references. Like *Talladega Nights*—Ricky Bobby," I added when he frowned. "Remember him? You called him Rickety Body—the *travesty*."

"Ah. Evidently, his is *not* an enduring tale." A sideways smile slanted over Cheriour's face. But it faded when another slow batch of thunder rippled by, this one sounding very much like a bowling ball charging down the lane but fizzling out before it hit the cones.

"You should rest, Addie." Cheriour touched the back of his fingers to my shoulder, above my arrow scar. "We'll train again later."

"Like hell we will," I grumbled. "Hurleigh's probably gonna show up here in a few hours, being all *come with me if you want to live.*"

Cheriour cocked his head to the side. "Tomorrow, perhaps. The storm will hold until then."

"Okay, Meteorologist Cheriour...if you say so." I slipped my arm through his.

Below us, the first group of horses stepped onto the beach as a monster wave ravaged the shore, sending blobs of white foam ten feet into the air. Five horses screamed and scattered, ignoring Braxton as he cooed, "Ach, it's a wee bit of water, laddies. Ye're alright."

Cheriour's chest heaved on a long, gloomy-sounding sigh.

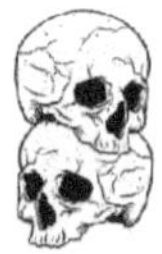

The clouds darkened throughout the day, and a misty rain blanketed the area by nightfall. The storm rumbled and roared but seemed to be stomping up the coast at the speed of a blitzed sloth (aka, it creepy-crawled one agonizingly slow mile at a time).

That night, even though I was bone-tired, achy, and snuggled against Cheriour (with little Splinter doing his civic duty to keep the girls warm) I couldn't sleep. Not even a light doze. And I wasn't the only one. Most people lay awake, whispering to each other, listening to the rain, and dreading the dawn.

But dawn didn't come. The pewter-green storm clouds strangled the sun. Midmorning was as dark as midnight.

It was almost Go Time.

As thunder rattled the barn, we shimmied into our

armor—if you could call the stiff leather vests and knee-high boots *armor*. And we saddled the horses beneath a pounding deluge—*not* an easy task, with the rain making the leather slimy and the horses jolting and jittering at every boom of thunder or sizzle of lightning.

As the other riders took their mounts and shuffled toward the sea, Cheriour and I hung back. Because we had one last—*extremely* unpleasant—task to do.

My boots went *squitch-squitch-squitch* when I walked back to the barn. Cheriour's went *squatch-squatch-squatch.* Almost in rhythm with mine. Kinda like a bad musical number, ruined only by the heavy *kerthunk-kerthunk-kerthunk-kerthunk* of the horse splashing between us.

"I hope to God Abs eats," I mumbled. "And we're not killing this poor horse for nothing."

As if understanding my words, the horse blew a nervous, cackling snort.

Cheriour stroked the animal's nose. "She's more likely to drink fresh blood," he said.

I didn't know this horse. He was brown, like 90 percent of them, but he seemed young, fit, and easygoing. I didn't know why he hadn't been picked to cross the ocean. And I didn't know why Cheriour had plucked him out of our surplus herd.

But I had a sick, slippery feeling in my gut as Cheriour and I led this kind, gentle-eyed animal to the guillotine (aka, the barn).

Inside, Abby Normal still stood in the center, her head hanging low, her eyes listless and unfocused. She didn't look up when we entered. Even when I clapped my hands against my thighs and trilled, "Look alive, Abs!" she barely blinked.

"C'mon, Abs!" I wrestled the door free of the wind and

slammed it shut, temporarily muffling the roar of the storm. "We're heading out, and I need you to hold down the fort for a bit. 'Kay?"

She swayed slightly, dragging her droopy lower lip through the dirt.

Overhead, thunder popped off with such force, it vibrated the earth beneath our feet.

The brown horse squealed and bobbed his head. Cheriour chuffed and patted the animal's neck.

At that, Abby Normal blinked sluggishly. Her head remained glued to the floor, but she rolled one red eye toward the horse.

"Yeah, we brought you something special." I walked over to her and rested my hand against her brow, tracing my thumb over the scar Hurleigh had left when he'd decked her with his wing. "It's the Deluxe Happy Meal—the finest grade-A horse meat in all of Sakar. You've earned it, girl-friend. So, take a load off. Chill for a bit. And, for fuck's sake, eat up. *Please.* I want that horse to be bone-dry by the time we get back. And *don't*"—I glanced at Splinter's enclosure, tucked in the farthest corner of the barn—"munch on Splinter as dessert. *Please.* He's an off-limits snack. Capiche?"

She made a low whuffle but never moved her eye off the horse, which spiked hope into my heart. It was the first time she'd shown interest in *anything* since the hellhound attack.

"We'll need to open the vein." Cheriour's knife made a soft *whoosh-ziing* as he whipped it from its holster. "She won't have the strength to do it herself."

He smoothly slashed a long line down the horse's neck —not severing the artery but still drawing ribbons of blood. And he cooed soothing nonsense words as he dragged the bleeding, wide-eyed animal to Abby Normal's side.

Abby Normal's nostrils flared, and she made low *hur-hur-hur* noises as she curled her lips over her teeth.

"Oh, *ew, ew, ew, ew*! Nope. *Noooope*. I can't watch this." I clapped my hands over my ears as I booked it out the door.

Cheriour emerged from the barn less than a minute later. "She's drinking," he murmured.

BOOM! Zzzzzaaaaapppp.

"Jesus!" I hissed when the latest thunder-lightning combo left my ears ringing.

Cheriour closed the distance between us and brushed my shoulder. "We have to go."

Yup. I'd gotten that memo too. *Loud* and clear.

Fifteen minutes later, I *squitch-squatched* back through the town, this time walking behind Cheriour and his burly mare. I clutched a water-slicked rein in one hand, and it was...deteriorating? Or something. It left my bare palm coated with a sticky brown residue.

On the other end of that viscid rein, Sacrifice trudged beside me, wet and stinking worse than a dog who'd found a deep puddle of deer crap to roll in. She kept sneezing, blowing misty puffs of rain and snot out of her nose.

As we slabbered past the barn, I peered through gaps in the crooked door, trying to gauge if Abby Normal was eating. But all I saw were blurred hunks of shadows.

Wind gusted by, pinging rain into my eyeballs. The barn loosed a long, harrowed groan as it fought to withstand the gale.

Sacrifice grunted and shifted sideways, her little ears splaying.

I absently reached up to bonk her nose. She jerked back,

her teeth clanking against her bit. And it wasn't a *"don't touch me"* move. More of a *"too fast, human!"* reaction.

I made the poor horse nervous.

Abby Normal was used to all my sudden movements and loud trills. She sometimes got irritated with me, sure, but she mostly let my anxious energy roll right off her shoulders. And I hadn't realized how much she'd adapted to me, and I to her, until now, as I stared at Abby Normal's shadowed sliver through the door while walking beside the very first horse I'd ever ridden.

A horse who reacted to every move and sound I made, and sometimes looked at me as though I had fifteen heads and spoke exclusively in Martian (*ack, ack, ack!*).

"Sorry, honey." I slowly stroked Sacrifice's nose. "You and I didn't get off on the right foot, huh? I'll try to do better this time."

So much had changed since Cheriour first plopped me onto Sacrifice's back. Kingdoms and cities had fallen. Summer had faded, and autumn was currently withering under winter's chokehold. People had died...more than half of those I'd journeyed with during those first few days were now gone.

I'd changed most of all. And I was *seriously* glad mirrors weren't a thing in Sakar because I probably wouldn't recognize my reflection. And not *just* because my frayed and weather-damaged hair was twisted into a sloppy, rat-nest braid. Even if I gave myself a hot bath, a well-needed blowout, and slapped a healthy coating of makeup over my face, I still wouldn't recognize myself. Because I wasn't the same Addie Collins who'd sucked down that caramel latte (with *extra* caramel, of course) on the way to work.

I couldn't even remember what a caramel latte tasted like.

But Sacrifice, who looked at me with those dark, soft, horsey eyes hadn't changed. She was the lone reminder of a different time. And a different version of myself.

And being reunited with her made my heart ache. Because sometimes I missed the old, naïve, stupid, vain, and blissfully ignorant Addie Collins.

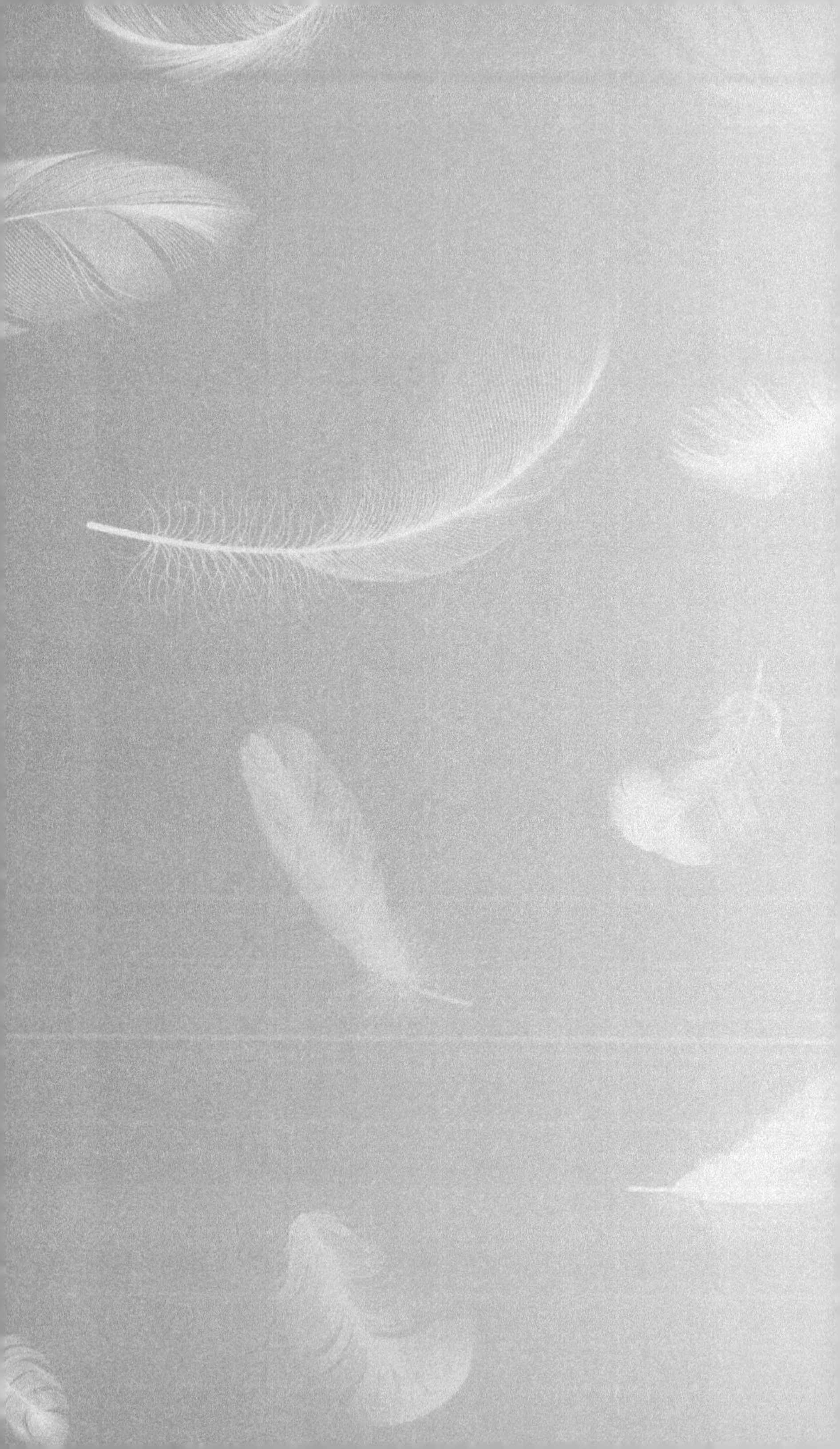

CHAPTER 27
JUMP SCARE

Forty-six horses and riders gathered on the edge of the cliff. And what a motley crew we were: a bunch of green-gilled landlubbers who looked ready to hurl at the sight of the rollicking waves below (Hurleigh was appropriately named indeed, har, har), and a cluster of horses who were telling us, in no uncertain terms, that they thought we were out of our fucking minds.

Most horses squealed, reared, and bucked (not always in that order). Some got fancy with their footwork and side-stepped into high-flashing dance moves. Cheriour had a hell of a time keeping his bay mare's feet on the ground. She repeatedly flung herself into the air, as though trying to sprout wings and fly off into the storm like Pegasus. Even Sacrifice was hard to hold. She shivered when the thunder clapped, and she was restless, swinging her shoulder into me, hauling at the reins, and getting pissy when I pulled back. Her eyes were blown so wide, the outer edges were all white.

This was going *splendidly* so far. A walk in the fucking park.

And the damn Celestial hadn't even shown up yet.

A minute ticked by. Two. Ten.

I stayed at the back of the group (because my Queen Bitch needed her personal space), but through the undulating throng of wet, writhing bodies, I caught glimpses of the savage waves torpedoing the cliffs.

Rain hammered us, and the wind seemed to blow in five different directions. It was cold. Miserable AF. And, my God, I'd already inhaled so much freaking water. I was either gonna turn into a fish or asphyxiate by the end of this.

"Yer sure he's comin'?" Braxton called.

Zzzzzzsssshhhhh.

Lightning zapped an oncoming wave, briefly casting an orange hue over the ocean.

And the preening peacock made his theatrical entrance.

He rose gracefully from the sea (still shirtless...surprise, surprise), slipping his bare feet soundlessly onto the clifftop. Beneath the inky, stormy daylight, his glistening wings looked almost black.

Devil's wings.

And his sudden appearance made for a *perfect* jump-scare. Our group turned into a brigade of screeching banshees as horses and people shrieked in panic.

Sacrifice whizzed sideways, tearing the rein through my fingers. I yelled and barely, *barely* clung onto her, getting some gritty leather burns on my palm for the effort.

"Easy!" Cheriour's drawling voice somehow cut through the wind, rain, ocean rumbles, and all the screaming. He grunted when his mare thrust herself into the air again, and then he stood still, stroking her neck, coaxing her to keep her feet grounded. "Braxton, calm the horses."

"Aye...a wee bit difficult to do when I myself *am not calm!*"

I couldn't see Braxton through the throng of people, but the frustration in his voice had teeth. His face was probably about as red as his hair.

Cheriour kept calling instructions. "Do not draw your weapon, Rhona. Kaelan, it's alright. Walk away for a moment to get your composure back."

Thank fuck he was here, keeping everyone and everything together. Because, y'know, I always had to make things worse, especially when I was freezing, tired, scared, and had a thousand-pound animal trying to rip my arm off.

"Here's a fun idea: next time, yell '*Boo!*' when you pop out of oblivion," I yelled at Hurleigh. "You'll *really* make everyone shit their pants..."

"Addie," Cheriour said. "Stop pulling on Sacrifice's mouth. If she won't be still, turn her in a circle."

Easier said than done. Despite her small size, Sacrifice needed more clearance to turn than a semi-truck. She kept her head sky-high the whole time, grinding her teeth around the bit, the whites of her eyes becoming more and more prominent.

"I will not be able to take you over the ocean." Hurleigh looked at me when he spoke, not at Cheriour or at anyone else.

If my hands hadn't been full with Sacrifice, I would've flipped him off. "You *can't?* Or you *won't?*"

"There are too many of you," Hurleigh said, "and your beasts will hamper your progress."

As soon as the words left his mouth, Deborah's bloodred

stallion slipped out of his bridle and tore ass back to the barn.

Something bubbled in my chest at Hurleigh's words. Relief? Anger? Disappointment? A bout of nervous gas? I wasn't sure. But, for a hot second, I thought the mission was canceled. He wasn't going to do it. We'd gotten ourselves all dolled up for nothing.

"You'll need to go *beneath* the sea." The next pop of thunder almost drowned out Hurleigh's words.

Almost.

Lightning cut diagonally across the sky, making the air sizzle. Sacrifice's nostrils blew so wide, I saw the pink lining the inside.

"I'm sorry, *what*?" I asked.

At the same time, Cheriour nodded and stroked his mare's neck, calming her before she leapt for the heavens again. "Understood."

A few people gave him nervous glances. Nathan, wrestling with a shrieking black and white mare close to the edge of the cliff, peered down at the ocean. Then he straightened and ogled Hurleigh with an almost comical *"are you shitting me?"* expression.

"Swimming? Are-are you telling us we have to *swim*?" A weird metallic taste filled my mouth, and a jolt pinged through my heart, as though I'd licked a battery to test if it still had juice.

"You'll not be swimming," Hurleigh said. "Bring your beasts to the beach..."

"The beach that's currently underwater?" I clarified.

"Move quickly. This storm will not last into the night, and I cannot help you once it ends." Hurleigh fluttered his wings...

Poof.

"Gah!" I squealed when he materialized in front of me, close enough for me to get a whiff of the briny seaweed scent clinging to his body.

"Dude, what the—" I started.

Sacrifice flung herself sideways, nearly snatching the rein out of my hand again.

"I trust you remember our discussion, Adelaide." Hurleigh flashed me a look of smoldering intensity that would've put Dwayne Johnson to shame. And then he *poofed* again, returning to the ocean.

"Oooh, you fucking—"

"Enough, Addie," Cheriour droned. "Be still." He pivoted to face me, cocking his head. Like he understood my fury but was reminding me this was not the time or the place for a hissy screaming match.

"Erm...Cheriour?" Braxton moved through the mass of horses. And, haha, look at that! I'd been right about his face being as red as his hair. He resembled a tomato. A *soggy* tomato. "We may have a wee problem," he said. "I've been telling the horses we're going *over* the water...and they haven't much cared for that, mind, but they were prepared. But now...some of them can't swim well, ye see..."

"We won't be swimming," Cheriour said.

"Eh?"

"Move to the beach!" Cheriour raised his voice so everyone could hear him.

A surge of unhappy grumbles rippled around the group. A few people coughed. Sneezed. At least three of them hurled their guts up, and those sticky *uuuurrrkkkk-bleggggh* sounds had a nasty, artichoke-y taste pooling in my mouth. But everyone still formed a single-file line and led their screeching horses down the twisting path to the beach.

"Braxton," Deborah called, waving her horseless bridle through the air. "Can you—"

"He's comin' back," Braxton snapped. "Oh, for feck's sake..." This came out in a vicious snarl when Natalia's plaintive cry rose from the beach. Her mare was, evidently, refusing to budge. "Give her a mo'...mayhap treat her a little more kindly, yeah?" Braxton said. "She's as scared as ye are."

"You alright there, Braxton?" I asked when he walked by, leading his brown mare.

"*No.*" And he went full demon with that growl.

I didn't blame him. This was pure madness. And I stood behind the group, still at the top of the cliff, getting a bird's-eye view of the clusterfuck below.

The beach was underwater. Angry, fizzling bouts of ocean poured over the rocks and engulfed the sand. People and horses stepped off the path and straight into the rampaging surf.

A wave stampeded in, munching up the rocks and the sand, the force of it knocking several people off balance. Natalia and Reece both teetered, fell, and disappeared beneath the foamy waters for several terrifying seconds. As others dashed to help them, horses got loose and created an unholy tangle at the bottom of the path, blocking others from coming down.

"Move along!" From somewhere on the cliff trail, Braxton's cracking voice rose above the hubbub. "Come now, *forward!*"

But the traffic jam didn't budge. Until Rhona bulldozed her way down the trail, shooing the errant horses aside, and lugged her quivering, brown-speckled stallion into the water. Quinn followed her...*very* ungracefully, getting dragged when his horse bolted from a wham of thunder. For a split, comical second, Quinn looked like a jet skier about to go skipping over the surf. And then he back-flopped, swallowing a big mouthful of water and retching it back up. Rhona had to grab his horse's reins to keep it from running off again.

With the traffic jam cleared, Deborah and her returned rogue sidled down the path. She boomed, "Oooh, it's bloody freezing!" as she tipped into the sea.

CRRRRRACCCKKK!

A bolt of lightning turned the world into a strobe light for two long seconds. Sacrifice screamed and whipped her head back and forth, and I yelled when the sticky leather reins flayed my palms.

"Addie," Cheriour called back to me as he prepared for his descent, "you're tense—"

"Gee, *am I?*"

"She'll not relax if you maintain that tension. Loosen your hold. She doesn't like her mouth pulled."

And then Cheriour descended, moving with his nimble ease. He oh-so-casually leaned forward at the end of the path to break through an oncoming wave, all while grasping his hopping mare lightly in one hand.

I skittered behind him, nonchalantly strolling through the water like a mermaid returning to sea.

Pffftttt, as if.

"Easy, Sacrifice. Go easy on me here," I murmured as we navigated the winding trail.

She snorted, sending a misty cloud of boogers into the rainy air, but seemed to heed my plea. Because she walked docilely. No leaping, crow hopping, or sideways jigs like the others had done.

"Good girl." I stroked her muzzle. "Good—*ooof!*"

My foot slid out from under me, and down I went, bashing my head against the stone and skidding down the last bit of path on my back. Stars erupted before my eyes, followed by a crap ton of foam as the surf crashed over me. But before I could take a big lungful of fresh, salty water, Cheriour grabbed my shoulder and hauled me to my feet, holding onto me when another wave barrel-rammed into my knees.

Meanwhile, Sacrifice ambled into the water and started playing. When the wave whooshed in, she made a loud squeal and pounced on it.

"What are you, part cat?" I laughed around a cough-sneeze combo—the saltwater freaking *ravaged* my sinuses. "Or part fish?"

Sacrifice shoved her nose beneath the water and blew bubbles.

But then the Proud Peacock returned, doing his Jesus stroll on top of the water, and Sacrifice's happy mood faded. But her tinny whine was lost amongst the fresh swell of shouts and whinnies.

"I'll give you a few moments to clear the rocks." Hurleigh stretched his glistening wings to their full width. "The sea is going to swallow you, and you must allow it to."

With that, he gave his wings a shake and *poofed* away.

"Stupid, cryptic...Sacrifice, come on!" A series of *crrc-crrc-cracks* erupted along my shoulder when Sacrifice threw her full body weight against the reins, scrabbling to get back up the path. "We're not going that way. We're...*ugh*..." I staggered into Cheriour, our wet bodies colliding with a resounding *smack*, when the tide ripped at my ankles, trying to tow me out to sea.

Cheriour widened his stance, keeping his feet rooted against the ocean's hold. As I leaned against him for balance, he curled his free hand over Sacrifice's rein and gave one little tug. She came right back to him. *Go figure.* I'd been pulling on her with all my strength, and she'd given me the middle finger.

Horsewoman extraordinaire, I was not.

"What did he mean?" Natalia's thin, frightened voice misted into the air. "The sea is going to *swallow us*?"

"We need to ride out," Cheriour said. "*Mount up!*"

"*Mount up?*" Natalia gaped.

"Where are we riding to, exactly?" I asked.

Cheriour angled his head, a very "where the hell do you think?" gesture.

"Ah. Into the ocean," I grumbled. "*Of fucking course.* How silly of me for asking..."

But as I shimmied around and got ready to mount, a breathless, red-cheeked Braxton came sloshing over. "Sacrifice must go first. She's the only one not afraid of the ocean." He patted his mare's neck, murmuring something unintelligible into her ear when she squalled. "The others will go no farther. They're scared, Cheriour. We're askin' too much of them. But Sacrifice...she has no fear of water. If she goes, it might convince the rest to follow."

"Might?" I asked.

"Aye. *Might.*"

"Then Sacrifice goes first," Cheriour said. "Braxton, help the other riders ready their mounts. Addie, take my horse." He extended his arm, offering me the reins of his flighty mare.

"Wait, what?"

"I'll help you mount her," he said.

The mare's squawks punctuated his words as she did another round of aerial gymnastics. It was barely an effort for him to hold the reins through her high-tootin' bucks.

But me? Sitting on her back? Ha. That wouldn't even be a full eight-second run.

Besides, I wasn't a dummy. I knew *exactly* what he was doing.

"No." I dug my fingers into Sacrifice's reins, pulling her away from him.

"Addie…"

"I said no." If someone was gonna get yeeted into the great unknown alone, it had to be me. *Had to be.* Because this whole debacle was my fault. I'd dragged half these people to Muirin; the other half had followed me here. And I'd be damned if I let any of them gallop off into the ocean of doom.

"I'm riding Sacrifice." I flipped her around, hefted my foot into the stirrup, and prepared to do an elegant, Clint Eastwood-esque swing into the saddle. But when I tried to jump, the tide snagged my foot, gluing it to the sand. I floundered and thwacked my chest against the saddle. "Okay…ummm…." I rubbed my poor, abused boobs. "I'm gonna need some help. Please? My foot's stuck."

Cheriour said nothing. Just bent, grasped my calf, muttered a drowsy "ready?" and boosted me into the saddle. The saltwater-and-rain mix made the saddle slicker than a Slip 'N Slide but turned my breeches into gritty, crusty sandpaper.

Beneath my legs, Sacrifice's stomach heaved on a downtrodden sigh. As though grumbling, *"Oh, good. This chaotic idiot's riding me again?"*

I stroked her mane and gathered the wobbly, limp-noodle reins in my hands.

"You'll need to push her." Cheriour touched his hand to my knee. The gentle, comforting heat of his skin seeped through my breeches and stilled my nervous shiver. "Sit back," he continued. "Push her forward. And keep your eyes up." He gave my knee a firm squeeze, and there was a flicker of emotion in his gaze. A twinge; there and gone.

Fear.

"Go, Addie." He stepped back, bringing his mare around so he could climb into the saddle.

But I hesitated, my trembling breaths puffing a janky beat as I stared at the lathered ocean through Sacrifice's ears.

"For feck's sake. Go!" Braxton's piercing shout made me jump, which made Sacrifice flinch and skitter to the right.

"Goddamn..." I hauled on the left rein. She angled her head into my left knee, but her body curved outward, continuing its right-hand trajectory until her hip dinged against a curved rock. Then she stilled and screamed in outrage.

"Forward, Addie!" Cheriour said. "Push her *forward*."

I kicked her with my right leg. She straightened herself with a hollow grunt. Then I dug both heels into her sides. *Go, go, go...*

For a terrifying half second, she coiled herself up but didn't budge. And I *swore* she was going to shoot into a vertical rear. But then she drove off her haunches and leapt into the surf.

I pitched forward in the saddle, going *"heeeecch"* when

the pommel caught me square in the crotch. "Motherfuck-er." I righted myself with a gasping cough. "These saddles need seatbelts. And better padding. And—*eeek!*"

Sacrifice nearly ran headlong into a chunk of stone. I sawed on the reins, pulling her around it. Then she bobbled when a retreating wave uncovered a serrated dip in the ground.

And a cold fist of fear punched a hole into my chest.

Because *too much* water was receding, and too quickly. Before us lay a maze of wet sand and scabrous boulders. The sea drew farther and farther away from the shore, as though inhaling, preparing to loose the mother of all waves upon us.

Sacrifice was oblivious, too busy stalking the last tendrils of water. For a second, two, twenty, all I could hear was the clinking and clanking of her churning hooves kicking up plumes of sandy pebbles. My breathing hitched as I zigzagged her around hulking boulders, piles of *zizzing* seaweed, and jagged potholes.

All the while, I kept my gaze locked outward, squinting through the darkness.

And then, for the second time in my life, I stared down a behemoth wave.

Rrrrrrrrrroooooooaaaaaarrrrrr.

The watery skyscraper tumbled toward us, buzzing with fury.

Sacrifice's ears shot forward. She took one look at that sucker, went, *"Hell naw, I don't like water this much!"* and came to a jerky, stiff-legged halt.

"You gotta go." I ran a trembling hand over her neck, even as I dug my heels into her sides. "It's...I know it looks horrifying, but it's not gonna hurt you!"

I hoped.

Sacrifice let out a long, piercing whinny.

Behind us...*far* behind us, another horse neighed a response. Maybe comforting her—or telling her she was screwed if she didn't turn back ASAP.

Clear the rocks, Hurleigh had said. And it made sense now.

We had to venture out to meet that wave.

Because if it came to us, even with the intention to carry us somewhere...well, it was still, y'know, *a wave*. A metric shit ton of water with fucking terrible aim. It'd shatter us against these rocks.

"Sacrifice...you gotta *go!*" I screamed. And I shoved my heels into her sides until my calf and thigh muscles threatened to explode, willing her, *pleading with her*, to canter forward. Away from the rocks and into the mouth of a Godzilla-sized wave. "Please. *Please.* Help me!"

And, miraculously, she moved.

Her canter was stiff and pogo-hoppy, her breathing heavier than a horny dragon's.

Or was that my breathing?

Or both?

Probably both.

Her wet, salty mane slapped my arms, and tendrils occasionally whipped my face. I winced at the stinging lashes but never stopped nudging her with my heels. The rain pelted us, its stinging droplets belting my cheeks and swarming my nose, making me feel like I was breathing water instead of air.

I was gonna drown before the big shebang had a chance to snuff the lights out.

"It's *not* gonna kill us!" I yelled, trying to comfort Sacrifice. And myself.

The watery monster stomped toward land.

And it was all so, *so* loud. The rain. The ocean. Sacrifice's terror. My own sounds of panic. I didn't know if anyone was behind me. I couldn't hear them. And I wasn't daring enough to look over my shoulder.

Maybe they'd wised up and scrambled back up the cliff, and I was all alone, galloping across the sand, driving myself and an innocent horse straight into hell's arms.

The sea will swallow you.

I couldn't breathe. White spots exploded before my eyes.

T-minus twenty seconds to impact.

Sacrifice made another piercing whinny and almost gagged herself on a mouthful of rain. No horses answered her. She screamed again. And again. Veins bulged in her neck. Her eyes, when I caught a glimpse of them, were white-rimmed and wild.

T-minus ten seconds.

A sob caught in my throat. "We'll be alright." I threaded my left hand through her mane, clutching it for dear life. "It's not going to hurt us. It's *not*."

But I squeezed my eyes shut as we smacked headlong into the water wall.

MARCO! POLO!

Pain!

Everything hurt. But not in a "we're getting pulverized" kinda way. This was a tight, tight, *tight* pressure. Kinda how I'd always imagined Augustus Gloop felt when he got slurped out of the chocolate river and smooshed into the tube.

I'd always felt bad for Augustus. Mostly because I *was* Augustus, living my best life, trying to eat all the sweets.

And now I *literally* was Augustus Gloop: being pummeled on all sides and squeezed into an opening I didn't fit through. Except he'd been in a tube made of plastic and metal. Mine was all water. And I had no idea where it would spit me out.

Beneath me, Sacrifice had stopped screaming and was now blindly plowing forward. And I couldn't help her. Couldn't comfort her. All I could do was hold on as the wave did its damnedest to pancake us both.

The water robbed me of my senses. Furls of foam pounded my eyes whenever I dared to open them. The warbled *rooooooaaaaarrrrrr* of the sea lolloped around in my ears. Unyielding pressure sandwiched me from all sides. And every time I inhaled, trying to find pinpricks of air, I swallowed big mouthfuls of ocean. My lungs ballooned with water—a bulbous, pulsating balloon that would grow and grow until...*POP!* Blood everywhere.

"*Guggh-heeugh!*"

A burbled huff-cry combo tumbled out of my mouth when the pressure abruptly lifted.

I choked, dribbling mucus and water all down my front, and inhaled air. Sweet, salty, *glorious* air.

Beneath me, Sacrifice sneezed and snorted, her sides heaving unsteadily as her body locked into a violent bout of trembling.

"It's alright." My voice came out in a croaky rasp. I coughed again, my lungs spewing up another mouthful of water, and patted Sacrifice's quivering neck. "It's alright. It's over. We made it...*somewhere...*"

As I lifted my head and stared at my surroundings, I saw nothing but murky black. Heard nothing but the *whoooosh-rrooooarrrr* of the waves.

"What—" I started. But then a big flash of light strobed overhead, and my mouth went dry.

Arched panels of undulating aquamarine walls surrounded us.

Water.

Those walls were made of *water*.

We were standing under the mothereffing ocean!

It was cold down here. And slimy. Globs of sizzling seaweed coated the ground. Some fish wriggled and flopped by Sacrifice's feet, their bugging eyes glinting through the blackness.

Whooosh.

Rooooaarrrr.

Whoooossssh.

Bang.

Each time the sea swelled with a fresh wave or thunder clanged, the walls heaved and quavered. Lightning struck every few seconds, sending snippets of light through the high-domed ceiling, which only made the unnatural atmosphere more sinister.

Sacrifice whipped her head up, as though just noticing our surroundings, and skittered sideways with a panicked chuff.

"Don't!" I cried, snatching a rein. Which, of course, only made her bolt harder.

Bzzzzzzt.

We collided with one of the ocean walls, sending a fine mist of salty water washing over us. Sacrifice squealed, ripped the rein out of my hand, and tore off in a stiff-legged, hoppy canter.

"Easy...easy..." I tried to coo as I snagged the reins back, but I was shaken—not stirred (har, har)—so my voice had the plinky quality of an antique wind-up doll.

Sacrifice billowed in protest and shot sideways, crashing into the wall again.

Bzzzzzzztttt.

With a cackling snort, Sacrifice halted with her legs splayed and her nose stuck up in the air.

"It's alright," I whispered. "It's—"

Blughugh.

She and I both jumped when the sound of retching filled the air bubble.

I whipped my head around.

A shadowed blob now stood a few feet away, emitting a series of stomach-curdling gags.

Zsssssshhhhhh.

The next bolt of lightning beamed a spotlight over the blob, and I blew out a relieved guffaw.

Cheriour!

He still sat astride his mare, both of them heaving.

"Addie?" His voice was a little nasally and a lot breathless as he swiped his hair out of his eyes and squinted, searching for me.

"Oh, *halle-fucking-lujah.* You made it! I—" Sacrifice body-slammed into the wall again and kicked out, almost catapulting me over her neck, and then she reared, screaming, when the other horses and riders began bursting through the water.

For several minutes, chaos unfurled. Horses smashed into the bubble and slammed into each other. Hoots and yaps rattled the dome as the riders fought to settle their mounts and settle themselves. Traveling via wave tube was *not* a pleasant experience. For anyone.

"Oh, bugger me." Deborah leaned over her horse's shoulder and blew oceany chunks onto the ground.

Other people choked and gagged. More sneezed. And the horses continued to twirl and trill, which set Sacrifice more on edge. As I tried to crack a joke ("Look at that. The gang's all here!"), she backed up, hit the wall again, and kicked out, spraying water all up my backside.

"Stop pulling on her." Cheriour pushed his mare to the front of the group.

"I'm not!" Although I was. Not intentionally, but fear had me white-knuckling the reins. I exhaled, pried my numb fingers open, and let the leather slip through my hands.

Sacrifice whimpered and decided this was *not* the time to be an antisocial ninny. She pulled the reins out of my hands, trotted to the herd with her tail tucked firmly between her legs, and plastered herself against the first horse she bumped into: Cheriour's mare.

"So, uh..." I swiped at my still-running nose. "That was an interesting trip, huh? I'm sure it cleared *everyone's* sinuses."

No one answered. Braxton looked almost ready to pass out. Deborah still seemed a little seasick. Quinn stared at the ocean walls, his jaw hanging slack (pretty sure he had some drool dribbling down his chin). Nathan and Natalia were both sneezing their heads off.

Even Cheriour was red-faced, wide-eyed, and disheveled. "Rhona," he called, his voice a little sharper than normal.

"I know." Rhona had nudged her prancy stallion beside us. "But I'll not be able to hold it for long."

"Give us as much time as you can," he said.

Cheriour's mare, only now realizing she had Sacrifice glued to her side, squawked and chomped her teeth. Sacrifice pinned her ears and swung her ass sideways, loading a kick.

"Ladies," I sighed, "can we not catfight?"

"*Tsssk,*" Cheriour hissed and flicked both their necks. They grudgingly stilled, although neither wiped the grumpy expressions from their faces. "We'll need to move *quickly,*" Cheriour called. "Stay together. The horses are frightened—"

"The people are too," Deborah huffed.

"And we won't have much light."

As he said that last bit, Rhona stretched her right hand above her head and...

I blinked once. Twice.

"Please tell me I'm not the only one who sees her hand glowing," I muttered. Because it literally looked like her palm had thousands of mini-LED bulbs implanted beneath the skin.

"Rhona's an Illuminator," Kaelan, wrestling with his skitzy gray mare a few feet away, said.

Illuminator.

I'd heard that before. Only once, in passing. When I'd first arrived in Sakar, Cheriour had been caring for an injured preteen boy. A kid who, sadly, had died on the trek to Niall.

"Liam is an Illuminator. He creates light."

So, this would've been that kid's power: casting wide beams of incandescent light from the palm of his hand. A human flashlight, and a damn good one. Rhona's palm illuminated the craggy path snaking through the cylinder of rolling water.

Let there be fucking light, indeed.

"We really are under the ocean, eh?" Braxton's strained voice floated through my ears. "If only Belanna had lived to see this..."

A wave *whoooshed* overhead, pulsating the water cylinder. Several people gasped.

"Be still," Cheriour droned.

"Should be an easy path through," Rhona said as she flicked the lights off and pushed her horse into a brisk trot.

With a call to "ride forward," Cheriour launched his jittery mare into a skippy jog behind Rhona. Sacrifice did a panic-scramble to catch up with them, and the rest of our ragtag crew sprawled out behind me.

Light on.

Rhona stretched her arm forward, double checking our path.

Light off.

We traveled in oppressive darkness.

Whoops, hollers, and profanities pinged off the back of my head as the group behind me tried to gather their bearings. There were lots of *kerthunks* as people steered their horses into each other and even more *bzzzztttssss* when they smacked into the walls. The horses, shockingly, had settled better than the people. Some yawped or squealed, but most thrummed along quietly while their riders played bumper cars with each other.

In front of me, Cheriour's mare pounded her hooves erratically against the ground, but I couldn't see him. Occasionally, if Sacrifice got close enough, I'd glimpse the wispy outline of his back. Otherwise? Black. I saw nothing but black.

And the *noise*. Between the blustering waves, the muffled rumbles of thunder, and the babble of nervous chatter from the group, my ears were ringing.

"This is freaky," I said. "I don't like it. At all. And what happens if a horse trips and falls flat on its face?"

About twenty people informed me, quite snootily, that horses were perfectly capable of seeing in the dark, and it was only us humans who were blinded down here.

"Jeez," I mumbled, "I didn't know."

Light on.

I blinked, clearing the sunspots out of my vision.

"There's a curve here." Rhona's glowing hand illuminated the shadowy bend in the water tunnel. "Stay left."

As I scooched Sacrifice over, and my eyes reacclimated to the light, I got a good glimpse of Rhona's hand. And...*yeeech*. Long, jagged stripes of red skin and pulsing blisters curved around her knuckles, as though she'd stuck her hand in front of a blowtorch.

These poor hybrids...my God. They—*we* were all cursed.

Light off.

Darkness swallowed us again.

Behind me, several people emitted nervous expletives.

And, y'know, I was me. Stuffy tension made me antsy.

"Have y'all ever played Marco Polo?" I shouted over my shoulder.

A few people hissed and barked at each other, but no one answered me.

"Yeah...I should've seen that coming. It's a game! You typically play it in a pool, but this trippy-ass water tunnel will make an okay substitute, as dark as it is. Because you'd normally have your eyes closed anyway. And it's *super* simple. I'll yell 'Marco.' Someone else yells 'Polo.' If I figure out who said it, I win. If I don't, you win. Easy-peasy. Wanna play?"

Someone directly behind me coughed. A horse whuffled.

And I took that as an affirmative.

"MARCO!" I boomed.

Sacrifice flinched and gave an indignant squeal.

"Oh, hush up," I chided. "This is a humans-only game. Sorry."

"Polo!" Kaelan's bemused yell sounded like it came from miles away.

"Whoop-whoop!" I craned my head, beaming over my

shoulder, even though I knew he couldn't see me. "Thank you, Kaelan, for participating. I knew I liked ya for a reason."

In front of me, Cheriour chuckled.

Light on.

A behemoth, hulking creature burst from the darkness, obscuring our path.

"*Cheriour!*" I screamed when he and Rhona almost ran right into the monster's open mouth.

Cheriour's wet ponytail whipped through the air, the only indication the creature had startled him, as he swung his mare around. "Go right," he called, sounding as cool as a cucumber, even as his mare erupted into a series of back-cracking bucks.

"Apologies," Rhona said over her shoulder. She also sounded unfazed. "I didn't realize the skeleton was so close."

Skeleton.

Not a monster.

Or, well, not a *living* monster.

"Oh fuck. Fuck. *Hoolllyyy fuck!*" I squealed, clutching onto Sacrifice's mane when she did a wild-legged cat leap past the beast.

The school-bus-sized skull stared at us with blank, bottomless eyes. A thick skin of barnacles and corals coated the bones, making the creature look less like a dead relic and more like a live (but sleeping) Godzilla. As though it would open its eyes at any second and go on a screaming rampage because we'd disturbed its slumber.

The thought had my poor, overstimulated heart trying to duck and hide beneath my stomach. "*What the hell is that?*"

"It's naught but a whale." Although Braxton was only a

few feet behind me, his words were barely audible over the raucous ocean (and the shrieks of everyone else who'd been scared shitless by the monster).

"Oh, sure, it's *just* a whale. You see how ginormous it is?"

"The poor thing is dead, Addie," Braxton said. "And it's only his wee head..."

"*Wee head*??"

"Aye. Only the head. The sea took the rest of his body. He can't hurt ye."

"He can't, sure. But there are *live* ones who can."

"Ach...whales have no interest in harmin' a human."

"That's a load of crock. You ever heard of Pinocchio? Or Jonas? Or Captain Ahab? I think they'd say something very different about whales..."

"*Arrrrggghh!*"

This time, it was not me who bellowed. It was a guy in the back of the group.

"*What was that?*" I yelled. "Is someone dying?"

"It's Iarla!" I recognized Deborah's laugh. "He's alright! But he's made a new friend."

"Get it off!" Iarla cried.

"Oh, but it'd be a shame to evict him. He's quite attached to you," Deborah chortled.

"GET IT OFF!"

"Ye be kind to that crab now," Braxton shouted. "We're traipsin' through his home."

Iarla gave another shorter, angrier yelp.

So, yeah, this water tunnel was filled with Godzilla-sized whales and killer crabs.

Suuuppper fun, right?

I wanted out. Desperately. I hated the way the blackness

loomed in front of us, like a snarling, sneering monster, ready to gobble us up.

And that skull...

A cold sweat prickled across my skin.

That whale was dead, sure, but what was stopping other sea creatures from entering our air tube? *Nothing.* We weren't surrounded by steel or plastic. Just water. If a hungry predator got a whiff of us and decided to indulge in some long pork, we were *fucked.*

In front of me, Cheriour's mare zagged away from... *something.*

My fear-addled mind convinced me she was fleeing from a shark's snapping teeth.

"Hmmmnnggghhhh ahh dmmmoooddd..." A string of panicked babbles poured from my mouth. I was so scared, I'd started speaking in tongues.

But it was a rock. Just a rock. Cheriour and his mare had zigged to avoid it.

Cheriour angled his head toward me, his brow pinched, and slowed his mare down, allowing Sacrifice to catch up. He said nothing, but I felt a smidge better cantering beside him. Especially when Rhona's light flicked off again. I could still see his face, shadowed as it was, and I could *feel* him. Our knees occasionally bumped when our horses swayed inward—and these were *not* pleasant bumps. We smashed into each other, almost busting kneecaps, and then Queen Bitch would do her "get outta my personal space" kick, which made Cheriour's mare pissy. And we'd straighten them up, only for them to spook and veer toward each other again.

"We're nearing the surface," Cheriour said after a long

stretch of this bump-and-go trek. (Had it been minutes? Twenty? Thirty? I had no freaking clue.)

"How can you—*oh*."

Lightning flashed, brighter than it'd been before. Because it had less ocean to go through to reach us.

That domed ceiling over our head was thinning.

"So...uh..." *Why* did my voice sound like Minnie Mouse? "What do we...I mean...we're not gonna pop right onto dry land, are we?"

"The water will shallow before it reaches the shore."

"So we're gonna surface and get pummeled by a wave. *Wonderful.*" I twined long strands of Sacrifice's mane around my hands. "*Fantastic.*"

The water above us thinned, and thinned, and *thinned*, until we crested the surface. There was another moment of blinding panic and pressure as the sea bore down, trying to shove us back into the air pocket, but then it gave up and spat us out.

More bedlam ensued as the horses splashed and flailed, struggling to find their footing in the rollicking surf. And, of course, my weirdo horse had to do an enthusiastic dolphin leap that sent me nosediving over her shoulder and straight back into the water.

I clawed my way back to the surface and watched my not-so-noble steed merrily skip her way to the shore, not giving two fucks that she'd lost her rider.

Cheriour looked over his shoulder to confirm I hadn't drowned, but his mare had already set sights on dry land and was barreling toward it like an out-of-control freight car.

So, I did the walk/swim of shame to the beach.

But at least I wasn't alone.

Quinn's horse had teetered sideways over one of the waves and unseated him.

"Fancy meeting you here," I chirped as I sloshed beside him.

Quinn bowed his head and scowled at the water, looking like a sopping version of Oscar the Grouch.

What an A-list team we made, as everyone coughed and wheezed their way into enemy territory.

Ramiel's minions had to be *quaking* in their boots at the prospect of facing us.

Bahahahaha. As if.

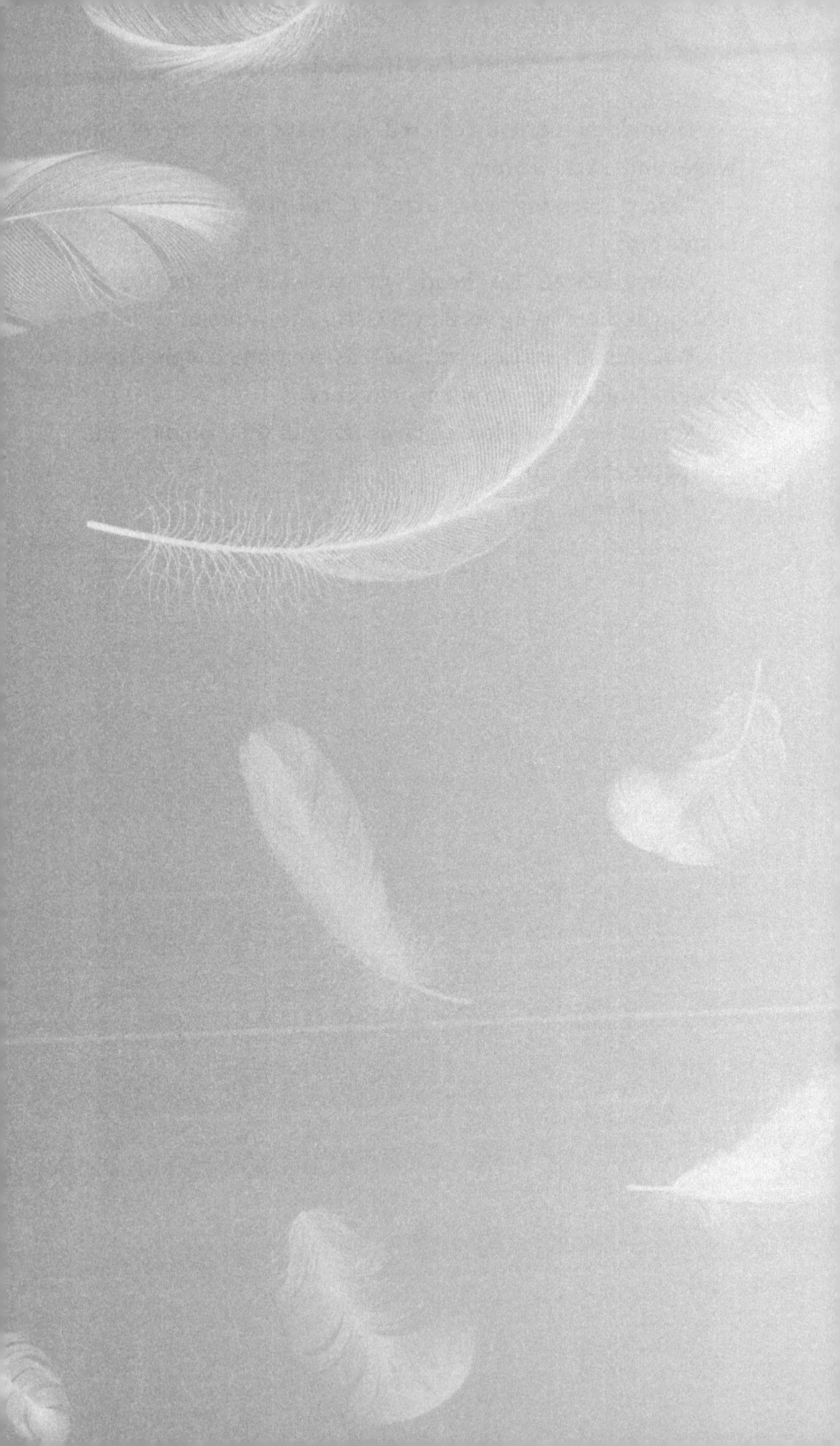

CHAPTER 29

BLOOD RAIN

Cheriour was shivering.

Mr. Macho, "I'm gonna rate a mortal stomach wound as a three on the pain scale because I'm a big strong He-Man and acknowledging pain is for sissies..." *He* shivered. Not much. But whenever we paused and I pressed myself against him, both hoping to absorb some of his body heat and share some of mine, I felt those light tremors pulsating through his muscles.

Meanwhile, I jittered like a crack addict coming off a ten-year high.

Our group had left the beach behind and the billowing, wild-eyed horses on the beach ("They'll not be forgivin' us for this," Braxton had said in a tired, slurred voice). And now, we splashed through the forest, up a steep incline, winding our way through withered trees and spindly undergrowth. *Relentless* curtains of rain pummeled us, which made it damn near impossible to see, as though we were watching the world through a waterfall.

And it was *freezing*. Easily in the thirties—*without* the

wind chill. But when you factored in those super fun fifty-mile-per-hour gusts that assaulted us every thirty goddamn seconds...

Oooh, yeah. This kinda cold had teeth. And it was giving us a big, sloppy hickey.

Someone grunted. A few other people stumbled and blew out aggravated snarls and curses. The visibility was so crappy, I couldn't even see who surrounded me. They were all wavery, waterlogged shadows.

Cheriour moved deftly over the soggy forest floor, stepping over roots and branches and gracefully navigating all the dips, rivets, and jutting patches of ground, all while dragging an anchor (aka, my uncoordinated ass) behind him. I clutched at his hand, my fingers shaking so hard, I kept accidentally raking my nails over his skin.

Faint noises trickled back to us. Shouts. Cries. The sounds of humans in torment.

My stomach *slished-sloshed* and then splashed all the way into my throat when I stepped wrong in a puddle and twisted my bad ankle. "O-o-ouch...*motherfucker!*" I hissed.

Cheriour stopped. Not because I'd tripped, although the pause gave me a chance to lean against him and shake the pain out of my throbbing ankle. But he'd cocked his head to the side, listening for something. After a second, he turned to the group, made a "down" gesture with his free hand, and dropped to a crouch.

We did a funky duck walk for the last several feet.

Well, to be accurate, Cheriour and the others did the duck walk. I got down into the deep squat, took two steps, and my thighs went "bitch, how fit do you think we are??" So instead, I crawled, dragging my knees through the mud and dinging them on the rocks and roots.

But I didn't feel any pain. I was too cold and, when we crested the incline and stared down at the city below, too shocked.

"W-whut i-i-i-in th-e e-e-vr-luf-f-f-ing f-u-uc i-ss th-is p-l-ace?" (English translation: "What in the ever-loving fuck is this place?") I plastered myself to Cheriour's side, pressing my hands under his gloriously hot (and slightly stanky) armpit, but I couldn't get warm. Couldn't ease the shivering. Because fear had started dancing those spindly, icy fingers along my spine, stealing any comfort Cheriour's presence provided.

"Keld," Cheriour said, a slight catch around the "k" the only evidence that he was shivering too.

"*K-killed?*"

"*Keld*," he repeated slowly, which made the word sound like a very drawn-out version of "killed."

And the place, with its murderous pronunciation, was aptly named. This freaking slum looked like it'd choke the life out of anyone who set foot there.

Hundreds of tiny, derelict houses twined around festering, mud-covered streets. And, I mean, calling these things *houses* was being generous. They looked like a bunch of wooden outhouses strung together. The only real buildings were smack in the middle of the town: a squat and sprawling gray-stoned fortress flanked by two long barns.

Wraiths infested the muddy streets. Some held whips, some clutched barely restrained hellhounds. And they leered as they prowled, their milk-white eyes focused on the working humans.

Working.

They were making these poor people *work*.

I mean, there was a freaking hurricane happening, but it

was the *perfect* time to garden, right? Or slaughter some animals. Or make repairs to the gaudy gold fountain sitting in the town square.

I dug my fingers into Cheriour's side as a woman, standing in a flooded field and plucking what looked like heads of lettuce, gave an almighty sneeze/cough combo, the kind that normally happened when someone was outside in a torrential downpour and got rain blown up their nose.

A nearby Wraith zoomed to her side.

Zooosh-SNAP!

Down came the Wraith's whip, its crack louder than the clap of thunder overhead. Even from this distance, with the wind dumping buckets of water into my ears, I heard the woman scream.

Zooosh-snap.

Zooosh-snap.

Zooosh-snap.

More whiplashes echoed around the city, mixing with the bloodcurdling wails and the pitter-patter of rain to form a macabre song. And each time one of those whips cracked down, crimson droplets spritzed into the air. Sometimes, if I had my eye on the right spot, and the Wraiths coordinated their beatings, it looked like it was raining blood.

"The last relic of an old world," Hurleigh had called this place.

It was hard to imagine *any* part of this world being more fucked up than Sakar, but apparently, I'd been living in a freaking utopia these past few months. At least compared to this place.

And this hellscape was what the Wraiths of Sakar were striving to recreate.

"God, Cheriour, these poor people..." My breath hitched as that all-too-familiar pain speared my chest.

"I know," he murmured.

The Keldians looked like skeletons. Worse—they looked like corpses. They had no muscle, fat, flub or roly-poly sections. They were just layers of skin stretched taut over jutting bones. Bones that were *seriously* underdeveloped. People were bow-legged, pigeon-toed, and spindly looking. Adults walked on limbs and cartilage barely refined enough to support a child.

There were kids down there too. Lots of 'em. And seeing the state they were in made it easy to understand why the adults looked the way they did. Malnutrition, illness, abuse, and overwork would all cause stunted growth. And those kids, even the stubby-legged toddlers, worked right alongside the adults, getting clobbered for being too slow or clumsy, or for crying, or...sometimes I couldn't tell why Wraiths hit people. Because they liked the *zooosh-snap* their whips made? Because they enjoyed watching blood run in rivers down a person's mangled skin?

Or maybe this was all part of the food prep for them, tenderizing the meat before they cooked it.

I didn't realize I was holding Cheriour with a death grip, clawing my nails into his armpits, until he grasped my hand and smoothed his thumb over my knuckles.

I'd probably been hurting him. But he said nothing as he turned to the group. "Quinn," he called. "I count seventy-three. Would you agree?"

Although only a few feet away, Quinn looked like a blurred object behind dingy stained glass. "Seventy-three Wraiths," he said. "But there's at least a dozen hellhounds."

Oh...haha. Apparently, we were supposed to be, y'know,

staking out the place. Counting the enemies. Being productive. Not staring blankly at the miserable mass of people.

"You're both wrong." This came from Deborah, who was on my right side, out of my line of sight. "Did you count the seven Wraiths by the well?"

"What well?" Quinn asked.

"Then you didn't include them," Deborah sniffed. "There's a well behind their fortress—you probably can't see it from your angle. But I'm counting seven Wraiths there."

"They'll be more in that fortress as well," Cheriour said. "Braxton, are you able to see anything?"

"Aye, there's a ruddy bitch takin' a shite by the pig pen," Braxton called from behind us. "Poor feckin' things, having to smell her—"

"I already counted her," Cheriour said.

"Ach, that'll be it, then. Except, as ye said, the ones inside. There's a wee rat in the fortress. All the Wraiths look the same to her, mind ye, but ye have no less than a dozen in there. Most are sleepin'—the lazy sods."

"I'd say we can estimate a hundred Wraiths," Quinn added. "At a minimum."

"Agreed."

My stomach gurgled. One hundred Wraiths. Forty-six of us. Those were some lousy odds.

But, astonishingly, a ripple of relief went around the group. *Relief.* At being *outnumbered*!

"That's not so bad, then." Braxton sounded more cheery than he had all afternoon.

"Should be easy enough," Deborah quipped.

A few other people murmured similar things. Kaelan, crouched on Quinn's other side, laughed—the kinda high-pitched, wavering chuckle you got when you'd been sitting on pins and needles all day, dreading something, and then realized the thing you were worried about wasn't all that bad.

"Y'all are freaking nuts," I grumbled.

"We've been outnumbered by worse," Braxton said. "And these Wraiths are fat and lazy. They'll not take much to kill. Ye'll see."

"Define *'won't take much to kill?'*"

"Addie." Cheriour gave my shoulder a firm tap. "Enough. Braxton." He lifted his chin over my head to stare at Braxton. "I want you to stay back with Pegeen. You're both best with the bow, and you'll see more than we will on the ground."

I had no idea who or where Pegeen was, but Braxton gave a long-suffering sigh. "Cheriour, I think yer mistakin' me for Belanna..."

"I'm not. You've an accurate shot. What you lack is patience. But you'll *need* to be patient today."

Braxton groused something that sounded suspiciously like "fuck this bullshit," (a phrase he picked up from me?) but said nothing else.

"We'll need to be quick," Cheriour continued. "Once we move and lose the coverage of the trees, we will be attacked."

"Remember, food and supplies are kept not only in the fortress but in the longhouses as well," Quinn added. "Take what you can, but don't overburden yourselves."

"What about the people?" I asked. From somewhere in the town, a child had started wailing. "You're not gonna bring mayhem into their home, steal their stuff, and *leave them* there, right?"

"They," Cheriour said, gently digging his thumb into my

palm, soothing my tense muscles, "will be your task." And then he raised his voice. "Kaelan, Rhona, Nathan...I also want you to stay back. You as well, Quinn. Addie will gather the humans from the city and send them to you. Get them to the ocean. They'll be frightened," he added. "Confused. They've never seen life outside Keld. They'll fear us as much as they fear the Wraiths."

"Well." I cleared my throat when my voice caught. "I'm kind of a pro at annoying people. If all else fails, I'll start blathering useless pop culture fun facts. They'll run into the trees to get away from me. Guarantee it."

Cheriour's mouth twitched.

Quinn turned to me, and the surging curtain of rain almost made him look...*soft*. As though he was smiling. Not in a *"har, har, you're so funny"* kinda way (because everyone *knew* I wasn't funny). More like a *"hmm, maybe I don't hate this bitch's guts"* sorta smirk.

But when I squinted, trying to figure out if the rain was bamboozling my eyes, Quinn shifted away. "Is everyone ready?" he asked.

After everyone *hmmmed* or muttered their affirmative, we stood and emerged from the safety of the trees.

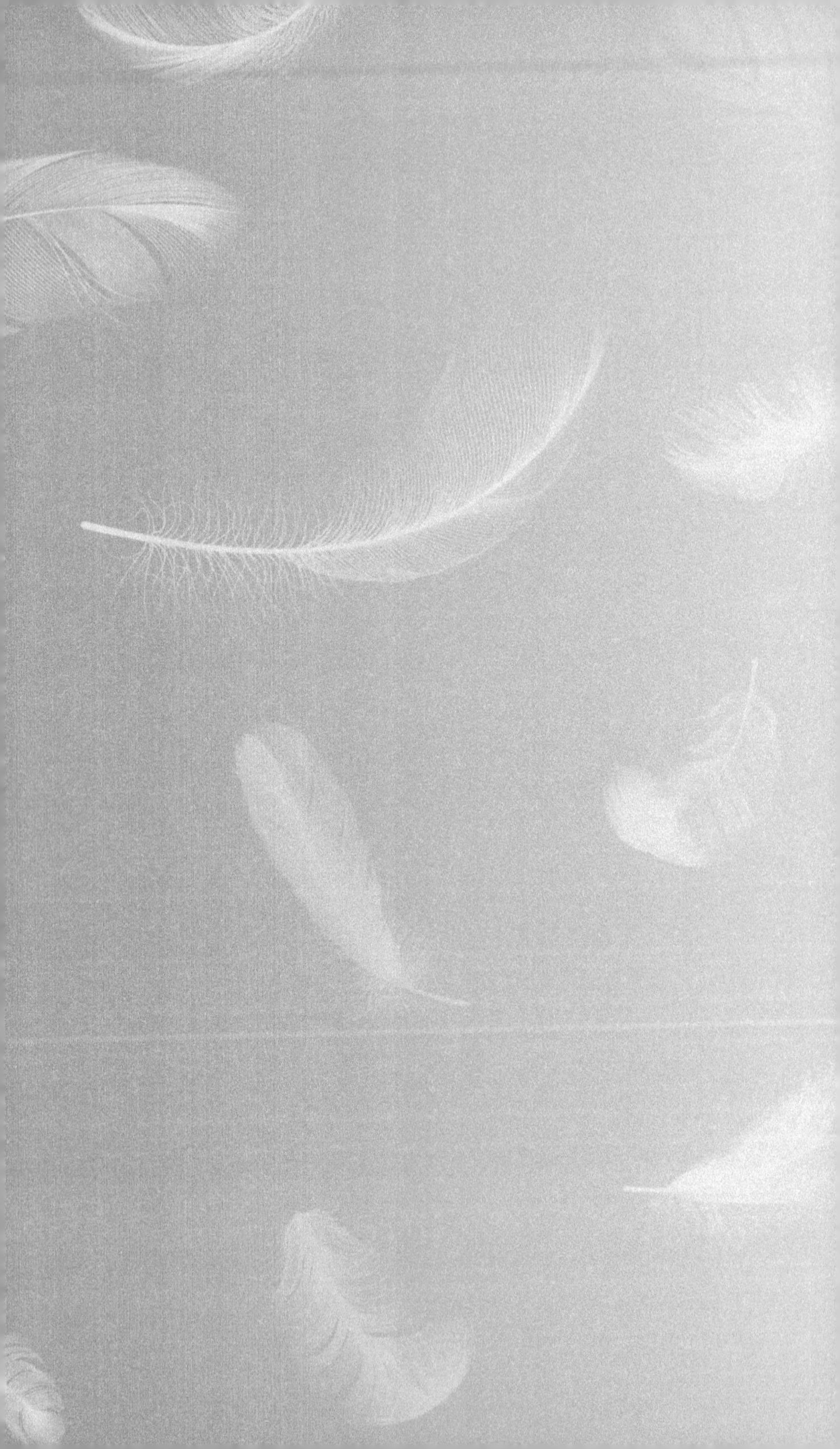

CHAPTER 30

THOROUGHLY CASTRATED

Cheriour led the way down the hill, guns blazing.

Not literally. *Obviously*. But he drew and threw knives so damn fast, he might as well have been firing bullets.

Bam, bam, bam.

Three Wraiths were kaput.

I slid down the muddy incline beside him, my wet hands fighting to get a good grip on my poleaxe.

Bam. Bam.

Two more Wraiths down.

I heard the whizzing of an arrow in flight, felt it whisk past my ear, and a sixth Wraith crumpled, clutching at the barb embedded in her chest.

Braxton gave a muted hoot.

And the rest of the Wraiths? They were *oblivious*. They were all facing away from the hill, and the storm was so tumultuous, they hadn't heard their comrades fall.

Huh. Maybe everyone had been right to be relieved...

"*Shite*...we've been seen," Rhona hissed from behind me.

Ooop, never mind. I'd jinxed it.

A rawboned, blood-soaked woman sat in the open doorway to her hut, using the slim overhang as an umbrella while she jerkily ripped feathers off a chicken carcass. She was the first to look up, the first to see us descending the hill. And the first to scream.

Soon, *dozens* of humans were screeching. Whether because they were afraid of us or terrified of being caught in the middle of a brawl, I didn't know. But as soon as they went off, the Wraiths were on high alert.

Cheriour's next knife missed. Or, to be more accurate, the Wraith he'd aimed at was as good, or better, at knife throwing. The Wraith ducked, freed a blade from his holster, and lobbed it at Cheriour's head.

The silver blade flashed through the rain. And I had one brief, panic-riddled vision of it smacking Cheriour between the eyes before he went full *Matrix*, bending over backward in the *nick of flipping time*. The knife trimmed the frayed edges off his beard but didn't hit skin.

But then the Wraith threw a second knife and almost took *my* goddamn head off.

"Fucking shit *bastard*!" I dove for the ground.

Whoosh.

The knife scraped over the back of my head, scratching my scalp. Meanwhile, my poleaxe slipped out of my hands, the shaft rolling and smacking Cheriour across the back of the legs.

Cheriour grunted as he freed his short sword and chucked it.

Thunk.

Blegh...guuuurggggllleeee.

The Wraith hadn't been so quick to jump out of the way

that time, and the blade speared his throat. He coughed, retched up two big mouthfuls of blood, and collapsed.

Other Wraiths swarmed around him. They gnashed their teeth and drew their weapons, their movements synching *perfectly* with the next clap of thunder. A scene that would've looked badass in an epic fantasy movie.

Except, y'know, this wasn't a movie. Those pissy, armed, and lethal AF monsters were *very* real. And now they were blocking our entry to the city.

My pulse roared in my ears.

Whoosh.

Zing.

Snap.

Thwack.

Gurgle.

Blades and arrows pierced the curtains of rain. Some of them came from my crew. Some came from the Wraiths. They all got jumbled in the storm-ravaged sky above my head. I couldn't tell who was shooting at who.

"Addie..." Cheriour scooted in front of me. Shielding me. "Get to your feet. *Go.* I'll watch your back. And retrieve my sword. Please," he added gruffly. "I'll take it from you in a moment."

I scrambled back to my feet and scampered around him.

"Your poleaxe!" he called.

Fuck me. I'd gone running off without it. Because *of course* I had. "One day, maybe this thing won't feel so freaking awkward," I muttered as I trudged back to get it. "But today is not that day." And then I booked it down the hill, running in a half-stooped position to keep my head on my shoulders. I still almost got nicked a few times.

"Shit, shit, shit..." I slid to a stop beside the fallen knife thrower and wrenched Cheriour's sword out of his throat. The Wraith's body twitched and spumed a gush of blood over my feet.

Footsteps *splish-slunked* through the mud behind me.

Ziiiiinnnnggg.

A sword whizzed past my right ear, and a burning sleeve of pain enveloped my right arm as the blade scraped my bicep, tearing my shirt and taking the top layer of my skin.

The wound wasn't bad. Bled like a mothereffer, but it was shallow. But the big slash in my shirt had me seeing red.

"Ooooh, you stupid, fugly *neanderthal!*" I jabbed my poleaxe back. A Wraith hissed when the pointy end *thunked* against his armor. "This is my *favorite fucking shirt!*" I spun, whipped the poleaxe around—

Thwack.

The Wraith collapsed well before the axe head zipped anywhere near him. A teensy dagger jutted from his right eye, the blade stuck between the slats of his helmet.

Cheriour.

Thank frick I had him as my guardian angel.

I blew out a misting breath, shoved Cheriour's sword through my belt loop, and grasped the hilt of the dagger. The sucker was really lodged in there. I yanked once. Twice. Each time, the still living Wraith twitched and flailed his arms, striking at me blindly. On my third attempt, the blade popped out of his eyeball with a wet *squap.*

The Wraith *keened.* Cursed. Blood geysered through his helmet slats. And coating the blade...

"Oh God. Dude...are these your *brains?*" I wagged the dagger under the rain, letting the torrent wash the ooey, jiggly chunks of...whatever that grayish stuff was off. "*Bleeegughh.* Get off...get off, get off, get—"

A small, plaintive whimper rose from behind me.

A few feet away, two kids huddled together under a narrow overhang, staring at me as though I was Medusa, sent to turn them to stone.

"Hey!" I cooed as I popped the brain-guts dagger into my belt and walked over to them. "No, no...it's okay..."

The little boy yelled and shoved his sister behind him, as though he thought his scrawny three-foot-six frame could protect her. "It's okay," I said again. "I'm here to help."

The boy eyed my poleaxe.

"This is for them"—I jabbed a finger at the writhing Wraith—"not you. 'Kay? I'm not gonna hurt you. Honest."

The boy reached an arm around, shoving his whimpering sister more firmly against his back.

Around me, the fight raged. Wraiths barked commands. The Keldians screeched and fled. The Sakarians fought brutishly. But in that moment, all I saw, all I cared about, were those two kids.

I dropped to a crouch, putting myself at their height, and leaned my poleaxe against my left shoulder. "It's okay." I winked. "I'm the good guy. Honest. And...wanna see something cool?" I rolled my torn right sleeve up to my forearm, exposing the bottom of my tattoo, where I had the colorful Marvel symbol medley.

The girl made a soft "*oooh.*" The boy said nothing, but he glued his eyes to Thor's hammer.

"It's pretty awesome, huh?" I smiled when the boy reached out and rubbed his thumb over the hammer, maybe trying to smear the ink or see if the tat had a different texture.

"That's Molinjr," I said. "It belongs to Thor. The God of Thunder."

And my timing was top-notch. As soon as the words left my mouth, a rumbling flash of lightning forked the sky above us.

The kids both jumped, stared at the sky, and then looked at me in utter awe, as though I was the Mighty Thor in the flesh.

I'd never felt like more of a badass.

"The storm's here to get you to safety," I said. "And so are we. Can you—Where's your mom? Dad? Parent figure?"

The girl lowered her head. The boy turned to the dumpy shack beside him with a pained expression on his face. "Papa didn't wake up," he sniffed.

"And your mom?"

Silence.

My heart crumbled. These poor kids. The boy was barely seven years old, the girl even younger, and they were orphaned.

"Alright, well..." I clasped my hand around the boy's bony wrist. "It's alright," I murmured when he flinched. "I won't hurt you. But I want you to take your sister's hand and follow me. Can you do that?"

The boy, still a little wary-eyed, nodded. The girl trembled when he grasped her hand.

They both screamed when a Wraith thundered by us.

Deborah chased after him, looking like a savage beast hunting its prey with the way her wet hair was plastered to her face and her lips were drawn back over her bared teeth. When the Wraith turned to her, blade drawn, she lunged and gouged his crotch. Not once. Not twice. *Three times.* The dude was *thoroughly* castrated.

"Get him, girl!" I whooped as I walked by.

Deborah angled her head and shot me a feral grin.

Note to self: Deborah was an *animal*. I'd never piss her off. Uh-uh.

The two kids trotted beside me, their little legs stumbling over Wraith bodies and squishing through the mud. Kaelan, bless his sweet, saintly soul, was already galloping toward us. "Most people sought refuge indoors when the fighting started," he told me, and then he smiled at the kids.

The girl shrieked.

Kaelan flinched.

"Oh man, Kaelan," I chuckled. "That beard's starting to scare the ladies. He won't hurt you," I said to the girl. "Honest. He's gonna take you away from here."

They both quavered when Kaelan gently took their arms, pulling them away from me. But he spoke to them in soft murmurs and walked with a stooped back so he didn't tower over them. They relaxed almost immediately.

Me, on the other hand...

"Shit!" I squealed as a sword *ziiinngged* above my head, catching the right side of my temple. Something hot and wet dripped into my eye as I stopped, dropped, and rolled.

Blood.

The Wraith swung her sword again.

"*Eeek!*" I pivoted to my knees, wincing when my kneecap ground painfully against my shin, and flung my poleaxe up.

Her blade scoured the shaft, making a godawful nails-on-chalkboard sound. But the bitch had two hands—*and* two weapons. The left held a whip. And she cracked it over my shoulder. *Hard.*

Pain exploded across my back as the whip bruised deep,

deep, deep into my skin. And it *itched*—the way a fresh, blistered sunburn would prickle and ache.

That fucking *hurt!* OMG.

And that was only *one* whiplash. What was it like for these poor bastards who got whacked every time they sneezed?

"You mother—" I shoved against my poleaxe with all my might. The Wraith took one step back, her whip hand recoiling.

Zoooosh-snap.

The second lash caught me across the face.

Burning, itchy pain devoured my right cheek and swelled the skin around my eye. Red swamped my vision. *Blood.* It trickled into my left eye from the sword wound and pooled in my right from the whiplash.

I fell back to my haunches, my mind soupy and dazed, and I swore I had some tweeting birds circling my head.

The Wraith raised her sword again.

And all I could think was...

Nothing.

I didn't think. Just grasped my poleaxe and swung it, like a batter wailing at a fastball.

"Take that..." The axe head punched through the armor at the Wraith's abdomen. "Fucker...*eeek!*"

A blade *thunked* into the back of her neck, pitching her forward and driving my axe farther into her stomach.

"Addie!" Cheriour sprinted toward me, pausing to wrench his knife free from the wheezing Wraith.

"Oooh, dude, you really *are* a savior...and a fucking saint..." I pressed my hand to the whip slash on my cheek and drew back with a hiss when pain rocketed through my eyeball. I couldn't see *anything* on this side. "D-did I lose my eye?" My fingers probed through the pain, trying to feel if I still had an eyeball.

"No." Cheriour knelt and ripped a piece of his shirt sleeve off, pressing the fabric against my face, ignoring me when I bit out a low "*fuck*" and sucked back. "You *almost* lost it."

He cleaned the blood out sloppily, pausing every few seconds to chuck a knife somewhere. "Can you see now?" he asked.

I blinked. Shook my head. Blinked again. My left eye had cleared, but everything out of my right side still looked like fractured pieces of red glass. "Yeah. Kinda."

"The rain will finish cleansing it," Cheriour said gruffly. "Quinn will heal it once we're done."

"Aw, but if he heals it, I won't get a fancy scar like yours."

The corner of his mouth curled. But then he plucked his sword and dagger from my belt and hauled me back to my feet, barking, "Do *not* stop moving." He shoved my poleaxe back into my hands. "You cannot be idle in a battle. Even to help a pair of children."

"They were scared."

"I know." He twisted and flung a knife over his shoulder. "But you don't have time for coaxing. Do what you must to move them. But do it *quickly*."

And so, I hauled my freshly one-eyed self back into the fray.

And the fucking Wraiths (y'know, the ones Braxton had called *fat* and *lazy*) nicked me at every turn.

"Fat and lazy my left tit," I hissed after I took down a spindly female Wraith who'd *bitten* me—sank her stanky, blunt teeth right into my hand—trying to steal my poleaxe.

I'd somehow managed to hold onto the weapon while I wrenched my knuckles out of her clamped jaw, and I swung it around at the right angle to hack at her neck. But now I had a bloody ring of teeth marks on the back of my hand.

By the time this fight was over, I'd have more holes in me than a piece of Swiss cheese.

The only good thing about all this?

The people of Keld stayed in groups. Maybe because they were scared and figured they were about to go out in a blaze of glory, so they wanted to cling to the people they loved most. Or maybe these huddles were the deviant protocols they'd been raised with: *"Stay in a group and hold hands so we can hit* as many of you as possible *with the whip. We're trying to break the Guinness World Record for most blood drawn from a single whiplash."*

Whatever the reason, it helped me.

No matter where I went, big groups of people waited.

They crammed themselves into rickety houses and barns, hid beneath shoddy overhangs, and stuffed into shit-riddled alleyways (a literal description—the alleys, mostly shielded from the rain, were *covered* in poop).

Bouncing from person to person would've taken *forever*.

Groups were easier.

I liked groups.

Loved them.

It was a beautiful thing, seeing clusters of twenty or more people take refuge in the woods.

But, with all the mayhem going on, my brain had gotten scrambled. The patient, calm spiel I'd had with the kids dissolved into a panicked ramble by the time I reached my fifth group.

"*Heeelllloooo* everyone! The rescue wagon is here! Jesus...

shoot, I didn't mean to scare you. I'm sorry." I'd burst into a barn and scared the bejesus out of everyone inside. One man comically flew backward, got his foot stuck in a bucket, and upended himself into a trough.

"I'm sorry!" I cringed as the man battered himself around in the water. "Please don't freak out. Okay? I'm not a Wraith. My name's Addie. I'm here to help. But I need to get y'all moving this way"—I jabbed my thumb to the door—"because I've got some friends with a getaway car. I mean... they don't actually have a car...I *wish* they did. But they're gonna get you out of here. Away from Uchen and the Wraiths. Away from *all* of this. We're going to help you."

No less than fifteen pale, wild-eyed faces stared back at me, all crammed into this shoddy, dark, and dank little barn.

"We'll *never* be free from the Wraiths," a scar-faced woman muttered.

"Won't pass the ocean," a knobby-kneed man cautioned.

"Don't worry about the Wraiths," I said. "They're so busy trying to figure out what hit them, they're not gonna stop you. As for the ocean..." I winked. "We've got a water-bender on our side. You'll go right under the surface and walk on the seabed. It's freaky, not gonna lie, but *sooo* cool."

Pretty sure they only understood half of what I said.

But the feeling was mutual, because they all spoke in a heavy, English-butchering accent, and I only understood half of what they said.

"There is no leaving. Many tried. And they aren't among the livin's now, eh?" A man rubbed at a seeping wound on his nearly bald scalp.

"Look, okay, you don't trust me," I tried again. "You have no reason to. I get it. But you can't tell me you haven't seen the Wraiths getting their asses handed to them tonight. By *humans*. That sight has to make you a *teensy* bit curious as to whether I'm telling the truth, right? We're clearing a path for y'all. I just need you to move your asses out of the city, and then you'll never have to get walloped with a whip again. Wouldn't that be nice, huh? To be able to sneeze in peace without some milky-eyed bastard getting all pissy about it...There ya go!" I squealed when they started shuffling forward. "Ándale, ándale! Keep your feet moving. Straight up into the woods. Y'all are gonna be sipping drinks around a fire tonight...Anyone who crawls outta the bowels of hell deserves *at least* one drink. Two would be best..."

Again, I wasn't sure if my words were getting through to them or if they just wanted to get outta dodge so they wouldn't die with my dulcet voice ringing in their ears.

I didn't care *why* they moved. As long as they moved.

As they dashed for the trees, skipping over the new speed bumps in their streets (aka, the hunks of mangled Wraiths), I sloshed back through the town and found my next group huddled in one of the yecchy alleyways between two rows of houses. Kids sat in stagnant puddles of human waste. The adults stood over them, watching me fearfully, their eyes bugging out of their sunken faces.

This was a *big* group; had to be at least forty people jammed into the alley.

I started my spiel, vowing to keep my voice light and friendly instead of scaring them with my over-excited trill. But they screamed before I got past the word "hello."

"Whoa, whoa!" I braced my poleaxe against my shoulder and held my hands out, palms up, showing them I wasn't hiding any secret weapons. "Easy. It's alright. Man, you're a tough crowd. I—*Jesus*." I flinched when they screamed again, shrinking back. "C'mon, I can't look *that* scary. I know I've got a swollen eye, but..."

My chest gave a sudden, almighty lurch, as though someone had snagged a fishing hook in my lungs and was reeling them in, *tearing* them up my throat and out through my mouth.

White checkerspots burst before my eyes.

Fuck. FUCK!

Had my heart finally decided to peace out? Was this what a heart attack felt like?

But as I staggered against a wall, slipping in a shit puddle, I realized the people in the alley weren't just screaming nonsense noise. They'd been yelling a *name*.

"*Ellard!*"

Bare feet slopped against the muddy street behind me.

The hook inside my chest went nuclear. White-hot pain mushroomed inside me, and it grew, grew, *grew*. I swore my insides were lit up brighter than the Rockefeller Christmas tree. Swore my skin was gonna bust open and spew radioactive hunks all over this alley.

"*Ellard!*" Several people cried.

The sloshing feet came to a halt.

I turned slowly, crying when that atomic fishing hook scourged my raw lungs.

A nightmare of a creature stood behind me: a buck-naked humanoid with craggy pewter-gray skin, piss-yellow eyes, and curved spikes along his shoulder blades. A monster I'd only seen once before, when Seruf dragged the Fallen Celestial Gabriel into Niall.

But this wasn't Gabriel.

This was a newcomer.

Ellard.

CHAPTER 31

THE DEPTHS OF A PLUMBER'S ASSCRACK

It took everything I had to raise my arms, turn, and whip my poleaxe around.

And it was an epic swing-and-a-miss.

The Fallen—Ellard—sidestepped.

The arc of my blow sent me bonking into the wall. I braced my left hand against the damp, moldy wood and fought to breathe as a massive, spiked balloon inflated inside my chest. My every inhale puffed it up, driving those barbs deeper into my lungs.

And the *screaming*...

I thought the piercing wails were coming from the people in the alley. "*Shut up!*" I hissed at them. "*Shut UP!*" Because it was *so loud*. Their voices grated long, juicy shreds off my brain.

But when I turned, peering at them through bleary eyes, they stared silently back. Terror contorted their faces, the kinda quaking fear that took the air right out of your lungs.

They weren't screaming.

So who the fuck was?

Not Ellard, although he was splashing toward me, arm outstretched. I swung at him again, and my blade made a diagonal swipe across his chest. I *heard* it scrape across his rocky skin, but it left no wounds. There was no blood.

Well...there was no blood from *him*.

But that brambly balloon swelled into my throat, blocking my airways, gagging me. I coughed once. Twice. Then cried when big, syrupy globs of blood gushed from my mouth.

What the hell was happening to me?

I sucked in a breath. Blood shot down my throat. I choked again and dribbled the sticky liquid down my front. All the while, those wretched screams dug their claws into my brain. And a low, demonic screech stitched itself into the ear-splitting soundtrack.

Me.

That guttural, animalistic howl had exploded out of *me*.

"*Addie!*" Cheriour's voice was so harsh, so lanced with fear, I almost didn't recognize it.

He yelled more than my name as he raced into the alley-way, chucking a knife at Ellard's head. But my name was all I heard before I buckled, landing with a heavy splash on the wet, shit-puddled ground. My hands clawed at my head, my chest, my skin. I tried to call out to Cheriour, to *plead* for help, but I couldn't.

I couldn't even *breathe*!

Each inhale injected liquid into my lungs. Each cough or exhale sent blood spritzing into the air.

Was this how I was gonna fucking die?

"Addie!" Hands gripped my shoulders, turning me onto my side, holding me as I heaved steaming wads of crimson.

I recognized Cheriour's touch, the scritch of his calloused fingers against the back of my neck.

"What happened?" Deborah's voice drifted over my head, barely puncturing the cacophony of agonized cries.

"I don't know." Cheriour's hands wandered along my body, pressing, searching for a wound. Something that would explain why my lungs had suddenly started hemorrhaging.

But I wasn't wounded. Not in a way that would cause this. I tried to tell him that, but I couldn't. All I could do was tremble. And gag.

"Deborah, Reece...keep Ellard back!" Cheriour called. "Nathan, see if you can convince these people to leave..."

The responses were muffled. Inaudible. Lost in the blaring caterwauls shredding my brain.

"Jonathon, tell the rest to fall back. We've done what we can here. And find Quinn." Cheriour's left hand remained steady as it poked and probed the front of my chest. But his right hand, resting on my shoulder, had a slight tremor. "I need him to come down here. *Now.*"

He didn't yell the words, but there was an authoritarian barb to his voice that left no room for argument.

I wanted to crack a joke about that—a moment of humor to break up the agony. *"Dude, that kinda voice is pure sex fodder. How much do I gotta pay to get ya to talk to me like that in bed?"*

But when I opened my mouth, all that came out was a frothy vat of crimson fluid.

The blood in my chest kept percolating, filling my lungs, and sloshing around the base of my throat. It tasted *awful*, like rancid butter that'd been chilling in a rusty dish for a few years.

"Addie…" Cheriour flattened himself to the ground beside me and pressed his ear to my chest.

I clutched at him. At his hair. His ears. The scruff of his neck. Whatever bit of him I could reach. Desperate to feel his warmth. His comfort.

"Be still," he murmured as he rubbed his thumb in soothing circles above my hipbone.

But the *look* on his face when he sat up…

Well, when you saw fear—raw, glassy-eyed *fear*—on a guy who was an expert at hiding his emotions, you knew you were fucked.

"What happened?" he asked. His gentle drawl was a balm against the high-pitched sounds echoing inside my head.

I tried to answer him, but all I did was emit wet *hurgh-hacks*.

Cheriour made a soft noise and swiped a lock of hair off my cheek, safely away from the mess I was making of myself.

I *hated* that small, sweet gesture. Because it made him seem…*lost*. As though he didn't know what else to do for me, so he was focusing on the only thing he *could* do: getting my hair out of the line of fire.

This really was the end of the road for me.

And I was terrified by how very *un*terrified I was. My brain whirled, telling me I *should* be afraid, but my body and my heart, both ravaged by pain and rapidly weakening, didn't give two shits.

Cheriour kept speaking as he crouched beside me. His words stopped making sense, but I clung to his molasses-y voice as the agony rampaged and screams pinged off my skull.

And then Cheriour's hands were under me, lifting me up and up and *up*. Too high. Too fast. My brain *whomp-whomp-whomped*. My blood-logged lungs heaved, searching, *pleading* for air. I coughed harder. *Deeper*. And the liquid I spat over Cheriour's neck and chest was different. Darker. More of a red-streaked chocolatey brown than bright crimson.

Yikes.

I didn't have to be a doctor to know that wasn't a good sign.

I gasped when Cheriour spun around the corner, away from the protection of the shoddy overhangs in the alley, and rain pelted my face at full force. Cheriour grunted, tucked my head under his chin, and slammed the heel of his boot into something.

A door.

He'd kicked down a door.

As the creaking *snap* filled my ears, Cheriour lurched into a building, pulling me out of the rain.

I blinked up at a pockmarked ceiling as he laid me on the floor, bundling me into a moldy pile of blankets.

A few minutes ago, I might've bitched that those blankets smelled worse than the depths of a plumber's asscrack. And I sure as *hell* wouldn't have let him tug one of those asscrack sheets over my chest. Because...*ick.*

But now...I didn't care.

"I won't be far." Cheriour grasped my left hand in both of his and pressed his lips to my knuckles. Then he stood and dashed through the gnarled door that now hung half off its hinges.

And then I was alone. In a dark, dank room, with a low, slanted ceiling. Surrounded by lumps of asscrack blankets, piles of clothes that had a sweaty sock odor, and spatterings of blackened hay. Which definitely meant this house—or barn, or workshop, or whatever this place was—had a mold man running rampant.

Mold man. Heh.

I hadn't thought of that in *years*.

Freda had said it once, when her basement flooded and a mold infestation took hold, despite the days she'd spent cleaning and drying everything. "The mold man snuck behind the walls," she'd said with false cheer as her hired (and very expensive) cleanup crew went to town with the bleach.

I pictured her walking into this building with her hands on her hips and her steel-gray hair twisted into a bun as she tutted, "The mold man certainly overstayed his welcome here."

I knew I was crying. But I had so much blood and rain-water on my face, the tears had gotten lost in the shuffle.

My coughing eased. It didn't completely go away, but I had longer breaks that allowed me to pull thin strings of air into my lungs. Molten blood still bubbled inside my chest. The burning sensation reminded me of the time I'd gotten bronchitis and had flayed my insides with my non-stop hacking. But this was *worse*. Bronchitis burn on steroids. My skin also prickled from the fresh claw marks my nails had left. The screams in my head had quieted, though. Somewhat. Enough for me to process other sounds: booms of thunder, alarmed yells, and metal clanging against metal. The uproarious noises of battle.

But the battle should've *ended*! We'd been kicking ass. Winning. We should've been able to snatch the last of the supplies, gather the rest of the people, and skedaddle.

Had something changed?

Or did those sounds exist only in my head? Like the screams had earlier?

That theory was blasted out of the water when the door creaked open a moment later, and Cheriour stepped into the room. Fresh gashes flecked his arms and hands. A shallow wound encircled his throat like a macabre necklace.

"What happened?" I tried to ask when he knelt beside me. The words came out as a long *buuuuurrrrpppppp*.

A tear trickled out of the corner of my eye.

He said nothing. Just stroked my hair until a sharp *ziiii-ing-WHACK* outside the partially open door sent him bolting back into the fight.

But he returned every few minutes. He never spoke. No placating, "it's going to be alright" statements, which I would've loved to hear, even if they were bald-faced lies. But he'd brush my hair, or lightly trace his fingers over my cheeks, and his hands spoke louder than his voice ever could.

I'm here. I won't leave you.

Every time he was gone, I stared at the ceiling, running movie quotes through my head, focusing on each wispy breath, and forcing myself to stay awake—to stay *alive*—so I could see him again.

On the seventh (or eighth) time, he walked in while I was internally singing "Be Our Guest" and silently panicking because I couldn't remember all the lyrics.

Be our Guest. Be our guest.

What comes next?

Heh, that kinda rhymes, though. Not really. Kinda. And—frick, what was the candle's name? He has a name. I know it. I've seen that movie a gazillion times. Why can't I remember it?

Cheriour rubbed his knuckles over my cheek, dragging me away from my *Beauty and the Beast* rabbit hole. I blinked, angled my head toward him, and tried to smile.

A second set of wet, cold hands brushed my knuckles, making me jolt and cough.

"What happened?" Quinn grasped my arm and pressed me down, keeping me still as I sputtered.

"I don't know." Cheriour sounded winded.

Quinn touched my chest—a short, feather-light tap. His fingers came away smudged with crimson. "How much blood has she lost?"

"Too much," Cheriour said.

A shout rose from outside. Cheriour drew his stubby sword and stepped back into the rain, closing the warped door behind him, leaving me in this moldy-ass room with a man who'd once tried to kill me because he'd gotten in a tizzy about the color of my eyes.

Fabulous.

"Addie..."

Quinn's clammy fingers continued to inspect me. And I *hated* how cold they were. And how smooth, compared to Cheriour's sandpaper fingers. I twitched. More blood erupted from my mouth.

Quinn pulled his wet sleeve over his hand and used it to mop up the fresh bouts of brownish-red liquid off my face. "Addie," he said again, more softly. "What happened?"

As if I fucking knew.

"Cheriour said he didn't find a wound. But, in my experience, small punctures can cause more damage than large ones. Did you feel any pain, at any point, around your chest? Or your back? Even if it was only fleeting?"

I shook my head. *Slowly*. But not slow enough to avoid another bout of wet coughing.

And Quinn sucked at concealing his emotions. All the color left his cheeks as he continued poking around my body, as though he thought I was too befuddled to remember if I'd been stabbed in the chest. His mouth drooped when his search came up empty.

He tried to heal me anyway. His fingers shook when he pressed them to my forehead and his power trickled through me, soothing the other aches in my body. But it did nothing to douse the flame-broiled blade rammed into my chest.

I retched again.

Quinn wiped the blood away again. And then he sat back on his haunches, raking his hand through his hair. "This isn't an injury," he murmured.

The door creaked. Cheriour stepped into the room, his eyes moving back and forth between Quinn and me. His fingers fidgeted around his sword, his shoulders tense and balled up beneath his ears, giving him a bit of a hunchback.

"I can't heal her," Quinn whispered.

Cheriour kept a carefully crafted mask of indifference on his face. "We can't stay here..." His mouth twisted as he fought for words. "The city is overrun. I've pulled everyone back. But the Wraiths are moving toward the shore. I—" His mask splintered. Pieces of it tumbled away, revealing the panic-stricken patches of heartache beneath.

An expression that had *my* heart aching.

This was *hurting* him.

Cheriour was a guarded guy. He kept people at a distance, schooled his emotions, and never shared anything personal. He'd basically surrounded himself with a fifty-foot privacy fence and communicated with the outside world through a peephole in the gate. But he'd lowered that gate for me and invited me inside. He'd let me see the sides of himself he hid from everyone else.

He'd made himself *vulnerable* for me.

Once you let someone in, you gave them all the power to hurt you.

I didn't *want* to hurt him.

But I was.

I wanted to hug him. Stroke his hair. Press my lips to his. Do *something* to ease his pain.

My hand flopped. That was all the movement I could manage.

He recognized the summons and came to me, dropping to his knees when he reached my side.

My watery vision bounced as I stared up at his face. Which was annoying, because I wanted to absorb every-thing: his emerald stare, the scar slashed across his left eyelid. Those high cheekbones—I *loved* the way they shaped his face—and the freckles dotting his nose. The lush curve of his lips, and the wild (but somehow sexy AF) tangle of his beard.

But as he leaned over me, his beautiful features mutated into a trippy Picasso painting. Because I couldn't *stop fucking crying*.

Cheriour bent and pressed a lingering kiss to my brow. It was the wettest, messiest smooch I'd ever gotten, but I savored every second of it.

Outside, multiple people yelled his name.

He drew back, his hand still cupping the curve of my cheek, even as his head lilted toward the door.

He *needed* to be out there.

But he *wanted* to be in here.

Quinn watched him with an odd, almost remorseful expression etched on his face. "Go," he said. "It's alright. I'll stay back and do whatever I can to bring her to the shore."

Cheriour's mouth pursed. But with a final, bittersweet caress, he stood. "The city is overrun," he reminded Quinn.

Quinn emitted a barking laugh. "I can steal through a crowded city. Easily."

Cheriour nodded. "The west side is the clearest. But Deborah said Ellard escaped to that side. He may still be there. Be careful."

"You as well," Quinn said.

It was only when Cheriour turned away that I noticed he had my poleaxe strapped to his back. And I had no friggin' clue *why* I found that comforting, but I did. Like there was a small sliver of me that would get to stay with him, even after the rest of me was six feet under.

And then he was gone.

Quinn immediately slipped his arms under me, tugging me against him. His movements were slow, *careful*, but they jostled me enough to slosh blood back into my throat.

"Addie, listen to me." Quinn mopped at my face when I coughed and wheezed in slithery lines of air. "I'm taking you back to Muirin. Whatever is happening, I *will* figure it out. Do *not* die."

I gave a wet scoff. He'd barked those words like a command, as though I could *control* whether I lived or died while I had nuclear bombs exploding inside of me. And why the fuck did he care? From the moment I'd set foot in Niall, the dude had slapped a neon sign on my back that said, "Addie Collins is the nastiest skank bitch I've ever met. Do *not* trust her."

But then Quinn murmured his next words: "He'd be devastated." And, with that heart-shattering line, he slipped out the door and into the rain.

I belched blood all over his shoulders and chest. He didn't flinch. I writhed, fighting for every teensy scrap of oxygen. He merely tightened his hold, shuffled my face more firmly into his shoulder to muffle my coughing, and kept moving.

Hordes of Wraiths traversed around us. I heard them stomping, yelling, and making aggravated *bleggghs* from being out in the downpour. They were literally *everywhere*. And Quinn craftily avoided all of them. He slunk around like a freaking cat, barely making a sound as he tiptoed through the alleys, staying in the darkest, stankiest sections. Periodically, he'd pause at a corner and swing his head out to listen for Wraiths, but he never stepped out into the open.

The dude was a proper sneaky-sneak.

But our progress through the city was agonizingly slow. And, well, *agonizing*.

Teeth savaged the inside of my throat, biting down to my chest, and then my diaphragm.

Heh. *Teeth*. Funny way to describe the pain. Made it seem like a savage monster was eating me out (and *not* in a fun way). Like in *Alien*, when the slimy, sharp-toothed extraterrestrial ripped its way out of Kane's chest—

Oh fuck.

Fuck, fuck...was that happening to me? Like, *for real?*

Did Sakar have parasitic aliens?

Had a *literal monster* been dwelling inside my chest cavity for the last few months, slowly consuming me as it grew strong enough to bust out?

And, as if to confirm my sudden frenzied theory, the

teeth inside me sank farther. *Deeper.* And gave a ferocious twist.

White ink blots exploded before my eyes. A bout of indecipherable phantom wails punched a hole through my skull.

I'm dead, I thought wildly.

The broken shards of my skull ground against each other as they rattled around, puncturing their jagged edges into my brain.

I have to be dead.

But why did it still hurt so much?

Brutal, vicious agony ensnared every fiber, every cell, every *molecule* of my body. And it wouldn't let go.

I screamed, although all that came out of my mouth was a bloody burble.

"Hold on, Addie…" Quinn's voice seemed miles away, even though he was still holding me.

Or was he?

As I thrashed, my elbow squelched into the mud.

I blinked once. Twice. Squinted. Peered through the blinding haze of white.

I'd been so consumed by the pain mauling my body that I hadn't noticed Quinn had put me down. Hadn't seen the half dozen Wraiths pouring into the alley.

Wraiths Quinn now fought single-handedly.

The cries detonated.

Was Quinn yelling?

Was I?

Or did the howls exist only in my head?

No idea.

But they got louder, and louder, and *louder.*

Make it stop! Make it stop! Please!!

I didn't know who I was pleading to, but I hoped someone had their listening ears on.

Please! Let me die.

The sensation inside my chest shifted, shoving against my breastbone so hard, my entire body bowed in a spasm. As I jerked almost into a sitting position, I saw him on the other side of the alley, watching Quinn war with the Wraiths.

Ellard.

Anger bubbled through my veins, pumping enough adrenaline into my body to dull some of the pain.

Ellard didn't notice me. His yellow eyes were focused on the Wraiths.

Wraiths *he'd* sent to kick Quinn's ass.

This was all *his fucking fault.* We'd been *winning.* For once. But then Ellard sauntered into town and...something had changed. *Everything* had changed.

And he'd sabotaged me. Somehow. I hadn't been in pain before he showed up.

This bastard had fucked all of us over.

My chest lurched again.

And maybe it was my oxygen-deprived brain cells thinking crazy thoughts, but I swore the...*thing* in my chest started fluttering. *Shoving.* Pushing me toward Ellard.

And y'know what, if some maniacal alien wanted to burst out of my chest and go chomp-chomp on Ellard's fugly face, so be it. At least I'd go out with a bang.

But I had to get to him before I blew into a gazillion pieces.

I upended another mouthful of blood onto my lap when I sat up. The world whooshed around me in buoyant circles, as though I'd been strapped to a rusty old tilt-a-whirl.

Be still! I moaned at the peskily rotating world. And then I cried. Because those were Cheriour's words.

"Be still, Addie."

I couldn't hear his syrupy drawl anymore. Even when I focused through the mayhem, my mind was only filled with the way he'd bellowed my name across the alleyway: that sharp, panicked cry.

Cheriour's anguish was Ellard's fault too.

And I wanted to make him suffer for it.

My knees were wobblier than a stack of cards as I stood, leaning against the wall for support. More spots ruptured before my eyes as my liquid-filled lungs stretched and stretched and *stretched*, rapidly reaching popping point.

But I dragged myself along the wall, one slow, laborious inch at a time.

With each wobbling step, I thought of Cheriour. And Braxton. Kaelan, Deborah, Quinn…all the poor bastards who came to this shithole with me and who now risked getting trapped here. *Because of fucking Ellard!*

Ellard still didn't notice me. Not until I tried to speak: "You stupid sack of shit! I'm going full Ramsay Bolton on your ass: I'll chop your dick off, cook it nice and crispy, and make you eat it!"

Of course, my words came out as a glob of blood.

But my sputtering caught his attention.

Before I lost my nerve (or my balance…or consciousness) I flung myself at him, grasping the side of his neck, my nails digging at his gray flesh.

Frothing rage rushed beneath my skin. *Burn, baby. Burn!*

And when my chest swelled again, the clawed creature finally, finally ready to bust through my flesh and bone, I didn't fight it.

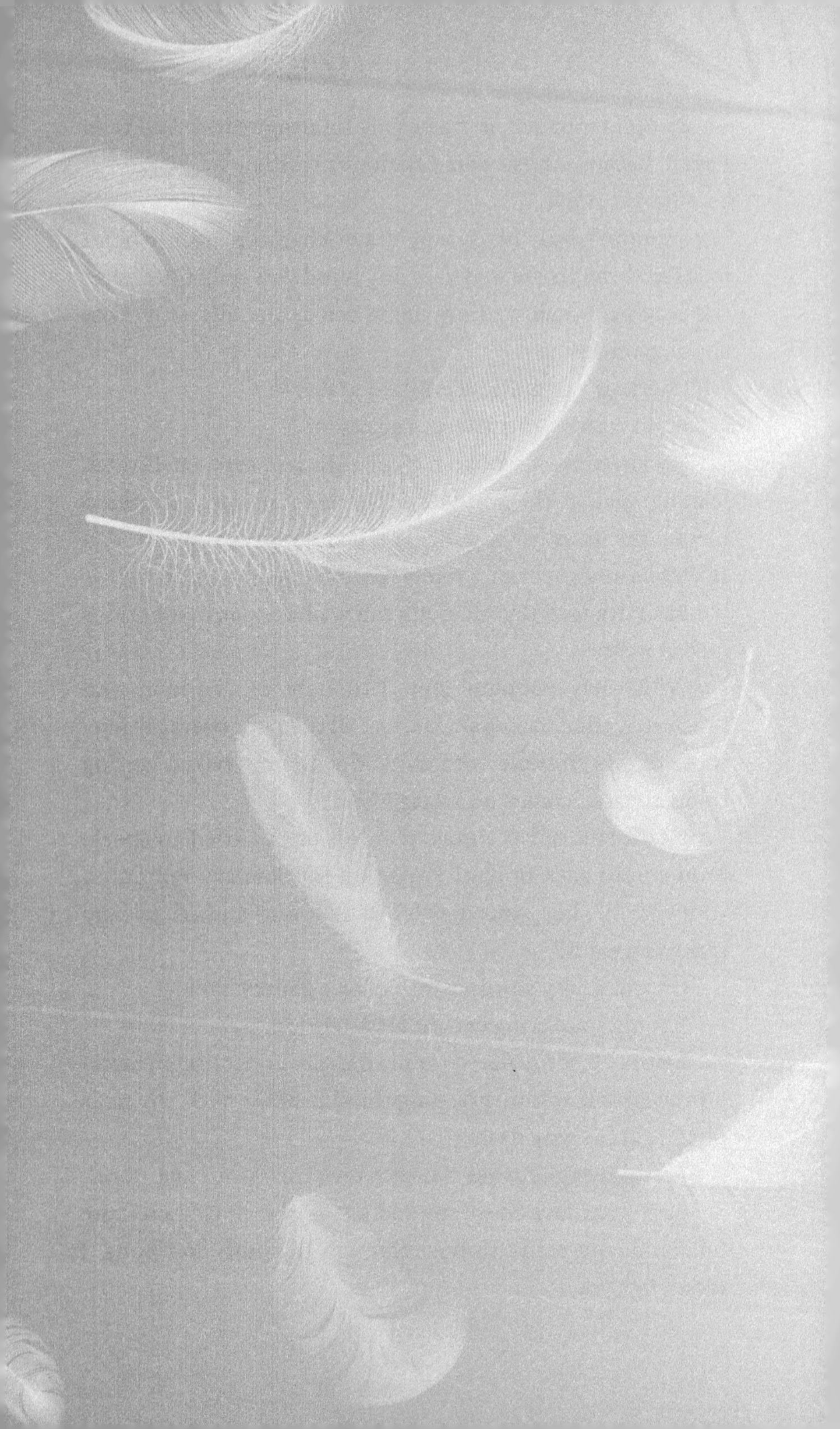

CHAPTER 32

WE ALL SCREAM FOR ICE CREAM

I choked on blood.

And then I vomited fire.

Literally.

I doubled over, mouth gaping, eyes bugging out of my head, as everything inside me went heave-ho.

"Aggghhhbbbbllleeeeegggghhhh."

Pop.

Something small, round, and slimy rolled up my throat and ping-ponged around the inside of my mouth.

"Mmmuh mmm mmmfphuh?" I whined. (English translation: "What the fuck?")

As the...*thing* tumbled over my lips, I raised my hand to catch it. It plonked onto my palm in all its obnoxiously bright, twinkling glory.

A *flame?*

Was that a freaking fireball?

Ellard stared at me.

I drew in a breath, readying myself to scream, but then I bit off with a cry.

Because I'd drawn in a *full breath*.

My airways were *clear*! And that first gulp of air, free of blood, was more satisfying than a sip of ice-cold beer on a hot summer day.

So, so, *so* freaking good.

But what in ever-loving fuck had just happened to me?

And why did I hock up a flaming hairball??

Because that was the best way to describe the flickering tongue of white-orange light. The thing was tiny—barely the size of my pinkie tip—but it was *fire*. A genuine, gyrating flame. And it'd come from somewhere *inside my body*!

Ellard barked something. A command. A cry. I wasn't sure.

I kept staring at the teeny flame in my hand, watching the mists of rain pitter ineffectively off it. I wiggled my fingers. The fireball rocked back and forth. And then thin, ear-splitting wails surged from its twinkling depths.

The same yells that had tried to blow my brain to smithereens.

"Gah!" I jolted and rammed my back against the wall.

The fireball oscillated in my palm, still screaming bloody murder.

Was this...

No. It couldn't be.

But what else *could* it be?

The sliver of Seruf's soul. Or Essence. Or whatever. The one Kylah said would latch onto my soul like a gooey piece of pre-chewed bubble gum.

It had to be. Right? I mean, humans didn't form fireballs inside their chests.

Right?

Unless hybrids did. Which...*yeech.*

But that still didn't explain why the fireball was screeching.

It had to be her soul.

And no wonder I'd felt like horseshit the past few months. This little sucker had been slow-cooking me from the inside. Now it was gone. And I felt *so much* lighter.

I was also light-*headed* thanks to the blood loss. But the weight in my chest, the aching twinges, had all vanished.

I loosed a wild cackle that would've fit on a laugh track for a cheapo haunted house. It sure scared the bejesus out of Ellard.

He stumbled back, tripping over his own feet, and got all shifty-eyed as he glanced between my face and the flame in my hand. And, *ooh yeah*, the anger came rushing back once I swung my gaze over his craggy-ass skin.

He continued his backward shuffle.

I lunged forward.

"Please!" His breath rattled when I snatched his shoulder in my left hand.

"'*Please?*' Are you fucking kidding me?" I yanked.

He *eeeped* and stumbled into my chest. The impact sent the back of my head cracking against the wall. Blobby stars floated before my eyes, ratcheting my rage up a few notches.

"You stupid, fugly sack of shit," I seethed. "What the fuck *did you do*? Why couldn't you *leave us alone*? God forbid we attempt to live some semblance of a normal goddamn fucking life in this goddamn fucking world..."

I raised my right hand, intending to ram that tiny flame down his gullet until *he* retched blood. But everything inside me screamed *no*.

Right idea.

Wrong spot.

Instinct drew me to his scraggy chest, so I thumped my hand against his bare breastbone.

Or *tried* to. The blow never landed. Instead, my hand passed right through him, the way it had for Seruf and Darragh.

The flame went neon, lighting up Ellard's greenish-gray flesh like a sickly looking Christmas tree.

He screamed.

I screamed.

We all screamed for ice cream. Har, har, har.

Yeah...my brain was officially fried.

Ellard twisted, wrenching my hand out of his chest. But the flame stayed with him. He staggered away, roaring, and crisscrossed his feet, tripping himself. His arms flapped as he teetered on one heel. And, *boom*, down he went.

I stumbled back, still bristling like a hissy cat, even as my knees knocked together.

"Addie!" Quinn's hands snagged my armpits, holding me upright. "What...?"

I didn't let him finish. Because that was the thing about anger: once it had its barby fingers in you, it was *really* hard to pry them loose. And sometimes you didn't want to. Without anger, I would've dropped into a dead faint. But rage kept the little blood I had left pumping. It made me feel awake and alive, even when my body moaned, *"Bitch...lie down!!"*

I shoved away from Quinn, accidentally ramming my elbow into his gut. "Sorry!" I muttered when he let out a wheezy cough. But I only glanced at him long enough to see the gashes swelling across his face and the tangle of dead Wraiths behind him before I whirled and screeched at Ellard, *"You fucking zombie piece of shit!"* Blood squirted from my mouth—but *not* because it was still frothing from my lungs. This was the leftover stuff. And, my God, the taste...

I needed a gallon of mouthwash, a fuck ton of toothpaste, and a jumbo bag of mints. Because that rusty/rancid butter flavor was...*blegh*. And Sakar (or Uchen) didn't exactly have a surplus of oral hygiene products, so I added *lingering blood breath* to the reasons I was pissed off.

Ellard slowly, discombobulately, got to his feet.

"Bastard!" I stomped over and shoved both hands into his chest. They didn't pass through him this time; my palms slapped coarse flesh, and the force of my smack sent him sprawling back on his ass.

As he fell, his arm flew up. Flames sprouted from his fingertips, despite the endless trickle of rain seeping into the alley. And he grasped at my shirtsleeves, trying to *burn me!*

I snagged his hand, wrapping my fingers around the flame. "Joke's on you, pal. I'm fireproof. And so is this shirt. You're going to have to do better than that if—"

"You killed Seruf?" The mournful timbre of his voice brought me up short.

Don't do it, Addie. Don't start pitying this bastard.

"I sure did." My teeth ground together.

"You—*what?*" Quinn yelped.

"And you're next, bucko." I clasped down on Ellard's hand, trying to shatter his bones.

"You carried this fragment of her Essence? All this time?" Again, Ellard went for the sucker punch with that doleful voice and those unsure eyes. And, again, he brought me up short.

Blood, Addie! You were drowning *in your own fucking blood. Because he...he...he did something...*

"I assure you, I did nothing to cause you harm," Ellard

responded to the words I'd obviously blurted. "It was Seruf's Essence. It *knew* me."

"*Knew* you?"

He nodded and jangled our joined hand, squeezing my knuckles, as though we were lovers holding hands during a moonlight stroll.

I tightened my grip, trying to pulverize his flame-wrapped fingers.

"It's been fourteen years." He loosed a breathless laugh as he watched the flame gyrate over our knuckles. "Fourteen years since I was able to do this..." He twirled his other wrist, summoning a volleyball-sized tongue of flame.

"You were a Firestarter?" Quinn rasped in my ear. He'd stepped forward, getting way too close to the deranged ex-Celestial with a fireball.

I ripped my hand away from Ellard and threw my arm across Quinn's chest, keeping him behind me.

Ellard looked up with a giddy and awestricken smile stretching across his face.

"I—you—do you remember me?" Quinn asked. "I lived in Darfield during your reign and was a member of the army there...a Healer."

Ellard's smile faded a smidge, but he didn't move. "That was a long time ago," he said. "You would've been a child."

"I was. And you..." Quinn shuffled forward again, pressing against my arm. "I-I did not know you were a Firestarter."

"Nor did I want you to know." Ellard rolled the fireball back and forth over his fingers. "After Seruf's tantrums, I was afraid you humans would fear me if you knew what I was."

"I don't think we could've," Quinn whispered. "The

people of Darfield adored you. You were gentle, and you used to give us gifts from the Celestial City."

At this, Quinn touched my shoulder, plucking at the fabric of my pink/blue shirt. Which, despite all my blood belching, still looked brand spanking new (minus, y'know, the goddamn tear in my right sleeve). Not a single speck of blood dotted the fabric, even though crimson blobs marred my leather vest, breeches, and boots.

Ellard gave another soft, breathy laugh as his eyes took in the sleeves of my shirt. "Ooh! I *thought* that was my old tunic. How *lovely* to see it again. I'd forgotten how beautiful it was."

"*Your* tunic?" I asked.

"Yes. It's *utterly* grand, is it not?" His eyes sparkled. "Do you know how such garments are made, little human? It's *quite* fascinating. You see, we collect the material from a dying star."

"A-are you for real?"

He glanced down at his bare-naked self as if to confirm he was, indeed, a bona fide zombie. "I believe I am real, yes. Unless I've died again and am merely waiting to reawaken —what a *dreadful* process." He shuddered. "But death has never felt quite this vivid."

"That was...never mind...So, wait, hang on...*Phew*, man, there's a lot to unpack right now." My poor brain was like an old, over-wrung sponge. "So, let's stick with the shirt. For now. Did you say this was from a *dying star?*"

"Yes."

"Are you being literal?"

He blinked.

"Did you *actually* fly to a dying star, squeeze its juices

out, make a shirt, and then...you *gave* it to the highest human bidder?"

"Well, I'd not intended to part with it," Ellard said. "But after several years of indulging in human festivities and meals, the shirt was getting rather snug."

I had to puff a laugh at that. *Had to.* Because I knew that feeling well.

"The last I'd seen," Ellard continued, "'twas a rather endearing human *male* who purchased that shirt. Tell me, little human, how did it come to be in your possession? It was passed down, yes? It always *fascinates* me the way you humans attach yourselves to inanimate objects, so much so that you deem it necessary to dictate who shall succeed you in the possession of such objects."

This dude was off his freaking rocker.

Before I could respond, Quinn talked over me. "It was Terrick who purchased the shirt from you, wasn't it? An older man—a Concealer."

Ellard's eyes twinkled. "Yes!"

"He must've gifted it to his daughter. Because"—Quinn's throat clicked—"Lass was wearing this shirt. The day I helped her escape Darfield."

"Ah..." Ellard dragged the word into a prolonged *aaaaah-hhhhh.* "I see. Hmmmm. And this Lass would've been the hybrid Seruf created, yes? Lasair?"

Quinn and I had *very* different reactions to Lasair's name.

He uttered a lonesome, "Yes."

I silently ground my teeth. Even after all these months, that name still spun my stomach around in a loop-de-loop.

Ellard laughed, although it was cold and humorless.

Kinda deranged. And the fireball cast some ominous shadows over his rain-soaked face.

My skin prickled, and I pressed my arm more firmly against Quinn's chest, making sure he kept his distance.

"If only I'd known Seruf's hybrid resided in my city," Ellard said bitterly. "What a different world this might've been." He fixed his eyes on the sleeve of my shirt again. "So, the tunic passed from mother to child, then?"

"*No.* I found it buried in the dirt," I snapped.

Ellard looked poised to give an indignant response about his precious shirt being treated like a plant, but then he groaned, doubled over, and clapped both hands to his head, smooshing his fireball over his scalp.

The fire didn't burn him. Obviously. But the flame shifted from his hand to the top of his bald, ridged skull, making him look like Hades from *Hercules*. Or the Heat Miser. Or one of their unholy offspring.

"Is that the flaming hairball cozying itself up inside you? It hurts, don't it?" I sneered. "Has the screaming started yet? That's the *best* part—like having the world's worst rock band screech-sing between your ears. Thank fuck I'm not dealing with it anymore."

"It's not..." Ellard raised his head and then stopped with a cry of pain. He squeezed his eyes shut, grinding his knuckles between his eyes. "Seruf's Essence is settled. It *belongs* with me. We were bonded."

"Bonded?" I asked. "As in, the kinky *'you're my mate'* kinda way?"

"There were four of us."

"Oh. So it was a harem, then?"

Ellard doubled over again with a long, strained sound,

then lurched to his feet, shaking, with a full flaming halo encircling his brow.

"Quinn...back up." I pushed at Quinn's shoulder. When he didn't move quick enough, I rammed my elbow into him. "Back the fuck up. Before—"

Ellard stretched a hand toward us. "Fear not," he murmured. "I'll not harm you."

"No? You realize you look like a lunatic pyromaniac right now?"

"I assure you," Ellard waved his arm, snuffing the fire, "I have spent a millennium controlling the flame. Ramiel's interference will not make me lose myself so easily."

Quinn made a strangled, panicked noise. "Ramiel?"

Ellard staggered into the wall and bashed his head against it. Once. Twice. *Three times.* Each one made a vicious *ker-thunk.*

"Ahhhhh," he sighed after he finished scrambling his already mashed brains. "That's better. Oh my...apologies," he said when he saw Quinn and I ogling at him. "That was quite startling to witness, I'm sure."

"Dude, you're out of your fucking mind," I said.

"On the contrary," Ellard chirped, "this is the first time I've been properly within my mind in a very long time. And I have you to thank for that, little human. Gifting me Seruf's Essence—"

"I would *not* call that a gift."

"—has helped me regain control. It's the first I've held an Essence within me since my mortal one dissolved." Ellard flashed a watery, loose-lipped smile. "Of course, it cannot sever my tether to Ramiel, not so long as he retains ownership over my Essence, but it's given me *strength* and *clarity.*" He sniffed and wiped at his nose. "Souls and Essences are powerful things, are they not? I've been without mine for so long, I've forgotten how fulfilling it is to have one. I've been *empty...*" His words melted into another groan. "This pain... it's not the Essence. It's Ramiel. He knows his tether has loosened. But fear not, humans, I *will* prevail—oh my...oh dear, oh *dear*...you may want to leave this place. *Quickly.* Ramiel knows you're here—my fault, I'm afraid. Please understand, I had no desire to betray you, but when I set foot outside the fortress and witnessed your valiant, if rather foolish, attempt to vacate the city, I alerted him to your presence. Inadvertently, of course. But now—my dears, he's sent Uriel."

"Who...?"

Quinn and I sounded like twin owls. "Who, who!"

"I know...I know. It's *dreadful*," Ellard said. "But there is hope! Uriel will not traverse the ocean. You can still get your people to safety!"

I whirled to face Quinn. He had the same pale, "*ooooh shit!*" look that was probably etched across my face. "Did anyone make it back to Muirin?" I asked. "Before, y'know, everything went to crap?"

"No," Quinn said. "The people of Keld wouldn't go near the ocean. We gathered them on the beach and had planned to send them in groups."

"Oh my," Ellard murmured. "That was not so prudent. Any left on the beach will perish."

"Shit!" I hissed. And my insides started aching again. Not as vigorously as before. My fear was a mewling kitten compared to the roaring lion Seruf's soul had been. But kittens had claws too, and they still hurt.

Everyone was on that beach. The Keldians. My friends. *Cheriour...*

And we were too far away, the storm was still too loud... We had no way of knowing what was happening down there.

Maybe they'd skedaddled while Quinn and I were chatting with Eccentric Ellard.

Maybe they were already dead.

"We have to go." Quinn must've been thinking the same as me because his face had turned a sickly grayish-white.

My tongue felt like a scratchy piece of gauze. *Blood-soaked* gauze. I swallowed but couldn't get the dry sensation out of my mouth. Or the taste.

A rush of exhaustion, of hopelessness, smashed into my bones. I would've collapsed if Quinn hadn't grabbed my arm. He pressed his other hand to my cheek. Not healing me, just peering into my eyes, studying me.

I probably looked like Casper the pasty white crack addict. Because now that some of my high emotions had burnt out, my weary muscles quivered, straining to hold me upright.

"Ellard." Quinn held me steady as he spoke over my head. "Could you watch over her while I return to the beach? She's lost too much blood and isn't fit to fight."

"Screw that. I'm going with you," I said.

"Addie—"

"I said, I'm going with you. And *you.*" I turned and jabbed a finger at Ellard. "How much control do you have right now?"

"I'll not burn you," Ellard said.

"That's not what I'm asking. Can you keep Ramiel out of your head for a little while?"

He gave another dry laugh. "Have I not been doing that very thing?"

"I dunno. From my vantage point, you seemed to be having some kinda fit."

"If Ramiel knew I was speaking with *you*, he would have sent Uriel to this spot."

"Right...well...okay. Then, can you help us out? *Please.* It's...you *know* the Celestials. And your little pyrotechnic displays could *really* come in handy."

Ellard bounced on his heels. "I've always had a fondness for humans," he said. "You're rather adorably tenacious creatures, are you not?"

"*Creatures*? For fuck's sake, we're not animals!"

"You are to me," Ellard said. "But you're animals I find endearing. It would be my utmost pleasure to assist you. As much as I am able to, of course." He ruefully reached over and tapped one of his shoulder spikes. "I am not what I used to be, and I cannot best my brethren in a fight."

My next words stuck to the roof of my mouth. I *really* had to twist my jaw and contort my tongue to spit them out. "But I can."

"Ahhhhh."

If Ellard made that obnoxious noise one more time, I was gonna clock him.

"Of course you can. Yes." He snapped his fingers, then chortled when a flame appeared in his hands. "And you're already quite accomplished at it."

Quinn pursed his lips, throwing me a dirty look that basically screamed, "*You lying skank. You told me you* didn't *know what happened to Seruf.*" But he only uttered a clipped, "Very well," as he pivoted. "Let's not waste any more time."

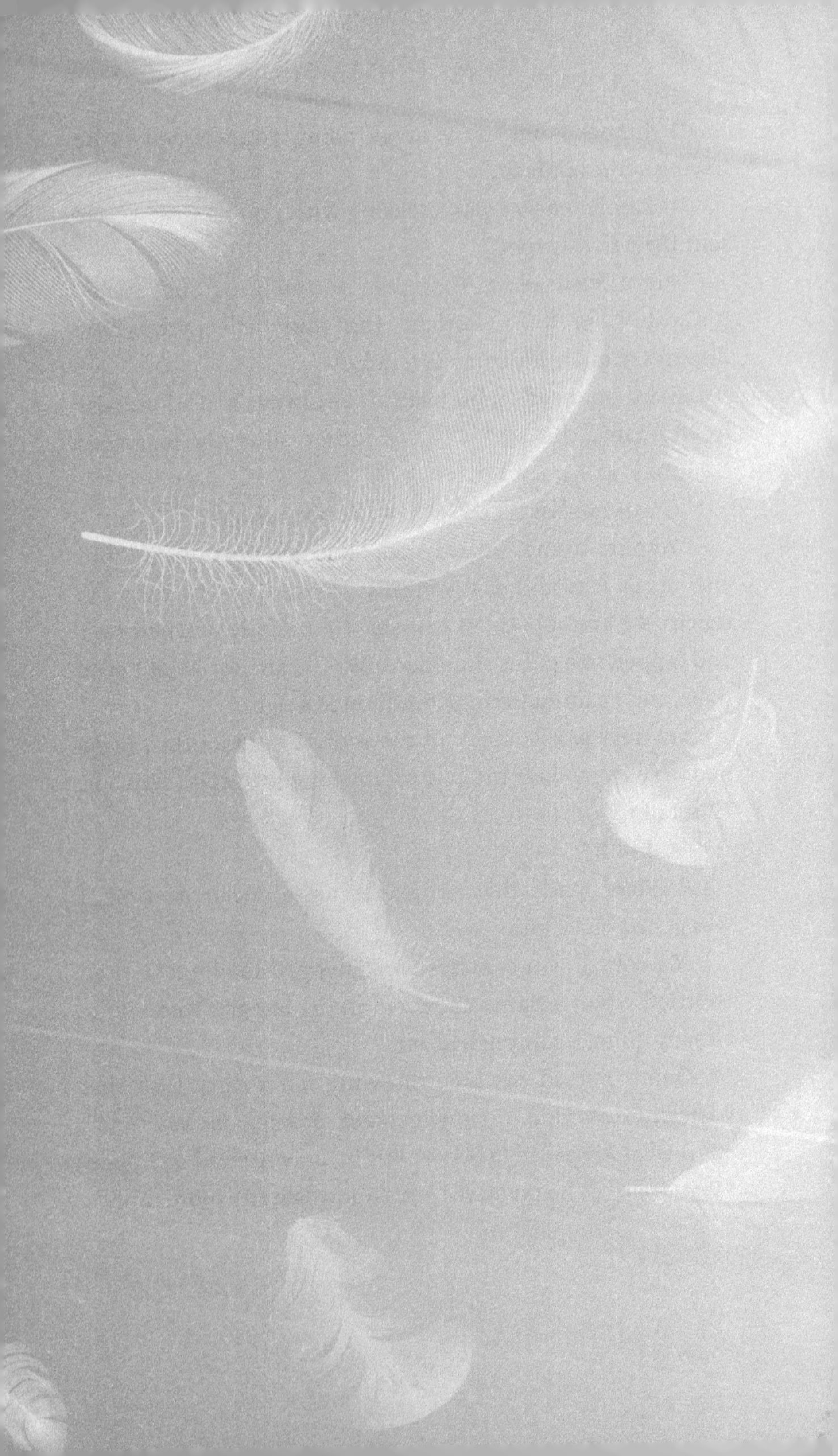

CHAPTER 33
B-MOVIE HORROR REMAKE OF LADY AND THE TRAMP

Even the endless torrents of rain couldn't wash the blood from the beach. And the scene bobbing between the trees as we made our way through the woods was pure *bedlam*.

My Muirin crew encircled the Keldians, trying to protect them from the hellhounds that dashed around, snatching at people's legs like massive, demented chihuahuas. The Wraiths zeroed in on the horses, probably figuring demolishing the getaway cars would throw a monkey wrench in the heist. Five corpses already crisscrossed the rocky sands, too far away and cleaved into too many chunks for me to guess who they were. Three dead horses also sprawled across the beach. One still twitched as the wound on its chest spurted. The other two were still, their legs stiff and straight. Other mangled animals littered the ground too. Pigs. Some chickens. A goat's body was flopped close to the hills, but its head had rolled down to the water.

My crew had snagged everything and everyone they could find in Keld.

And we were about to lose all of it.

"They need to get their asses in the water!" I called, and then I squealed when a root nabbed my ankle. I fumbled to my right, pinging off Ellard, who moseyed along with his head clutched in his hands. "Sorry," I mumbled to him once I got my wobbly legs sorted again.

Note to self: speed walking through the woods, in the rain, while blood-deprived, was *not* a good idea. If my klutziness didn't get me, the lightheadedness would knock me on my ass at some point.

Quinn walked on my other side, his head slightly cocked, watching my clumsy progression. He never offered to help, but he stayed close. Y'know, in case I timbered.

"They're too frightened of the water," Quinn said. And then the blood rushed from his face when his eyes snapped to something on my right side.

"Ooooh boy. Do I even wanna look?" I heezed.

"Uriel," he muttered.

"Man...why'd you tell me that? Now I've *gotta* look." I craned my neck, peering through the trees and rain. On the far right edge of the beach, a few dozen yards away from us, a golden wing fluttered between two hunch-backed rocks. And then the Celestial himself stepped forward, placing himself smack in the middle of those boulders.

My God.

Uriel was a fashion *disaster*.

Those gold wings were gaudy enough. The fact that he'd paired them with a laminated black and gold suit...*yikes*. Way too much bling-bling. And none of it looked good against his ivory skin and white hair. He should've been decked out in all *silver* with that complexion. Or a different color palette entirely. Some slate gray, sea foam, or pine green...

Why *the fuck* was I nitpicking his sense of style? Jesus. I had bigger things to worry about.

Like the lone, dark shape that jogged along the beach, sword drawn, preparing to meet Uriel head-on.

Cheriour.

Of fucking course he'd volunteer to drive Mr. Gold Bags away. Of *course* he'd go alone, armed with only his piddly knives, stubby swords, and my poleaxe, all of which would do absolutely *nothing* against a Celestial.

Fucking macho, self-sacrificing bastard.

I loved him.

But I would wring his goddamn neck if we lived through this.

"He's keeping Uriel away from the others," Quinn said in response to the tangent that hadn't stayed in my goddamn head, as per usual.

"I get that," I said. "I'm still gonna wring his neck. You!" I whirled and snapped my fingers under Ellard's nose. "Still in the driver's seat?"

He frowned, and then giggled. "Ah! Is that one of your humanisms? If you're asking whether I am in control, the answer is yes."

"Good. Can you go help the macho bastard with Mr. Gold Bags over there—Cheriour and Uriel," I clarified when Ellard gave me a foggy look. "Can you keep Uriel from pummeling Cheriour's ass?"

"Cheriour," Ellard turned the name over in his mouth. "Cheriour. Cheriour?"

"The fuck are you doing? He's not Beetlejuice! Just..." A glimmer of gold caught my eye as Uriel whipped a wing through the air, nearly clocking Cheriour in the head. "*Help him!* Please."

"Is this the Reaper Cheriour you speak of?" Ellard swung his head toward the fight unfolding at the rocks.

Reaper?

Like...*Grim Reaper?*

"Ummmm, I dunno," I stuttered. "Maybe? He was a Celestial...Can you..." I trailed off when Cheriour burrowed a knife into Uriel's wing.

Uriel gave an almighty bellow that ripped across the land faster than a hurricane-level wind gust.

Cheriour back flopped onto the sand.

Half the people, Wraiths, and hellhounds on the beach toppled.

And that vicious gale snaked through the trees to bowl us over too. I hissed when my ass *kerthumped* over a jagged stone. "Oooh, ouch, ouch, *ouch*...What the *hell* was that?"

Ellard had done a clumsy somersault. Now he sat up, unsticking the wet leaves from his head. "Uriel is a Messenger"—he twitched and smacked the heel of his palm against his temple—"with some control over the wind."

"Well...that's fantastic. We've got three Elementals crammed into this teensy corner of the world. Let me know when Earth shows up, 'kay? Because then it'll be a *real* party." I squinted and exhaled when Cheriour gracefully flipped back onto his feet. "Can you please help—oh, okay... *thank you!*"

Ellard was already moving away from me, silkily navigating his way down the rocky path toward Uriel while periodically smacking his temple. And I couldn't tell if he looked a little green in the gills because he was teetering on the edge of losing control, or if it was because, y'know, he naturally had zombie-green skin.

Quinn grasped my hand, pulling me to my feet. "You get as many people as you can into the water," he said. "I'll help keep the Wraiths back...*ooofff!*"

Uriel's second yell sent another puff of wind pinwheeling across the land. This one walloped us from behind, shoving us through the last line of straggly trees and bitch-slapping us onto the beach.

The landing gave my tailbone a good thwacking.

Quinn did a full back flop and made a strained *eeeeuu-uggh* as the air rushed out of his lungs.

This time, I had to pull him to his feet.

"That's the worst feeling, ain't it?" I asked as he sputtered. "When you get the wind knocked out of ya. But I've heard if you smack someone's chest *real hard*, you can knock the wind back in." I'd never heard this before in my life. "You want me to smack ya?"

Quinn shook his head and lurched forward, drawing his sword.

"Spoilsport," I muttered.

He and I made a *bang-up* duo as we sprint-staggered across the sand, wheezing up a storm.

"Addie!" Braxton, standing beside three wildly panicked horses and one tubbo pig, was the first to greet me. "What in fecking...Deborah said ye were *dead*! Feckin' shite!" He whipped his bow out, nocked an arrow, and drilled an oncoming Wraith.

"You *were* bloody well dead!" Deborah was only a few feet away, trying to dig a cart out of the sand. "With the way you bled..."

"Yeah, well, hell barfed me back up," I mumbled. "Probably so I could figure out what the fuck y'all are doing... *eeek!*" A hellhound zoomed around me, gnashing its teeth.

Quinn speared it with a well-placed underhand blow. Then he dashed through the fracas to see who needed healing or help.

I tried to ignore the way my knees knobbled together when I came to a stop beside Braxton. Tried to ignore how heavy and burdensome the rain felt as it slugged my body, as though the heavens were dropping anvils on me. "Why, *why* are you still here?" I gasped. "You should be halfway back to Muirin!"

"Ach, it's been a feckin' disaster." Braxton shot three more arrows. Each *creeeeaaaak-thoooom* of his bow was punctuated by a low "feck" or "damn bloody cads" or whatever other expletive he was in the mood to spew. "The horses won't go back in the water."

"Neither will the people," Deborah called. "And with bloody Uriel—"

As if responding to the sound of his name, Uriel blessed us with another booming yell and trouncing billow of wind.

I fell. *Again.* My spindly legs struggled to hold me up when I *wasn't* getting body checked with a murderous gale. Everyone else managed to brace against it and stay upright.

Braxton threw his hand down to help me back to my feet.

One of his horses shot sideways, nearly trampling the poor, pudgy pig, and ran headlong into a Wraith.

"Ach, ye fecking blighter!" Braxton screeched as he whisked around, bow raised.

The wind stole his first arrow, but the second hit home.

The Wraith collapsed. But not before he got a few good gouges into the horse's neck. The animal screeched and danced on its hind legs as a goopy crimson ribbon curled along its shoulders.

"What a *fucking mess.*" When I spat sand and rainwater out of my mouth, a few leftover flecks of blood went flying. "Okay, let's try to get somewhat organized here. Deborah, the carts *have to* go last. If they go at all—how the hell are you planning to get them under the water?"

"They're weighted," Deborah said. As if that explained anything.

"Okay. Well, focus on the people and horses first. Then figure the carts out. Braxton, is Sacrifice still...They didn't kill her? Right?"

"She's over with Kaelan," Braxton said. "She's a tough old lass. Not so easy to kill. But she's become testy with us..."

"Can you get her into the water?"

"Kaelan's been tryin'..."

"But what if *you* were leading her? To give her an extra boost of confidence. Would she go?"

Braxton paused and rubbed his hands over a gray horse's muzzle. "I'm not sure. She might...she's a wee bit braver than the rest. But even the brave ones have their limits."

"Can you try?"

Braxton sighed. "These horses are never goin' to forgive us."

"If we get them to Muirin, at least they'll be alive to hold that grudge," I said.

"Aye. Well, I'll do me best to sort the animals. Ye"—he jabbed a thumb at me—"need to help sort the people."

"I'll work on it." Out of the corner of my eye, I caught two mottled hellhounds slurping a woman's tendons out of her busted leg, like some B-movie horror remake of *Lady and the Tramp.*

And I was suddenly...*exhausted.* The kinda fatigue that rattled your bones and had gallons of tears shoving against your eyeballs, trying to pop them out of their sockets. There was so much mayhem. So much blood. So many screams...

All I wanted to do was lie down, clap my hands over my ears, and zonk out. Because where could I even *start?* I had no weapon. There were people, animals, and objects scattered all over the goddamn beach. And the notion of getting all of them into the water, under the waves, and through the ocean tunnel seemed as outlandish as getting booted to a rudimentary fantasy world while picking up a goddamn pizza.

But then I saw the kid—a Keldian—snap back at a Wraith.

The other Keldians were all clustered together, watching helplessly as Wraiths burst through the shoddy protective circle my crew had tried to form. A herd of sheep surrounded by a pack of wolves.

But one of the sheep had fangs. And he used them to bite back.

The tall, haggard boy couldn't have been more than sixteen, if that. He had a baby face but also sported the sagged, worn look of someone in their eighties. And he seemed about as fed up with life as a crotchety eighty-year-old.

When a Wraith barked in his face and lashed her whip at him, he lunged. Armed with nothing but his bare hands and teeth, he climbed onto her shoulders and attacked *viciously,* ripping her helmet from her head and digging his teeth into her ear.

She keened and chucked him off her.

He sprang right back to his feet.

When she pivoted and cracked her whip over a group of people, the boy rushed forward, raising his needle-thin arms to deflect the blow away from the others. The whip flayed his skin, but he didn't flinch. Hatred gleamed in his eyes, and his boxy jaw was set in a grim line. He was ready to go out swinging.

And, y'know what? People followed brave souls like that.

So maybe my task would be less exhausting than I'd thought. I didn't have to coax every single Keldian into the water. I only had to convince *one*.

"Hey." I scuttled over and tapped Deborah's shoulder. "Can I get you to help me with something...? *Eeerggh!*" I grunted and clutched onto her when another ear-splitting burst of wind threatened to bowl us over.

Fire erupted at the far end of the beach, where Cheriour and Uriel were locked in battle. I caught the flames out of the corner of my eye, but I didn't look that way. I *couldn't*.

"You needed my help to stand upright?" A slow smile twisted around Deborah's mouth that was probably meant to be humorous, but it looked creepy AF the way it leered at me from beneath the thick globs of rain-slicked blood covering her face.

"That too. But...*Oh shit!*" Some Keldians had gone down in the wind blast. The Wraiths hadn't. And now those milky-eyed bastards were dragging people bodily back toward the city.

Our window of opportunity was closing. *Quickly*.

"Okay." I sniffled and swiped at the rainwater and snot running from my nose. "You see that kid there...No, not him…" Deborah had pointed at a wailing toddler. "The *other* kid. He just got smacked with the whip."

"That one?" She jerked her thumb at a screeching baby.

"I guess kid means something a little different to you, huh? No, the *man* in the front. Black hair. Yeah, yeah! Him!" Her finger had finally landed on the scrawny spitfire. "Can you go grab him for me?"

"Grab him?"

"I need him."

"For what?" Deborah snatched a galloping hellhound by the scruff of its neck, yanked it against her chest, and hewed at its underbelly until its entrails twined around her axe.

Yum.

"He and I are going swimming. I'd go get him myself, but Cheriour has my poleaxe. And I'm…" I held my hands out, palms up, watching them jitter. "I don't know that I'd be any good for fighting anyway."

"The people won't go into the water," Deborah said.

"He will. I'll bet ya anything. That kid's got spunk. And if I get him to go in, and Braxton gets Sacrifice in, everyone else will follow."

She gave me an exasperated "*this is the kinda crazy talk that got us into this mess*" look. But then she turned and marched up the beach.

The boy, now bleeding from multiple lashes, had locked himself in a duel with the Wraith, fighting tooth and nail to seize the whip. Deborah strolled up, separated the warring duo, and swung her axe at the Wraith's neck. *Pop* went the Wraith's head from her shoulders.

The boy yelled when Deborah seized the collar of his threadbare shirt and dragged him behind her.

"Uh…oh boy. That's *way* harsher than I would've done

it." I jogged to meet them. "Okay, well, thanks for grabbing him," I said as I shooed her hand away and beamed at the boy. "Hey there!"

The kid reared back and—*whack!*—sent an open-handed slap across my face.

Ouch! Goddamn, that kid had a turbo jet attached to his swing. I saw stars. Big ole spiky ones. Broiling pain bubbled across my cheeks and straight down my neck. "*Excuse me,*" I hissed as my nose twitched, "we use our *words* to communicate 'round these parts. Not our fists—*ah!* That goes for you too!"

Deborah had *thunked* the back of the kid's head.

"Can y'all be civil for a sec?"

The boy glowered at me.

Deborah gave a noncommittal, "Humph."

"My name's Addie," I said in the sweetest, falsest customer service voice in my arsenal. "This lovely lady— who saved you from a Wraith, I might add—is Deborah. We're trying to help you."

"By drownen' us in the sea!" the boy spat.

"Oh, c'mon now. I'm sure you're a smart kid. Use your head. If we *wanted* to kill you, why in the hell would we go through all this? It's a lot easier and quicker to slit your throat."

He lifted his chin defiantly.

"I'm *not* gonna slit your throat, by the way. And neither is she." I stared pointedly at Deborah as she hulked and paced beside us, a caged mama bear, loaded with rage and ready to rumble. "And we want you to go into the water because that's the *only* way we can get you off this shitland."

The boy started to say something. Stopped. Started

again. Stopped.

His gears were grinding.

"There we go. *Now...*" I winced when more flames fumed in the distance.

We had no time.

"Listen." I scuttled around to the boy's side, slinging my arm over his shoulder. "You and I are gonna go for a swim. *Together.*" I gave him a gentle push toward the ocean.

He grunted and *definitely* thought about being a stubborn shit, but he moved into a stiff-legged shuffle when I raised my brow at him.

"There's a tunnel down there," I added, trying to sound nonchalant.

Big mistake.

The boy ground to a halt and threw his weight backward. And this poor kid was so thin, he barely pulled me.

"Ah, c'mon, kid. You see the size of me? You ain't gonna move me so easily."

"Me name is *Garvin*," he spat.

A pang shot through my heart, so sharp, I actually had to check to make sure I hadn't been shot.

Garvin.

The name of my old Breakfast Club pal. The dude who turned everything into a question, and who'd died, brutally, on the streets of Niall while trying to help me get people out of burning buildings.

There'd been nothing I could do for that Garvin. But *this* Garvin I could save.

"A handsome name for a handsome man," I trilled. "Listen, Garvin, I'll strike a deal with ya. We'll go out into the ocean. If I'm bullshitting you and there is no tunnel, you get permission to stab me. Deborah!" I called over my shoulder. "Do you have a weapon you can—yeah, that's perfect!"

Deborah had pulled a knife out of her boot, still giving me a "bitch, you're crazy" expression.

"Give that to our new friend Garvin," I said.

"Are you *sure* this is a good idea, Addie?" Deborah stretched her hand out, handing the hilt of the knife to Garvin.

He grabbed it off her so quickly, so snappishly, he almost sliced her hand.

"It's a *perfect* idea," I said. And then I clapped Garvin's shoulder. "There. You've got a weapon. I've got nothing." I held my arms out to prove it. "And this is the deal we're gonna strike. If we go swimming, and there's no underwater tunnel, you've got permission to put that knife into my chest. If the tunnel is there, you and I are going to come back to shore, and you're gonna help my crew get the rest of your friends into the water. Sound fair?"

Garvin harrumphed, clutched the knife, and stormed toward the water.

"I'll take that as a yes. But wait!" I sprinted to catch up to him. "You *do* know how to swim...right?"

Garvin paused and paled as he watched the white-capped waves. "No."

"Well, *crap*. Okay, hold onto me then. I'm no Michael Phelps, but I'm a professional doggy paddler."

I held out my arm. He grudgingly took it. We sloshed into the sea, both of us wincing as the cold water gnawed at our waists.

The surf swelled, rolling a wave toward shore. Garvin gasped, clawing his nails into my hand.

"We're gonna dive," I said. "Straight in. Keep holding my

hand, and it'll be easy-peasy, I promise. And take a deep breath...*now!*"

I lurched into the wave, dragging Garvin behind me.

The foamy, salty water tickled my nose. The few mouthfuls I accidentally swallowed burned my raw throat.

Garvin's fingers clawed at my right arm as I doggy paddled down, down, *down.*

Seconds passed. Too many of them. My lungs tightened, and panic curdled my stomach. Where was the tunnel? Had Hurleigh taken it away already? Or was I swimming in the wrong damn direction?

My eyes stung as I fought to keep them open, trying to get my bearings, but I couldn't see *anything* through the murky waters. Not that seeing would've done me much good anyway. The ocean didn't have street signs to point me in the right direction.

Beside me, Garvin writhed, and his eyes bugged out of his head. The knife slid out of his other hand—he was too panicked to realize he'd dropped it. Blobby bubbles fizzed from his mouth as he loosed a silent scream.

I propelled my weary legs through the water, taking us farther down, even when the tide thrashed us about and the water pressure pushed and squeezed at our bodies.

My lungs puffed up, desperate for oxygen.

Please, please, please let it still be here!

The pressure built. And built. Splintering my skull. Mashing my brains into a pulpy juice.

Please tell me I did not just kill this poor kid!

"Uggghh!" I screeched when my face smacked against the ground.

Dry ground.

I inhaled, tasting more blood from my freshly broken nose. Moist, salty air filled my lungs.

The tunnel was still here.

Thank fucking God.

Garvin landed in a crumpled heap beside me. He picked himself up, peered through the darkness at the undulant walls, and screamed.

And I screamed. Because that was my default reaction.

"Holy crap, kid. Don't do that!" I clutched a hand over my racing heart. "I'm old! The ticker isn't as good as it used to be."

Garvin staggered away from me and smacked into one of the water walls.

Bzzzzzttt!

At its angry buzz, he flew away with a cry. "Wha—I—no —" Nonsense words leaked from his lips as his saucer-wide eyes absorbed his surroundings.

"Oh no. Uh-uh. I recognize that look." I snapped my fingers to snag his attention. "We don't have time for you to have a meltdown. I'm sorry. I know they're therapeutic, and you're free to have all the meltdowns you want later. But right now, you gotta help me." I stood and snatched his shoulders, forcing him to stand still. And I fought to keep my voice steady, remembering all the times Cheriour's quiet timbre had calmed me.

Cheriour...

My insides squirmed again. I *needed* to get to him. If Uriel killed him...If I never got to say goodbye...

If I had to see him turn into a zombie...

"I need you to help me," I said again. And I was shocked by how drawling my voice sounded, as though I'd been temporarily possessed by Cheriour's spirit. "This tunnel will take you to a place called Muirin. It's...I mean, it's not The Ritz, but you'll be *safe* there."

"The Wraiths'll follow," he said.

"No. They won't. This tunnel...it...er...it's magical. It only allows humans to pass. If the Wraiths try to force their way in, they'll drown." Ooof, that was a slippery lie. Sure, the Preening Peacock (aka, Hurleigh) would probably flip and demolish any Wraiths he saw crossing into his realm, but I figured it'd be best to leave him out of the conversation. The kid was already overwhelmed. "Garvin, listen, I *need* you to help get everyone into this tunnel. The same way you and I got here. Anyone who can't swim can go with one of my people."

Garvin's eyes shot in every direction, trying to absorb the rippling water walls, the roar of waves, and the occasional (and rapidly dulling) sparks of lightning.

"Can you help us?" I asked. "So we can help you?"

Slowly, uncertainly, Garvin nodded.

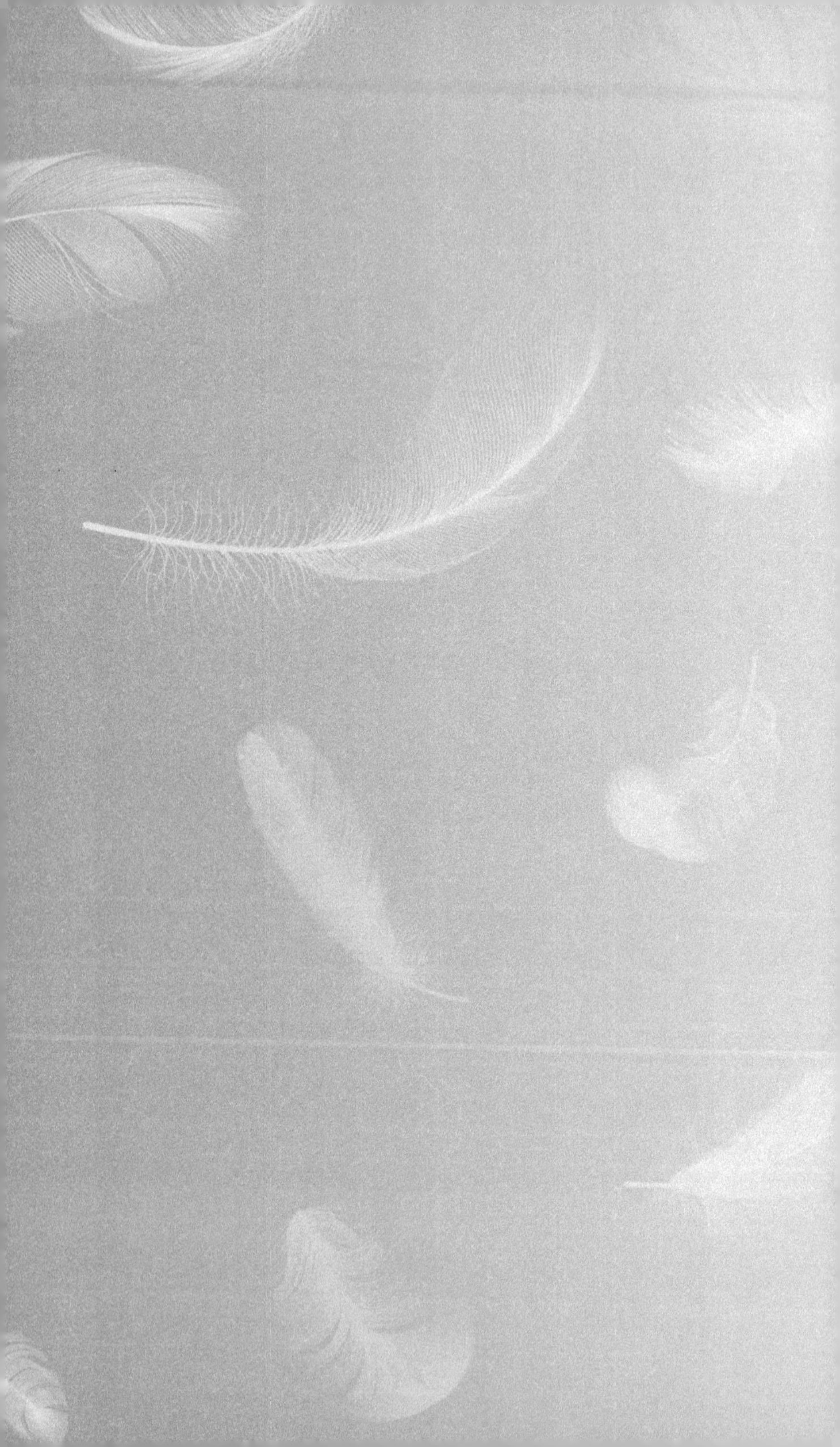

CHAPTER 34

HUMPTY DUMPTY

The rain had slowed to a sputtering drizzle when Garvin and I spurted out of the water. Thick black clouds of smoke sulked over the beach, like a giant, poofy dragon hovering over its kill.

I couldn't see Cheriour anymore. Or Uriel. Or Ellard.

But Uriel's yells were still in full surround sound, complete with immersive effects (aka, the nasty pufts of air he burped out).

So, I took off, not bothering to explain or help Garvin round the Keldians up.

A hellhound yapped and broke away from the group to chase me.

"Addie!" Quinn shouted as he did a sloppy sword chuck at the hound. It wasn't a fatal hit, but the hound halted when the blunt edge of the blade pinged off its back, which gave me a head start.

"Addie, what are you doing?" Quinn bellowed.

I said nothing. Just kept running.

My thoughts sprinted ten times faster than my weary

legs. A good thing. Because it distracted me from how rubbery my muscles felt.

"How did you kill Seruf?"

"I don't know!"

"You destroyed her Essence."

How *had* I killed Seruf? What kick-started my power?

I needed to figure this out. And stat!

As I dashed, the sticky smog reached out, enveloping me in a loving embrace. It smelled of burning cheese on a charcoal grill, and it soothed the raw rasp in my throat—like sucking on a cough drop after a prolonged bout of choking—but did nothing to ease the rattling pain in my lungs.

I streaked through the smoke, huffing and puffing worse than the Big Bad Wolf. Some vapors shifted, curling away and revealing the brawl happening at the other end of the beach.

Cheriour stood with his back toward me, holding a sword in his left hand and my poleaxe in his right. Ellard crouched on his left side, his arms swathed in fire. Uriel raged in between them, angry, disheveled, and bathed in the bright, silvery blood oozing from his damaged right wing.

I was still so damn far away....

My breath caught when Uriel whipped his bleeding wing toward Cheriour.

Cheriour met the blow head-on and drove his short sword into the golden feathers.

"Ummph!" Pain rocketed through my leg as I caught my heel in a divot. I hit the deck, twisting my ankle, whacking my elbows, and gnashing my teeth against my tongue, drawing more blood.

The world tipped sideways on me.

I dug my fingers into the wet sand, holding on until my surroundings stilled.

My body was officially on E, and that little *"oh shit"* light had flicked on. But I could run an extra two miles on empty. I *had* to.

It took three tries to get my legs back under me, and then another half a second to convince them to move again.

In that time, Cheriour had stabbed Uriel twice more. Ellard had burned him. And Uriel had given Cheriour a nice slash along his back.

Hurry! I screamed at my body.

The rocky sand grasped at my feet, trying to cement them in place. I dug down, ripping my feet out of its snare, and focused on anything, *everything*, except how tired I was.

"Evidently, you do *know how you killed Seruf. And you are capable of doing it again."*

How? *How, how, how?*

Something about that night at Niall and the day of the hellhound attack had been different. Something I said or did or thought had awoken the Kraken (aka, my Soul Stealing ability). But *what?*

In front of me, Cheriour shuffled sideways in a slinky walk, never crossing his feet over each other, his eyes fixed on Uriel.

Uriel plucked a knife out of his wing, chucked it aside, and *poofed*, sending a spray of glowing blood into the air.

Cheriour pirouetted in a half circle and plunged the queue of my poleaxe into the ground.

No. Not the ground...

Somehow, Cheriour had known the *exact* spot Uriel was gonna *poof* to, and he'd driven the poleaxe through Uriel's right wing, staking it into the sand.

The dude had a sixth sense.

And so did Ellard, who zipped to Uriel's other side and grasped the left wing in his fire-soaked hands.

Uriel's roar sent another gust of wind spiraling over the beach.

Bam! I faceplanted into the lazy trickle of a wave that barely reached this section of the shore. Salt flumed into my mouth, making me gag.

Uriel's yell snaked overhead, twirling in time with the gust. And it wasn't an echo as I'd assumed before. The wind...*carried* his scream. Because that dulcet tone feathering through the air was crystal clear. And *loud*, as though Uriel was standing over me, booming directly into my ear.

A Messenger, Ellard had called him.

Uriel wasn't blasting cold air for shits and giggles. He used the wind as a megaphone and could probably stretch his voice for *miles*.

He yelled again. And again. And again. Each time sending more and more violent gusts. Until Cheriour rammed a knife down his throat, silencing him.

For now.

I bunched my legs up, screaming when my right knee scraped against the saltwater-soaked sand. Blood dribbled through the jagged hole in my breeches.

Fan-fucking-tastic.

Who needed blood, anyway?

I sure didn't.

My body ran fine on sarcasm and spite.

I gritted my teeth against the pain as I stood and started my hobbling jog again.

I was *so close* now.

Ellard bailed. He doddered away, doubled over, and pounded his flame coated fingers against his skull.

Another minute or two of running, and I'd get there. And then...and then...

Think, Addie! Something flips the switch. Something turns *that power on. A thought, a feeling, a bad bout of gas...think!*

But my brain went offline with a buzzy *"noooooo!"* when Uriel plucked a mini boulder off the ground—literally, that sucker was as big as me—and threw it. *One-handed!* As though the massive rock weighed no more than a baseball.

The boulder swiveled toward Cheriour's head.

My stomach flew into my throat.

Cheriour did a duck-swerve combo and almost, *almost* got himself out of the way in time. But the boulder was too big, and it came on too fast.

Thwack.

The corner clipped Cheriour's temple.

"NO!" I gasped.

Cheriour tumbled ungracefully, getting his legs tangled together. He shook his head once. Twice. Even from a distance, I saw the dazed "huuuurrrr, what just happened?" look on his face. Blood painted his right cheek.

Uriel reached for another boulder.

Ellard still had his back turned and was too busy trying to smack some sense into his brain to see what had happened.

My mouth went bone dry. "Please...no..."

I pumped my arms, pleading, *begging* my legs to give me more. One short burst of speed. Enough to close the distance.

They wouldn't. *Couldn't.*

My heart ricocheted around my chest, and a deep, raking itch peppered my skin.

Cheriour blinked again. And sluggishly, so very sluggishly, picked up his sword.

Uriel gave his new boulder a mocking shake.

"DON'T!" I screeched.

Ping!

This time, I *felt* the switch flip.

A shrill ringing filled my ears, distorting the sounds of the ocean, the rain, the sharp babbles of battle...as though I was listening to all of it through a set of crackling, water-damaged speakers. My vision blurred and bounced. And then...*bam*. Uriel was suddenly lit up brighter than a thousand-watt bulb. The light shone right through his gaudy laminated suit, giving him the appearance of an ugly shag lamp. Long wires of LED strips (aka, Uriel's blood) slithered along the beach. One of them wove all the way to where Cheriour sat, still trying to collect himself.

Both Cheriour and Ellard remained dim.

Which was odd.

Ellard had Seruf's soul, and that bitch had all the razzle dazzle, but it didn't shine through him. And Cheriour still had a soul—right?

Right?

But why did they both look as faded as a candle burning through the last of its wick?

Was the dimness because they were Fallen?

"*Shoooouuuucccckkk!*" I was so distracted ogling the dull pallor of Cheriour's skin that my toe got stuck in a rut. I pinwheeled my arms, caught myself in time, and breathed a "*halle-freaking-lujah*" when that bright light veil remained over my eyes.

I'd have to worry about Cheriour's soul another time.

My power tap was turned on now. I had to *keep* it on.

Almost there!

Uriel threw his boulder.

Cheriour did a janky somersault to avoid it and hurled a knife. It missed by a country mile.

"Hold on!" I tried to yell, but all that came out was a winded wheeze.

Uriel made this bubbly *uk-uk-uk* sound (courtesy of the torn vocal cords Cheriour had left him with) as he ripped his wing out from under my poleaxe. His luminant blood spritzed everywhere: all over the ground, the rocks, and across Cheriour and Ellard. Seriously, the scene was beginning to resemble a night at a bad rave.

I was only a few feet away now.

Ellard was still trying to perform a self-exorcism.

Cheriour got to his feet looking steady but heavy-footed.

"*Stand aside!*" The words rocketed out of my mouth.

Ellard jumped and whacked his head in earnest.

Cheriour turned to me, his face white beneath the splotches of blood.

Uriel *laughed.* Silently, of course, but mockingly.

Ooooh, this cocky, gaudy idiot was *going down.*

His chest glowed like a neon dartboard, and I was dead set on hitting the bullseye.

As I stumbled into him, hands outstretched, his eyes blew wide open. There was recognition on his face now. *Fear.* But it was too late. Because I'd thrust my hand into his chest and plopped into his soul tunnel.

It was every bit as loud, bright, and trippy as Seruf's had been. The swirls of blinding color were something out of a psychedelic nightmare. Blurs of people flounced sideways, up, down, all around, like a shifty, mirror tunnel in one of those god-awful carnival fun houses. The voices...Well, thankfully, I didn't hear any abused kids wailing this time, but that didn't make this trip any easier. A grating sound-track of panicked cries, angry shouts, and violent accusa-tions ripped into my eardrums.

"*I trusted you!*" That deep bass voice had to belong to Uriel. "*You sent her there to be* murdered*! Do not try to deny it.*"

Seruf's smirking face, framed by those stylishly dark curls, appeared in front of me for a split second before she flipped over my head and out of sight.

"*I did.*" Ramiel stood below me, dressed in his trim and prim three-piece suit. "*Seruf no longer had the desire to help us achieve our goal. She'd become too attached to the humans. But rest easy, my brother, her death was not in vain...*" As Ramiel lifted his hand, inspecting underneath his nails for dirt, he got whisked off to the side of the tunnel.

My head ached. So did my legs. And my lungs.

Shit, my *entire body* pulsated with pain. But I ignored it and kept moving.

Uriel keened, his resonant yell only marginally higher than the cacophony around me.

More voices and faces ricocheted around me, most of them unrecognizable.

Except for one.

The purple-eyed Lasair.

A scrawny, teenage version of her oscillated over my head while a petite adult Lasair did a jabby, angry stomp beside me. In both versions, Lasair's eyes were bitter. Hollow. She had that resting bitch face down pat.

But it was adult Lasair who spoke, in short, snappy tones:

"They cared not for me. They are pitiless creatures, so driven by their own fears and prejudices that they would not extend a hand to help a frightened child. So, yes, I would turn on my kin as they once turned against me."

Jesus. This bitch was my *mom*?

I couldn't even *imagine* her raising a kid. *"You spilled your milk? You pitiless creature! I shall take the rest of the food away from you as you took it away from yourself."*

But the teenage Lasair, revolving slowly above me, had none of her adult counterpart's haughty arrogance. Her eyes, angry as they were, also shimmered with fear and pain.

That poor kid had seen trauma. Lots of it.

Adults usually only became prickly if they'd grown up with no other way of defending themselves.

Lasair's adult apparition melted into the air over my head. The teenage version paused, let out a screech that had flames bursting from her skin, then vanished in a puff of smoke.

Seruf reappeared and did a crazy boing from my left side to my right, all while cackling and fussing with her (admittedly gorgeous) hair.

Ramiel floated back into the picture, this time decked out in a suave navy suit with a cornflower-yellow tie and pocket square. A toddler tottered at his right side, bawling at the top of her lungs. Red blotches stained her pudgy cheeks, and tears streaked from her clenched eyes. Her teeny hands were balled into fists, thwacking him every time he tried to pet her fuzzy blond hair.

"Come now, Adelaide. It's not so terrible once you've gotten used to it," he said.

Ummmmm...what??

I blanched.

No. No way. Uh-uh.

That little tater tot wasn't me. *Couldn't* be.

But those tubby cheeks were awfully familiar.

And the hair...

Ice spiked through my stomach when the toddler opened her eyes.

Her vibrantly *purple* eyes.

What the fuck?

Ramiel and Mini Me cartwheeled over my head, leaving me surrounded by an endlessly churning wheel of strangers.

"You wretch!" Uriel's baritone voice filled my ears, momentarily drowning out the other sounds.

I shook my head, trying to whisk away the cold sense of dread the sight of Mini Me had left behind, and ground my teeth. *Takes one to know one, right?*

Uriel emitted a low, humorless laugh. "You took Seruf's Essence and gave it up? Instead of embracing its power for yourself?"

Seruf was a toxic pain in the ass. And so was her Essence. I wanted no part of that.

Again, that bitter laugh filled my head, but there was a high-pitched quality to it now. "You've weakened yourself, Adelaide..."

Addie.

"You'll not be able to claim my Essence as easily as you claimed Seruf's."

You sure about that? I dug my heels into the...well, I mean, I wasn't exactly *standing* in the soul tunnel. My physical body probably hadn't even moved. But I dug my mental heels into the figurative floor. *I've been told I'm a bullheaded bitch.*

"That may be so. But you lack the strength."

I'd say Ramiel disagrees with you. My legs were gassed. Each sludgy step was agony. *He sent Seruf to Niall so I could off her. I'd bet anything he just did the same to you.*

"I have been loyal to the cause, and to Ramiel, since the war began." Uriel used much more emphasis than would've been needed if he truly believed his words. "I was sent here because the humans of Sakar breached the shores of Uchen. I am to remind you of your place in this world."

Oh, is that all? I scoffed. *Silly me. Of course you were the only man for that job. I mean, the Wraiths've got two left feet on the battlefield, and their little dogs are useless, so Ramiel had to send the big, bad Celestial to scare off the naughty humans. It makes perfect sense.*

"Your tone suggests you jest."

Of course I jest! Dude, wake up! Nobody sends a CEO to do the tedious grunt work. And Ramiel didn't give two shits when Seruf died. He wanted me to kill her—he was proud of me for doing so. Cold people like that usually don't give a fuck about loyalty. And he knows I'm here. Doesn't he? When did he send you? After Ellard saw me that first time?

Silence.

I'll take that as a yes. And I'd bet my fucking soul he wants me to dust you the way I dusted Seruf. Dude...he slapped you on death row. And you're too freaking dumb to realize it.

"You speak of what you do not know—"

Oh, I know plenty. I might've only had the displeasure of meeting him once, but I've dealt with people like him before. He's a slippery son of a bitch, isn't he? Real good at sweet talking. Those types hug you from the front and stab you in the back. Guarantee it. You were bamboozled, buddy.

Uriel went silent again.

Another voice rose. This one different, muffled, as though someone was talking to me from behind a steel door.

"Addie, come back..."

Cheriour.

My heart leapt.

"Don't do this," Cheriour called. "We have Uriel contained now. Come back. *Please.*"

Never let it be said that Addie Collins denied a pleading man.

Luckily for you, I said to the still silent Uriel, *I'm* not *a dumb-dumb that gets burned twice by the same thing. I won't take your Essence.*

"You have not the strength to take it," Uriel said again, still using way too much emphasis.

And, y'know what? I *had* to prove the smarmy bastard wrong. So I dove forward (or sideways, or upward, or backward...it was impossible to gauge directions in here), scrabbling, straining, and screaming at my body to move. Just two steps. That was all.

One step.

"Seruf was not loyal to the cause," Uriel barked. "She was *expendable.* I am loyal. He'll not forgive you for killing me."

Maybe. Maybe not. I funneled everything I had into that next step: my rage, hatred, fear...*everything. But you're not gonna live to find out, are ya?* And there it was. Step number two.

"You'll *destroy* your human soul if you keep claiming ours." Uriel went into full, shrieky panic mode with that trilling line.

I know. That's why I'm not taking yours today. But don't ever fucking tell me I can't. *I'm* choosing *to spare you. Remember that.*

"Addie!" There was panic in Cheriour's voice too. Duller than Uriel's, but I'd never, *ever* heard him snap a word out that fast before.

My stomach flip-flopped. *I'm coming!* I called silently to him.

Once, y'know, I figured out how to get out of this tunnel.

"Addie, *listen* to me," Cheriour called again. "Come back!"

I stopped.

Stopped moving.

Stopped struggling.

I closed my eyes and stayed still, breathing and clinging to the steady line of Cheriour's voice.

And the people, the shouts, the tunnel...it all melted away.

It was *that easy* to back myself out of it.

I blinked and let out a shocked *"iiiicccccckkk"* when I found myself holding onto a torso without a head. Or arms. Or legs.

"Ficking—ferking—*fucking hell*!" My tongue spluttered the words.

Uriel's disembodied chest still rose and fell with wavering breaths. The serrated remnants of his gaudy suit were glooped with glowing, silvery blood, as though someone had woven patchwork patterns of sterling silver into the fabric and then popped some Christmas lights underneath to give it that extra *spark.*

The glowing blood enveloped my hands too.

And the sight was so...*bizarre.* I didn't know whether it

was terrifying or funny. Whether I wanted to laugh or scream. So I did both. A leam.

My hands slid out of Uriel's chest with a squelch, and his disembodied torso flopped to the ground, heaving with short, pained breaths.

I teetered backward and bounced off something solid.

Before I could twist my head to look at him, Cheriour gently spun me around.

"I think..." I swallowed when Cheriour cupped my cheek. "Humpty Dumpty here...we should scatter him around a bit. Make it harder for the king's horses and king's men to put him back together again. Har, har, har. Get it? It's a nursery rhyme."

Cheriour huffed and yanked me into his chest, smooshing my face against his bloodstained vest. His arms squeezed a little too tightly to be comfortable, and his chin dug into the top of my head.

It was a sucky hug.

But I clung to him just as tightly, raking my nails along his back and burrowing my head into the sweaty, stinky crook of his neck.

We were both shaken. And terrified to let each other go.

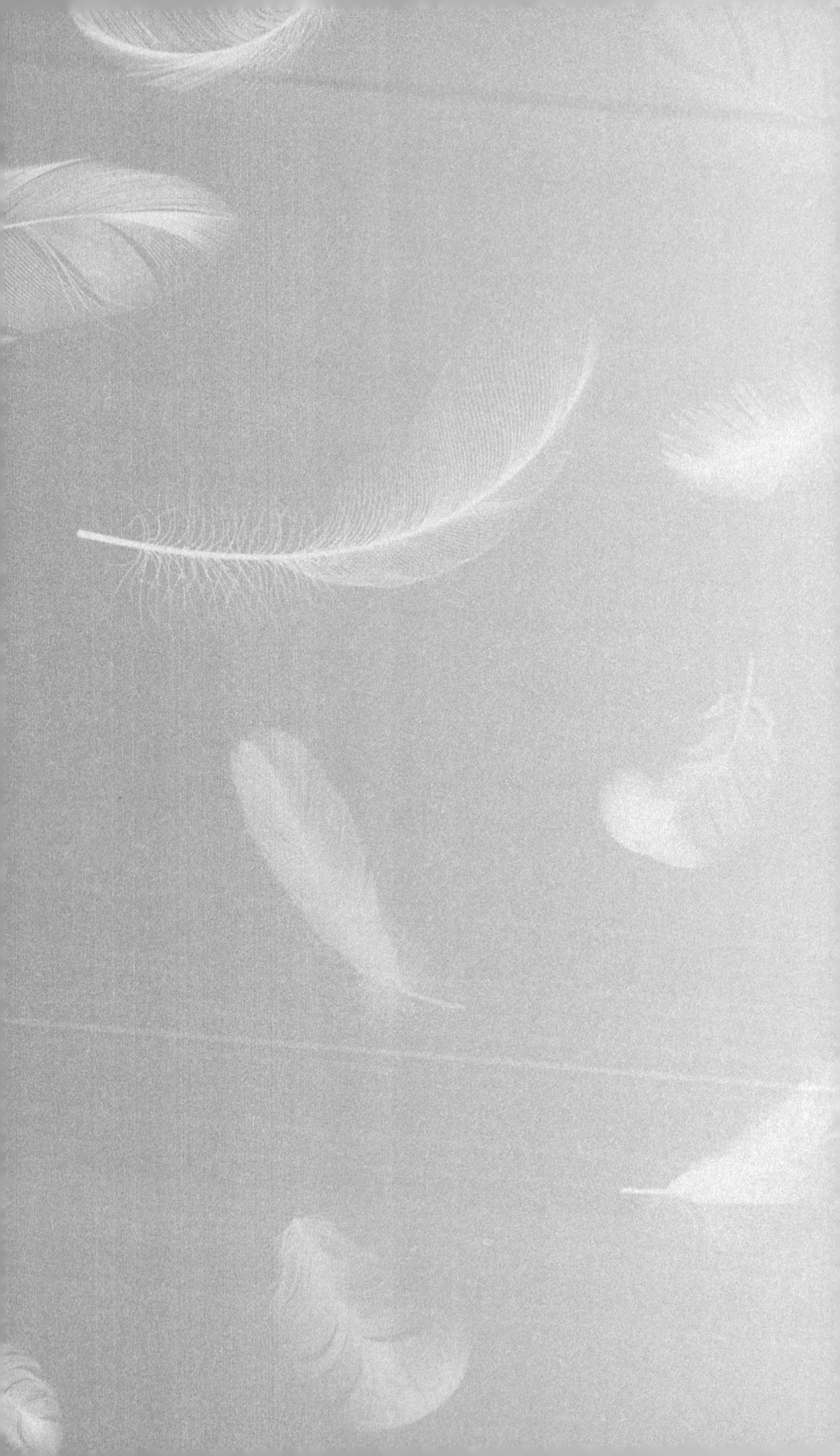

CHAPTER 35
A FUCKED-UP FIGMENT OF A FUCKED-UP IMAGINATION

The cold brutalized me.

Maybe my overwrought body had finally crapped out or shock had me ensnared in its icy grasp, but I *couldn't get warm.*

I burrowed myself against Cheriour, trying to steal his body heat, but he had none to give. I might as well have been hugging a popsicle.

"Jesus, dude." I rubbed at his back, trying to create friction. "Are you—"

I froze.

Because my fingers didn't coast over damp, blood-soaked leather. They bumped over hard, craggy skin. And my thumb brushed against a very large, very pointy spike protruding from his left shoulder.

Ice jangled in my stomach.

No.

No. He wasn't...

He couldn't be...

Right?

I wriggled out of his bone-crushing embrace. "Cheriour, what—" I bit off with a scream.

Because the Cheriour standing before me, emaciated, and swaddled in sickly green skin, was *not* the Cheriour I'd embraced seconds ago.

"Cheriour?" My voice broke around the word.

He snapped his head in my direction. There was no recognition in his blank, piss-yellow eyes.

"Cheriour...what happened?"

He bared his spiky teeth in response.

"He's dead, Adelaide."

"Motherfucking sack of shit!" I squawked when Hurleigh *poofed* beside me, ruffling water out of his wings and drenching me with bitter droplets.

"He's *not* dead." I wrapped my arms around myself to still my shivering. "He's still standing. And moving. And b-breathing."

Hurleigh raised an eyebrow. "Very well. I'll use the correct terminology. He *died,* and then he rose again. Thus, he is *animated* but *unalive.*"

"He was *alive* two seconds ago!"

"It takes naught but a second to stop a mortal's heart, especially when you plunge a blade into it."

I had a knife in my hand. No idea how it got there, but I had that bad boy in a white-knuckled grip.

Blood slicked and swirled along the blade.

Cheriour gnashed his teeth at me again, his eyes drawn to a droplet of crimson dangling off the edge of the knife.

"I didn't...no...I *couldn't*..." My heart hammered somewhere near my esophagus, choking me. "I *love* him."

Hurleigh smacked his wet wing against my back. "Then why did you stab him?"

"*I didn't!*" I shrugged away from him.

"You did. You simply felt no remorse upon doing so. The more you use your power"—he *thwacked* the wing against my chest—"the less you'll feel. This is a *good* thing, Adelaide."

"*Stop it!*"

"If you want to kill Celestials, you'll need to accept that some humans will die." This spank walloped my cheeks.

"STOP!" I screamed.

And then I blinked.

Cheriour vanished. Hurleigh too.

Everything had disappeared: Uriel's jigsawed body, Ellard, and the beach.

Only the ocean remained.

And, once again, it spat a massive wave at me.

I tried to run. Tried to scream. But the surf clung to my ankles, rooting me to the spot, and a big bubble of blood erupted from my mouth.

I squeezed my eyes shut.

"Sakar is dead, Adelaide," Hurleigh called before the wave guzzled me into its icy depths.

I gasped. Sputtered. Thrashed.

A warm palm skimmed my cheek, and Cheriour's voice murmured in my ear, "Be still, Addie."

I wrenched my eyes open and found myself staring at... at...

I blinked.

Cheriour—the red-blooded *human* version of Cheriour —blinked back.

A dream.

That whole nightmare had been, *literally*, a nightmare. A fucked-up figment of my fucked-up imagination. Nothing more.

"Gahhh...blah...ugggh..." I was so *relieved* to see those gorgeous green eyes, my brain shot into a different hemisphere and discovered a new language.

"It's alright, Addie. Be still." He squeegeed a washcloth against my bare shoulder. Lukewarm water trickled along my skin, plinking into the pool below.

Water?

I twisted my head.

"Why—" My voice broke. I cleared my throat, wincing when more leftover blood flecked over my tongue. "Why am...naked...in water trough?" Did those slurred words even make sense?

"You were covered in blood," Cheriour said.

And the water lapping at my body was, indeed, bright pink.

A shudder wracked through me. "Sss cold." Why did talking hurt so much?

Cheriour scooted closer and lightly tugged me forward, pressing my wet, naked chest to his warm, clothed one. "I know." He tightened his grip when I shivered. "I'm nearly done."

I angled my head again, a strange sense of déjà vu tingling in my chest when I recognized my surroundings.

The barn at Muirin.

It was dark, lit only by the dancing flame in the firepit, and vacant, save for Abby Normal. She stood in the center of the building, still bandaged out the wazoo but more alert than she'd been in *days*.

She whuffled when she noticed me staring at her.

"How?" I croaked. Because a few seconds ago, I'd been hugging Cheriour beside Uriel's body, and now I was bathing in a dinky wood trough, back in the relative safety of Muirin. And I had *no idea* what had happened in between.

Had I passed out?

"You didn't," Cheriour said.

"Huh?"

"You didn't faint." His hands moved over my bare body, scrubbing gently. So, *so* gently, as though he was cleaning a baby bird instead of a fully grown woman. "You walked to Muirin. Along with the rest of us. And you fell asleep upon returning. Do you not remember?" A frown puckered his brow.

Nope. I had zero memory of that. Not even a shadow of a memory. Just that weird sense of déjà vu, like my brain knew something was missing from the archives.

It should've concerned me—that my body had gone on full autopilot while my mind had fritzed and shut down.

But I was so...*tired*.

And cold.

And when Cheriour untwisted my braid, massaging water into my scalp...well, was there anything more relaxing than a scalp massage?

My heavy, aching eyes slipped shut.

There was nothing refreshing about this slumber. It was a deep, dark, bottomless ocean.

Occasionally, I managed to paddle my way out of it.

The first time, I found myself sitting against Cheriour's chest as he tried to coax me into eating and drinking.

The water tasted like dirt. And metal.

And the goddamn porridge...

Bug guts, I'd called it once. This crap was the slimy sludge from hell.

"It's not bug guts," Cheriour sighed when I weakly, but adamantly, slapped his hand away.

"Looooksssss it..." I slurred.

But I ate it. Because he was a persistent bastard, and I was too tired to put up a fight.

And when the black tide swallowed me again, I didn't have the strength to battle it.

The sound woke me up next.

It *shouldn't* have. I'd been in the depths of my blackout sleep, and the noise was little more than a light hum, but it somehow dredged me back into the waking world.

Darkness surrounded me. The air was mostly quiet, save for the random throaty snores and garbles from the dozens of people sleeping around me. Obnoxious, sure, but not enough to wake me.

So what had?

I gasped when something tightened around my torso, squeezing the air out of my belly. A soft whine ghosted across the back of my shoulder.

Cheriour.

His arm twitched, his legs shifting restlessly beside mine. His skin, when I touched his hand, was sticky with sweat.

"Hey." I tapped his knuckles. "It's alright..."

No response other than him kicking out and ramming his knee into my backside.

"*Ouch*...goddamn, you got some bony freaking knees. Cheriour...hey..." It took a lot of energy to turn myself around. Because A. my body still felt like a sack of disconnected bricks, and B. he was squishing me. But I wriggled until I finally faced him.

He was out cold, but his face was contorted in pain.

"It's alright..." I traced my fingers over his cheek, gently probing the fresh crescent-shaped scar that curved along his right temple.

His eyes opened, but they were dull and blank, as though his body had awakened but his mind was still trapped in a dream. Tears trickled in zaggy trails along his sweat-slick cheeks.

A sharp, slippery pang shot through my heart. "It's alright," I repeated as I wiped the moisture from his eyes and pressed my brow against his. "I mean, you're kinda breaking my ribs here...but it's okay...what's a few broken bones between lovers, right?" I kissed his nose, his eyelids, his cheeks, all while stroking his face and murmuring to him.

He stilled, his arm relaxing around my midsection and the tight expression of pain loosening, leaving him more relaxed than I'd ever seen him.

I pressed my mouth against his, gingerly sucking his lower lip between my teeth. He groggily returned my kiss in a messy, sleepy smooch.

I didn't want to wake him the rest of the way, so I drew back and tenderly finger-combed his hair, soothing him into a peaceful sleep.

And then I cried. How was it possible to care for someone this much after only knowing them a few months?

How was it possible to become so bonded with a person that their pain became your pain?

"You're killing me here, Smalls," I whispered, then laughed. "Gosh, you'd *hate* that movie, wouldn't you?" I booped his nose. "How did I fall in love with someone who wouldn't like *The Sandlot*?"

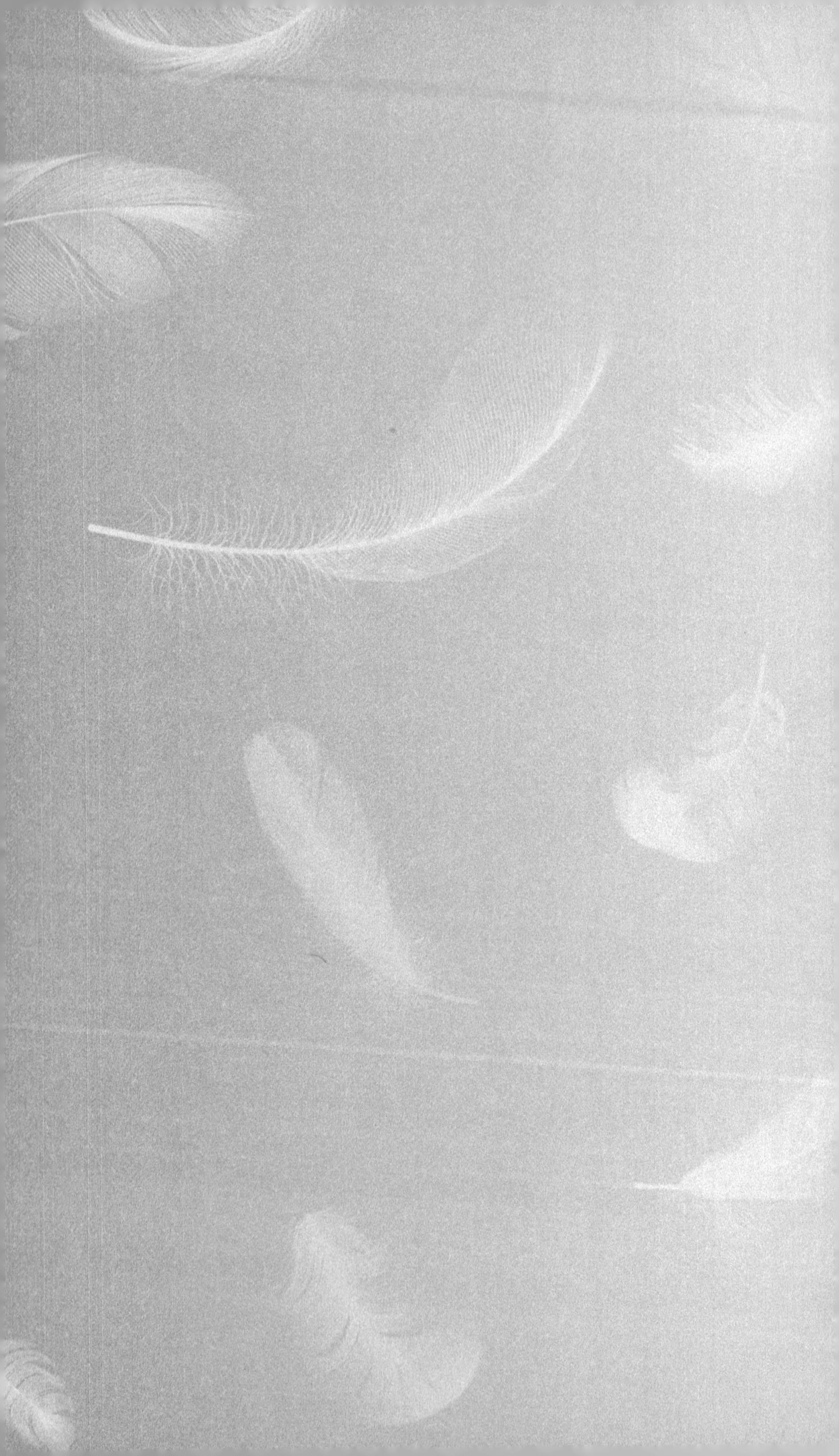

CHAPTER 36

THE DRUNKEN QUARTET

I slept for decades and awoke a creaky old fart who'd let her life and youth slip away.

Not really.

But I felt like absolute *dogshit* when I fully emerged from the blackout sea, all achy and brain-foggy. My stomach gnawed with hunger, and my dry throat burned hotter than the Sahara Desert.

But I was alert...ish. Enough to be aware of the scratchy sandpaper blankets I'd been swaddled in. To feel the warm bundle of Splinter's body nestled against the side of my neck. To have my mouth water as I got a whiff of...*something*. Beef broth. Maybe? And to get pricks of panic when I peered around the cold, empty barn and didn't see Abby Normal.

An icy wind crept through the narrow slats in the wall, brushing against my back. Although the fire still crackled in its pit, it didn't do much to keep the chill away.

I shivered as I shifted out of my blanket, clutched Splinter in one hand, and stood from my rumpled floor bed.

Error, Error!

My brain fuzzed. The world whirled and teetered faster than a spinning top.

"Nope. Not doing that." I plopped back down. Standing was *not* in the cards for me yet. But I could manage sitting. Poor Splinter didn't want me upright at all, though. He gave me this bleary-eyed "bitch, how dare you?" look and dove back under the covers.

At the same time, the door behind me banged open, sending streams of bitterly cold air into the barn.

I pivoted, winced when my ears *whomp-whomp-whomped*, and blinked until the white streaks framing my vision faded.

A dozen people tumbled into the barn looking red-cheeked and miserable.

These were all strangers—faces I'd never seen before.

Keldians.

The woman at the front of the group jumped when she saw me and sent her sword clattering to the ground. The sharp noise made everyone else jump, and several other people dropped their weapons.

"I know it's cold," came Cheriour's droning voice as he sauntered in behind them, "but take more care with your weapons. We've only a limited—"

He paused when he saw me sitting up, and his lips twitched, but he turned back to the Keldians again, ignoring me for the moment. "A limited number with us," he continued. "In battle, you will be even more limited. You must learn to hold your weapons. Even when something startles you."

These poor people were *visibly* uncomfortable being armed with pointy objects. A few of them sighed in relief as they shuffled across the room and offloaded their weapons on...

I squinted.

"When the hell did we get that?" I asked.

Because people were slotting their weapons into a nifty wooden rack, which was tucked oh-so-neatly into the back left corner of the barn.

"I built it," Cheriour grunted.

Of *course* he had.

Cheriour stood silently at the doorway, watching the group to make sure they hung their weapons correctly. He only turned to me again when the last person left the barn.

Ran from the barn was more apt description. That shaky, wild-eyed guy looked ready to beg to be sent home—*away* from us whack-a-doodles.

I knew that feeling. *Ooooh*, I knew it.

"They've been here *a day*, and you're already putting them through training?" I tutted at Cheriour.

"Three."

"Huh?"

"They've been here for *three* days."

"Shoot. Really? I've been out for *three days*? No wonder I feel like roadkill."

"You pushed yourself too far. And I let them rest a day before I began training," he added.

"How *generous* of you."

Cheriour huffed and pulled the barn door shut.

I peered out before he did, glimpsing the hordes of people working and chatting outside in the gray-hued sunlight. I still didn't see Abby Normal.

"Where's Abs?" I asked. "Is...she's..."

"She's healing," Cheriour murmured. "Quickly, now that

she's resumed eating. Braxton and Quinn have been walking her."

My eyebrows rose. "Braxton and *Quinn*?"

"She needed to move. Her legs had begun to swell."

"And *they* volunteered?"

"I believe there was a game to determine who would walk her. They lost."

"Oh jeez. Tweedle Dee and Tweedle Dum. How's that been going?"

An amused smile graced Cheriour's lips. "Abby Normal has been tolerant." He crossed to the fire pit, chucked another log into it, and fumbled with the black kettle suspended over the flames.

"Where the heck did we get that? Oh, no," I groaned when he ladled goop into a slanted wooden bowl. "That better not be bug guts. Don't think I don't remember you spoon-feeding me that shit...*ooh*, wait." I inhaled when he pressed the bowl into my hands. "This actually smells *good*." But I grimaced when I peered over the rim at the wobbling brown goo. "Kinda looks like diarrhea, though."

"Goat stew," Cheriour said. "It's for tonight. But I'd rather you eat some now."

"Tonight? What's—oh, *goddamn it*." Apparently, I'd lost the ability to talk and slurp at the same time, because I sloshed hot stew all down my front. "What's tonight?" I asked as I mopped myself up.

"We're celebrating." Cheriour moved across the room, running his hands over the weapons on the rack, adjusting each one to make sure they hung *perfectly* straight.

His little OCD tangent was adorable considering this was the guy who used his floor as a trashcan.

"Celebrating *what*? The disaster at Keld? That—

hmmmm, oh my *God!*" I'd taken a proper gulp of the stew. And maybe I was just *reeealllyyy* hungry, but goddamn, this was the most savory thing I'd ever tasted. *Ever.* A beef copycat (aka, goat meat) wrapped in a zesty mixture of spices and tomatoes...*hmmm.* "This is so freaking good! *OMG.* Anyway, *why* are we celebrating that debacle?"

"It wasn't a debacle," Cheriour said. "We returned to Muirin with enough supplies to last the winter. And nearly three hundred citizens of Keld."

I choked on my next mouthful. "Three *hundred?*"

Cheriour inclined his head. "Two hundred and eighty-four, to be precise. But when you first heard the count, you said, 'Round that shit up. Three hundred's a more impressive number.'" His screechy impression of my voice might've been freaking *hysterical* if he hadn't followed it up with a stern stare. "Do you truly not remember returning to Muirin?"

My déjà vu Spidey Senses tingled. Because that was 100 percent something I would say, but I couldn't *remember* it. "No. Should I be concerned about that?"

"I don't know," Cheriour mumbled. And then he shifted around the room, sorting the baskets of food that now lined the corners of the barn, inspecting the meats and fish hanging on the walls, checking the weapons again, frowning when he found some that weren't sharpened to his liking, and tearing through the barn like a tornado in search of something to sharpen them with.

The dude was the definition of organized chaos.

"Can you sit down? Or something?" I asked. "You're exhausting me."

He turned, raising an eyebrow.

"You never stop moving! Can you take five and sit with me for a bit? Please?"

He did, but only after he grabbed two swords, a whetstone he found buried near the wood stack (he pew-pewed the logs all over the floor in search of that stone), and a flask.

I took the flask when he handed it to me, and even the gritty dirt water it contained was *delicious*.

Hocking up Seruf's soul must've fried my tastebuds.

Cheriour touched my shoulder and began to sit beside me.

"Don't crush Splinter!" I cried.

He sighed, plucked a grouchy-looking Splinter out from the blankets, and plopped him on my lap, where he harrumphed and sulkily curled up on my thigh.

Poor Splinter. His life was *soooo* tough. Having people constantly disturbing your beauty sleep was a fucking tragedy.

"There is wine for tonight." Cheriour lowered himself down beside me, pulling one of the swords over his knee.

I almost spat out my drink. "And you gave me *water*?"

His mouth twitched. "You can have the wine later. For now, your body *needs* the water."

And, once I'd consumed the dirt water, my body *needed* the bathroom. So I disturbed Splinter again. This time, he did a stompy march back to his cage, chittering like, *"To hell with all of you!"*

I moved with a stiff-legged waddle to the bathroom (aka, the bucket I took to the back corner and squatted over) and was utterly *exhausted* by the time I sat beside Cheriour again. So I rested my head on his left shoulder and watched him scrape his whetstone against the blade. The sound was a grating *rrrrrriiiiiinnnnkkkk*, but it was melodic.

Quiet. My eyes grew heavy, and a buzzy fog wrapped around my brain.

"Hey," I mumbled, "before I pass out, can I ask you something?"

"Hmmmm."

"Were you a Reaper? Was that, like, your Celestial status? Or did I dream Ellard saying that?"

"Yes." Cheriour tapped his finger against the edge of the blade, testing it. "I was."

"Huh. *Interesting*. Did you do the whole 'emo black cloak and scythe' getup?"

"I had no need for a scythe."

"So you totally did the emo cloak," I guffawed. But then thorns ensnared my stomach, strangling the laugh as other thoughts, memories, and dreams popped into my head. "If you...Is Ramiel going to control you the way he controlled Ellard? When, y'know..." *When you die.*

Those words stuck to the roof of my mouth.

Cheriour stilled. "Yes." The word came out in a bored drone, but a tension spasm gripped his back as he said it.

I snuggled more firmly against him and kissed his cheek, relaxing again only when he resumed sharpening the blade.

"Y'know." I pressed my lips to the chiseled line of his throat. "I hope you weren't cursed with bl-bl-black wings." A jaw-cracking yawn gripped me. "When you were a Celestial. That would've been too much emo, even for you. Especially since everyone else has obnoxiously bright wings—although you're not ostentatious enough to pull those bold colors off. You'd rock a silver, though. Something light. Classy looking. Or—"

A deep, throaty belly laugh rumbled through Cheriour.

"Uh...did I miss something?"

He angled his head and smooched my brow. "My wings *were* silver, Addie."

"Really?"

"Hmmm." He nuzzled the top of my head. "How did you guess?"

"Pure freaking luck, really. But I did work at a hair salon, and color matching *used* to be my specialty." I squeezed his midsection. "I kinda wish I could've seen them, though. Your wings. I bet they were beautiful."

"I wish you could've seen them too," he whispered.

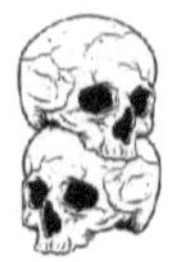

"*Aaaand the Lus—Lass-Lasssssie she suld—sold her arse at the pub, for any old—*" hic "*bloke lookin' for a hurty—hearty rub.*"

Braxton cackled as he finished his Grammy Award-winning melody and guzzled more wine, spilling most of it down his shirtless front when he decided to mimic a "*hearty rub.*"

"That's lovely," I chortled. "A star in the making."

Sharp peals of laughter echoed around me, not necessarily because of Braxton's *wonderful* rendition. But when three hundred people stuffed themselves on beef substitute and booze and gathered outside around *two* bonfires...*oh yeah*. Shit was getting loud. Lots of shrieking laughter and animated conversations. Tons of bad singing. Spatterings of discombobulated dancing.

I freaking loved these kinda nights...even if I, sadly, couldn't join in on the drunken festivities.

Blood loss did *not* pair well with red wine. My head had gotten woozy after a couple of sips. Which sucked because the alcohol would've kept me warm.

It was a poopy night: frigid, foggy, and damp—not enough to snuff out the massive fires, but enough to make my skin sticky and Cheriour's hair *super* frizzy. Twenty minutes of finger combing hadn't been enough to tame those wild strands, so I'd begun braiding them instead.

He and I sat a few feet away from a Flaming Tower of Pisa (aka, a badly lilting bonfire). Although the fire kept my front toasty warm, the bitter air slashed at my back. I even had a blanket draped across my shoulders, and the cold *still* cut through. And the rock I sat on was more frigid than a damn ice cube, even after a solid twenty minutes of having my ass to warm it up.

Cheriour reclined on the frozen ground in front of me, using my shins as a backrest as he frowned at the rumpled piece of paper in his lap. A paper he was currently sketching on, although how he wasn't giving himself a headache trying to sketch beneath the flickering firelight, I didn't know.

Abby Normal stood beside us. She was still bandaged and had a creaky old lady shuffle when she walked, but she watched the undulating mass of fire-lit bodies with bright, interested eyes. Not in a *"hmmm, a moving buffet"* kinda way; more like the intent, judgy way I used to watch bad reality TV.

A woman staggered past us doing the "my bladder is gonna burst" toddle. She was one of the Keldians—and I'd already scared her earlier by asking if I could give her *gorgeous* strawberry-blond hair a trim. Because, y'know, those frayed ends were sending me an SOS. But the woman apparently thought hair trimming was a violent activity. She'd gotten all pale and stammery and had *begged* me not to.

So, yeah, lesson learned. Haircuts were scary around these parts.

Abby Normal snorted when the woman walked by. The woman squeaked, "*iiiiccckkk*," and dashed off.

"Abs." I tapped her chest when she whuffed and bobbed her head. "You're *sadistic*."

Cheriour *hmmmmed* at his paper, then emitted a soft sigh when I ran my fingers back through his frizzy curls, finishing the braid I'd started. It wasn't my neatest work, but the four plaits arching across the top of his head already looked badass. Very Viking Warrior-esque.

"Do I want to know what you're doing?" His charcoal piece made a prolonged *scritch-scritch* as he shaded something on the page.

"Let it be a surprise," I said. "You're gonna look fab-u-lous once I'm done."

"Hmm…"

I laughed and dropped a kiss to his forehead.

And I wished desperately that my brain would *turn off* for a few minutes so I could enjoy this night with him. But my thoughts churned and churned and *churned*, as unsettled as the sea below our cliffs.

I thought of Ellard grappling to keep Ramiel from taking control, and my heart hurt as I pictured Cheriour one day fighting the same battle.

I pondered the flashes I'd glimpsed of Uriel's memories: the grumpy-faced Lasair, Mini Me standing beside Ramiel. Now that I'd seen him with his grubby hands all over my kid self—*another* childhood memory that I didn't remember…

Well, he'd once barked at me for using *his* power.

"You dare to use my power against me?" had been his exact words.

It didn't take a rocket scientist to put two and two together, but I didn't want to acknowledge it. Didn't want to make it *real*.

And my power...

I'd done a lot of thinking about that. Too much.

"If you continue to use this power, you will change."

"Evidently, you do understand how you killed Seruf. And you are capable of doing so again."

Kylah's warning about it and Hurleigh's insistence that I use it were two sides of the same coin.

I had the power to kill Celestials, but wielding it would shred my soul.

I had the ability to save everyone I cared about, but I'd lose my humanity in the process.

"You're quiet tonight," Cheriour mumbled.

"Am I?"

"Hmmm."

Another bout of drunken singing started up. Nathan did a weird jig around the second fire, babbling a bawdy tale about a male prostitute. Meanwhile, Deborah swayed in front of our fire, crooning about someone losing their heart to a doomed love. Quinn had started jamming away on overturned buckets like Ringo Starr rocking on his drum set. And he was *good*. It was hard to hear over the Drunken Quartet, but some drumline solos still drifted over. The dude had serious rhythm.

"It's kinda hard to talk with all this going on," I chirped.

"It's never stopped you before," Cheriour pointed out.

"Well...I don't wanna steal anyone's spotlight. Y'know?"

He sighed and rested his little stump of charcoal against the paper as he leaned more fully into my legs. His left hand twined around my calf, rubbing gently. "Don't dwell on your thoughts, Addie. Not tonight."

"Who says I am? I'm just enjoying the music."

Cheriour kneaded my calf, and then he grabbed his piece of paper, holding it over his head for me to see what he'd been drawing.

And, okay, it wasn't enough to take the dread away, but it did make me smile.

Because there I was, crouched over Sacrifice's withers as the two of us barreled into a massive wave. The sketch was only partially complete—he hadn't filled in Sacrifice's tail, and her hooves were shapeless blobs since he hadn't finished shading the water around them. But it was a badass picture.

Even Abby Normal seemed to agree. She leaned over and gave the paper a few wet sniffs.

"Don't blow your snot on it, Abs." I bonked her nose. "And that was the ballsiest thing I've ever done," I said to Cheriour. "I only pissed myself a *teeny bit* while doing it."

He squeezed my calf again and pulled the drawing back onto his lap.

"You've got mega talent, dude," I said. "We should hang that on the wall once you're done. Start an art gallery for ya. Back home, you could'a made some serious bank being able to draw like that, especially if you did commissions. We could've gotten you set up on social media, posted a few images, and you would've been *drowning* in commission requests."

Cheriour let go of my calf and resumed sketching, as though satisfied that I'd started babbling again. So I kept talking as I finished his braids, offering commentary about the music ("Do y'all know any songs that aren't about heartbreak or prostitutes?"), laughing at Braxton's mini strip show ("Pulling off his shirt is one thing. The second his pants come off, I'm outta here."), and joking about Kaelan's awkwardness when Aria and Natalia dragged him before the fire and began dancing with him. "Ain't he your adopted kid or something?" I nudged Cheriour's shoulder. "Why didn't you teach him how to dance?"

Kaelan looked so adorably flustered as he stumbled his way through the movements, trodding on their toes.

"He can dance." Cheriour vibrated with a low chuckle. "When he's not nervous."

Soon, more people were dancing in front of us. Cheriour had to give up on his drawing when the twirling, swirling, sloppily drunk bodies obstructed his light.

He leaned back again, now massaging my other calf, looking the picture of contentment as I tied off his last braid with a leather strap. "This looks *sooo* cool." I rubbed my fingers over my handiwork. Tightly woven plaits encircled the top of his head, but I'd tapered the two middle ones off halfway so some of his gorgeous (if slightly puffy) curls still spilled over his shoulders. "Any chance I can convince you to leave this in for a bit?"

He said nothing.

Which meant he'd leave the braids alone for a while.

Around us, more people burped up drunken ballads—thankfully veering away from achy breaky hearts and sexcapades. These tunes were cheery and vaguely familiar, as though they were bits and pieces of popular music from a bygone era.

I tapped Cheriour's shoulder. "Know any of these songs?

Because you would make my fucking year if you joined in on the karaoke."

He turned and raised his eyebrow in a *"not in a million years"* look.

"Come on," I laughed. "One song. Please? Or I can serenade you?" I threatened.

When he said nothing, I belted out the chorus to *Don't Stop Believing* at the top of my lungs. Totally off-key, with my squawking *"cat yowling in heat"* singing voice.

Cheriour couldn't even suppress his wince.

"That's it, Addie!" Braxton stood several feet away, arms outstretched as he whooped and sang along, butchering all the words.

"Please stop," Cheriour grunted. But there was laughter in his voice.

It was infectious. I screeched out a few more notes, just to see him grimace again. And I would've kept going, but Cheriour stood then, placed his drawing beside my rock, and held out his hand. "Do you want to dance?"

Glee burbled in my stomach. "Really?"

He inclined his head, a lopsided smile tugging at his lips. "You wanted to before. And I said I would."

I squealed as I grasped his hand and allowed him to sweep me off my feet.

Not literally. Obviously.

But, my God, he was a *good* dancer, every bit as graceful and elegant as I'd imagined. His arms encircled my waist, thumbs kneading my hips, while I wrapped mine around his neck. And he moved in a languid rhythm, his feet shuffling to a beat only he could hear, as he deftly steered me around the drunken buffoons and their wild twerking.

When Rhona and another woman fumbled into us,

blinded by their teary-eyed laughter, Cheriour swept me into a smooth spin to avoid them.

"Huh…" I rested my head against his chest, trying to ignore how off-kilter the pivot had left me. "Rhona has a laugh button. Who'd've thunk it?"

Cheriour's chuckle rumbled beneath my ear.

"Then again, there was a time I didn't think *you* had a laugh button." I lifted my head and snatched his smiling lips in a soft, suckling kiss.

We both broke off giggling when Kaelan did a wobbly mamba and nearly crashed into us.

"Thank you," I said when Cheriour drew me more tightly against him and sashayed out of Kaelan's path of destruction. "And not *just* for getting me out of that firing line…"

Kaelan *thumped* into Braxton, who turned and gave the poor, flustered kid a big, wet smooch on the lips.

I smiled and nuzzled my face into Cheriour's neck, reveling in the way his entire body vibrated with his laughter. "Thank you for humoring me. With the dancing. This is perfect."

His arm swept silently over my back.

I wished I could've said I felt better as we swayed in a loving slow dance, but I didn't. Not really. My mind still whirled in time with my churning stomach.

All I could think about was how much I loved this man in my arms and how I would do anything, *anything*, to save him.

Even give up my soul.

"I suppose you're here to die. Like the rest of us."

The words Cheriour had spoken to me all those months ago had hit the nail on the head, and he hadn't been aiming, just swinging his blunt instrument around to show me how much Sakar would hurt.

But I *was* sent here to die. Not *with* the humans. *For* them.

Or, to be more accurate, my *soul* was sent here to perish.

A few months ago, this thought would've made me *rage*. And I'd've refused the responsibility. I didn't sign up to be a self-sacrificing hero. Nobody wanted that job. Not even the superheroes in the comics.

But now...

I cared too much. These people were my friends. Cheriour was my whole fucking heart. I *would* save them.

The Celestials started this stupid war and trapped these people in the middle of it, and then Ramiel dumped his Wraiths in Sakar to crank up the misery.

That suave bastard was also holding Cheriour's soul hostage.

I wanted to end it. All of it.

Even if it meant hunting Ramiel to the ends of the earth.

Even if it meant my own destruction.

TO BE CONTINUED...

eyed boy who still thinks she can be saved. But as Lass struggles to control her volatile powers, she slowly transforms into the monster the humans believe her to be. And even the boy she loves is in peril...

Hunted by Fire is a dark romantasy novella filled with gritty action, starcrossed romance, found family, and a lethal heroine.

Buy Here!

She wants to watch the world burn. He still believes she's worth saving.

After a lifetime of cruelty at the hands of humans, Lass escapes to Uchen—a Celestial-ruled land rich in splendor and innovation. For the first time, she feels safe, powerful, and *free*. And then she meets *him*—Ramiel, the infamous Conqueror. He's enigmatic and kind, and unravels a history of this world that further darkens Lass's heart toward the humans.

But a return to Sakar, and a run-in with the cocky blue-eyed boy, shatters everything she'd come to believe about humans, Celestials, and herself.

Now, caught between two worlds, Lass must decide where she belongs...

And that decision may just break her heart.

Betrayed by Ash is a grimdark romantasy novella filled with gritty action, star-crossed romance, found family, and a lethal heroine.

552

Addie's Rockin' Playlist

1. Carry on Wayard Son - Kansas
2. Beam Me Up - P!nk
3. Remember Me This Way - Jordan Hill
4. Weight of the World - Citizen Soldier
5. Once Upon A December - Christy Altomare
6. Dancing on Broken Glass - Poets of the Fall
7. Feels Like Tonight - Daughtry
8. Wake Me Up When September Ends - Green Day
9. Under Your Scars - Godsmack
10. Sounds of Someday - Radio Company
11. Danger Zone - Kenny Loggins
12. Changes Are Coming - Daughtry
13. To Build A Home - The Cinematic Orchestra, Patrick Watson
14. Time - Hans Zimmer
15. Run Boy Run - Woodkid
16. Circles - I See MONSTAS
17. Point of Know Return - Kansas
18. (Don't Fear) The Reaper - Blue Oyster Cult

19. Dust in the Wind - Kansas
20. Bad Moon Rising - Creedence Clearwater Revival
21. Come Sail Away - Styx
22. Surive - Peyton Parrish
23. Heavy Is The Crown - Daughtry
24. Break Into My Heart - Daughtry
25. Dearly Beloved - Daughtry
26. Darkness Before The Dawn - Caleb Hyles, Lacey Sturm, Judge & Jury
27. Northwest Passage - Jonathon Young, Caleb Hyles, Colm R. McGuinness, RichaadEB
28. Eye of the Storm - Jonathon Young, Judge & Jury
29. Battle Cries - Peyton Parrish
30. Ragnarok - Peyton Parrish
31. Sound The Bugle - Bryan Adams
32. Spooky Scary Skeletons - Jonathon Young, ToxicxEternity
33. Into The Nothing - Breaking Benjamin
34. Fight the Tide - Jonathon Young, Colm R. McGuinness, Judge & Jury
35. Safe and Sound - Kurt Hugo Schneider
36. Go the Distance - Peyton Parrish

Acknowledgments

Buckle up, Buttercup. Because I'm gonna get sappy.

To be completely and totally frank, this book almost didn't happen. The original launch of Fires of the Forsaken (the dual POV version) flatlined. *Hard.* And one thing they don't warn ya about in the "Publishing for Dummies" handbook is how unbelievably gutting it is to have a passion project, something you've poured your entire heart into, fail. It was rough. And there were multiple times I'd considered ramming an axe into this book, and the rest of the series, and walking away from it. But I didn't. Because these characters have a chokehold on my heart. I'll never abandon them. And, honestly, this story is pretty freaking awesome. It was a fight to get it published, but I can't even tell y'all how unbelievably proud I am of it. Well, I mean...I *could* tell you, but that'd be a whole long-winded essay that I won't subject you to. LOL. But this is, by far, the best book I have ever written.

And I am fortunate enough to be surrounded by a lovely community who helped get this book to this point. So now I'm gonna slather them with some sappy accolades.

To Adina, Brindi, and Devon, who provided the best

moral support and nursed me through my lowest points...I flipping love you guys. Your support and friendship mean *everything* to me. I actually don't think I could continue on this roller coaster publishing journey without you. (And these are authors, y'all. You should be checking out their books. Because they're amazing and deserve all the praise).

To my beta readers Stephanie, Alix, Jayden, Jasmine, Marje, Gloria, and Hannah...I'm so unbelievably grateful to have had you on my team. Y'all rocked those beta reads, and helped shape this story into its current kick-ass version. Thank you. So, so, freaking much.

My editor, Meg, is an absolute rockstar as well. Because not only do I dump these massive doorstoppers on her lap (aka, my books), but I send them with 20 pages of notes and then I beg her to help me unpretzel this pretzel story. And she comes through! Every single time. I love ya, Meg! Thanks for being awesome!

I gotta give a special shoutout to my mom. She's been the biggest cheerleader for this series from the beginning... and I mean, the beginning beginning, back when I wrote the sloppy 2008 version of these books. She's devoured each and every version of this story, raved about it, gotten excited whenever I dropped snippets, and is still steadfast in her belief that this series will one day be a bestseller. She's liter- ally my number one fan. And, mom, I love ya for that. You'll always be #1.

Lastly, I want to thank you, my dear reader. Because it means the world to me that you've picked up one of my books and given it a go. So, thank you. A million times over. *Thank you.* I hope you felt all the emotions while reading this one, and I hope you love these characters as much as I do.

I know I've left Addie and the gang on a bit of a cliffhanger. But worry not! I won't leave them there for long.

OTHER BOOKS BY STEPHANIE E. DONOHUE

Standalones

Windsong (2022)

Bewitched by the Sea Monster (2025)

The Across Time Series

Fires of the Forsaken (2023)

Ashes of the Earth (2024)

Embers of the Damned (2026)

The Across Time Companion Novellas

Hunted by Fire (2024)

Betrayed by Ash (2025)

Cursed by Ember (2027)

ABOUT THE AUTHOR

As a child, Stephanie E. Donohue roamed Narnia with the Pevensie siblings and rode the Hogwarts Express with Harry and his friends. She never tired of discovering new and magical worlds through the pages of a book. And, when the yearning to explore still wasn't satiated, Stephanie turned to writing. With a pen and a few sheets of paper, she learned to craft new worlds, and vibrant characters to explore with.

That passion has never died. Stephanie still enjoys writing stories that take readers on exciting, and sometimes danger-ous, adventures.

When she's not writing, Stephanie can usually be found cuddling with her two cats, obsessively re-watching The Office, or rocking out to a Pound Fitness class.